THE IMPERTINENT
MISS TEMPLETON

LYNN MESSINA

potatoworks press
greenwich village

To Barbara,
who always makes me laugh

CHAPTER ONE

As Miss Tuppence Templeton had never had her sleep interrupted by a pair of thieves who'd stolen into her room in the middle of the night, she wasn't entirely sure of the protocol for such an event. She was reasonably confident, however, that the intruders were not supposed to stand over one's bed and bicker.

"A poke is harmless," the first prowler said impatiently.

"Harmless, yes," the associate conceded, "but frightening too. Imagine if you were sleeping and a stranger woke you with a poke."

"Almost that exact occurrence happened to me, if you'll recall, and I was fine," the first voice insisted.

"He wasn't a stranger, and you were hardly fine."

The trespassers were female, Tuppence thought, lying still, her eyes firmly shut. She could tell their sex from the pitch of their voices, which, at a whisper, were remarkably similar.

The original speaker sighed. "Very well, then. What do you propose?"

"Perhaps a tap," her accomplice suggested.

This seemingly reasonable recommendation elicited an immediate and inappropriately loud giggle. "In what appreciable way is a tap different from a poke?"

While the second intruder detailed the many things

1

that separated a tap from a poke—pressure, vigor, intention, et cetera—Tuppence considered her options. Obviously, she couldn't pretend to be asleep forever. Even if her uninvited guests didn't intend to wake her up as soon as they settled on a method for doing so, she could hardly let them leave without discovering the purpose of their visit.

Given her unimpressive standing in society, Tuppence couldn't imagine what the pair hoped to achieve with their two A.M. break-in. By all accounts, Miss Tuppence Templeton was an unremarkable creature: plain of face, slight of build, quiet of voice. At five-and-twenty, she was a confirmed spinster, as firmly on the shelf as any copy of the *Complete Works of William Shakespeare*. She'd had her chance, of course—three glittering seasons in which to nab a husband—but she had failed so spectacularly to garner any attention, let alone a single measly suitor, that her parents decided it was more practical to put her to work. Why pay a governess to educate her two younger sisters when she was more well-read than an Oxford don?

Was it a sort of punishment for failing to establish herself?

Yes, Tuppence rather thought it was. Her mother had been a reigning beauty in her day and her father a much-sought-after parti. Both believed that one got out of society what one put into it, and they were very cross at Tuppence for not throwing herself into the social whirl with sufficient vigor.

Neither understood that their daughter was incapable of throwing herself into anything. She walked thoughtfully, carefully, sometimes even eagerly, but always with measured steps.

Impatient, annoyed and more than a little embarrassed to have produced such a lackluster offspring, Lord and Lady Templeton decided Tuppence would be more useful behind the scenes, working to ensure her sisters didn't suffer the same disappointing fate as she. They were in London now for the come-out of Hannah, whom Tuppence was charged with squiring around. In the blink of an eye, she'd gone from governess to companion. It was, she readily acknowledged, a very short trip.

"To be clear, then, you're endorsing a tap—"

"A gentle pat."

"On the arm."

"Perhaps the back of the hand would be better."

Listening to the first prowler's hefty sigh, Tuppence realized with surprise that she'd just discovered the first remarkable thing about herself: Her mind had a tendency to wander when strangers stole into her room in the middle of the night.

This was a good thing, she decided. It meant she kept a cool head in a crisis and didn't panic.

Or maybe it was the opposite. Perhaps she was so frightened, her mind was taking refuge in the familiar and the mundane.

Unwilling to dismiss anything out of hand—there was that cool head again!—she considered for a moment the possibility that she was terrified, then decided it couldn't be true as she displayed no physical signs of distress. Her heart was not racing in terror or anxiety; her breathing was calm and even.

If anything, she was intrigued and curious.

Again, she marveled at their presence in her room and wondered if they could have made an egregious mistake. Like her, the Templeton town house was nondescript and people often rang the bell in error. Perhaps her trespassers had meant to break in to the residence next door. If their behavior so far was anything to judge by, then they were certainly not the brightest or most professional housebreakers she'd ever come across—although, to be accurate as well as pedantic, they actually *were*, for the two women were the first and only housebreakers she'd ever come across.

Nevertheless, the more she thought about it, the more convinced she became that her guests had meant to invade the bedchamber of Viscount Headfort next door. He was, after all, a notorious rake, and surely a notorious rake was a more likely target for a late-night visit than a mousy spinster stuck at the beck and call of her siblings.

As entertaining as she found the farce being enacted over her sleeping form, Tuppence decided that it had gone on long enough. The early-morning hours were fleeting, and her intruders would no doubt want to move on to their proper quarry before the sun rose. Additionally, Hannah had a busy day planned for her, and Tuppence could ill afford to lose even one hour of precious sleep. Given her lowly status in the household, she would be expected to give French lessons to her younger sister Caroline before her lazy charge ordered her first cup of chocolate.

Smothering a yawn, Tuppence rolled over, sat up, blinked at the figures barely visible in the dim light of the dying fire and said, "Before you poke, pat, tap or otherwise prod me awake, I must inform you that you missed your intended target's bedchamber by one entire town house. Viscount Headfort lives next door. I'd like to console you in your failure by assuring you it's a common mistake, but you are actually the first ones to make it, which is, I suppose, an accomplishment in and of itself. Now, if you would quickly and quietly show yourselves out the way you came, I'd be very grateful. Actually, no," Tuppence added with another yawn, "given your record so far, I don't trust the pair of you to safely find the exit. Very well, I will escort you myself."

Rather than take offense at this long and somewhat impertinent speech, the first intruder turned to her partner in crime and said with a trill of satisfaction, "I told you she was perfect."

"I didn't disagree with your assessment of her suitability," her accomplice said calmly as she squinted her eyes in the inky darkness. Then she walked over to the fireplace, removed a candlestick from the mantel and used the dampened embers to light it. "I simply suggested that bursting into her bedroom in the middle of the night was perhaps not the best way to make her acquaintance."

"Ah, a candle. Very clever, Vinnie. I do think I shall help myself to one of those as well. You don't mind, do you?" she asked her host, whose wide-eyed wonder was easier to see now that a taper was lit.

Bewildered by the circumstances, Tuppence withheld her approval of the candle-lighting scheme, a development that had no effect on her visitors' behavior. With the addition of the second taper and then a third, she could make out the features of the women's faces and was shocked to discover her intruders were none other than the Harlow Hoyden and her twin, Lavinia.

Her confusion deepened at the sight of the notorious young women who were known for doing what they pleased despite the consequences. Tuppence had never spoken to either highflier, and her conviction that there must be a mistake grew stronger. "If your intended target was not Viscount Headfort, then perhaps you meant to seek out my sister Hannah. She's just out this year and has made quite an impression on the *ton*. Her room is two doors down and across the hall. I must warn you, she's a much sounder sleeper than I, and a gentle tap on the arm would hardly be sufficient disturbance to wake her. I suggest you consider a hearty shake of her shoulders. Now, if you'll excuse me, I'd like to get some rest. Do tell Hannah I said hello."

The Harlow Hoyden, who had become the Duchess of Trent upon her marriage, sighed with satisfaction, gave her sister an I-told-you-so look and sat down on the edge of the bed. "It is an absolute pleasure to meet you, Miss Tuppence Templeton. I'm—"

"I know who you are," Tuppence said, slowly realizing that the only person in the room who had made a mistake was her. These women were there to see her—*her*, mousy little Tuppence Templeton. She couldn't imagine what she'd done to bring herself to the attention of the

Harlow twins. In the two months since her family had come to town, she'd done little more than escort Hannah from one affair to the next. Once her function had been fulfilled—that was, after her sister had been successfully delivered to the event—she would retire to a quiet corner to mark time with the other companions. She knew how dreadfully boring her existence must seem to outsiders, the young things who laughed gaily at every witticism their beaux uttered and the married ladies who cast coy looks at men such as Viscount Headfort, but there was an honesty about the way she lived her life that she relished. And the other companions were not quite the dull fish society assumed them to be. Many of the women she conversed with regularly were intelligent and interesting, and she genuinely enjoyed her interactions with them.

But such minor delights as these were hardly the sort to have drawn the notice of the Harlow Hoyden.

Thoughtfully, Tuppence said, "I'm surprised to discover you know who I am."

The Marchioness of Huntly wasn't as forward as her duchess sister, and rather than make herself at home on the bed, she pulled over a chair. "Of course we know who you are," she said, sitting down. "We were presented the same year. You wore a lovely dress to your come-out ball. It was white, of course, but had a royal blue–and–white sash, which made me desperately jealous. Being blond, I was forced to wear pastels. If it wasn't pink, it was lilac or pistache."

Delighted to be remembered—and in such vivid detail!—Tuppence sat up further in the bed, brushed the blankets aside and curled her legs underneath her. "I recall your come-out ball, as well. I tripped on the way into supper and you graciously caught my arm and helped me regain my balance."

"Actually, that was I," said the duchess, with a wide grin. "And it only seemed fair that I help you remain upright when I was the one who knocked you over in the first place. My intentions were good, I swear. I was trying to escape the clutches of Mr. Bertram, who had declared his eternal love only seconds before. I was not then, nor at any time later, in the market for a husband, but even if I had been, I would never consider a beau who had made his declaration on the way to claiming a prawn."

Sparing only a thought as to how a woman who'd never aspired to having a husband managed to nab such a coveted one, Tuppence laughed and commended the duchess on her scruples. "I'm not even remotely romantic, and yet I, too, would be put off by the alarming practicality of his approach. Verily, one doesn't want a lover to waste away whilst repining, but skipping a meal or two would not be entirely inappropriate."

"My rejection had no ill effect on his appetite at all. He ate six prawns in rapid succession and then moved on to the roast widgeon."

Tuppence's eyes brightened at once. "I remember the roast widgeon! It was sublime."

"My mother would be happy to hear that," the duchess said. "She thought the plum sauce was too heavy. She complained about it for days."

"It was prepared beautifully," Tuppence said. Then she added, because it was very unlikely the Harlow Hoyden and her infamous sister had come to her bedchamber to discuss events that had transpired six years ago, "Now, on to the matter of your presence here. Are you *entirely* sure you didn't mean to disturb someone else's sleep? As I said, my sister, who is in the middle of a brilliant season, is just down the hall. She'd be delighted to meet you—both of you," she added with a darting glance at the other woman. "She fairly worships your grace. She aspires to a duchy as well."

"And she has taken Emma as her model?" the marchioness asked with a horrified glance at her sister. "Please extend my sympathies to your mother."

Although Tuppence dipped her head in acknowledgment, she thought it was an odd thing for the first female member of the British Horticultural Society to say. The Harlow Hoyden's exploits were famous, yes, including a mad dash to Newmarket in a curricle to break Sir Leopold's record, but they were all minor peccadilloes compared with her sister's recent behavior. Petitioning for membership to the society had been scandalous enough, but it had been widely assumed that, once her goal was achieved, she would do the decent thing and quietly withdraw. No lady of proper upbringing would be so cruel as to inflict her presence on her more serious-minded colleagues.

But, to Tuppence's delight, Lavinia Harlow had held steady, refusing to stand down, and tongues had wagged about it ever since. The dowagers were aghast, the pinks were appalled, the swells were horrified, and even the regent himself had been heard muttering about her impudence. How dare she invade their inner sanctum? How dare she discomfit these fine gentlemen in their own citadel of knowledge? How dare she undermine their solemn pursuits with her trivial female presence?

Did the words *male bastion* have no meaning whatsoever to her?

As harsh as the criticism had been, the new marchioness seemed unmoved by it, a posture aided, no doubt, by the support of her husband, who had been a respected member of the British Horticultural Society for years and who had proposed her name for membership in the first place. It also didn't hurt that her brother-in-law and fellow member, the influential Duke of Trent, had lobbied for her inclusion.

"I appreciate your modesty," the duchess said, "but do be assured that it was your sleep we meant to disturb. We are here to ask your assistance with a gravely important matter."

"It's true. We do need your help," the marchioness said. Then, with a censorious glance at her sister, she added, "Although I do believe the meeting could have been contrived in a far less dramatic fashion. Over tea, say, in your mother's drawing room."

"Too risky," her grace insisted. "Nobody must know we are working together."

Tuppence's lips twitched at the duchess's confident assumption that an alliance had already been formed. "*Are* we working together?"

"Of course you're free to decline our request for assistance," she conceded graciously. "But our research reveals you're an intelligent woman with a strong sense of right and wrong. I'm sure once you've heard all the facts, you'll be eager to lend us a hand."

"Your research?" Tuppence asked, amused by the prospect of anyone, let alone the fashionable Duchess of Trent, launching an investigation into her life. She could only imagine what tedious reading that was: Subject woke up, taught siblings to conjugate French verbs (*parle, parles, parle, parlons, parlez, parlent*), accompanied sister to Lady Newlyn's rout, sat with other companions in corner, conversed with other companions in corner, drank warm lemonade with other companions in corner, accompanied sister home, went to sleep.

Little in her routine changed from day to day save the verbs (*donne, donnes, donne, donnons, donnez, donnent*).

"Our research," the duchess said firmly. "You sold your grandmother's garnet-and-opal ring in order to buy Miss Carsdale's companion passage home so she could take care of her sickly mother. You presented evidence to Lady Harkness that proved her butler was pilfering the silver, not her daughter's governess, as she originally believed. You sent a letter to Lord Featherweight telling him to cease his attentions to Lady Sophia or you would be forced to make sure he was unable to devote his attentions to any lady in the future. The last was very ominously worded. Was it a death threat?"

Although Tuppence was taken aback by the question, for she was not accustomed to being asked if she'd threatened to take a life, she was more shocked by the list the woman had managed to compile. Nobody but the parties involved knew of the events, and she couldn't imagine any of them making an honest confession to the Duchess of Trent—certainly not Featherweight, who'd left for the country soon after, chased out of town not by her but by his creditors.

The stories were true, of course, but they sounded far more ennobling when detailed one after the other. Yes, she *had* helped Martha arrange travel home when her mother fell gravely ill and Lilly's mama refused to advance her salary to cover the cost of the coach. It was the only decent thing to do. But her actions weren't entirely selfless. The ring in question had belonged to her grandmother, a tyrannical woman who had pinched her cheeks more than she'd patted them and who took great joy in silencing her with thunderous looks. Tuppence relished the idea of the heirloom ring—a heavy, bulbous affair that never sparkled—being worn on the pinky finger of an elaborately turned-out parvenu. And for the proceeds of the sale to go to improving the circumstances of one lowly companion! Such generosity was anathema to everything her grandmother held dear.

The poor woman must be rolling in her grave.

Or so Tuppence dearly hoped.

When Tuppence didn't respond immediately, the marchioness, assuming she was unsettled by the revelation of so much private information, rushed to assure her it would remained confidential. "Our associate is very discreet in both his methods and his demeanor. He won't tell a soul what he's discovered."

As relieved as Tuppence was to hear it—and as interested as she was in learning how their so-called associate uncovered so many of her secrets—she was more alarmed by their estimation of her character. No good could come of anyone having such a positive impression of her.

"I believe Miss Templeton is more worried about

what generous deed she'll be asked to perform in the future rather than the discovery of the kindnesses she's done in the past," the duchess observed, humor glinting in her eyes.

"Naturally, yes, I find it somewhat concerning when a duchess and a marchioness break in to my room in the dead of night to recruit my help in the service of an important matter. It does seem to portend something dire or at the very least inconvenient," Tuppence noted soberly.

Her grace laughed, and a dimple peeked out from her left cheek. "You're right. I've made a career of causing inconvenience to others, and I regret doing so again. I truly do. If we had another option, then we would have spared you this intrusion. But we've exhausted all our avenues and come to you in humility to respectfully request your help."

Tuppence very much doubted that the woman who set an African deer free from the Royal Menagerie and then married a duke could be humbled by anything, but she didn't question her sincerity. It was enough that the Harlow Hoyden perceived herself to be humbled. "Very well. I'll listen."

The marchioness smiled with relief and reached out to clutch her host's hand. "Thank you," she said, squeezing her fingers lightly and then immediately letting go. "We realize there's no advantage to you in agreeing to help us. It would be a selfless act of kindness."

Although she nodded, Tuppence didn't entirely agree with this observation, for she was beginning to see the advantage of an association with the Harlow twins. Life rarely surprised her, and when it did, it was stingy with its wonders. The big revelation of the week before had been that her thirteen-year-old sister, Caroline, had actually studied the vocabulary list. She still spelled only fourteen of the twenty words correctly, but it was a vast improvement over the nine she'd gotten correct on the previous exam.

But now life had thrown an unexpected development in her path, and she found the prospect of the unknown oddly exhilarating. The last time she'd felt like this was early in the season, when she'd waited in the darkness of Lord Peterson's carriage for Featherweight to appear. He'd concocted a nefarious scheme to compromise Lady Sophia in order to secure her lavish dowry for himself, and discovering his intentions, Tuppence had taken the girl's place. How angry Featherweight had been when he detected her plain features in the dim light of the coach and not his rich quarry! His fury, swift and intense, turned his face as red as a strawberry and spread down his neck and up his ears. Tuppence was unsettled by its ferocity, but she held her pistol steady as she threatened to damage a vital part of his anatomy if he persisted in his ruthless pursuit of Lady Sophia. Then she very pointedly and accurately aimed her gun at the relevant body part to drive home her intentions.

There was something in that moment that she found very satisfying. It was not, she thought now, the danger that gratified her but the confrontation itself, meeting one's adversary on the field of challenge and outmaneuvering him, either with wit or brute force.

There were few things Tuppence loved more than a challenge, and conceding that truth for the first time, she realized she would probably agree to whatever the Harlow sisters asked of her, for she knew it would comprise a very great challenge indeed. Easy tasks walked in the front door and had tea in the drawing room; only difficult ones invaded your sleeping chamber at half past two in the morning.

Determined to reveal nothing of her thoughts, Tuppence nodded noncommittally at the marchioness and asked her to proceed with her request.

"It has to do with the hose," her ladyship announced.

To be sure, Tuppence was not expecting that. "The hose?"

"Yes, the hose. The ordinary garden hose, to be exact," the marchioness explained. "The garden hose is typically made of leather that's been stitched together. It works well enough, but its utility is hampered by the material's lack of elasticity. It will burst, you see, rather than stretch when the water pressure is too high, which is—"

Her sister cut her off with a flutter of her hand. "Yes, yes, the contemporary garden hose is an entirely desperate affair. It deserves to be consigned to the rubbish heap of history along with corsets and mattresses stuffed with grass and leaves." She turned to Tuppence with an amused gleam in her eye. "Vinnie is passionate about hoses and can run on for hours about their inadequacy. But we don't have hours if we want to be out of here before your maid comes in to light the fire. Suffice to say that Vinnie, perceiving the contemporary garden hose's deficiency, very cleverly invented another, which employs Indian-rubber to increase the leather's elasticity. It's really quite brilliant how she deduced that a process invented by a shoemaker to increase his shoes' imperviousness to rain and puddles might also improve the elastication of the hose. Having made this hypothesis, she painstakingly—"

Now the marchioness interrupted with an impatient hand gesture. "And if we let Emma run on about my brilliance, we will still be here when the maid comes to damp down the fire in the evening. The relevant piece of information is that I invented a new type of garden hose."

"And then promptly abandoned it," the duchess said disapprovingly.

Her sister glanced at her deprecatingly and then looked at Tuppence to clarify. "I went on my wedding trip."

"For two months," her grace said with a moue of disgust.

"Yes," Vinnie agreed serenely, "I went away with my husband for two months. And while I was gone—"

"While she was gone," the duchess interrupted, too annoyed to let her twin tell it in her calm tone, "an amoral wretch filed for the patent on her invention."

Tuppence, who had been enjoying the interplay between the sisters, the easy rapport with which they teased each other bearing no resemblance to the way she and

Hannah rubbed together, straightened her shoulders and looked at Vinnie in surprise. "Your actual invention?"

"Yes," she said firmly. "My actual invention."

"Are you positive?" Tuppence asked. "If the Indian-rubber process you based your innovation on was widely known, then perhaps another inventor worked out a similar contrivance that bears a striking resemblance to yours."

The marchioness shook her head. "No, the formulation on the application is identical to mine, and as Emma was explaining, I worked on my device for months, altering the recipe by minute amounts of turpentine and other ingredients until the elasticity attained the ideal consistency. I cannot believe that someone else would have settled on the exact same formula. Similar, yes, perhaps even disconcertingly alike, but not identical in each measurement. As well, someone looked through my notes. I did not think much of it at the time because I assumed one of the servants disrupted them on accident, but in light of Tweedale's application, I see now that someone broke into my lab and copied the information. It's the only explanation that makes sense."

"The person who did this was motivated by malice, pure and simple, and hiring someone to steal the formula is a minor transgression compared with his other sins," her grace said. "First he tried to keep Vinnie out of the horticultural society with lies and deceit, and when that failed, he sought to humiliate her publicly. We've thwarted his every attempt, the last of which was both treasonous and violent, and with the help of the Runners have driven him from the country. And yet even from another continent, he has resurfaced to bedevil us. I shall not bore you with the petty details of the fierce rivalries in England's gardening community, mostly because I've never cared enough to discover them. Rest assured, however, that the enmity between the British Horticultural Society and the Society for the Advancement of Horticultural Knowledge is so great that a member of the latter wouldn't hesitate to steal an invention from a member of the former if it would increase the illustriousness of his own organization, which Vinnie's hose does. It's a towering achievement that any group would eagerly take credit for."

Vinnie nodded. "I want to demur, but what Emma says is true. Having one of its members receive the patent for my gardening hose would be a huge coup for the Society for the Advancement of Horticultural Knowledge."

Now Tuppence's interest was piqued—she truly could not imagine anything more fascinating than the internecine infighting among gardening zealots—but she refrained from satisfying her curiosity for particulars and instead asked the women if they had any proof of their claim. Even as she voiced the query, she wondered how such a thing could be proved. Would a document signed by a solicitor attesting to the date of one's creation have any bearing on the case? To whom would one present such a document? To the head of the patent department? *Was* there a patent department? She had no idea.

Even though she'd no cause in her five-and-twenty years to acquire knowledge about patents and the procedure for securing one, she suddenly felt her education was sadly lacking in this area. It represented, she thought, a general neglect of subjects not directly related to her welfare.

While she was questioning the usefulness of her schooling—aside from instructing her younger sibling in verb conjugation, she'd few opportunities to show off her fluency in French—the Harlow Hoyden emphatically said yes, they had proof. At the same moment, her sister said no.

"We can," said the duchess. "All we have to do is summon all twenty-five members of the British Horticultural Society to appear before the Home Secretary and swear to Vinnie's invention."

Unmistakably appalled at the idea of calling on her fellow members to give evidence on her behalf, the marchioness turned bright pink. Before she could respond, however, her sister added, "There are, of course, procedures in place for making a more standard claim against a patent application, but I refuse to even entertain the option. For one thing, there's no guarantee that justice would prevail, and for another, history must clearly and uncontestably show that Vinnie invented the modern gardening hose. If we raised a challenge, there would always be a suspicion that it wasn't true—as if someone had put a parenthesis around her name with a note saying, 'maybe or possible inventor of the modern gardening hose.'"

To Tuppence, this logic was irrefutable. However the matter was resolved in the courts, few people would find it possible to believe that a woman had done something first or that she'd done it better.

Being of a practical bent, Tuppence asked her visitors if they'd considered offering a bribe to a carefully selected person in a position of authority who could make the problem go away. In her experience, money resolved most, if not all, situations in a satisfactory manner.

At this query, the duchess smiled with delight and darted a triumphant look at her sister, pleased, it seemed, by their host's ready grasp of the facts. "Considered, adopted and abandoned. The patent process is remarkably complicated, requiring almost two dozen signatures, stamps, warrants and seals, and every step of the way, it's overseen by an official whose position requires little work but offers great remuneration. A man who is paid well to do nothing isn't interested in being paid very well to do something. I'm appalled by the lack of industriousness even as I'm impressed by the surfeit of integrity."

Tuppence noted the wry humor in her voice. "I suppose there's some consolation in knowing one's trusted officials are worthy of one's trust."

"And that's why we've come to see you," the marchioness said, "though I must apologize again for the poor timing of our visit. Emma insisted it was the only way, and although she does have a flair for dramatics, I'll concede that our plan hinges on nobody suspecting a link between us and you."

"Ah, yes, your plan. Do tell," Tuppence said, more intrigued than ever. Above all else, she loved things that *hinged* on something else. "How do I fit in?"

"Prickly Perceval," her ladyship announced with a grin.

CHAPTER TWO

Although Tuppence had been unable to imagine what the young woman would say, the name she let slip was somehow beyond her comprehension. "Prickly Perceval?" she repeated, not sure she'd heard it correctly.

But Vinnie nodded firmly. "Prickly Perceval."

Still not understanding, Tuppence furrowed her brow and looked from one sister to the other. "Prickly *Perceval,*" she said with extra emphasis on the second name as though *which* Prickly might be the source of her confusion.

Alas, there was only one Prickly Perceval in the known world.

"Yes, Prickly Perceval," her ladyship confirmed.

At once, the image of harshly pinched lips under thundering black brows flitted through her head and before she could stop herself, she flinched. Her last run-in with the notoriously caustic gentleman had been far from pleasant, which was surprising, for only minutes before she'd saved his sister from almost certain ruin. She hadn't expected him to prostrate himself before her in gratitude, but a sincerely delivered thank-you would not have been amiss. "I'm sure I can't be of service in any matter that involves Prickly Perceval. We have but the thinnest of acquaintances," Tuppence said.

"True," the duchess said, "but he owes you a favor."

At this reasonable-sounding observation, Tuppence guffawed. She didn't mean to let forth such an indelicate bark of laughter, but she couldn't stop herself. The idea of the famously surly lord acknowledging a debt to anyone, let alone a dowdy spinster who interfered in matters that were none of her concern, was vastly amusing. "I doubt he sees it that way. In fact, I'm sure he'd argue that 'tis I who owed him a favor for the honor of extricating his sister from the clutches of a callous fortune hunter."

The Harlow Hoyden's lips twitched as she conceded the veracity of this statement. Nicholas Perceval, the eighth Earl of Gage, was not known for his humility. Indeed, his opinion of himself—his intelligence, his importance, his lineage, his position, his stature, his knowledge of arcane Parliamentary procedure—was said to be as high as the heavens, and in a much discussed illustration by a caricaturist named Mr. Holyroodhouse, his ego, in the form of a heraldic shield with feet, was shown floating amid the clouds.

As was typical of the arrogant noble, he'd sent a bill to the proprietress of the printshop demanding his share of the sales. His commercial bent earned him further scorn in a second drawing that depicted him sweeping the entrance of Gage Hall like a merchant.

"Whatever pose Lord Gage chooses to affect," her grace said, "the fact remains you performed a great service for his family and he owes you a debt of gratitude."

As simplistic as this logic was, Tuppence refrained from pointing it out because she wanted to hear the rest of their plan. The inclusion of Prickly Perceval made the scheme entirely untenable, of course, but she wouldn't share that bit of information until her curiosity had been appeased. "And once Prickly acknowledges his debt?" she asked.

"You request a favor," her ladyship explained.

Again, the cold black eyes of the Earl of Gage flashed through Tuppence's mind, and she couldn't conceive of a circumstance less likely to happen. She considered herself an intrepid soul—anyone who would pull a gun on Lord Featherweight had pluck to the backbone—but even she lacked the courage to request a favor of Prickly Perceval. She'd been the target of his derision once before and would do everything in her power not to suffer the humiliation again.

Clearly, that meant she couldn't possibly assist the Harlow Hoyden and her sister in their endeavor to outwit the patent department. They'd have to muddle through without her, something she thought with some disappointment they'd most likely do very well.

Rather than admit her cowardice to the two women before her, who struck her as fearless with their curricle races and horticultural memberships, she asked what the favor entailed.

"A tour of the Patent Bill Office," the duchess said.

How simply she stated it, as if asking Prickly Perceval for a tour of anything were a banal activity. And this—requesting to be shown the Patent Bill Office! Was there any desire more absurd or strange? How would she explain it? What possible reason could she give to justify her sudden and bizarre interest in an obscure governmental agency? She had no history with the law, no knowledge of its workings, no familiarity with its machinations. Such an appeal would make her seem like a complete nodcock, at once utterly ridiculous and ridiculously affected.

If Prickly Perceval didn't immediately deride her request, she would be tempted to do it for him.

Then another thought struck her, more terrifying than the last: What if Prickly said *yes*? What if the Harlow sisters were right and Prickly was cognizant of the debt her owed her? She would be forced to spend an untold amount of time in his presence, perhaps an hour, maybe two. He might even insist on driving her to the office, which would mean an entire carriage ride—there *and* back—in his company.

Oh, the horror.

Something of her shock must have shown on her face because the marchioness quickly added, "It sounds outlandish, I know, but it's not as implausible as it might appear. The matter of patent reform is being discussed in the House of Lords, and your father is on the select committee investigating the law and practice of attaining a letters patent for an invention. Lord Gage is head of the committee and will easily understand your interest when you explain your father has sought your opinion. As a dutiful daughter, you wish to provide informed counsel and cannot do so without firsthand experience."

Ah, yes, *easily*, thought Tuppence cynically. It was just an easy and simple matter of professing Lord Templeton's interest in her opinion and doors would magically open. Nobody would ever question the veracity of that story because it bore such a startling resemblance to the truth.

And horses could fly and pigs could solve mathematical equations and she herself was having tea with the prince regent later that day to discuss the novels of Mrs. Radcliffe.

The truth was, Lord Templeton, while perhaps not the most hardheaded didact in the entire kingdom, refused to accept guidance from his peers. His intractable belief in his own rightness was legendary, and he would hardly take advice from a woman, certainly not one whose inability to nab a husband proved her lack of usefulness to her family and mankind.

At this thought, a wave of sadness washed over her, and she ruthlessly squashed the dismaying bout of sentimentality. As if self-pity had ever done anyone a speck of good!

She took a deep breath, raised her eyes to the marchioness and said, "And after Lord Gage grants my wish and leads me on a tour of the Patent Bill Office, what do I do next?"

"You will observe from the periphery of your vision a slip of paper peeking out from behind a cabinet," Vinnie said.

"I will, will I?" Tuppence said, seeing not just the outline of the plan but its details as well. "And I suppose I will make a great show of picking it up and examining it."

"That would be helpful, yes," her ladyship said. "If you so desire, you may read it aloud or you may simply hand it to the clerk."

"Or I could hand it to the earl," Tuppence suggested, "so he may have an opportunity to examine it, as well."

The Harlow Hoyden smiled and her dimple peeked out. "That's your prerogative, of course, but I imagine, as the head of a select committee investigating the defects of the intricate and difficult patent process, he'll be very interested in your discovery."

Tuppence nodded. "He will no doubt be dismayed to learn that important documents, such as the Marchioness of Huntly's application for a new and improved gardening hose—dated, I presume, several weeks before the other petition—are falling behind cabinets."

"I should think he'd be very horrified indeed," her grace said.

"And the poor clerk, too," Tuppence observed, "who will be shocked to find that an application he's never seen before has somehow gotten lost amid the clutter. I should think he'd want to stuff it back behind the cabinet and pretend it never existed."

"An understandable instinct," the duchess agreed with a grin.

"But with Prickly Perceval there to witness his carelessness, he'll be forced to address the matter by entering the marchioness's application into the public record," Tuppence said, feeling some sympathy for the blameless clerk. If the man was clever enough, he would immediately turn around and blame the oversight on a colleague who had the misfortune to be absent from the office. "Which will invalidate the first application *and* validate any suspicions Prickly might have that the procedure for securing a patent is in desperate need of repair."

Tuppence had to admit it: The plan was good. At

once practical and Machiavellian, it had a sleek simplicity that augured well for its success. As the author of more than a dozen schemes herself, she knew the challenge was figuring out how to make sure the players responded properly to a particular circumstance. A few of her plots had nearly unraveled when the target behaved in an unexpected manner. Mr. Cragledale, for example, who was supposed to be horrified at finding himself alone with an unmarried young woman, instantly threw himself at her, his lips nearly scraping her left ear before she was able to propel him back and secure his agreement to provide his sister's former companion with an excellent reference.

The duchess was right, of course, about one thing in particular: The plan did hinge on there being no discernable link between the Harlows and Tuppence Templeton. It was her genuine lack of interest in the injustice she was to uncover that made the discovery beyond reproach. What cause would anyone have to raise an eyebrow or cry foul?

Several pieces of the puzzle were still missing, of course, including how they would arrange for the marchioness's application to drop behind the cabinet in the first place and from whence they would get the application itself. It could not simply be a petition written and signed by the inventor, for that would prove nothing. No, it would have to be a document endorsed by an official of some consequence to give it legitimacy. That meant either recruiting an important official—which, if they succeeded in doing, then would not need the rest of the plan—or forging the document themselves.

Tuppence found she desperately wanted to know the rest—and not merely because having an incomplete picture of something always drove her a little mad. As ridiculous as it was to be plotting the infiltration of the patent office in her bedchamber at three in the morning, she was enjoying the experience, particularly the novelty of discussing the details of a scheme with other schemers. Tuppence Templeton always worked alone.

Because she'd never had coconspirators before and because she didn't have them now, for she knew she would have to decline their request, Tuppence spoke sharply to hide her disappointment. "How grateful inventors everywhere would be to you if they could only know of your kindness."

She had intended to give offense, but the Harlow Hoyden took none. "It goes without saying that our motives are purely selfish, but we always like to leave things in a better condition than when we found them, and fortunately for us the patent system has much room for improvement."

"Truly," Vinnie added, more sensitive to the slight than her sister, "the current system is unwieldy and expensive, and the average inventor can ill afford the time or money it requires to attain one. As Emma said, the favor we do is for ourselves, but others will benefit as well."

Tuppence nodded because she imagined it was true. Although she didn't know anything about how one secured a patent, she did know administrative offices in general tended to be large, complicated and governed by small-minded despots who loved to enforce obscure rules.

Or, at least, that was what her father had said too many times to count.

Regardless of the Harlow sisters' altruism—whether an intended objective or an advantageous consequence— she would not help them achieve it, for she would not risk another confrontation with Prickly Perceval.

As a rational human being, Tuppence knew the humiliation she'd suffered at Prickly Perceval's hands had been exaggerated in the month since it had happened. At most, the stinging set-down he'd subjected her to had lasted five minutes. In truth, it was probably more like two. And yet her mortification was made more acute by her own outsize expectations. Like everyone else, she knew the sneering earl by reputation, and when devising her scheme to save his sister from ruin, she'd imagined earning his gratitude and doing what the *ton* considered impossible: securing his friendship.

Obviously, there was no way to make up for three un-inspiring seasons or to undo half a decade of spinsterhood, but she'd thought if she could only perform that one tiny miracle—win the respect of the supercilious lord—it might burnish her own reputation just a little bit. People would point to her and remark in hushed tones how she, the un-assuming Miss Templeton whom nobody ever noticed, had somehow charmed civility out of the beastly Prick.

It was a foolish fantasy, and it horrified Tuppence to the center of her being to know she was capable of such ridiculous drivel. It was only that the circumstance had seemed so right for a wondrous event: the giddy weekend party in the country, the innocent girl, the ruthless fortune hunter, the sinister society matron who showed her guests to the wrong rooms. All it needed was the swashbuckling hero to swoop in, save the damsel and thwart the villain.

And Tuppence did—she swooped and saved and thwarted with ease and effortless grace—and all she want-ed in exchange was a thank-you and perhaps a lightening of Prickly's famously thunderous countenance. That was it: sincere gratitude and a look of kindness. She didn't even aspire to a smile.

What she got, however, was the reprimand of a life-time, an excoriation so severe and unkind, she felt as if she were the villain of the piece. How dare she imperil his sis-ter further by not immediately informing him of the dan-ger! How dare she attempt to resolve the matter on her own! How dare she consider herself better equipped to handle the situation than a man of one-and-thirty!

How dare! How dare! How dare!

On and on the litany went, the volume of his voice growing louder and louder, the force of his anger growing stronger and stronger, until she felt no larger than a mouse squeaking helplessly under a broomstick.

Well, there's your miracle, Tuppence thought cynically:

The Earl of Gage transforms interfering spinster into scrambling vermin.

No, Miss Tuppence Templeton would not be confronting Prickly Perceval again. She would sooner tell Prinny to his face that he should limit the number of fruit tarts he ate.

Realizing there was no reason to keep the Harlow twins in suspense about her decision, Tuppence opened her mouth to politely decline their offer. Before she had said three words, the duchess jumped to her feet and gestured for her sister to rise as well. "We really should let Miss Templeton get some rest. We've made our case as eloquently as possible. Now she must be allowed to think on it and arrive at a sensible decision."

Although the marchioness seemed as surprised as Tuppence by the abrupt movement, she quickly stood up. "Yes, yes, of course. You must take some time and think about it. We don't want to rush you into anything."

"Of course you mustn't rush into a decision," the duchess agreed with a bright smile, "but you mustn't *not* rush either. The fraudulent application is with the Lord Privy Seal, and we all know what that means."

Tuppence didn't have a clue what that meant, but its significance had no bearing on her answer. "I can tell you right—"

Emma cut her off again. "You will be at Lord Clerkenwell's ball tomorrow evening, I trust? Of course you will. You said your sister is making her come-out this season. You can give us your answer then. We can't be seen speaking to each other, but never fear, we'll devise a means of communication."

"But I know—"

The duchess refused to let her finish. "It's three in the morning and you are clearly too tired to gather your thoughts properly. Indeed, the circles under your eyes are vast and your skin is a little gray. You must get to sleep at once. When you wake up, have a nice filling breakfast—

may I suggest eggs with kippers—and take an inspirational walk around the square. Then, if you're feeling clearheaded, you may decide. If you are still too tired to come to the right decision, take a little nap and think on it some more."

Tuppence's lips twitched as she realized the Duchess of Trent was determined to keep her in a continual state of repose until she was ready to offer her help. Smothering a grin, she tried one more time to announce her decision, but her grace blithely interrupted with an effusive compliment on the commode along the far wall, which she attributed to George Hepplewhite, although it was in fact by Sheraton.

"You might as well give up," the marchioness said softly to Tuppence as her sister wrongly identified the maker of the bedstead in her enthusiasm to admire it. "Emma has spent her whole life hearing no. She knows when it is coming and is well adept at putting off the inevitable."

With a heavy sigh, Tuppence turned to the other woman and smiled sadly. She couldn't explain why she felt as if she was letting her down. Vinnie and her sister had stolen into her room in the middle of the night like thieves and requested an impossible favor. *She* had done nothing wrong, and yet she felt compelled to apologize. "I'm sorry. I really am."

Her ladyship reached out and grasped Tuppence's hand warmly. "You mustn't feel bad. Emma likes to couch things in as dramatic terms as possible, but we do have other options. You were our best hope but certainly not our only one."

Although Tuppence didn't believe that was true, she greatly appreciated Vinnie's graciousness in saying it, for it absolved her of responsibility. The relief she felt at the absolution, however, was immediately undercut by a sense of cowardice in feeling it. She wasn't a spineless creature, to be sure, but nor was she the fearless heroine of her imaginings.

The truth, she assumed, lay somewhere in the middle.

While Tuppence was reassessing her bravery, the Harlow Hoyden walked over to the northern window, threw open the sash and looked down. Tuppence stared agog as she realized that was how they'd gained entrance to her room.

"We climbed up the oak," the Harlow Hoyden explained, correctly interpreting her host's expression. "All very safe and sturdy. You're extremely lucky to have such a viable option directly outside your bedchamber window. In our country home, I had to make do with a dogwood tree, which, as you know, is really just an overgrown shrub. It was absolutely useless."

"It flowered beautifully in the early spring," her sister said, explaining its use. Then she turned to Tuppence and thanked her for her hospitality. "I'm especially grateful you didn't scream for help when you realized your room had been invaded."

"I am, too," the duchess said, "although, unlike my sister, I paid you the compliment of expecting you would not. You are far too intrepid to swerve into a panic over a little break-in."

It was, Tuppence thought, perhaps the highest compliment anyone had ever paid her, and knowing how little she deserved it, she smiled uneasily and thanked the women for dropping by. It was an absurd thing to say—they had hardly paid her a social call—but in the awkwardness of the moment, she could do nothing but fall back on years of breeding.

"Nicely done," the Duchess of Trent said, her tone full of admiration for her lovely manners. "My mother-in-law would be very impressed."

Her sister laughed. "No, she would be horrified that you have one leg over a window sill and are two stories up."

The duchess clutched the side of the window with one hand as she tugged her skirt over the sill with the other. "Actually, she wouldn't care about the height. A lady being astride anything would be horrifying enough."

"True," Vinnie allowed as her sister effortlessly transferred herself from the window to the tree. "Good night, Miss Tuppence. We will see you later at Lord Clerkenwell's ball."

"But we won't speak to you," the duchess said from her perch on the bough of the oak tree, "because we mustn't reveal our connection. But know that we're very grateful. Now please go to sleep. You have much thinking to do."

Tuppence watched silently as the Marchioness of Huntly climbed over the windowsill, slid into the tree and followed her sister branch by branch to the bottom of the oak. When they reached the ground, neither woman looked up. Rather, they straightened their dresses, smoothed their hair and walked toward the street as if nothing untoward had happened. Quickly, they disappeared from view, but Tuppence remained by the window for a long time afterward, inexplicably reluctant to go back to sleep.

CHAPTER THREE

To be clear, Nicholas Perceval, the eighth Earl of Gage, did not consider everyone in the entire kingdom of England and Ireland to be a buffoon. He thought Hobson, his butler in Belgrave Square, was fairly competent at his job and particularly good at discouraging visitors from staying above twenty minutes. He respected Mr. Grovely, who, in overseeing the wine cellar at Brooks's, frequently met his expectations and sometimes exceeded them, such as when he decanted a remarkably fine 1798 Château Lafite. He admired William Barnes, the *Times'* special correspondent who reported on European affairs with clear-eyed common sense, and he appreciated the services of Mr. O'Connell, a deputy in the Clerk of the Parliaments office who dispatched his duties with almost alarming efficiency.

Among his own set, it was harder to find men whom he esteemed, for their ability to engage in intelligent conversation was hobbled by their somewhat limited fields of interest. Dandies thought only of the cut of their coat, Corinthians only of the grace of their jab, and rakes only of the depth of their pleasure. There were some exceptions to this general rule, of course. Lord Addleson, for example, was famously in thrall to his tailor and yet could debate a parliamentary bill with impressive cogency. And Viscount Denbigh, whom one rarely found more than ten steps from a whist table, could discuss the plays of Christopher Marlowe with wit and perception. Yes, there were certainly bright spots among the *ton* to whom Gage was happy to devote his time and attention.

The vast majority of his peers, however, were bottle-headed clunks who couldn't defend an argument even with a sword and two liveried servants holding the victim still. Naturally, Gage didn't go in search of quarrels, but nor did he shy away from them. Indeed, he relished the opportunity to refine his thinking and was peeved by people whose resolve crumbled under the first hint of interrogation. The earl didn't care about right and wrong, for the truth was a paltry thing easily influenced by clever rhetoric. No, what mattered to him was the ability to articulate a position and assiduously defend it. He had no patience for people who muttered incoherently or stammered in confusion. Prickly Perceval asked for only one thing: For you to speak clearly, concisely and convincingly. Comply with this request and he will pay you the highest compliment of listening.

It was, Gage believed, a fairly unrigorous standard, and he couldn't understand why so few members of the *ton* were able to meet it. He knew cleverness wasn't contagious—it couldn't be acquired simply by being in the same room as an intelligent person—but surely logic and reason could be taught. Despite having undergone the same general education as he, many of his peers seemed to have learned little beyond how to acquire gaming debt efficiently. If only they had also acquired the mathematical skills necessary to dispatch their financial obligations with equal effectiveness.

Of course, the Earl of Gage hadn't met *every* member of the beau monde. In fact, he made it a matter of policy to meet as few as possible. This year, however, he was stuck squiring his younger sister around and was therefore required to attend a seemingly endless string of social events. Balls, routs, musicales, garden parties, weekend parties, dinner parties—the itinerary was exceedingly tedious, and in two brief months, he'd been forced to interact with more dullards and bores than he had in the whole of his previous one and thirty years.

If only the girl would get herself leg-shacked! He'd presented her with several fine prospects, gentlemen whom he'd investigated personally and judged to be entirely adequate. None of these suitors seemed remotely interesting to him, for they were first-born sons with more hair than wit, but they all came from established families with well-managed estates and reasonably full coffers. Most of them were young, some of them were handsome, and all of them were eager to marry a woman with a significant dowry. Letty's portion wasn't immense, but it was large enough to attract ne'er-do-wells and fortune hunters, something his sister seemed to find vastly amusing. Being the target of greedy villains was nothing to laugh about, and yet he couldn't convince Letty to take the matter seriously. An ardent devotee of Minerva Press novels, she relished the idea of being the heroine of her own story— which was utter nonsense, of course. Miss Leticia Perceval was merely a minor character in her brother's narrative and would one day play a supporting role in her husband's.

It was this misguided sense of self-determination, this inexplicable conviction that she had the right to make her own choices—and wasn't he letting her, by permitting her to select a husband?—that had led her to think she could handle a scoundrel like Mr. FitzWalter all on her own. What an irresponsible act! What a thoughtless decision! What an overweening conceit!

True, a crisis had been averted. The villain's plan to get Letty drunk with rum-soaked muscadine ice and have her delivered to his room so that *she* may compromise *him* had been scotched. But the fact that the weekend party hadn't ended in his sister's ruin was merely a function of good luck, not skill or planning. How easily and swiftly the situation could have gone the other way.

He knew, of course, that it wasn't entirely Letty's fault. As headstrong as the girl was, she'd never think to take on a fortune hunter all by herself. No, the blame for that misguided assumption rested firmly on the shoulders of that busybody woman with the plain brown hair. What was her name?

Gage shook his head, unable to recall it now. In truth, he doubted he'd ever known it. He couldn't imagine why he would have, as the only thing more intolerable to him than a man with no conversation was a woman with no conversation. A gentleman at least would prattle on about matters he had some knowledge of, if not interest in, but a lady could speak for hours about things of which he was completely ignorant. Like gloves, for example. Letty could chatter about gloves—style, length, color, material—as if they were the most significant item in the world and not a sundry fashion accessory to protect one's hands against dirt and the elements.

The woman who had led Letty astray was even worse, for she had nothing at all to say for herself. Having put his sister at further risk, she could only stare at him in blank-faced horror as he called her to account for her reckless-ness. Her silence spoke volumes, and he knew she'd real-ized the error of her ways as he made a catalog of her ter-rible decisions. If he'd given her the opportunity to apolo-gize, he was sure she would have taken it, but he'd been too angry to linger. He had made one promise to his par-ents before they died—of putrid fever within days of each other when he was only seventeen—and that was to take care of his sister. He might not enjoy the responsibility and he might resent the intrusion it imposed on his well-ordered life, but he took it seriously and he'd be damned if Letty found herself riveted to a hardened fortune hunter just because one overly confident, interfering female thought she had things firmly in hand.

It was he, in fact, who had ultimately settled the mat-ter of FitzWalter, threatening the young man, an insolent puppy of only three-and-twenty, with debtor's prison if he ever came within ten feet of his sister again. And it was no idle threat, for Gage had made a full investigation of the villain's financial situation and stood in possession of several of his IOUs. He was ready and willing to send him to Coldbath Fields at the slightest provocation.

Fortunately, the scoundrel had heeded his warning, leaving London immediately for Hillpoint Castle, the country estate of his guardian, Lord Wallasey. Gage knew where he was because he'd sent an investigator to Herefordshire to make sure he arrived safely. FitzWalter was a feeble enemy, to be sure, and no longer a menace, but the earl believed in being thorough. He would not let a mouse upset the apple cart for want of attention.

He was thorough now as he surveyed Lord Clerkenwell's ballroom and noted several young men who were on his list of approved husband candidates, such as Viscount Aldford and Mr. Kenworthy. The former was dancing the quadrille with a blond-haired beauty who far outshone his sister, a circumstance that Gage thought deserved further consideration, for many young bucks counted comeliness as among the chief requisites for marital affection. Examining Letty with a disinterested eye, Gage conceded there was room for improvement. Like him, she had the bold features of the Percevals—the dark, deep-set eyes; the aquiline nose; the square jaw—but whereas these attributes gave him a pleasingly masculine look, they seemed to overwhelm his sister. Her black brows were a shade too heavy and the set of her mouth a tad too obstinate. More curls would no doubt do the trick, just a few more framing her face to soften the angularity of her features. Her dresses could probably benefit from a slight alteration as well. More pearls, perhaps, or rosettes, something to brighten the pastel confections she was required to wear as a young lady in her first season.

Contemplating how to achieve these goals—would embellishing the gowns suffice or was another trip to the dressmaker in order?—Gage felt a shiver of disgust as he recognized how far he had fallen: reduced not only to chaperone but to lady's maid as well.

Would there be no limit to his humiliation?

That Letty was doing nothing to end his suffering there could be no doubt, for rather than smiling endearingly at an eligible suitor, she was speaking quite earnestly to a young woman on the other side of the dance floor. On the face of it, the woman posed no threat to his sister's prospects, for she was a plain little thing with not much to recommend her, but by cornering Letty's attention, she risked undermining his entire project. His sister couldn't meet and beguile the man she was to marry if she didn't meet or beguile any men. Conversation with one's peers was all very good, provided, of course, that one could stand one's peers, but such niceties were a luxury that would have to wait until after the nuptials.

With this thought in mind, he strode across the ballroom to interrupt his sister's tête-à-tête and was surprised when the nondescript creature, seeming to perceive his intentions, flashed a bright smile at him. Without question, Gage was used to such treatment: In the months since he'd begun escorting his sister around, he had learned that one could not put an item on the marriage mart without finding oneself similarly listed for sale. With his rank and wealth, he soon realized himself to be the target of every coy miss and matchmaking mama in the city. The simpering nonsense he'd had to endure reaffirmed his decision to seek romantic company from among the skilled courtesans of the demimonde. It was impossible to say which was worse—the trivial blather of schoolgirls or the sycophantic acquiescence of their mothers.

As accustomed as the earl was to being greeted with an eager smile, he found himself taken aback by this one, for there was something different about it. There was a sharpness to it, perhaps even a bite, and as he drew closer, Gage saw that the woman was past the first blush of youth. She was, he thought, as old as five-and-twenty.

Letty also smiled at him as he approached. "Ah, Nicholas, your timing is impeccable, for Miss Templeton and I are in need of someone to voice a deciding opinion because we can't agree on who is the greater villain: Count Wolfenbach or Lord Liverpool."

The question did not surprise Gage. Of course his sister was ardently debating scoundrels from her favorite Gothic novels instead of courting a future husband. Rather than air his frustration, he said amicably, "I would love nothing more than to settle the dispute but I'm not familiar enough with either character to have an opinion."

Miss Templeton looked at him sharply. "You do not know Lord Liverpool?"

"Is it so surprising that I don't share the same taste in literature as my sister?" he asked, slightly amused himself. "Which novel is he from? *Orphan of the Rhine* or *Necromancer of the Black Forest?*"

"Neither," Miss Templeton said matter-of-factly. "He's from Westminster, as the Earl of Liverpool is generally known as the prime minister of the United Kingdom. Surely, you've heard of Parliament. I was given to understand from your sister that you've participated in it."

Now it was Gage's look that was sharp. "You're comparing one of our country's leaders to a cartoonish villain in a Minerva Press novel?"

If she heard the offense in his tone, she didn't acknowledge it. "Yes, and finding him wanting."

"Which is perfectly absurd," insisted Letty. "Count Wolfenbach killed his wife's true love and locked her in a closet with his bloody corpse."

"The Corn Laws," Miss Templeton said simply.

"He then kept her imprisoned in a castle for nineteen years and told her her son was dead," Letty added.

"The Corn Laws," Miss Templeton repeated.

"He murdered an elderly woman," Letty observed.

Unswayed, Miss Templeton shook her head and said yet again, "The Corn Laws."

Letty turned to her brother with an exasperated sigh. "See why we need an arbiter? Miss Templeton will not listen to reason."

"Nor will your sister," Miss Templeton said, looking at Gage with equal frustration, "for she seems to believe the suffering of the few outweighs the suffering of the many."

"Suffering?" Letty echoed. "He drugged his own servant with opium and burned him to death."

"Bah!" her friend said with a dismissive wave of her hand. "Burning to death is much preferred to slowly starving, which is the fate of thousands of children in our country, thanks to the artificially inflated price of corn."

Then both women turned to look at the earl with an air of expectation, and Gage realized he was curiously unwilling to take a position. He had supported the Corn Laws because it had seemed reasonable to him that farmers would be worried about the price of corn once grain imported from the Continent entered the market. Their concerns had in fact been justified, for the price per quarter of corn dropped a precipitous fifty percent in three years. And yet what Miss Templeton said was also true: The tariff kept the price of food high, and many families were too poor to feed their children properly.

The matter was clearly an issue of some complication, and reducing the prime ministership of the Earl of Liverpool to a one-on-one competition with an absurdly evil villain in a Gothic novel hardly served anyone's dignity, least of all his. And yet giving any answer that included Count Wolfenbach would make him feel like a damned fool.

Instead, he said the first thing he could think of: "Why don't you discuss gloves?"

Letty looked at him as if he had suddenly sprouted another head, which, he readily conceded, was an entirely fair response. He couldn't imagine any topic less worthy of discussion.

"Gloves?" his sister said with a confused glance at her friend. "What could one possibly have to say about gloves?"

"Quality," he said, standing firmly by his long-held belief that it's better to defend a point than to abandon the field. "Which material is best? What style is most appealing? There is much about gloves to spark a hearty debate."

"Ours gloves are white and made of silk and extend beyond our elbows," Letty said, still clearly puzzled by her brother's sudden turn to frivolity. He must be making a joke, she thought, although he did not have a history of such behavior. The Earl of Gage was always very serious. "All the women here are wearing white silk gloves that extend beyond their elbows. It is not a contentious topic."

Miss Templeton tried to smother a smile and failed. "Your brother is not as daunting as I remember."

Surprised to discover they had already met, Gage examined the young woman before him for signs of familiarity but could find nothing that resonated. Up close, she was as unremarkable as she had appeared from afar. Her features were ordinary, if perhaps a little delicate. Her hair was an indifferent shade of brown, too light to be rich and too dark to be vibrant. Her lips were a slender strip of pale pink that he could easily imagine narrowing further in a pinched moue of disgust, and her eyes were dull and brown, like bark.

She looked, he decided, like a governess who was perpetually disappointed in her charges. Even when a smile had flitted across her face, she still had a general air of dissatisfaction. He was reluctant to add to it but could see no advantage to be gained in claiming an acquaintance he did not recall. "I'm afraid I must request another introduction as the first one has slipped my mind."

At once, her demeanor changed as the gleam of amusement entered her eyes, lightening her appearance strikingly. "Oh, no, this is terrible," she said with what struck him as genuine distress. "I was relying on our prior association to convince you to aid me in a future endeavor."

He smiled, something he very rarely did in a crowded ballroom, particularly in the third month of squiring around an unmarried sister who seemed disinclined to remedy the situation, and said, "All is not lost. I'm sure a word or two will be enough to remind me of our previous meeting."

"One word, yes," she said, her lips twitching in amusement, "that would certainly do it. FitzWalter. Mr. Horace FitzWalter. No doubt you now recall how I saved your sister from his evil clutches and how you owe me a favor in return, a favor that I would now like to claim if it isn't too inconvenient."

But the Earl of Gage didn't need a whole word. A single syllable was sufficient. No, not even that—with the first flush of the F sound, the entirety of their previous interaction had come flooding back.

Gage straightened his shoulders and glared at the presumptuous ninny who had almost ruined his sister. Was this really the same woman? He hadn't retained a single detail about her in his memory, dismissing the interfering upstart only seconds after he'd stalked away from her, and looking at her now, he decided that was entirely understandable. Her appearance was ordinary in every way, save her dowdiness, which felt excessive or aggressive in its drabness, and perhaps her eyes.

Yes, her eyes, he thought, which seemed to sparkle now with satisfaction, as if his oversight had somehow given her the advantage.

It was absurd, of course, for nobody got the advantage over him, not his peers in Parliament and certainly not this imprudent little nobody.

How dare she persist in her absurd belief that *she* had done *him* a service! Was her grasp on reality so tenuous, her understanding of logic so meager, that she truly believed her cobbled-together plan to derail Mr. FitzWalter's evil scheme had had any long-term effect on his behavior? Surely, her naiveté was as problematic as her confidence.

"No," he said severely, "it is *you* who owe *me* a favor for not telling your parents about your disastrous interference in my sister's life. Say thank you now and we'll never mention it again."

He expected her to cower. Most people—men and women—cowered when he addressed them in his commanding tone, imbued with all the imperiousness of a general ordering troops around the Continent. Yet this brazen female, this slip of a girl, really, as she barely came up to his shoulder, stood unflinchingly before him, amusement still glinting in her eyes. He could not fathom where the self-possession came from, for if he could remember anything about her from their last encounter, it was how easily she'd yielded to his superior understanding of the situation. She'd been too intimidated to mutter an apology, but if she'd had the ability to compose herself, he was confident she would have expressed her regret.

That was only a month ago and yet how dramatically things had changed.

"Goodness, my lord, you seem still incapable of fully comprehending what transpired that night. I wonder if this a persistent problem for you." She turned to Letty and asked with seemingly sincere concern, "Does this happen frequently? Is your brother's ability to grasp basic facts often impaired? Perhaps he sustained an egregious head wound as a child. Have you consulted a physician? I can recommend an excellent one in Croyden Lane. I'm sure it's nothing a good blood letting won't fix."

Gage let her talk. Although he was silently seething at her impertinence, he was curious to see just how far she would take it. Would she, by the end, have him consigned to the insanity ward at Bethlem Royal Hospital?

Unconcerned for his dignity—or, it appeared, for her own—his sister giggled and said, "Our Aunt Josephine once mentioned that my uncle dropped him on his head as an infant, but it wasn't from a very great height, a mere six inches if the story is to be believed. But I cannot conclusively say that isn't the source."

Knowing he was being provoked was all Gage needed to stop himself from rising to the bait. He detested giving in to the expectations of others, especially when their hopes were clearly apparent, so he said with a calmness that bore no resemblance to his earlier tone, "I believe the problem is your inability to grasp basic facts. After your futile attempt to thwart FitzWalter, and here I will applaud your noble if ill-advised efforts"—he could be condescending too!—"I routed the villain with a threatening letter, leaving him in no doubt of his perilous future should he persist in his attentions to my sister. That is how *I* remedied the situation."

Given the rationality of his explanation, Gage expected to see some sign of remorse, some indication that she understood how easily he'd solved a problem she'd made worse with her reckless intervention, but her face revealed no contrition. If anything, she seemed even more amused.

"I don't know what information your missive contained, my lord," she said silkily, "but my own informed him that I would reveal every detail of his venal scheme to his famously straitlaced guardian, Lord Wallasey, if he bothered Lady Letitia again. He complied with my request because he knows I have proof in the form of a letter I tricked him into writing to his confederate, Mrs. Shipton, confirming the details of his plan at her country party— which is how *I* remedied the situation."

Dumbfounded, Gage stared at the girl, not entirely convinced she wasn't a figment of an overly tired imagination. In recent days, he'd been struggling to balance his responsibilities in Parliament with his obligations to his sister and as a result had missed several hours of sleep per night. He could think of no explanation for how a woman could have such an irrational amount of faith in her own abilities other than she wasn't real. He'd expressly told her that he would handle the matter of FitzWalter himself, and to discover that she had not only ignored his directive but blithely continued with her foolhardy plan horrified him in a way he'd never experienced before. He was unaccustomed to not being immediately deferred to, especially by a dull and colorless female with no prospects.

No doubt it was her poor prospects that made her so bold. She clearly had nothing to lose on the marriage mart and lacked the imagination to understand what could be at stake for women with a higher market value.

As much as he wanted to rail at her, he realized the situation would not be aided by his indulging the prickliness for which he was famous. Instead, he would give her the cut direct and insist Letty have no further dealings with her.

Before he could implement his plan, Miss Templeton said, "And because I handled the problem so adeptly, for your sister was just telling me she hasn't heard anything from Mr. FitzWalter—that is, in case you're wondering, how we got onto the topic of villains in the first place—you now owe me a favor. I will understand, of course, if you choose to disavow all knowledge of the service I've done you. You are a gentleman, and although your kind treats each other with the utmost respect, you have a different standard for women. If you *are* to renege on your obligation, I hope you won't feel too bad about it, as it's really not your fault. You are merely a victim of your own nature, and I'd as soon grow cross with a turtle for moving slowly."

Gage could see what she was doing, for the maneuver was so blatant even a blind man could trace its outline, but he felt trapped by it nonetheless. He could still give her the cut direct or he could subject her to one of the acerbic set-downs for which he was famous, but either option served only to give her the upper hand. She was expecting him to behave in an imperious fashion, to fall back on the une-quivocal privilege bestowed by wealth, rank, gender and breeding, and he could far too easily envision the glint of amusement that would enliven her eyes as he strode away.

He refused to give her the satisfaction.

And yet the thought of acknowledging an obligation that didn't exist was equally infuriating.

Surely, there was a third possibility he had yet to con-sider, and to buy himself time to think of it, he looked at his sister, who was, by all appearances, enjoying herself immensely. The depraved minx! It was all her fault he was in this fix in the first place. If she had just confided in him about Mr. FitzWalter's wicked plan to compromise her, he could have been spared the unpleasantness of this scene, particularly Miss Templeton's egregious condescension.

And then he realized: What was good for the goose was good for the gander.

"I am delighted to assist you, Miss Templeton," he said with such uncharacteristic smoothness that none of his intimates would have recognized him, "because I could never refuse a damsel in distress. You may talk of obligations and favors all you like, but such things have no bearing on my willingness to extricate you from a situation from which you are unable to extricate yourself. You need only ask and I will do whatever I can to solve your problem for you."

She didn't like that. Oh, no, she did not like the implication of helplessness, especially the female kind, and her lips pressed into a thin line of displeasure. Happy to have the advantage for the first time in the conversation, he leaned back on his heels and waited to see how she would respond. Her options were even more limited than his own because she was the supplicant in this situation. She needed something from him, and he wasn't going to give it without first extracting his pound of flesh. Before he was done, he'd have an apology for interfering in his sister's life and a promise never to do so again. Indeed, he would go one step further and make her swear not to "help" anyone else's sister either. He was not used to seeing himself in a philanthropic light, but if he could spare another man the unpleasantness of dealing with Miss Templeton, he would be happy to make an exception.

Given the angry press of her lips, the earl expected a heated outburst or at least a cry of frustration as the woman realized she'd been bested at her own game. But the Templeton chit didn't give him the satisfaction. Instead, she took a deep breath and heaved a comically loud sigh of relief. It was so hefty, he was surprised the curtains on the far side of the ballroom didn't flutter.

"And here I was, afraid you would set conditions before committing yourself to rescuing me from the miserable debacle that is my life," she said, her mouth settling into a grin as she warmed to her new tactic. "You have no idea how much of a damsel in distress I am, my lord. Indeed, my trials make the life of poor Julie de Rubin, the heroine of *The Orphan of the Rhine,* seem like a placid lake in Hyde Park. The help I need is extensive, and given your fine speech, I know you won't cavil at providing everything I require. Should I give a full account now or should we arrange another meeting, perhaps with your secretary to make a record? There are fourteen items in all, but some explain themselves. Like item number six, for example, which is to negotiate a fair price for a new horse at Tattersall's. You've done that before, I trust, and successfully, one presumes, so you are in no need of guidance from me. I will, of course, set aside time to advise you on various strategies should you require it."

Amusement danced in her eyes as she fluttered her lashes in feigned concern. He imagined she'd have to think long and hard to come up with fourteen different tasks for him to perform, but he didn't doubt she could do it. And like the twelve labors of Hercules, the assignments would be difficult and tedious, and she would discover some way to find fault with how he handled each one.

Although part of him—a very, very small part of him—admired the clever way she'd wiggled out of the trap he'd set, the earl was extremely annoyed to find himself outmaneuvered once again. She was right: He *had* committed himself before making conditions, a tactical error he regretted the second she'd drawn his attention to it. The failure stemmed from the disparity of their situations. Being a man, he was used to dealing honestly with his fellows; as a woman, Miss Templeton was accustomed to using trickery and wiles to get her way.

It was little wonder he was no match for her.

Determined to end the exchange as quickly as possible, he said, "Although I'm not surprised to learn you have hours to spend bracketed with my secretary, my time is far too precious to be thus consumed. Instead, why don't you tell me the first item on the list right now and I will endeavor to address the matter as quickly as possible so that we may consider it settled."

"Of course, my lord," Miss Templeton simpered as she lowered her eyes in a show of deference. "Your time is so much more valuable than mine, and I'm mortified to think of my taking up a single moment more than is necessary. I do so humbly apologize for forgetting for even one moment how incredibly important you are and how incredibly unimportant I am."

Relieved that the girl wasn't entirely lost to reason, the earl nodded because he knew this sensible statement to be accurate. As a member of Parliament working on key legislation that would affect the welfare of the country, he was indeed more important. Additionally, he was a man of strong intellect who knew how matters should be handled. Having been given the gift of intelligence, he never hesitated to use it, particularly while in the company of those whose understanding seemed to be less than keen, a description that, sadly, appeared to apply to the majority of the *ton*.

Gage knew his mental and social superiority to be undisputed fact, and yet there was something about the way she stated it that made the idea seem ridiculous. It was as if she were mocking him by aggressively affirming the things he knew to be true.

Obviously, that suspicion was way off the mark. No woman, not even the delusionally self-assured Miss Templeton, could believe she was his equal, or, heaven forbid, his superior. Being of relatively sound mind and body, she had to realize her position in comparison to his. If she were to die tomorrow, the country would be unaffected.

Her parents would mourn, naturally, and her siblings, if she had any, would weep, but the course of liberty and justice would continue unabated. In *his* absence, however, the lives of ordinary Englishmen would worsen as the rules of the land became ever more elaborate and unfair. He did not discharge his duties out of a desire to improve the lot of common folks—although, to be clear, he believed that the lot of common folks could and should be improved—so much as from a need to eliminate the waste and inefficiency created by needlessly cruel and complicated laws. The Earl of Gage cared less for the struggle of the farmer to feed his family than the struggle of the farmer to attain a license to make candles in the privacy of his own home. Pragmatically, he understood the need for taxes, but the way the government created a dozen steps in order to collect a dozen payments offended him on a fundamental level. Levy the duty once, all of it, whatever the sum, and be done with it.

"At last we agree on something," Gage said with an approving nod. "I'm gratified to discover you have the capacity to be sensible, Miss Templeton. Until a few moments ago, such clear thinking seemed beyond your ability. Now, as we said, a single favor so that I may solve one of the many problems that plague your calamitous life. What shall it be?"

Miss Templeton's eyes narrowed again in displeasure, but she didn't hesitate to respond. "A tour of the patent office."

Rarely had the Earl of Gage been so surprised. Even her previous exploit of trying to single-handedly rout Mr. FitzWalter paled in comparison with her request to see the patent office. That episode, while foolhardy, ill-conceived and potentially disastrous, offered a hint of glamour and derring-do. Clearly, Miss Templeton saw herself as the heroine of her own story, just like his sister, and her involvement made a sort of topsy-turvy sense. Given the inevitable dreariness of her life—for how could a spinster's life be anything else—it was little wonder she would seek out adventure wherever she could. But the Patent Bill Office was dreariness incarnate. It was a cramped room with little natural light and a bevy of squinty-eyed clerks who growled in annoyance every time someone dared to enter their domain. The floors were dusty, the walls were sooty, and the desks were stained with decades of ink. Those who stepped within its bleak confines had all hope for a glorious future slowly drained from their bones as they wended their way through the costly and byzantine process of acquiring a patent.

The Patent Bill Office at Lincoln's Inn was where dreams went to slowly suffocate to death.

Because the request was so unexpected and, frankly, bizarre, the earl opened his mouth to ask why in God's name would she want to visit such a wretched place. But even as his lips began to form the words, he recognized the strategic mistake and immediately changed course. Asking questions would only prolong their interaction, and that was the last thing he wanted to do. Furthermore, it was no business of his why she wanted to do any of the things she did. As long as she stayed out of his sister's path, their association was at an end. All he had to do now was make sure Letty understood that, as well. He couldn't let her headstrong whims undermine his resolution.

"A tour will be arranged posthaste," he said calmly. "My secretary will see to the details and meet you and your companion at Lincoln's Inn at the prescribed hour."

"That is perfect, my lord. Thank you," she said, leveling a sweet smile at him. "And of course I understand your wish to delegate the responsibility to a subordinate. I don't question your manliness at all."

No insult had ever more cleanly hit its mark.

The earl straightened to his full six feet and three inches, glared down at the brazen upstart with thunderous brows and said with cold menace, "I beg your pardon?"

Knowing her brother's temper and the sure signs that

he was at risk of losing it, Letty took a step back. Miss Templeton, either oblivious or incapable of feeling fear, leaned forward as she answered the question—which, any dunderhead could tell, wasn't actually a question. It was an outright repudiation.

Perhaps, Letty thought, considering a third option, Miss Templeton was a few feathers short of a duck.

"Truly, nobody would judge you harshly for wanting to avoid further contact with the woman who bested you. Well, perhaps a few small-minded people would," Miss Templeton conceded with gracious reluctance, "but you mustn't count me among their number. Indeed, if any one of them had the nerve to criticize you in my presence, I would heartily defend you."

She wrinkled her brow in concern, as if genuinely worried on his behalf, but the earl was onto her tricks by now. He knew everything she said was the opposite of what she believed. "Bested me?" he asked, struggling to hold on to the little control he had. To reveal the extent and depth of his anger would be to let her win. And she must not win.

Taking a page from her book, he decided to affect amusement. He filled his lungs sharply, pictured Gage Hall on a beautiful Derbyshire morning in late spring and twitched his lips purposefully. "Bested me?" he asked, pleased that his efforts paid off. He sounded thoroughly entertained by the daft idea. "Your version of events is delightful. Yes, let's say you've bested me a dozen times over. How pleased you must be with yourself. Would you like to take a bow? May I provide an ovation? Your ego seems to need constant bolstering; otherwise I can't imagine why you tell yourself such stories. Bested me." He shook his head as if highly entertained by the notion and had the satisfaction of seeing a wave of pink creep up her neck.

She was capable of feeling shame.

Good, the earl thought.

Despite her embarrassment, she didn't back down, and Gage, who only moments ago wanted nothing more than for this conversation to be at an end, was strangely pleased that she extended their encounter. He was, he realized, interested in seeing what she would do next. Every time he thought he'd trapped her in a corner, she'd somehow managed to slither free.

Her cheeks still red, Miss Templeton laughed nervously and averted her gaze while conceding he was correct: Her conviction that she had bested him in the FitzWalter matter might have been a *bit* overstated. "Considering the situation, I'm rather glad it will be your secretary who will accompany me to the patent office."

Hours later, Gage still couldn't say what exactly had motivated him to act in such a perverse manner—it could have been the relief in her voice or the prospect of furthering her discomfort or plain old curiosity about why she wanted to visit that godforsaken place—but for some inexplicable reason he insisted on escorting Miss Templeton to Lincoln's Inn himself.

At once, her eyes, now wide with surprise, flew to his, and he thought he detected in their brown depths a flicker of some deeper emotion. Trepidation, he supposed, well pleased by the development. Finally, he had the upper hand. Determined to retain it, he allowed Miss Templeton no time to speak. Rather, he told her to expect him at her town house two days hence, bid her a curt good night and strode away without pausing to make sure his sister followed.

CHAPTER FOUR

Tuppence couldn't stop shaking. The moment Lord Gage had spun on his heels, the second he had walked away, the tremors had started, first in her left hand, then in her right. Before she knew it, both arms were trembling and her teeth were chattering with such ferocity, she feared her jaw might shatter.

It was nerves, she knew. The conversation with Prickly Perceval had been the most nerve-racking experience she had ever endured in the whole of her life. Awaking in the middle of the night to find two strangers hovering over her bed was a trip to the circus in comparison.

And to speak to him so boldly! Tuppence still couldn't believe she had accomplished the feat with such composure. Her voice had sounded so assured, and her eyes never wavered. Inside she was a mass of quivering anxiety, but outwardly she was calm and composed. Miss Templeton was hardly what one would call the shy and retiring type—she had gone toe-to-toe with Mr. FitzWalter and Featherweight, among other adversaries—but those previous confrontations had been carefully mapped out in advance. Tuppence was too cautious a creature to rush her fences and always researched her subjects with painstaking thoroughness. Only when she felt confident she could predict her opponent's every move did she seek to engage him in battle.

Her run-in with Gage, however, bore none of the hallmarks of her usual work. She had been neither methodical nor meticulous, jumping in on impulse when it became clear he had no idea who she was. Tuppence had no illusions about herself. She knew where she fell in the hierarchy of memorable women—well below diamond of the first water and only a notch or two above maiden aunt—but she and Gage had had a Significant Incident. With unerring precision, he'd decimated her confidence and demolished her poise, reducing her to a shuddering, stammering mass of feminine uselessness unable to defend her very reasonable actions. She had routed a villain, she had gathered evidence of his perfidy, and she had ensured that the reputation of an innocent girl would remained unblemished. She'd achieved all these objectives with a minimum of fuss and without anyone discovering the truth, and yet, in the wake of the earl's venom, she had been incapable of speech. He had railed and she had cowered.

For Tuppence, the encounter had been profoundly unsettling, and to discover that her tormentor had no memory of her only a mere four weeks later somehow made the suffering more acute. It had seemed to her to be a gross breach of etiquette, for at the very least a tormentor should be able to recall the faces of his victims—all of them—even the Earl of Gage, whose victims were legion.

Enraged by the lack of courtesy, appalled by the surfeit of disrespect, she immediately began to bait him. She'd been sincere in her refusal to help the Harlow twins, but now she was grateful to have a goal to work toward. Tuppence always performed better when there was an objective to keep in sight. Tweaking the earl's ego for the sake of tweaking his ego would have been gratifying, of course, but it was nothing compared with the satisfaction of knowing she was moving him in the direction she wanted him to go. That he didn't realize she was controlling the conversation surprised her, for she'd assumed a man who insulted others on a daily basis would be more awake to the game. It had been, she thought, almost a little too easy to get him to agree to take her to the Patent Bill Office, and suddenly she was struck by the unnerving possibility that he'd let her get away with it because he was plotting his own move. The idea caused her heart to pound uncomfortably in her chest, and, shaking more forcefully, she ordered herself to calm down and think logically. To what end would the Earl of Gage try to manipulate her? She had nothing he could want. Indeed, she had nothing that any gentleman of the *ton* would want.

No, the simple explanation was the most likely: She was of such little interest to his lordship that it hadn't occurred to him to look for tricks. Being beneath his notice made her above suspicion.

Tuppence would have to use that to her advantage the next time they met, which would be, she realized, in two days' time. Thinking of what was yet to come—the carriage ride to the patent office, the carriage ride from the patent office—she felt a fresh wave of dread overtake her. How far away was Lincoln's Inn anyway? Twenty minutes? Thirty?

The thought of being confined in a small space with the Earl of Gage for any amount of time made her stomach clench uncomfortably. Famous for his disdain of pleasantries, he would no doubt make the experience as disagreeable as possible by staring at her in silent contempt. He would certainly not exert himself to entertain her with polite conversation.

And good thing, too, she thought, appalled by the idea of a tête-à-tête with Prickly Perceval. She couldn't even imagine what that experience would be like: Would he bestir himself to be civil? *Could* he? His contempt for the opinions of others ran deep, and she doubted he could bring himself to agree out of a desire to be kind. Whatever she said, however sensible, he would find fault with it, for that was the way he worked. Being of superior mind, bearing and importance, he alone possessed all the correct views.

But what if I don't say anything sensible, Tuppence thought, her heart tripping in excitement as an idea occurred to her. It would be perverse—oh, yes, very perverse indeed, for utter silence benefited her as much as him—but forcing him to listen to a litany of absurd and baseless theories would be highly amusing as well. She could bore him with stories about a towering snow creature said to torment mountain villagers in Italy and the dragon-like being that haunted the deepest reaches of a lake in Prussia. Both beasts figured prominently in *The Casket of Lord Mantini,* and although each one was proved to be a hoax by the end of the novel—the work of the villain who sought to drive his young cousin over the edge into madness in order to inherit her fortune—the descriptions Mrs. Willesden provided were detailed enough to make them believable for a little while. Miss Templeton felt sure she could do them justice.

How would Prickly Perceval react to a lecture on snow creatures and dragon beings? He would, of course, be tempted to correct her gross misunderstanding of the natural world, but any attempt to educate her would make him appear as foolish as she. What would he do—cite facts that conclusively proved there was no such thing as a ravaging man made out of snow? To not argue with her, however, would be to offer tacit agreement that such creatures did exist, an option that would be intolerable to a man who prides himself on always being right.

Perhaps, Tuppence thought as a slow grin spread across her face, he will default again to the very pressing matter of women's gloves.

She didn't know what about the Corn Laws had required him to seek shelter in such female frippery, but she could only conclude it was a reluctance to choose a side. It should have been easy enough, given that one of the contestants was a fictional character from a Gothic tale, and yet he remained unwilling to say something he didn't quite believe.

There, she thought, another chink in his armor.

Settling on a tactic for their next confrontation made her unbearably eager to employ it, and her limbs, which had finally stopped shaking, began to tremble again, this time with impatience. It was an absurd reaction to have because, despite her recent show of courage, she was still terrified of the man. No one else, not even her parents at their most disappointed, had ever made her feel less than herself, and she couldn't easily overcome the fear that he would do so again.

The strange mix of seemingly irreconcilable emotions—anticipation and dread—unsettled her, and she sought to relieve her anxiety with a distraction. Hannah, she thought, turning her head in several directions as she looked for her sister, whom she hadn't seen in ages. Her last sighting of her had been on the dance floor in the company of Lord Hughland, a calm, brown-haired gentleman with impeccable manners who was first in line for an earldom. During their brief conversation earlier, he had not only remembered Tuppence's name (and what she looked like!) but a few of her interests as well, inquiring about her latest visit to Hatchards and whether she had been able to find Dr. James Currie's biography of Robert Burns, as she had intended. At nine and twenty, he had just enough wisdom and gravitas to keep her increasingly unruly sister in line, and she hoped they would make a match of it. Hughland's fortune was not great—his father had lost a significant sum in a canal scheme in South America—but the Templeton girls had not been raised to expect excessive material comfort. A sturdy house, a dependable mount and half a dozen durable dresses were all they needed to be happy.

At least, it was all Tuppence needed, and judging by her parents' bitter acceptance of her unmarried state, it was probably all she was going to get. Indeed, the seven gowns currently hanging in her wardrobe had better be durable, as they were very likely the last seven gowns she would ever own, assuming she didn't set up a dressmaker's shop in the attics of their house.

Or would the cellars be more appropriate for commerce? It was, she supposed, a matter of how many steps one's clients were willing to climb up and down.

Shaking her head over such foolishness, for she was an appalling seamstress, always pricking her finger with a needle and bleeding on her samplers, she craned her neck and spotted Hannah near the refreshments table. She was drinking lemonade and talking to a blond woman in a white dress with pretty pink rosettes. Although Tuppence had not made her acquaintance, she recognized her immediately as Miss Emily Armitage. Like Hannah, she was having her first season. Unlike Hannah, she was quiet and biddable and rarely more than a step away from her anxious mother, who hovered with agitated suspicion as if Count Wolfenbach himself were about to claim her precious youngest daughter for the waltz. Tuppence couldn't imagine why the concerned mama considered all social events, including Lord Clerkenwell's ball, to be fraught with danger, but she respected the desire to stick close to her charge.

It was something she should probably do more often.

Aware of her duty, Tuppence decided to join the group at the refreshments table. As independent as Hannah was, she was still new to the social whirl and as susceptible to the wiles of a practiced charmer as any country miss. So far, only respectable partis had shown interest in her, but it was just a matter of time before one of London's more well-established rakes took notice. Her spirits were too high to go undetected for long.

Tuppence smiled at the turn her thoughts had taken. Now she was the one behaving as if Count Wolfenbach were among the guests.

How utterly ridiculous.

"I would advise you to take two steps back and act surprised," a low-sounding voice—seemingly male—said in her ear.

Taken aback by the peculiarity of the directive as well as the oddity of its issuance, Tuppence raised her head sharply to protest and found herself confronted with a gangly youth in a purple waistcoat.

"Perfect," he said with solemn approval. "Now two steps back or you're about to get very wet indeed."

Tuppence complied with the strange order. She couldn't say why, but at his words, she took the recommended steps back and missed the worst of the spill by barely an inch. Red liquid splattered her gown just as the glass hit the floor and shattered into a dozen pieces. At once, the young man's cheeks turned a bright shade of pink, and as a footman ran over to clean up the broken glass, he began to stammer out an apology. Shocked by the events, Tuppence stared as he offered her a handkerchief and, leaning close, quietly introduced himself as Philip Keswick, cousin to the Duke of Trent.

"It was Emma's idea," he continued, his tone assuming an air of authority it had previously lacked. "Says I have a reputation for clumsiness so nobody would blink twice if I spilled my wine on you. Ain't so! A few unfortunate bobbles doesn't make one a raggedy mister. But you know Emma. Can't reason with her once she sets her mind to something."

Although Tuppence didn't know the Harlow Hoyden very well, she thought in this case her assessment was on the mark. Just a few months ago, Keswick had made a cake of himself in Hyde Park by losing control of his velocipede and knocking over an unfortunate young woman whose only offense had been standing in the middle of a walking path.

"Accidents happen," she allowed graciously, wondering what would ensue. She didn't doubt this contrived mishap was part of an elaborate ruse to arrange a secret meeting with the duchess. She had observed the conversation with Prickly Perceval and now wanted to know its substance.

As if on cue, Philip said, "Come, you must dab that with sugar before it sets."

Tuppence's mouth twisted into a wry smile as she contemplated the misplaced optimism of his statement. It was unlikely that sugar or any other ingredient would save her gown, which now bore more than a dozen marks—some round, some squarish, all entrenched. The forest-green silk would have little use as anything other than a rather elegant rag. It was disappointing because its retirement brought the grand total number of her dresses down to a meager six. But it wasn't the worst thing, as it was by far the least flattering gown in her collection.

While a footman quickly swept up remnants of broken glass, Phillip discharged his duty, leading Tuppence across the ballroom. She didn't know where they were going. The retiring room was behind them, so that wasn't to be the site of their tête-a-tête. Perhaps the terrace. No, she thought, the night was too warm and welcoming to afford them sufficient privacy. Could he be leading her to the kitchens? Surely, not even the Harlow Hoyden was so bold as to arrange a private discussion in their host's scullery. But he had mentioned sugar so it wasn't entirely implausible to—

Suddenly an arm snaked out seemingly from nowhere, tugged her elbow and pulled her behind a thick velvet curtain. The fluidity of the movement amazed her. She felt as if she had been jerked about and yet the curtain barely fluttered. Only the most observant guest would have noticed anything amiss, and Tuppence doubted such a person existed.

"I appreciate your taking the time to meet with me," the Duchess of Trent said smoothly, as if greeting a caller in her front parlor. Tuppence half expected her to produce a pot of tea, a plate of biscuits and a table to set them on. "Our presence will be missed if we're gone too long, so I will be brief. When is your trip to the patent office?"

Although everything that had happened since the

moment Philip told her to take two steps back had been unexpected, the duchess's apparent omniscience astonished her the most.

Before she could even form the question, the other woman answered it. "I knew you wouldn't be able to resist a challenge. Naturally, you doubted yourself, for it's very hard to be brave at three o'clock in the morning. We all tend to cower under the covers at that hour. But I knew in the light of day, after a good night's sleep, your courage would return. And it has. When do you go?"

Tuppence knew the duchess's understanding of the situation was imperfect—her actions had been spurred by perversity, not audacity—but she liked this description of herself, so she didn't quibble. "Very soon. Only two days."

The narrow frame of time struck Tuppence as problematic, for there were still many pieces of the puzzle to put into place, but the Harlow Hoyden merely smiled and said, "Perfect. The sooner the better. Once I know where exactly in the clerk's office the lost document is to be found, I'll convey the information."

"I look forward to it," Tuppence said, smothering a smile as she tried to imagine what unconventional method the duchess would employ to deliver the vital intelligence. Truly, she wouldn't be at all startled to discover a note concealed in one of her tea cakes.

The duchess nodded firmly, then reached out and squeezed Tuppence's hand in a gesture more suited to her sister. "Thank you," she said with earnest sincerity—yet another surprise. "I'm sure who holds the patent on a watering hose seems like a trivial matter to you, for it seems that way to me, and I'm deeply grateful that you've agreed to help despite that."

"No, your grace," Tuppence said with more vehemence than she intended. She knew how easily women could be erased. She herself felt as if a little more of her disappeared every day. "History isn't trivial."

Either her words or her vehemence resonated with

the Harlow Hoyden, for she smiled kindly and said, "Please, you must call me Emma. Stiff-necked formality is for disapproving society matrons and the broadsheets, not trusted allies."

Being on a first-name basis with a duchess was a coup in any circle, and it struck Tuppence as particularly fitting that her greatest social achievement was to be confined to a slender group behind a heavy velvet curtain. Fashionable at last! How her parents would stare in wonder if they but knew it.

"Very well. Emma," Tuppence said, emboldened by the irony of the situation and her liking of the woman. "I must admit to an indelicate curiosity about the other aspects of the scheme, especially as you don't seem stymied by how little time you have to pull them together. You have the documents all ready to go?"

"We do. My associates are nothing if not efficient," she said with a modest amount of pride. "I won't reveal any details out of respect for the guilty, but a remarkably talented forger has re-created the home secretary's signature with such accuracy that the man himself would swear on a stack of Bibles that he signed Vinnie's petition. It's unfortunate that forgery is an art that must be practiced in secret, for it must be dispiriting to succeed at something so well and not be able to display your skill. I was very grateful to find such a person, as falsifying a convincing signature for Viscount Sidmouth's was the largest obstacle we had to overcome. But we sorted that out quickly enough, arranged for a sworn declaration, and paid you a visit to finalize the scheme. All that remains is the placing of the documents in the patent office, which will be taken care of tomorrow night."

"You arranged for a sworn declaration?" Tuppence asked, taken aback by how casually she'd said the words.

"Yes, all patent applications must contain a sworn declaration."

"But that must be done before a magistrate," she pointed out.

"For patents, it's a master in chancery," Emma explained.

Although Tuppence wasn't familiar with the minutia of the kingdom's judicial system, she recognized a more ominous-sounding office when she heard it. "I don't understand how you can contrive that, as it's impossible to forge a memory. Surely, the master in chancery will not be able recall an event that never happened."

"It seems daunting," Emma agreed, "but Mr. Davidson Berwick's fondness for gin made it an extremely easy problem to solve. Blue ruin has impaired his faculties to such a degree he can recall only a fraction of the petitioners who actually stood before him in Southampton Buildings. Vinnie's watering hose will be just one more contraption he can't quite remember."

"How fortuitous," Tuppence said without a hint of mockery. The master in chancery's destructive habit struck her as a stroke of luck for the Harlow twins.

"It was, yes," Emma said, smiling wide enough for her dimple to peek out. "I can't help but feel as though providence itself wants Vinnie to be properly credited for her invention. Now we really must return to the ball before anyone notices we're gone. You sneak out first, and I'll wait a full minute, then follow."

Tuppence readily agreed that their presence would soon be missed, although she meant the duchess's rather than her own. The only person who would look for her was Hannah, and then only when she needed something, such as permission to dance the waltz—which she knew she wouldn't be granted.

Exiting the confined space seemed simple enough to Tuppence, but before her fingers touched velvet she was treated to a five-point treatise on how to slip through a curtain without making a ripple. It was, according to the duchess, more of an art than a science, which, she hastened to add, was a good thing as Vinnie was the scientist in the family.

Amused, Tuppence listened as Emma explained what she called the principle of wind manipulation and decided that the Harlow Hoyden had had a far more interesting career than anybody suspected. No wonder she'd been such a pariah before her marriage—she clearly had little respect for social conventions—and yet Tuppence was surprised that society had yet to embrace her more fully, for she herself was thoroughly charmed by her grace's enthusiasms. She thought it was delightful that she'd not only mastered the practice of curtain sneaking but developed a theory about it as well. Implementing rule number four (holding one's breath for a count of seven), Tuppence realized she felt inordinately sad that her relationship with the young duchess was to be confined to dark corners. She would have very much enjoyed talking to her in the light.

CHAPTER FIVE

If there was one thing the Harlow Hoyden resented about her change in status, it was the insistence that she should allow other people to do her dirty work simply because she had somehow acquired a duchy. The very idea was insupportable. Indefensible. Unendurable. Imagine—sending your subordinates on a mission that you yourself did not lead. The Duchess of Trent was no ramshackle customer to consent to such dereliction of duty, and she was heartily offended that anyone would believe for even a moment that she would. She, not some underling, would be marching into the inner sanctum of the patent office that night, her head held high.

Or, to be more accurate, sneaking in with her head tucked tightly against her chest. Emma was, after all, a seasoned campaigner and knew better than to stomp around enemy territory drawing attention to herself.

Certainly, she understood why husbands might object to such schemes, as they were high-strung creatures who worried about succession and social standing and the safety of the people they loved. But for a comrade in arms at whose side one had fought many skirmishes to take an exception was entirely inexplicable, and Emma stared at

Mr. Squibbs, confused by his insistence that she let him go in her stead.

"I know how to pick a lock without damaging its mechanism," she said.

The gentleman, broad-shouldered and trim, bowed his head. "I know."

"I can pry open a window using a wedge-shaped metal device," she pointed out, listing yet another of her accomplishments.

Mr. Squibbs lowered his head a little more. "I know."

They were in the cheerful parlor off the front hall that Emma called her office. Although she had lobbied for a space in the servants' quarters, perhaps a large closet near the kitchens, Trent had insisted she take this room, with its generous bouts of midmorning sunlight, bright yellow wallpaper and comfortable settee. The whole effect was a warm and welcoming place where people, to her chagrin, felt warmed and welcomed. She'd been seeking a refuge from the duties and obligations marriage to a duke conferred and had unaccountably wound up with the family hearth.

"I can open a safe by divining its combination from the sounds it makes—a skill not required for this operation but one of which I'm in full possession," she explained.

If anything, the dark-haired man seemed to shrink a little more into himself. "I know."

"I do all these things exactly as you've taught me. In each case, I follow the Squibbs method to the letter. I have nothing but respect and admiration for your expertise."

He nodded slowly, his expression a complicated mix of pride and shame.

"I've never had a more adept student."

She accepted this compliment with a subtle dip of her head. "You are willing to concede, therefore, that I'm entirely capable of handling an assignment like this on my own."

"Yes," he said quickly and without hesitation. "You have all the skills required to achieve your goal."

"Then I cannot understand why we're having this

conversation, Mr. Squibbs," she said, her tone as calm as it was confused, as if all she sought was enlightenment. "By your own admission, I have the training and the skills necessary to succeed. If there isn't a single concern on which to base your objection to my breaking into the patent office and planting the petition documents, then I can't comprehend why you would object."

With quiet deliberation, London's greatest lockpick straightened his shoulders for the first time since entering the room via the side-street window, looked the Harlow Hoyden directly in the eye and said, "Your husband would skin me alive if I let you go."

Now the Duchess of Trent pointed her finger accusingly as if he had just finished off the last Shrewsbury cake and exclaimed, "Ha!"

The shout of triumph unsettled Mr. Squibbs, who had been prepared for her anger, and he stared at her, fully aware that the interjection was somehow worse. "Ha?" he repeated.

"You admit it," she said, striding across the room until she was a mere six inches from her target. "You're more afraid of Trent than you are of me."

He didn't even need to respond; his look of surprise said it all.

The Harlow Hoyden shook her head sadly. "You wound me, Mr. Squibbs. Truly, you wound me to the quick."

Genuinely fond of the duchess, Mr. Squibbs hated to think he'd offended her in any way and rushed to assure her she was terrifying. "Indeed, your grace, you're the most terrifying woman I've ever met."

Grateful for the compliment, Emma nodded her head and said thank you. She had little time to savor the tribute, however, for he immediately ruined it by adding, "But your husband would knock me flat if I let you put yourself in danger. You know he would. Then he'd throw my body into the Thames."

Unsurprisingly, this comment drew a hefty sigh from

the duchess, who didn't consider her actions to be the consequence of any man's largesse. She knew Mr. Squibbs felt obliged to the duke, whose concern for her welfare stemmed from sincere affection for her person. During an earlier incident, in which she had saved England from a traitorous spy and possibly a French invasion, he had promised Trent to keep an eye on her. That compact was precisely the reason she'd kept Mr. Squibbs ignorant of the finer points of her plan. She had been trying to protect him from his own sense of loyalty.

And yet he still figured out the details and betrayed her.

"Tell me, Mr. Squibbs," she said thoughtfully, "who sought you out in a rundown tavern on the docks and offered you a lucrative assignment?"

The lockpick swallowed, unsure where she was going with this line of questioning but confident it wasn't anyplace good. "You, your grace."

Emma nodded. "And who encouraged you to expand your underground network and offered tactical support on how to do it?"

"You, your grace," he said, his cheeks starting to turn pink.

She nodded again. "Correct. And who introduced you to roast stubble goose with applesauce and insisted you take home all the leftovers, as you had discovered it was the finest meal in all the kingdom?"

Now his face turned entirely red. "You, your grace."

"Yes, that's right, I did. And this is how you repay me?" she asked, her tone a daunting mix of disappointment, surprise and confusion. To her credit, she seemed well and truly baffled by the development. "By sending a note to my husband's club telling him I plan to break in to the Patent Bill Office this very evening? Indeed, in but a few hours. Do we not have our own compact of trust and understanding? Is there no honor among conspirators?"

With every word she said, the lockpick seemed to deflate a little more. Unable to meet her eyes, he looked at the floor, at the ceiling, at the desk in the far-right corner. Pressing her advantage, the duchess announced that the special bond she had always felt between them had obviously been one-sided.

"Leave off abusing our associate," ordered a voice from the doorway. "You have achieved your goal of making him feel like dog excrement on the bottom of your slipper. Do show a little mercy."

Emma stiffened her shoulders and turned around slowly to see her husband enter the room. Dressed in evening finery—blue coat with gilt buttons, buckskin breeches—he looked handsome, urbane and confident. She found everything about his appearance insufferable, from his immaculate cravat (the Waterfall, as usual) to his preening smile, which he made no effort to hide. The answer to the question she had posed to Mr. Squibbs couldn't be any more apparent: She wasn't terrifying at all.

Nevertheless, she addressed Trent with what she considered to be quiet menace. "I'm happy to now that I have a better target."

The duke grinned even wider, unperturbed by the anger that smoldered in his wife's eyes. "As always, I'm delighted to be of use," he said smoothly. Then he turned his attention to Mr. Squibbs and offered his sincerest thanks for the other man's assistance. "I know the situation cannot be easy for you."

Given how grossly this observation understated the case, Mr. Squibbs decided it was best not to respond directly and instead announced that he would take his leave. Trent insisted the little man avail himself of the front door, as he was a welcomed guest in their home, but the greatest lockpick in London insisted it would do irreparable harm to his reputation to be seen departing a duke's residence by such conventional means. "Especially at this hour," he explained before darting a hesitant glance at Emma.

The duchess saw his uncertainty and instantly felt better. "Yes, Mr. Squibbs, thank you for standing as such a great friend to both of us. I can only hope that one day you will hold me in the same esteem as you do my husband. Until then, I will do everything in my power to earn it."

Interpreting her statement as a thinly veiled threat of reprisal, Mr. Squibbs again held his tongue and dipped his head in silent acknowledgment. Then he thanked them both for their patronage and slipped silently out of the window.

Emma watched him leave, envious as always of the grace and fluidity of his movements. He could swing his body over a sill with the ease of a cat bounding from a tree. After he was gone, she turned to her husband and considered her options. Without a doubt, venting her spleen on the proper target would be quite satisfying, for she was indeed furious at his manipulations. Scheming under the table with one of her most valued associates, one of her most trusted recruits, was infamous, and it would serve him right if she cultivated new underworld connections.

Although that was definitely an idea worth consider-ing—and she was extremely vexed with herself for not coming up with it sooner—she didn't have time to think about it now. Mr. Squibbs had been right to reference the hour. It was growing late, and all the best miscreants were already out in the city, hiding in shadows and creeping un-der staircases. She had no time to waste.

Hoping to strike the perfect note of annoyed and re-signed, she said, "If you'll excuse me, I think I will retire for the evening. As you've successfully scotched my plans, I'm going to read a book on the history of medieval tor-ture instruments. Perhaps it will have instructions on how to build an iron maiden in one's sitting room. Good night, your grace."

Trent responded to her pointed threat with another broad grin, which enraged Emma further. Nobody conde-scended like a duke, with his coronet embossed with jewels and his four hundred years of ancestors lining the great hall. He was very pleased with himself, and why not? He'd gotten his way. People moved to his bidding like pieces on a chessboard.

Even as her anger rose, she resolved to swallow it, for she had a mission that required her attention. Would she remain as even-keeled in the morning? The answer was very likely no. Her husband knew exactly how she felt about the matter of Vinnie's patent, for they'd had a vigorous argument about it when they'd discovered what the villainous Luther Townshend had done. Even exiled on another continent an ocean away for murderous deeds, he'd managed to create mischief by sending the details of Vinnie's invention to a member of the rivalrous gardening society. In selecting Matthew Hobart Tweedale, Baron Tweedale, he'd picked the ideal accomplice, for the gentleman was as full of blather as a gossipy old biddy. He loved nothing more than to embellish a story or crow over the misfortunes of his peers. If anyone would delight in being thought the inventor of a clever new contraption, it was he, for he wasn't at all clever. He was venal and vain and prone to puffery, and every interaction was another opportunity to pass on rumor and speculation.

The thought of such a buffoon taking credit for Vinnie's invention made Emma so angry she could hardly speak. Having his name appear anywhere in the general vicinity of her sister's watering hose was unacceptable. All reference to him had to be expunged from the public record.

Anything less would be failure.

She'd explained this calmly to Trent four weeks ago, when news of Tweedale's application first reached them, discovered, thank goodness, by a member of Mr. Squibbs's network who worked in Chancery Lane. Being a gentleman—and a titled one at that—her husband had not quite grasped the urgency of the matter. He believed if Vinnie lodged a caveat against the petition, the court would readily comply with her version of events and grant the patent to her, not the imposter Tweedale.

Emma found such sanguinity to be as ridiculous as it

was naïve. Only someone for whom the system had always worked could have so much faith in it.

"If I were you," Trent said matter-of-factly as she swept by him, "I'd wear the mazurine blue."

Emma paused with her hand on the doorknob, fully cognizant of what his seeming non sequitur implied. Nevertheless, she affected confusion and looked at him with her blue eyes open wide with incomprehension. "Excuse me?"

"To break in to the patent office. I advise you to wear the mazurine-blue dress," he explained. "Despite how effortless Mr. Squibbs makes it look, I find climbing over windowsills to be a dirty business best suited for dark colors."

She wasn't surprised that her husband knew what she was up to. Her history of not abandoning the field was well-documented, and his grace would naturally assume she wouldn't do so now. He could make all the assumptions he wanted, however. She would hold the course and admit nothing. Coolly, she said, "Thank you, your grace. I'll keep that in mind if I ever have occasion to break in to the patent office."

"You are welcome to spend the rest of the night in this room claiming ignorance, for I would deny my wife no pleasure," he said mildly, "but I have a petition for a modern watering hose to plant. I trust you'll excuse me?"

Now Emma froze, for she knew Alex was too respectful of her feelings to toy with them. Deliberately, she raised her eyes to meet his. "Why?" she asked.

He leaned against the mahogany desk in the corner of the room and considered her thoughtfully, his dark, fathoms-deep eyes unusually serious. "Because I'm here," he said simply. "Because while playing a hand of whist at my club, I got a note from an associate telling me the details of my wife's scheme, including her intention to break in to Lincoln's Inn in two hours' time. Because of that note, I was able to come home at once and put a stop to it. And that seems patently unfair to me. I'm grateful to Mr. Squibbs, of course, and would have him do nothing different. But that doesn't change the fact that you were right when you argued that I don't know what it's like to be treated unfairly by the world. I don't know. What I do know is the perniciousness of Luther Townshend, and if his last act of malice before disappearing into the wilds of New South Wales is to try to deny Vinnie ownership of her own invention, then I'll be damned if I won't do everything in my power to stop him. Now I believe you have a document with the forged signature of the home secretary on it around here. I'd like to peruse it while you change into your skulking clothes."

Needless to say, Emma appreciated her husband's open-mindedness and ability to admit when he was wrong. It was, she thought, one of the most attractive things about him and a trait she found herself physically drawn to time after time. Nevertheless, she was peeved that he'd needed convincing. Her word should have been enough.

But the peevishness was minor compared with her relief that she wouldn't have to slip laudanum into his claret. Getting the right dosage was always a little delicate. "I'm not going to kiss you," she announced, her mood light as she contemplated how much easier breaking in would be with his help. By all measures, he was her most trusted ally and his presence improved any situation.

As the duke hadn't been expecting a kiss from his wife, he accepted this announcement with a curt nod of his head. "All right."

"I'm not going to kiss you because if I start, I won't stop," she explained as she walked toward where he stood against the desk, "and then we'll miss our window, and Miss Templeton's tour of the patent office in the company of Prickly Perceval will be a complete waste of time, and I'll have to break in to her bedchamber at two o'clock in the morning again to request another visit with the earl, which I know for a fact won't go over well, for we barely succeeding in convincing her to do it the first time. But I want to kiss you." As she spoke, she looked deeply into his eyes, which flashed with desire both breathtaking and familiar. Her pulse raced as she leaned so closely forward he could feel her breath on his cheek. Her hand brushed his thigh as she reached for the drawer only a few inches to his left and withdrew Vinnie's patent application. "I want to kiss all of you right now."

Calmly, as if he weren't craving his wife with every fiber of his being, Trent nodded and said, "I appreciate your forbearance."

"But I'll wait until we're in the coach coming home," she said, her cheeks dimpling as she smiled. Then she handed him the petition and left the room to change into her skulking clothes, which included but was not limited to her mazurine-blue gown.

CHAPTER SIX

What the eighth Earl of Gage did not know about the appearance and behavior of snow creatures, he was more than happy to theorize.

"The tendency is to imagine a wholly unfamiliar being made out of entirely familiar elements," he said as the coach turned right onto Wigmore Street. The vehicle lurched over a hole in the road, and Miss Templeton, ensconced on the bench across from him in a mustard-yellow dress that had seen much better days, steadied herself with a hand on the door. "An especially large dog, for example, with icicles hanging off its gnarled fur like pine cones from a tree. It's a natural inclination, for our imaginations are constrained by the limits of what we can envision. You're thinking, of course, that I've presented a contradiction of an irreconcilable nature, for to form the unfamiliar from the familiar would be to create something already known."

In truth, Gage didn't believe Miss Templeton was actually intelligent enough to formulate this observation on her own. Their previous interactions had revealed an obstinate mind, a fondness for flawed logic and an inability to comprehend the obvious. Aware of these defects, he nevertheless credited her with the ability to make the astute remark. It was something he did from time to time to enliven a tedious conversation—create an incisive counterargument to his own excellent point. It ensured that both ends of the discussion lived up to his standards.

"Familiar elements can create only a familiar whole, although it might not seem familiar at first glance," he continued on her behalf. "Most monsters appear that way only out of the corner of our eye. When considered head-on, in the bright light of day, they're revealed to be what they always were: an oversize dog well in need of a bath."

Miss Templeton made an unintelligible reply, presumably a murmur of assent, for even she couldn't be so inured to reason as to disagree with her own theory.

"Although that point of view has its merits," he conceded generously, "I believe a case can be made for the opposite. Imagine, for instance, a bear with fur as white as snow so that it may blend in to its environment. If such a creature were to approach, seemingly out of nowhere, on its hind legs, towering at least a foot taller than the tallest man, you would unambiguously—"

"No," Miss Templeton said.

It wasn't the rudeness of her interruption that surprised him, for he expected nothing less—or more—than shabby etiquette from such an injudicious miss. No, it was the firmness of her tone that caused him to stiffen his shoulders. Speaking to him with clipped impatience, as if *he* had somehow offended *her*. What insufferable audacity!

Possessing himself of his full seated height, he stared down at her and said coldly, "Excuse me?"

"Of course, my lord," she said with an affable smile. "I understand what it's like to get carried away by one's argument. However, as I was trying to say when your enthusiasm caused you to run roughshod over me, I don't believe the familiar and unfamiliar are irreconcilable."

It was a rebuke! Without question the frumpy little scold in the well-worn yellow dress was taking him to task for his conduct. He didn't respond immediately, for he was too startled by the development to issue a set-down.

No matter. The impudent chit had more to say.

"All new worlds are made from the mundane objects of our own. That's what makes them so remarkable," she said. "Consider ice."

As she spoke, Gage had the unpleasant sensation that he was about to be subjected to a lecture. He couldn't be certain because it had happened so infrequently in his life, even at Oxford, where one encountered lecturers everywhere one turned, but there was something alarmingly familiar about the tenor of her speech. He could hear his own conversational authority in the way she told him to consider ice.

Confident in her point, she continued without waiting for his consent. "It's an unremarkable element, merely water frozen from the cold. We have it nightly flavored with lemon or white currant, and we slip on it when alighting from our carriages in February. Yet when Coleridge describes it, it becomes something new, thrilling and strange," she explained. Then she rested her elbows against her knees and leaned forward, her eyes seeming to sparkle with golden flecks as she said,

"And through the drifts the snowy cliffs
Did send a dismal sheen:
Nor shapes of men nor beasts we ken –
The ice was all between.

The ice was here, the ice was there,
The ice was all around:
It cracked and growled, and roared and howled,
Like noises in a swound!"

Now the earl *knew* he was the victim of a lecture, for only an edifying sermon on an arcane topic would contain a quotation from Samuel Taylor Coleridge.

Already appalled by her manners, he was suddenly aghast at her presumption. How dare she think he would allow himself to be treated as such in the comfort of his own coach! Despite the constant demands on his time, he had condescended with all due courtesy to accompany her on a tour of the patent office, and this was how she repaid him? Where was the humility? And the gratitude? The keen awareness of her place? She was but an aging spinster well on the shelf. It was her duty to make herself as agreeable as possible in all situations. To that end, she was supposed to say, "Yes, my lord," and "You are correct, my lord," whenever her opinion was sought. She wasn't supposed to contradict him, especially not when he himself was in the midst of doing that very thing. No, he didn't happen to have "The Rime of the Ancient Mariner" at the ready to establish his point, but that was only because he didn't need to enlist the words of other men to win an argument. He was persuasive enough on his own.

And yet even as he chafed at her impertinence, he found himself impressed with her erudition. The Coleridge quote effectively demonstrated her contention, and he recognized it most likely for the same reason that she had memorized it: because it made him alive to the possibilities of the world.

Aware that his thoughts had taken a fanciful turn— next he'd be crediting her with a fondness for Henry Fielding simply because he himself had enjoyed *The History of Tom Jones*—the earl gave her a stern look and asked with marked distrust, "How do you know Coleridge?"

Miss Templeton primly flattened the wrinkles on the front of her hideous dress, a waste of effort, as far as the earl could tell, and said that she'd read it for her study on the literature of polar exploration. "I'm examining first-person accounts of Arctic voyages from the perspective of the modern Gothic novel, which employs many tropes of the ice-bound region. My dissertation seeks to understand the very nature of nature itself, which seems genuinely indifferent to the suffering of humanity. It's only at the extremes of the world—the poles, if you will—that the truth reveals itself."

Unable to recall when he'd heard a more remarkable speech, Gage said, "Really?"

He'd meant to utter the word with arch disbelief, a practiced affectation that had withered opponents at his club and in Parliament, but instead he sounded a note of genuine surprise. Indeed, to his own ears, he seemed at once curious and impressed.

Shaking her head, she smiled brightly and said, "No, no, of course not. I'm not writing anything as high-minded and complex. It's merely that you appeared so taken aback by my familiarity with Coleridge, I felt compelled to present a convincing explanation. The truth is, I love to read and have a wide range of interests. It is, I know, a defect of the mind for a female to enjoy anything other than Minerva Press novels and assure you that I'm taking care of it posthaste. I've consulted with a physician who has located the part of my brain that is inappropriately inquisitive, and he's scheduled a trepanation for Thursday. By this time next week, I'll be able to quote only passages from *The Mysteries of Udolpho,* assuming, of course, that the hole in my skull heals in a timely fashion. I've been warned it may take up to two weeks."

She was teasing him. Gage didn't have to see the impish gleam in her eyes to know she was making a cake of him and serving it to the room on a silver platter. It was obvious from the fustian she spouted, nonsensical jibber-jabber of the most ridiculous kind. He waited for the outrage to come, for if there was one thing Nicholas Perceval loathed more than mockery, it was conversation that did not serve a function. Nothing she said had any value to him. Her inane words not only failed to advance his understanding, they worked to undermine it.

And yet the annoyance didn't come.

He couldn't comprehend why she spoke such drivel.

She was a woman, of course, and the vast majority of her kind chattered endlessly without purpose. But the earl was not so firmly ensconced in his prejudices as to ascribe that motive to her now, for Miss Templeton's ramblings were far too pointed to be the offhand consequence of her sex. It was almost as if she'd resolved to unsettle or exhaust him with her nonsense, a goal she would have achieved with ease if she'd taken bonnets or embroidery as her subject. She hadn't, however, chosen to dwell on those banalities and instead talked of Arctic exploration and trepanation. The leap from one to the other was so effortless, Gage could not help but admire the elasticity of her mind.

It was because of that appreciation that he decided not to dampen the moment with cold silence or a chilly reply that would end the exchange. Rather, he sought to provoke a response by displaying a surfeit of esteem. "May I congratulate you, Miss Templeton, on graciously accepting the limitations of your sex? It's appropriately womanly of you not to insist on the right to enjoy a wide variety of reading materials. I would have expected you to react differently and am very encouraged by this show of good sense."

To Gage's delight, Miss Templeton's eyebrows knitted with indignation and the color rose visibly in her cheeks. Then, just as quickly, a look of suspicion overtook her features as she tried to decide if he was serious in his remark.

Good, he thought.

Miss Templeton, however, did not stay discombobulated for long. After a pause during which she examined him with a thoughtful tilt of her head, she said, "Thank you, my lord, for reaffirming my decision, for I know how little a woman's opinion matters in determining her own future."

Although she said it sweetly and with seeming docility, he heard the calculated humility and recognized the comment for what it was: a pointed critique of the way he was handling Letty's affairs. As always, the criticism irked him, but he was too entertained by her deftness in issuing it to let his hackles rise. Instead of addressing her comment, which, he knew, would lead to a quarrel and hurt feelings (hers, naturally), he asked which part of the brain housed one's reading preferences. Without pausing a moment to consider her answer, she indicated a spot a mere inch above her left ear and explained that it was reassuringly close to the area that supported reason. Its location was a stroke of good luck, she explained, because Dr. Singleham—and just like that, her fictitious physician had a name—would be able to modify her ability to argue at the same time.

"Two problems solved for the price of one," she said, "for I'm so dreadfully weary of outwitting men."

Her statement was meant to goad him into replying defensively, but Gage didn't rise to the bait like a fish to a hook. He wanted to know more about her upcoming procedure and asked question after question as if administering a test to a promising student. His intent was to confuse her with the particulars, but she answered his queries with so much precision and detail he could practically see her two days hence in the examination room (red walls, brass sconces, anatomical charts) on a table (mahogany, padded, tilted back), letting Dr. Singleham (gray hair, distinguished nose, two-inch scar on his chin from a grouse-hunting accident in his youth) bore a hole into her skull with a round, saw-like surgical instrument.

The interrogation of Miss Templeton was so engrossing, the earl was surprised to discover they'd arrived at Lincoln's Inn. Having resigned himself to an interminable coach ride talking about the weather—and considering his guest for the day, he'd have thought himself fortunate if the conversation actually rose to that level of triteness—he now felt disappointed that the time had passed so quickly. From the moment she'd dismissed his remark about the pleasantness of the day in favor of her own implausible comment about snow creatures, he'd had known himself to be entertained.

And now they were there, in front of the imposing

stone structure of the government building, with its pristine white facade and classical pediment.

"We have arrived," Gage said.

Miss Templeton examined the dignified structure and smiled. "So I see."

At once, the earl's coachman appeared at the window and opened the door. Gage climbed out of the vehicle, then offered his hand to help Miss Templeton alight. With what seemed to be the first hint of sincerity she'd displayed all afternoon, she thanked him for his assistance, and it was only then, as he was assuring her it was his pleasure, that it occurred to him to wonder why she'd asked for this visit. She was unconventional, to be sure, but even in the annals of eccentric behavior, an expedition to the Patent Bill Office was a strange request.

As he led her to the door of building number ten, he said, "Miss Templeton, I don't believe you've told me why."

She furrowed her brow, as if confused by the sudden change in conversation. "Why, my lord?"

"Yes, why you desired to visit the Patent Bill Office," he explained.

"Oh, yes, why, of course, why, yes," she said. "My father, you see. Yes, my father is on the committee to reform the patent process, as I'm sure you know, and I wish to be prepared should he consult my opinion on the matter. Given my propensity for books, I tried to read up on the procedures, but there are disappointingly few tomes on the subject so I decided to acquire firsthand knowledge." She glanced at him briefly as they crossed the threshold and added with a sly smile, "Perhaps I will write a useful dissertation on patents before my operation on Thursday."

The explanation made sense to Gage, particularly the part where she thought so well of herself she assumed her opinion would be sought by her father. It would not, of course. Lord Templeton was far too stubborn and arrogant to confer with anyone about anything, let alone a female who had failed in her purpose of finding a husband on crucial governmental business. But that also fit with what he knew about Miss Templeton, for her sense of the world rarely coincided with reality. Here was a woman who truly believed she'd saved Letty from a blackguard. More than that: She had managed to convince herself that he owed her a debt of gratitude for the effort.

In these particular ways, Miss Templeton's answer was entirely plausible.

And yet he knew it wasn't true because she'd stumbled over it. 'Twas a minor thing, a gaffe so slight it might not have happened at all, but he'd noticed it precisely because it was out of the ordinary for her. During a twenty-minute interrogation, she hadn't faltered once, issuing elaborate fabrications with the skill, grace and assurance of a master spy. Then, when confronted with a straightforward question that required naught but a simple answer, she stammered with uncertainty.

Her recovery had been almost instantaneous. Within a few heartbeats, she was back on terra firma, tempering a reasonable explanation with an absurd footnote that referenced a familiar topic, but he wasn't fooled. She was up to something, and although he couldn't fathom what it was, he didn't doubt it had something to do with her overweening self-confidence. She probably imagined she was in the process of saving some other unfortunate gentleman's sister.

He decided he didn't want to know.

Then just as swiftly he decided he *did* want to know.

If the object of her desire had been more common-place—if, for example, she had lied to gain entry to Almack's or the Brighton Pavilion—he wouldn't have given the matter another thought (save to spare a condolence for the soon-to-be-bedeviled brother). But the patent office was such a dull and dreary destination, he couldn't help being intrigued by her interest. It was among the worst places in London, a dark little room stuffed with bumptious functionaries who believed their work alone kept the empire running smoothly.

Even *he* didn't want to be there and he was in charge of overseeing its overhaul. It was a massive undertaking, and like every other system in the world, it had its detractors and its champions. Having developed without intention over several centuries, the patent process was riddled with wastefulness. Unfortunately, every inefficiency had its beneficiary, which made his task twice as difficult, for no one with a comfortable sinecure was willing to relinquish it without a fight.

Just thinking about the obstacles to reform put him in a disagreeable mood, and by the time he held the door to the small office open for Miss Templeton, the expression on his face was black.

The room's occupants turned at the scrape of the door, their faces twisted into dark scowls before they recognized the earl and immediately lightened their expressions.

Forced smiles, Gage noted, but he appreciated the effort.

"Good afternoon, my lord," said one of the clerks—Jeffries, the earl thought—who immediately stood up and bowed his head. "This is a pleasure we weren't expecting, but of course we're prepared for it. We are always prepared for anything, my lord, as such vigilance is required by our work."

To be fair, the earl was not unsympathetic to their plight. The process of attaining a patent was tortuous, and rarely did an aspirant enter their office in anything resembling good humor. The first step required an inventor to confirm that a patent for a device like his had yet to be issued, a task that would be simple if all patents were in the same place. Alas, they were not. Rather, patents were filed in one of three offices in Chancery, obliging a patentee to search all three at great expense of time and convenience.

It was little wonder, then, that by the time an inventor entered the Patent Bill Office—step number five—he was out of patience. It was an unfortunate thing for him, as he still had thirty or so more steps to navigate.

Gage's first recommendation to the committee to re-form the patent process was to combine the three offices into one. His next was to abolish the Office of the Chaff-wax, for the post served no other purpose than as a way to extort more fees from the public. The earl was not op-posed to the crown collecting payments from its popu-lace—indeed, he saw no other way for the kingdom to function—but he felt it was incumbent upon it to come up with more legitimate ways than simply charging for the preparation of sealing wax.

He would be happy to head up the Chaff-wax Dis-bandment Committee should the interminable business of reforming the patent system ever be resolved.

Oppressed by the weight of duty, Gage felt his re-sentment rise against the woman who had brought him there. It was, as he had tried to observe in the coach ride over, a remarkably pleasant day, and he'd much rather be out riding in Hyde Park or driving along the Heath.

Abruptly, without an introduction to either the clerks or the topic, he launched into an explanation of what hap-pened in the gloomy little room. "The Patent Bill Office is an adjunct of the attorney-general, whose chambers are near enough to exert its influence and far enough not to be contaminated with the tedium of this bureau. A petition, once signed by the home secretary, is brought to the attor-ney-general's office, which delivers it here so that the clerks may prepare a report. If the report is positive, the application is returned to the home secretary, whose office prepares a warrant, which is sent to the prince regent. Once his signature is secured, the warrant is returned yet again to the home secretary, who signs it himself before returning it here, to the Patent Bill Office. These clerks draft the regent's bill and write a brief summary. Then they make two copies—one for the Signet Office and one for the Privy Seal Office. Then the engrossing clerk prepares the final version for the regent's signature. The final ver-sion goes to the attorney-general, who signs it; to the home secretary, who signs it; and to the regent, who also signs it."

The Earl of Gage paused here to take a deep breath and decided he had spent enough time detailing the labyrinthine process. He turned to Miss Templeton, who stood only a foot inside the doorway, for he had not allowed her to enter more fully, and said, "I could go on. Attaining a patent is an epic worthy of Homer, and its cast of characters is legion. We are but halfway through and have yet to meet the Lord Keeper of the Privy Seal, the Clerk of the Lord Keeper of the Privy Seal, the Clerk of the Signet, the Clerk of the Patent, the Lord Chancellor, the Lord Chancellor's Purse-bearer, the Clerk of the Hanaper, the Deputy Clerk of the Hanaper, the Deputy Sealer, and my personal favorite and the man to whom I one day hope to compose a farewell sonnet, the Deputy Chaff-wax. The duties of this office, however, conclude after act two, so we are free to take our leave of these fine men. Do make your goodbyes in a timely fashion, Miss Templeton, as I don't like to keep my horses waiting for long."

As his intentions could not have been any clearer, he expected swift compliance with his request. He knew his companion's understanding was sometimes impaired by a lack of common sense, but even she could not mistake the situation. It was time to depart.

Miss Templeton nodded and smiled at the clerks, as if ready to leave, but she in fact made no move to go. Indeed, she skirted around the earl and stepped deeper into the office. She looked at the clerk who had greeted them upon their arrival. "What's your name, sir?"

Uncertain how to proceed, the clerk darted a look at the earl and then back at the young lady. As there seemed to be no way for the man to extricate himself without giving offense to one or the other, Gage reasonably assumed he would defer to him. He was, after all, the one who had a significant amount of control over his future.

But the clerk chose Miss Templeton.

"Jeffries, miss. My name is Jeffries."

"It's a pleasure to meet you, Jeffries," she said with a dip of her head. "I very much appreciate your letting us interrupt your day and hope you won't mind if I try your patience just a little bit longer with a question or two. You see, the earl, in his enthusiasm to detail the exciting and prestigious process of patent attainment, elided a few details. For example, the report you prepare for the attorney-general. Can you tell me a little bit about what's in it?"

Realizing there was no way to route Miss Templeton, Gage sighed loudly and closed the office door. Then he leaned against it and indicated with a look that Jeffries may continue.

In greater detail than was necessary, the clerk explained the information contained in the report, such as the legality of the invention and whether it was appropriate for the crown to grant the patent. Miss Templeton nodded thoughtfully and asked if she might see such a report. Jeffries's colleague, Polk, leaped to his feet and brought the document he was currently working on over for her inspection.

Although these matters seemed cut-and-dried to the earl, Miss Templeton managed to stir up controversy with her questions, and the two clerks vied for the pleasure of supplying the answer, sometimes bickering with each other over minor details.

"I'm not implying that skill accounts for it," Jeffries said, concluding a long thesis on the challenges of locating caveats, "but I do have the most success when it comes to finding them."

"But that boast must come with its own caveat," Polk said, twittering in appreciation of his own cleverness, "as my colleague tends to take only applications that he recalls seeing a caveat for in prior searches."

"I believe that's what he meant by skill," Gage said from his spot against the door, his voice dripping with boredom.

Polk had the decency to flinch at his tone, but Miss

Templeton continued as if he hadn't spoken. "And a cave-at is an instrument by which one can request notification if an invention similar to the one outlined in the document is submitted for a patent?"

"Precisely, yes," Jeffries said, then anticipating her next question, added, "They're stored in the cabinet by the window."

Gage bit back a growl of frustration as Miss Temple-ton walked over to inspect yet another cabinet. He had been in the Patent Bill Office half a dozen times and never noticed how many cabinets there were to inspect. If forced to describe the interior of the cramped room by memory, he would have listed six desks, three lamps and a bookshelf.

He considered huffing loudly to make his impatience known, but his impatience already was known to Miss Templeton and deemed a matter of no importance. Short of tugging her out of the office by her arm, he couldn't figure out how to draw this visit to a close.

And then suddenly the situation was of interest, as he came out of his reverie to notice Jeffries casting guilty looks in his direction and the color in Polk's face rising.

"What's the matter?" he asked, stepping away from the door. In half a dozen strides he was next to them, looking over Polk's shoulder at a piece of paper he held in his hands.

Miss Templeton shook her head. "I don't quite know. They're both quite distressed by a document they found behind the cabinet."

"It's a petition," Jeffries squeaked.

"Indeed," Gage said, his tone deceptively mild. "I wonder if putting it behind the cabinet is the best way to store it. As Miss Templeton has been so kind as to make us all aware, this room is besieged with storage options."

"It fell," Polk said. "Behind the cabinet. It fell. This application was submitted two months ago."

The earl wasn't surprised to discover a petition had fallen behind a cabinet, for the system was too convoluted not to have its victims. Thirty-five steps meant thirty-five opportunities for blunders.

"Process it," Gage snapped, annoyed nonetheless by this evidence of inefficiency. It was one thing to suspect it and another entirely to see it gathering dust behind a cabinet.

"At once, my lord," Polk said.

"And alert the petitioner to what has happened," he added briskly. "No doubt he's anxious to hear something."

The clerk nodded. "Yes, I will alert"—he perused the document for a name—"Lavinia Dryden, the Marchioness of Huntly, immediately."

"A female?" Gage said.

Polk squinted his eyes to make sure he read it correctly. "Yes, my lord, a female, and she has invented a new watering hose."

"What was wrong with the old one?" the earl asked.

"I don't know, my lord," Polk said.

"It's not elasticated enough," Jeffries said. "It bursts when too much pressure is applied."

Although the information was by all measures arcane, the earl didn't pause to wonder how the clerk had acquired it. He was anxious to leave Lincoln's Inn and salvage something of the day. It was too late for a run in the park, but it would soon be the fashionable hour, which was an excellent opportunity for Letty to meet potential suitors. If they left now, he would have just enough time to eat at his club before going home to change, for he was, he realized now, quite hungry.

Miss Templeton, having no respect for his appetite, expressed amazement at Jeffries's knowledge and insisted he account for it. After accepting her congratulations with a blush that rivaled his colleague's, he explained that he had seen an application for a similar device only a few weeks before.

"I wrote in the attorney-general report that the invention was uncontested and should be approved," the clerk said.

"The inevitability of such a development was so high,

you didn't even have to say the words," Gage replied with an air of resignation, for he was not master of the clerks. Their problems were not his problems. And yet he was there, a member of the House of Lords, and couldn't pretend to not know what he did know. "Very well, then. Alert the other applicant as well. Since there were no caveats at the time of his petition, the patent will be granted to the person who applied first, which appears to be the Marchioness of Huntly. I trust you've learned your lesson well."

"What lesson, my lord?" Jeffries asked.

"Don't look behind the cabinets," he said.

Although he was entirely sincere in his statement, Miss Templeton laughed and assured the clerks he did not mean a word of it. "I trust it goes without saying that the earl has too much respect for you and the office you represent to advocate for you to be derelict in your duty. In truth, I think this is a happy discovery, for now that you're aware that such a thing can happen you can compensate for it. I would advise a weekly inspection of all cabinets, wardrobes and desks done on a rotating basis."

Of course Miss Templeton had just the prescription and no compunction in applying it. She was, as Gage had known from the start, a busybody with an inflated sense of her own judgment.

"Now that Miss Templeton has so kindly clarified what I truly meant," he said, pausing to wonder if the interfering minx actually just told him he was welcome or if he'd imagined it, "it's time for us to take our leave."

Miss Templeton, who was no better at making brief goodbyes than she was at containing her opinion, offered lavish thanks to the two clerks. "As the earl explained when we arrived, my father is on the patent committee and he doesn't often seek my advice. When he does, however, I want to be ready, and thanks to you I'll be able to discuss the matter with intelligence and insight. I'm remarkably grateful."

She was also grateful to the earl for giving her the opportunity to acquire the knowledge and expressed her appreciation the entire way home. Her color high, she chatted happily about being a source of comfort and inspiration to her father, a situation she had yet to acquire but felt was very possible now that she'd familiarized herself with his work. All she had to do was convince him of her worth, and the formula for that was simple: information plus persistence equaled value.

It was a persuasive argument, but the earl was not persuaded. It wasn't her sincerity he doubted. He believed her enthusiasm to be entirely genuine. By all accounts, Tuppence Templeton had gotten exactly what she wanted out of the expedition to the Patent Bill Office.

The problem was, Gage couldn't figure out what that thing was, for it surely was not the knowledge she'd professed to desire. The dowdy busybody with her tales of trepanation was playing a much deeper game than she let on, and he'd be damned if he let the matter rest before he knew the whole of it.

CHAPTER SEVEN

The carriage ride home had been the hardest part for Tuppence. Sitting across from the earl, prattling on about wanting to make herself indispensable to her stiff-necked gobble-cock of a father! What self-control it had required not to preen in victory, not to stick her head out the window and yell in giddy triumph, "I did it, I did it, I did it!"

Because she had done it. And so unobtrusively! One moment she'd been asking about the procedure for settling a caveat and the next she was staring aghast at a seemingly misplaced file on the verge of being lost to history.

All she'd had to do to arrange it was drop her glove next to the cabinet and wait for one of the kind clerks to retrieve it. Jeffries and Polk almost bumped heads competing for the honor, and both sets of eyes appeared to notice the forlorn document at the exact same moment. Jeffries reached for it, conceding the pleasure of the glove to his colleague, and perused the first page. He recognized immediately what it was and he kept his head low, darting a surreptitious glance at the earl in hopes that the member of Parliament wasn't paying attention.

He wasn't and then he was.

Gage's response had been everything she could have

wished: reluctant interest tempered by tedium. In a more patient mood, he might have been inclined to examine the petition personally or consider the problem thoughtfully. But he wanted out of the office and insisted on the easiest solution, which played exactly into the Harlow sisters' hands.

Everything about their plan had been faultless—even the thin layer of dust sprinkled on the application was impeccable. It was, she thought, although her education in these matters was somewhat limited, exactly the amount that would accumulate in two months.

She'd been so anxious this morning that something would go wrong. Slipping out of the house unnoticed was usually easy enough, for no one kept track of her comings and goings as long as the purpose of her errands benefited the members of her family rather than herself. Today, she was ostensibly running to the lending library to pick up the newest Eliza de Roche tale for Hannah, although, in truth, the novel was already tucked in the top drawer of her vanity. In order to ensure freedom of movement, she often took out a dozen books at one time and then doled them out in small parcels over a period of several weeks.

It had never failed her before and yet as she had strode through the corridor to the front door to meet the earl in front of her house, she was dreadfully afraid someone would stop her.

When nobody did, she began to worry the file would not be lodged in the location the duchess's note indicated, for it seemed to her as if so many things could have happened since her grace placed it there. The porter charged with maintaining the office, for example, might have spotted it and tossed it in the trash. Or an impertinent mouse could have inadvertently pushed it deeper behind the cabinet while inspecting the area for cheese.

And there had been so many cabinets! She'd been truly horrified when she'd stepped into the room and found it stuffed with furniture for the storage of documents. It had felt as if fate were playing a cruel joke on her, and she had to smother a very strong desire to turn and run. But she'd stood her ground, took five deep breaths to calm her nerves and recalled the map the duchess had supplied in her missive. Just like a diagram designating where a treasure of great worth was hidden, X had marked the spot.

Tuppence's relief at the success of the mission was so intense, she felt an almost irrepressible urge to tell the earl about it.

Well, not *him* in particular. She just wanted to share her triumph with someone, anyone. If she had been in the coach with her father, she would have been overcome by the same desire to confess.

And yet some part of her knew that wasn't entirely true. As sincere as the impulse to exult in her victory was, she wanted the earl's acknowledgment more. Maneuvering two governmental clerks into doing exactly what she required was satisfying, of course, but it was nothing compared with manipulating his lordship. He was, as she knew he'd be the first to admit, an impregnable object impervious to the whims of others. 'Twas impossible to get him to do one's bidding.

Impossible for others, perhaps.

Having accomplished her goal so effortlessly, Tuppence felt as if the score between them had been settled. He'd decimated her composure with his humiliating reprimand, and she had skillfully directed his actions in ways he didn't understand. They were equals now.

Comfortable in their new status, Tuppence wanted to laugh with him about the events of the afternoon—for example, the expression of utter annoyance and disbelief when he realized he would not be leaving the patent office a mere three minutes after he'd arrived. His boredom during the visit had been of epic proportions, and even if she hadn't had reason to linger, she would have extended their stay for as long as possible simply to tweak his temper.

Naturally, Tuppence wasn't so intoxicated by her own success to think for a moment the Earl of Gage would be anything but enraged by her teasing. Prickly Perceval could hardly accept pricks to his ego. But there had been moments in the carriage ride over when he appeared to be a more even-tempered man with an easy sense of humor. She'd been surprised, certainly, by his willingness to play along with her absurd story, but she'd laughed with delight at his dozens of questions about the doctor—his schooling, his war record, the exact arrangement of the anatomical charts in his examination room—and enjoyed the challenge of staying one step ahead of him. She also admired how perfectly he aped her tone, issuing barbed insults in the tenor of compliments.

The interlude had truly been amusing.

Tuppence knew it was odd to have such a positive feeling toward London's most notorious misanthrope, and she resolved, as she paced her room an hour after returning, not to dwell on it further. The afternoon had been an interlude, an isolated event that would not recur. It was more pressing that she figure out how to convey word of that day's success to the Harlow sisters. Sure, she could send a brief missive now announcing the success of their operation or she could wait for their next social event and the first available curtain for a tête-a-tête. But neither plan was satisfying, for she wanted to tell them of her triumph immediately. The Duchess of Trent and her sister were the only two people she *could* tell.

She looked at her window and considered the Harlow approach, which consisted of waiting until after midnight, scaling the side of a building if an obliging tree could not be found and catching one unaware in one's bedroom. It would not work, she realized, for two reasons. The first was simple: She wanted to tell the two sisters at once, and they lived in separate residences. The second was harder to pin down but more daunting: As both women had husbands, a visit could occur while their husbands were being…husbandly. Even with her limited experience, she knew that marital relations were random and sporadic and nothing she wanted to stumble into or over or upon.

Staring out the window, she noticed that the day's fine weather had held. The sky was the same cloudless blue now, at four o'clock, as it had been hours ago when she'd climbed into the earl's carriage. The conditions were excellent for strolling, and she didn't doubt the turnout for the fashionable hour would be high. Although not a regular like Beau Petersham, the Duchess of Trent had been known to go for a drive in Hyde Park. Perhaps she would be there today with her sister.

Even if they weren't, visiting the park would give her something to do other than pace her bedroom wondering what was next.

Pleased with her decision, she set out to find her sister, for the only way her mother would consent to the plan would be if it furthered Hannah's prospects. Her eldest daughter's desire for a little fresh air and enjoyment was a paltry reason to tire the horses.

Hannah was in the front parlor, sipping tea and admiring a blossom-pink ball gown in the Empire style in *La Belle Assemblée*. The new issue of the ladies' magazine must have arrived very recently, for the only time her sister closeted herself in a quiet room was to pore over new fashions.

"That's a pretty dress," Tuppence said, settling into the armchair across from her sister. "The color would look lovely on you."

Her sister immediately agreed. "With my rosy complexion almost everything looks lovely on me. It makes it so hard to pick out dresses. You're so lucky that only one shade of blue flatters your pallid skin. Just once I'd like the pleasure of turning the page and thinking, I can't get that dress because it would look awful on me." She sighed and shook her head. "It would be so much easier to bear if Mama understood, but she thinks I want too many things. It's the *things* that want *me*."

It didn't matter how many times Tuppence had heard this lament before—and it had to number in the hundreds by now—she still felt an almost uncontrollable urge to giggle. Her sister's outsize sense of affliction was a constant source of amusement. "I know, darling. It's no wonder you want to hide in here on such a beautiful day. You're far too fragile to withstand the constant scrutiny of the *ton,* which will surely be out in full force today. You're almost out of tea. Shall I ring for more?" she said, knowing the answer would ultimately be no. The only way to get Hannah to do something was to make her think it was her own idea.

Her sister looked out the window, as if noticing the sky for the first time. "It is a beautiful day," she murmured.

"Yes. Just imagine how crowded the park will be. Dukes, earls, viscounts, marquesses everywhere you look," she said as she listed the categories of potential husbands that appealed to Hannah. Using the term itself would have been too obvious. "No room to maneuver at all. It sounds appalling. This is much better. A fresh pot of tea, fashion magazines. You're so clever, darling."

Even as Tuppence tucked into a tea cake, Hannah jumped to her feet and announced she had to change for a drive in the park. The idea of all those dukes and earls rubbing shoulders on South Carriage Drive was more than she could bear. "I know the favorable weather will make it an intolerable crush, but we get so few perfect days. It's a moral obligation to take full advantage. Do be ready to leave in forty-five minutes."

Pleased with how biddable everyone was being today—her sister, the Earl of Gage, even her mother, who agreed to accompany them—Tuppence presented herself at the front door after only forty minutes. Hannah took another fifteen, despite her own eagerness to be on their way.

As expected, the park was indeed thick with carriages and onlookers, and Hannah spotted many familiar faces. Her popularity was evident in the number of young men who stopped to address her and the society matrons who smiled in greeting. Lady Templeton watched her second-eldest daughter field the attention with skill and acuity, delighted to have raised at least one child who knew how to behave in public.

"You see how she looks down as she laughs?" Lady Templeton said to Tuppence. "That's how you display deference and respect. You always looked everyone straight in the eye, including your father and myself. It's mortifying, your sense of confidence and entitlement."

Years ago, this sort of criticism cut Tuppence to the quick, and she would disappear as quickly as possible to her room to try to figure out why she couldn't do the particular thing right. Why *couldn't* she just keep her eyes tilted down like she was supposed to? It seemed like an easy enough task for all the other young girls having their first season.

Slowly, however, it dawned on her that it wasn't merely one thing or two things or seven things she couldn't do right. It was everything. Nothing about her was suited to the London season. If she wanted to fit in and achieve the stated goal of her presence there, she would have to change every single thing about herself. Her parents thoughtfully gave her many opportunities to tailor herself to the occasion, introducing her to a seemingly endless parade of second sons,

whose expectations were as lowered as her own. Even if she were capable of modifying her behavior to win their affection, she knew she could not sustain it over a lifetime and to do anything less would be to ensnare a man under false pretenses. If a hopeful young lady pretended to be a certain way, then she was obligated to stay that way for the rest of her life.

With that as the alternative, settling into spinsterhood was the far more appealing option.

Since her mother's observation required no response, Tuppence didn't make one and instead examined passing carriages for either one or both of the Harlow twins. At one point, she saw Mr. Keswick, the duchess's cousin-in-law who had arranged their meeting behind the curtain, but he was too far away to converse with. She considered hailing him across the lawn but realized that such an action would be too conspicuous for the situation. If she wanted to call that much attention to the association, she might as well go ring the bell in Grosvenor Square.

More than an hour later, she'd all but given up hope and was wondering how long they would linger among the crush of carriages when she observed a phaeton with the Duke of Trent's crest driving toward her. At last!

Excited, she almost raised her voice to call out in greeting, but fortunately reason prevailed before she could make such a revealing mistake. Her greeting the Duchess of Trent and the Marchioness of Huntly as if they were old friends would raise eyebrows in several quarters, including her own. She could scarcely imagine her family's reaction. Hannah would be astounded, yes, but also angry that Tuppence had formed such a socially advantageous connection and not shared that information with her sister. Her mother would most likely be stern and censorious, for the Harlow Hoydens were hardly the rigidly respectable company the Templetons aspired to.

Of course, if it was Hannah who established the relationship, Lady Templeton would heartily approve, as everything her second-eldest daughter did was correct and precisely measured to improve the fortunes of the family. Even her acts of willful disobedience, such as dancing the waltz before gaining approval from the patronesses of Almack's, were lauded for their audacious bravery. One had to take bold steps to make oneself stand out in a crowded field.

If only Tuppence had done something daring to distinguish herself…

Cleary, Hannah was once again the most reliable route to getting what she wanted. All she had to do was put a flea in her ear about *not* introducing herself to the Harlow sisters and then sit back and let audacious bravery take its course.

It was almost *too* easy to arrange.

Smiling, Tuppence leaned forward to speak softly to her sister, but just as she did, she became aware of a curious sensation. It was like a tingling on the back of her neck, and, unsettled, she turned around to find herself suddenly confronted with the severe gaze of Prickly Perceval. Struck, she held herself steady, oddly unable or unwilling to break the contact. He wasn't very near, at least a dozen feet away, and yet she felt as if she could reach out and touch him.

This, too, was an unnerving sensation.

It was also one created entirely in her own head, for his lordship, observing nothing amiss, dipped his chin in curt acknowledgment of her presence and turned back to his sister, whom he was driving.

Tuppence remained still for another moment, her eyes transfixed on the earl's austere figure as she tried to understand what had just occurred. Her reaction to his lordship had been unprecedented, and the only possible explanation she could think of was the awkward timing of his presence. He'd appeared at the precise moment she had meant to establish contact with the Harlow twins. That disquiet she felt was really anxiety at realizing he would have caught her in the act. The truth of their scheme would have been exposed.

Yes, she decided, that was exactly the cause, and she was grateful to Letty for offering a distraction for her brother. He wasn't paying attention to Tuppence now, but it was better to let the moment pass without risking revelation. She wouldn't try to talk to the duchess or her sister, and when their carriage passed a few moments later, she contented herself with a knowing grin and a firm nod. Although it had been abrupt, the message was clearly received, for both sisters returned the smile and nodded back.

The exchange was not the thrilling recital of her derring-do that she'd anticipated telling, but delivering a communication with silent intrigue like a master spy provided its own satisfactions.

Pleased with the machinations of the day, Tuppence waited patiently while her mother and Hannah conversed with society matrons, fellow young ladies and the unattached sons of respectable gentlemen. Several times, she felt the urge to turn around to see if Gage was still behind her, but she kept her eyes trained forward. Showing too much interest in his lordship would raise suspicions, particularly in the breast of the subject himself. The danger wasn't that he'd think she was romantically inclined toward him, for no human being could be so misguided as to believe that impossibility, but rather that he'd start to wonder if there was something a little havey-cavey about their visit to the Patent Bill Office.

That he must never do.

Two days later, Tuppence was still looking for an opportunity to discuss the patent application with one or both of the Harlow twins. She was as eager as ever to tell someone about her clever discovery of the missing document, but she was more impatient to hear what had happened next. Had Mr. Jeffries indeed alerted the marchioness to the office's egregious oversight? Was Vinnie's application proceeding apace? Had an irate and distraught Lord Tweedale presented himself at the Huntly town house demanding satisfaction? Surely, the garrulous lord would not accept the setback in silence.

Tuppence had so many questions and no answers. She wished there was a socially acceptable way to invite a pair of sisters to your bedchamber after midnight for a private conversation. Alas, there was not.

And tonight offered no hope, for she was stuck at Almack's—a venue so unappealing, no young woman who wasn't in the market for a husband would voluntarily cross its threshold. The assembly rooms were hot, the refreshments were stale, and the company was ruthless in its assessment of the other guests. The few times Tuppence had attended during her come-out had been a miserable exercise in humiliation, as she learned her dowdy looks were meager compensation for her drab dowry. She was not a wallflower by nature—her intelligence was too lively for introversion—but the constant criticism of her mother and the general indifference of potential suitors had quickly eroded her confidence. It was much easier to say nothing than to worry that every word she uttered was wrong. From there, it was but a short walk to the wall, where she firmly planted herself for the next two seasons.

She'd felt some anxiety at returning to the site of so much misery, but Tuppence was delighted to find herself unaffected by past failures. Thanks to that lively intelligence, she knew the problem wasn't her; it was a system that made no adjustments for people like her. The strictures of the marriage mart fit only a narrow portion of society. Indeed, it seemed to be only wide enough to accommodate Hannah and one or two young ladies with equally elegant figures.

With this thought in mind, Tuppence secured a spot along the perimeter of the room and sipped tepid lemonade. Her vantage offered both an unrestricted view of her sister as she sparkled up at the unassuming Lord Hughland and a safe remove from the fray.

It was a position she would be happy to maintain for the rest of the evening. No doubt she would be joined at some point by other companions seeking a quiet moment and would not want for intelligent conversation.

No sooner had she thought about convivial company than a deep voice next to her announced, "You're looking well, considering your upcoming ordeal."

Tuppence was startled to find the Earl of Gage next to her and startled more to find out she couldn't say the exact cause of her surprise. It was shocking, certainly, that the renowned curmudgeon would seek her out when he'd been so eager to remove himself from her presence a mere two days before. But his demeanor—affable, amiable, maybe even a little amused—was just as astounding. He mimicked her posture, resting his shoulders against the wall, and she wondered if it was the first time he'd allowed himself to relax his stance in public.

His words, as well, were a cause for astonishment, for the famously terse Prickly Perceval never wasted his breath on nonsensical prattle.

"My upcoming ordeal?" she asked, her eyes still trained on her sister. Because they were equals now, she didn't feel obliged to immediately give him her full attention. She would turn her head to look at him eventually when she felt enough time had passed to make the action seem leisurely.

"Your procedure with Dr. Singleham, which is scheduled for tomorrow at nine-thirty in the morning. I believe the good doctor prescribed nine hours of uninterrupted rest prior to the event," he said, displaying his watch, which showed the time to be a little after eleven. "It doesn't seem as though you're going to get it unless you leave right now, but your sister appears unlikely to fall in with that plan. Nor Lord Hughland, for that matter."

Once again, Tuppence couldn't say which surprised her more: the fact that he remembered such idiocies or that he chose to speak of them.

"I postponed it," she explained, turning now to look at the earl. As she did so, she was in for yet another shock: Posed like this, comfortably against the wall with an agreeable expression on his face, he was handsome. His foreboding features—the straight nose, the sharp cheekbones, the piercing eyes—lost some of their menace, and marveling at the difference, she felt her heart skip a beat. "I've discovered that I'm not quite as weary of outwitting men as I thought."

The earl smiled in response, and Tuppence felt her heart dart wildly in another inexplicable leap.

"What about using me?" he asked without a hint of bitterness. "Are you weary of trotting me out like a pony to do your bidding?"

Tuppence turned white.

Within a moment, a single moment, all color drained from her face as the truth struck her. He knew the truth. He knew everything. He'd figured it out.

How?

She'd been circumspect in her behavior. Every move she'd made had been thoughtful and considered. Nothing she had done could have given away the game.

Well, obviously, *something* she'd done had given it away. But what? At once, her mind called up the scene at the Patent Bill Office. She saw Jeffries at his desk, standing upon their arrival, and Polk tipping over his teacup as he also got to his feet. The earl, standing firm in the doorway, greeted the clerks with—

Stop it, Tuppence thought, resisting the urge to shake her head as if to clear her mind of these images. It didn't matter how Gage knew. Knowledge was irrevocable, and worrying about its acquisition left her vulnerable. She needed to focus her attention on building her defenses and deciding how to respond in a measured way that would protect her from harm. If only the earl's tone had been bitter! Then she would have had some measure of the depth of his resentment. This amiability, in contrast, was like a bottomless pit.

Her first impulse was to deny the charge. The earl might think he knew the whole story, but unless the Harlow sisters had indeed confessed the details, his knowledge was purely speculative. With that shaky foundation, she could perhaps brazen it out with wide-eyed declarations of innocence and pursed-lipped proclamations of confusion. It had worked with Mr. Hittles when he'd accused her of stealing his cloisonné snuff box. She had taken it, of course, to prove to his employer that he was the man who had accosted Miss Saunders, for that lavender-cardamom scent was unmistakable. But the gentleman had not only believed her protestations, he'd apologized with an agitated air for wrongly accusing her of the crime.

It would be foolish, however, to equate Prickly Perceval with the hapless Mr. Hittles, for the former was by far the sharper customer. He would never accidentally spill his snuff in the hair of the lady onto whom he was pressing his unwanted attentions in the shrubbery at Vauxhall. Indeed, she was fairly certain he would never spill anything, let alone at such an inopportune time.

No, lying to the earl wasn't a reliable tactic. He would most likely see the sham for what it was, and the attempt to gull him would serve only to anger him more. He was a straight-as-an-arrow fellow and would appreciate being treated as such.

With a surfeit of calm she wasn't feeling, she said, "I could not have done it without your help, my lord. Your impatience to leave made it all possible, and for that I thank you."

Her admission surprised him. He'd assumed she would deny it or at the very least dissemble in hopes of leading him down the garden path, and this straightforward acknowledgment left him momentarily nonplussed. It was clear from his expression that he'd been determined to press the matter, but her good-natured ownership of the truth left him nothing to press.

He actually had to gather his thoughts.

It did not take long. Gage was a shrewd debater and experienced orator and knew how to neatly align his argument with the facts. But the adjustment wasn't instantaneous, and in the moment it took him to recover, Tuppence caught a glimpse of uncertainty on his face. There was, she decided, something very appealing about seeing those black eyes narrowed in bewilderment.

"And I must thank you, Miss Templeton, for not forcing me into a game of cat and mouse," he said, his tone both menacing and flat. "My time is far too important to waste trying to extract the truth from a triviality like you. As I observed on a previous occasion you are a sadly misguided woman of questionable intelligence with an overdeveloped sense of your own competence. I was appalled by you the first time we met, and further acquaintance has convinced me only that my opinion of you was still too high. I don't know what your purpose is in trying to subvert the United Kingdom's patent process and I don't care. Whatever underhanded business you hoped to accomplished has been thwarted by me, and that is all that matters. I had considered pressing charges, for your actions are by every account illegal, but I do not want your father to learn the truth. I understand he already finds you a failure as a daughter, and I would not like to make his suffering more acute."

It was a good speech. Indeed, a very, very good speech, for with each word Tuppence felt another part of her wither—first her heart, then her lungs, then her knees. Bringing her father into it was a particularly brilliant stroke because it was the truth. She could mount a reasonable defense against the rest of his claims, but there was nothing she could say to counter her father's suffering. It was wholly and completely true. She *was* a failure as a daughter, a fact her parents liked to remind her of by word or deed almost every day.

She had not, however, expected to be reminded of it here, tonight, in the assembly rooms at Almack's. Her mother had begged off from the outing, and it was only she and Hannah, who, though unimpressed with her as a sister, gave her existence too little thought to bother questioning her adequacy.

The desperateness of the situation was her own fault, of course, for she would not be so hurt now if she hadn't let her guard down with Gage. To think she'd dared to consider them as equals. What an impossible notion! She could never be his equal, not while she was so tightly constrained by society's disapproval and his freedom had no limits. The advantage was all his, and pressing it was how he'd humiliated her the first time. And now he'd done it again.

There was an inevitability to their relationship, if the accumulation of a few random encounters could be described as such, and it was something she'd intuited the first time they met. It was the reason she had said no to the Harlow sisters' original request. At the time, she hadn't been able to explain to them or even to herself what exactly she was so afraid of, but she realized now that it was this moment. This humiliation had always been in the wings, waiting for her.

Having her worst fears proved right, however, did not exempt her from the consequences of her actions. If she had remained firm in her refusal to help, the Harlow sisters would have been forced to devise another strategy to ensure proper credit for the marchioness's invention. But having gone with plan A, they were no longer afforded the luxury of plan B. That was her fault.

As withered as she was, Tuppence knew she had to do something to try to salvage the situation.

To bolster her courage, she recalled the look on Featherweight's face in Lady Sophia's carriage when he discovered she wasn't the well-dowried ingénue he planned to compromise and wed. For a moment—for just the briefest span of time—she could imagine him slowly squeezing the life out of her as he released his fury. Then calmly she withdrew her weapon, a fully loaded pistol with which she was an expert shot, and told him how the rest of the scene would be played.

This time she wouldn't be telling her quarry anything. She would be asking, and asking required humility.

Taking a deep breath, she said, "You are correct, my lord, in more ways than you know. I *am* a failure and have indeed failed in many things, including this, but I would beg that you hear me out, for the story is a little more complicated than it would appear."

By all indications, the earl seemed ready to storm off. Her words, far from placating him, seemed to enrage him further. His eyebrows drew together in a slashing line, making his already angry expression appear thunderous. Nevertheless, he stayed where he was against the wall, his shoulders stiff.

"It was not my intention to subvert the United Kingdom's patent process," she said softly, "or indeed any process. I was trying to right an injustice as a favor to a friend. You see, the garden hose in question was not invented by Lord Tweedale, despite the fact that he submitted a petition that would award him the patent. It was invented by the Marchioness of Huntly." Now the expression on his face was disbelief. Of course it was. If his incredulity hadn't been so predictable, then none of this duplicity would have been necessary. "I know it's hard for you to believe that because you're a man and you don't think a woman is capable of such invention. I do not say that accusingly or even critically, my lord. It's difficult for anyone to believe that a woman can do something better than a man. That was why the marchioness and her sister came up with the plan to make it seem as though the marchioness's application fell behind the storage cabinet."

"You have been told a Banbury tale, Miss Templeton," his lordship said with mild scorn, "and I'm surprised that someone with even your meager intelligence can't see through it."

Tuppence nodded, accepting the insult. His opinion of her was of no consequence. "Do you recall who the Marchioness of Huntly is?"

The earl sighed heavily, then answered, "The Harlow Hoyden's twin sister, the former Miss Lavinia Harlow."

"She's also the first female member of the British Horticultural Society," Tuppence said, "a position that isn't without its difficulties. As you can imagine, not every member of the society was pleased with that development, and one gentleman in particular devised a scheme to punish her for her daring. It did not prevail, for the marchioness and her family thwarted his intentions and advised him that a long-term stay in New South Wales would be the best way to ensure his continued good health. The villain left, but from his haven in Australia, he devised a new scheme—to wit, providing the specifications of her invention to a member of a rival gardening organization. That is Lord Tweedale. He did not invent the modern elasticated hose. Indeed, I very much doubt he knows anything about hoses at all, let alone how to increase their elasticity using India-rubber and turpentine. All the information he submitted on his application was stolen from Lady Huntly."

Gage's stony expression did not change as Tuppence related these facts. "Correct me if I'm wrong, Miss Templeton, but you did just say 'rival gardening organization.'"

"Yes, my lord, I did," Tuppence said, disconcerted by both the tone and substance of the question. It wasn't the detail she'd expected him to focus on.

With a thoughtful nod, he straightened his shoulders, took a step away from the wall and looked at her with faint disdain. "Ordinarily, I'd be in favor of a young woman doing whatever she could to make herself as feminine as possible, but with you, Miss Templeton, I would advise the opposite approach. Postpone your procedure indefinitely. Don't let the good doctor—Mr. Singleham, if I'm remembering correctly—perform a trepanation, for your brain is already so corrupted by Gothics, books about polar exploration might be the only thing tethering you to reality. To my mortification, I found myself highly entertained by your flights of fancy in the coach the other day. I thought your ability to describe the doctor's office in such precise detail was marvelous. But I see now that you are unable to distinguish between reality and fiction. The lively thoughts in your mind present themselves as facts and that I do not find entertaining. I find it horrifying and pitiful. It also further explains your actions in regards to Letty. I'm no longer baffled as to why you thought you could handle the situation on your own. In your mind, you're not a dowdy spinster but a heroic young lady who has accomplished any number of wondrous feats. My sister's life, I'll thank you to remember, is not an opportunity for you to display your heroism. Please keep your distance or I will be forced to take steps to ensure you do. Good evening, Miss Templeton," he said and walked away.

And indeed his contempt for her was so complete he did in fact just walk away—not stomp or stalk or stride with great purpose. He merely ambled across the room as if stepping away from a refreshments table with soggy meat pies.

I am a soggy meat pie.

Although the room was hot, Tuppence felt cold. It was as if ice suddenly filled her veins, and she was deathly afraid she might start to shake.

Or cry.

Or cry *and* shake.

She wouldn't do either. No, she absolutely would not disintegrate into a shuddering pile of female weakness in the middle of Almack's. Her reputation, as meager as it was, could not withstand the spectacle.

Ordinarily, she wouldn't have cared one way or another what the *ton* thought of her. Society had dismissed her years ago, and she had kindly returned the favor. But she didn't want the earl to know how thoroughly he'd leveled her, for she hated that he had the ability to bring her so low. Nobody else could make her feel like a slab of dirt on the bottom of the hem of scullery maid's dress. It was so devilishly unfair. The pompous nodcock skewered her for being unable to distinguish between reality and fiction when he himself couldn't make the distinction. It wasn't her fault he was ignorant of the finer points of the rivalry among competing gardening societies.

It was this aspect of his response—the glaring injustice of his scorn—that cut through her quivering despair and kept her spine as straight as a rod. She stood there, firm and tall against the wall, for the rest of the evening. The minutes passed slowly, for she seemed unable to get her mind to work properly. Every attempt to focus her thoughts on a particular subject dissolved into a self-pitying rant directed at herself, at Gage, at the Harlow sisters, at herself again, even at Letty for allowing herself to get into such a ghastly scrape in the first place. Around and around her mind went, spewing rage in random directions, picking a target and just as inexplicably letting it go.

Her mind spun and spun, and then it was time to leave. Hannah professed exhaustion as a young man who wasn't Hughland praised her stamina.

"She danced every dance," he said with an admiring shake of his head. "She didn't sit a single one out."

Hannah twittered in delight and pointed out that many young ladies had been just as popular. The young man insisted that couldn't be true, her sister insisted it had to be, and the argument, as teeth-achingly sweet as treacle, continued until Mr. Quilltop handed Hannah up to their carriage. He promised to call on her the next day as he closed the door, and Tuppence, grateful to him and Hannah's other beaux for not trying to run off with her sister while she was too distracted to notice, said she was looking forward to seeing him again.

CHAPTER EIGHT

Honest to a fault, the Earl of Gage didn't know the first thing about engaging in stealth-like behavior. He'd never inquired about a man's health without caring about the answer, complimented a host without admiring his hospitality, or sought the opinion of a peer without respecting his intellect. He had little use for by-rote courtesy and set the bar for approval so high few could meet it. This demanding combination ensured that he rarely had to put himself out for anyone, and as he contemplated the Marchioness of Huntly, who was talking sedately to Sir Charles Burton across the drawing room floor, he realized he wasn't sure how to proceed. He had no more experience striking up a conversation with a stranger than he did acquiescing to a simpleton.

His usual straightforward approach wouldn't further his cause, for flat out asking her to detail the process by which she invented her garden hose was antithetical to his purpose. He was there to gather intelligence in order to form his own opinion as to whom the patent properly belonged.

As unsure as he was, Gage knew one thing for certain: Dithering would resolve nothing. Determined, the earl strode up to Burton and asked him how his conservatory, which was currently undergoing a renovation to improve its drainage, was fairing. A week earlier the man's grumbling about the inconvenience of having a dozen workmen tramping through his home in their dirty boots had thoroughly ruined his lordship's late-afternoon meal at Brooks's. He had been seeking quietude and had instead been subjected to a loud and loquacious list of grievances.

Now he commiserated with the gentleman about the upheaval construction can cause in one's home and invented his own tiresome project to complain about. Although he'd never personally indulged in the practice before, he knew people often established a connection by sharing tales of mutual suffering.

At once, Burton's features lit up, and he launched into an account describing the desecration of his grandmother's beloved rug—which had been rolled up and stored in the linen closet, where it should have been safe from harm.

"But the conservatory desk had to be moved to the front parlor," the baron explained, "which crowded out the leather chairs, which in turn had to be moved to the linen closet, which was in constant use because the workers were so dirty, and you know what happens whenever a pickax enters an establishment."

In fact, Gage did not, but professing ignorance might have resulted in the acquisition of that knowledge, so he smiled and gave a hearty yes.

He felt like a complete imbecile.

Burton laughed in sympathy, then gulped in horror when he realized he'd been so distracted by his own misery that he'd failed to introduce Lady Huntly. His effusive apology was waved off by the young marchioness, who clearly appreciated a good desecrated-rug story.

"It's a pleasure, my lady, to meet the first female member of the British Horticultural Society," he said, carefully inspecting her demeanor for some indication of discomfort at finding herself in conversation with the target of her scheme. To his consternation, he was unable to detect anything, for her blue eyes sparkled with naught but interest, and he couldn't decide if he was impressed by her composure or appalled by it. "You must be a very remarkable young woman to have realized such a daunting achievement."

The marchioness smiled and demurred at this description, assuring the earl that she was in every way ordinary and that the time had simply come to expand the society's ranks.

This display of humility did not sit well with Sir Charles, who disliked the implication that the British Horticultural Society was subject to the laws of time or inclined to accept just any woman with a fondness for roses. "Lady Huntly is indeed remarkable," he said, "for she's not only a gifted horticulturalist with a keen understanding of drainage systems but an inventor as well."

Gage, who had been wondering how to turn the conversation from conservatory renovations to garden hoses, lifted an eyebrow in feigned surprise. "An inventor?"

And still the Marchioness of Huntly maintained her poise. By neither a flicker of unease nor a titter of self-consciousness did she reveal the truth of their association. She remained so calm and unperturbed by his interest in her invention, he began to suspect anew the veracity of Miss Templeton's story. Although he could conceive of no advantage to be gained by shifting responsibility for the petition affair to the Harlow twins, he allowed for the possibility that the impertinent chit was playing a deeper game. Knowing how befuddled her mind could be, he wouldn't have been surprised if she had created the episode out of whole cloth.

Lady Huntly might be as much Miss Templeton's victim as he.

Yet as soon as he had the thought, he dismissed it, for the woman who had accompanied him to the Patent Bill Office wasn't the type to get befuddled or confused or perplexed. On the contrary, her mental acuity had struck him as razor-sharp, which was why he was there cozying up to her ladyship. Despite the insults he'd dealt the young woman—deeply felt at the time, for he'd been embarrassed and angry—he had a grudging respect for her mind. If she believed the Marchioness of Huntly was the true inventor of the modern elasticized gardening hose, then he had to consider the possibility that the Marchioness of Huntly was indeed the true inventor of the modern elasticized gardening hose.

He didn't want to make the concession and resented the fact that he seemed incapable of controlling his own impulses. His original plan for the evening had not included attending Lady Salcomb's fete with Letty and their aunt. Rather, he'd arranged to meet Lord Carroll at his club for a hand of whist. Up until the moment he'd climbed into the carriage with his sister, he'd truly believed he would pass a few comfortable hours at Brooks's with an old friend. And yet somehow he found himself sending a footman with his apologies.

It was absurd, but he couldn't let the matter rest. Immediately following their visit to Lincoln's Inn, he'd tried to convince himself that he didn't care what the impertinent miss was up to. So she'd lied to gain entry to the patent office—'twas no business of his why. He'd almost persuaded himself that was true when he'd spotted her in Hyde Park a few hours later. His eyes had been drawn to her immediately, the way she sat quiet and stiff in the carriage with her family comparing starkly with the animation she'd displayed in his coach that afternoon. He'd fully expected her to perk up when she saw Lady Huntly pass with her sister, for what could be more natural than to share the very strange development of finding her lost patent application only a few hours earlier? When she didn't hail the marchioness, he was struck by the oddity, and then the sly young lady nodded with meaningful intention. It was a moment rife with significance, and although the earl didn't comprehend it fully, he understood enough to realize the two women were involved in the deviousness together.

He'd expected Miss Templeton to deny it. For two days, he'd imagined their confrontation, the contrived look of surprise when he made his accusation, the false innocence when she claimed to have no idea what he was talking about. Respecting her intelligence, he'd envisioned an extended game of cat and mouse, with him ultimately overcoming her lies.

Instead, she had confessed. Calmly, without any defensiveness, she had acknowledged that, yes, her discovery had been arranged in advance. And then she thanked him! Owning no shame or limit to her impudence, she had the audacity to express her gratitude for his help in accomplishing her goal.

Her behavior was beyond anything he'd ever known.

Provoked by her display of cavalier satisfaction, he had issued the cutting set-down she'd deserved. And that was when the proceedings took an unexpected and unnerving turn, for rather than making a bold case in defense of her actions, she humbly submitted. Watching her, it seemed to him almost as if she'd folded up into herself until she was a compact little box on the floor of Almack's. Inexplicably, this pose as well as her agreement that she was a failure infuriated him. It was, he thought, anathema to everything she was for her to meekly accept defeat. The misguided Miss Templeton was too stubborn and confident to actually believe she'd ever failed at anything, and yet she seemed utterly deflated.

Then, while he was still trying to figure out why he felt so unsettled by that development, she'd launched into a ridiculous story about the Marchioness of Huntly being the true owner of the patent. It was in every way absurd to believe a young lady reared in the gentle arts of womanhood—watercolors, pianoforte, sewing, French—would have the wherewithal to create a new and improved watering device. Did Miss Templeton think he was a simpleton to believe such a whisker? Did she think him a green lad still wet behind the ears?

If he hadn't been so impatient to leave the Patent Bill Office, he would have realized at once how ridiculous it was to attribute the invention of a complex mechanical device to a genteel young lady. But Miss Templeton had known how very eager he was to leave, for he'd stood in the door practically tapping his foot in annoyance, and she'd used that against him. The last thing he'd wanted to do when the clerks held up the misplaced application was open an investigation. Far better to award the patent to the first petitioner and apologize to the second.

Matter resolved.

Now may we please go?

Yes, the Templeton chit had known exactly how to take advantage of his inattention, and she'd tried to do it again, at Almack's, when she claimed Lord Tweedale was motivated by a deep-seated dislike of a rivalrous horticulture organization. Of all things inconceivable! Only a woman steeped in Gothic fiction could come up with such a preposterous plot twist.

Clearly, she had been making a May game of him with her tale, as she had with Dr. Singleham, only this time he wasn't part of the joke. He *was* the joke. That she had so little respect for him made him furious, and he gave her a scolding worthy of her mockery.

But that was Wednesday night and now it was Saturday, and with the passage of time came the cooling of his temper. With a calmer head, he reviewed the exchange and could not comfortably dismiss Miss Templeton's humility as mere show. She seemed genuinely determined to efface herself in the furtherance of the marchioness's cause. Unable to explain that and uneasy with the lack of understanding, he decided to investigate and sought out the Earl of Moray at Brooks's. Naturally, he could not bring himself to ask the British Horticultural Society member if his organization was locked in deathly battle with another group with similar interests, but a few questions about the ideal method for growing orchids soon elicited a bitter

tirade against the Society for the Advancement of Horticultural Knowledge. Gage, who regularly belittled fellow
members of Parliament for their incompetence and facile
ideas, was taken aback by the depth of Moray's bile.

With less reluctance than he would have expected, the
Earl of Gage acknowledged that at least some of Miss
Templeton's outrageous tale was true. That did not mean,
however, that he was ready to accept all of it. A clever dis-
sembler would know the most convincing lies are mixed
with the truth.

Moray's rant against the Society for the Advancement
of Horticultural Knowledge, with its "wrongheaded approach to scientific exploration" and its "staggering inability to cultivate a half-decent *Cymbidium hookerianum*," continued long after Gage's interest had subsided. Rather then
try to gently extricate himself from the conversation,
which was more of a monologue than a discussion, the earl
decided to simply walk away. He sketched a bow before
leaving, a courtesy he didn't feel the situation required, as
Moray's angry soliloquy had already violated the basic rules
of polite society, and strode into another room to play
hazard. For several minutes more, he could hear the faint
rumble of the earl's wrath.

While the caster rolled the dice, Gage considered how
to confirm or refute the rest of Miss Templeton's story.
Despite the new information, his mind simply could not
conceive of the possibility of a gently bred woman inventing anything other than mischief. Letty, for example,
danced gracefully, sang beautifully, and poured tea elegant-
ly. She knew how to draw a fairly recognizable rose, how to
inquire after the health of a dowager without implying she
was feeble, and how to converse with members of Parliament in French. Her talents were womanly, appropriate and
unobtrusive. She would never have the effrontery to invent
a mechanism before a man had a chance to perfect it.

But just because his sister was the epitome of female
circumspection did not mean other women were, and he

could not deny the possibility that Lady Huntly was indeed the rightful owner of the patent.

To find out the truth, he overcame a lifelong policy of not intruding in other people's business and struck up a conversation with the Marchioness of Huntly with the intention of ascertaining what she knew about elasticized garden hoses.

Now that Sir Charles had obligingly introduced the topic, Gage was at liberty to ask relevant follow-up questions.

"I've never met a lady inventor before," he said, his tone slightly in awe.

Once again, her ladyship minimized her accomplishment. "My sister would be very cross with me if she heard me say this, but it's not as impressive as it sounds. I merely improved the elastication of the watering hose, which was prone to bursting when too much water passed through it, as leather alone lacks the required flexibility. I'm really more of a tinkerer."

Imagining that her assertion was probably closer to the truth than her petition asserted, the earl said, "How very clever. I suppose you used Amazon rubber as your main ingredient."

The marchioness tilted her head with curiosity. "I'm not familiar with that type. I used a variety known as India-rubber."

"Ah, yes, of course," he said with a knowledgeable air, as if everything he knew about rubber had not been acquired in the past four and twenty hours. "You added copper arsenate to increase the malleability of the India-rubber, I trust."

"I found turpentine to be ideally suited to my needs," she said.

The earl nodded thoughtfully, as if both chemicals had suited his needs at one time or another. "I imagine adding a good liter to the mixture also produced the desired result."

Her ladyship laughed, then immediately apologized

for the ill-placed humor. "It's merely that it took me months, my lord, to arrive at the ideal measurement to increase the elasticity of the rubber while not harming the seams of the leather," she explained. "That was the single biggest challenge. Truthfully, I'm surprised I'm not still in the Duke of Trent's conservatory increasing the amount of turpentine by tiny increments, as the process was so long and painstaking."

Although the entire conversation had been carefully planned to provide Gage with the information he sought, he found himself smiling sincerely at the frustration in her tone. He knew what it was like to work for months in pursuit of an elusive goal. "I think perhaps you were being needlessly humble when you described yourself as a tinkerer, my lady. Your contribution seems to be far more significant. However did you come up with such a creative idea?"

She smiled again, revealing a dimple. "And now you will know my characterization was accurate, for I got the idea from Mr. Samuel Brill, a shoe manufacturer who used India-rubber to improve his shoe's imperviousness to water. I merely adapted his innovation for my own purpose. I even visited his factory to get an inside look at his process."

Sir Charles bobbed his head with fond appreciation. "You see, this is why we deigned to allow a woman into our prestigious group. She's clever enough to modify someone else's invention rather than start her venture from scratch. And she had the temerity to call it a matter of timing. I would never have imagined in a million years that I myself would consent to a female member of the British Horticultural Society, but Lady Huntly is a charming exception to her sex. We're lucky she's a rarity. Otherwise, we might be overrun with females."

He shuddered as if to underscore this horror, and the marchioness, clearly determined not to give offense, laughed as if the sally were genuinely amusing. It was not, of course, for the baron's attitude toward her ladyship was both condescending and proprietary, as if she were some sort of creature he and his fellow members had adopted as a symbol of their open-mindedness and goodwill.

To his utter surprise, Gage discovered he was offended on her behalf.

Impressed with his own wit, the baron added, "If we admitted the ladies, they would no doubt spend all their time redecorating the society's offices. You know how they are with settees. Never sat on one that didn't need reupholstering."

Although the earl shared Sir Charles's view that women were drawn to superficial and trivial endeavors, he expected the marchioness to hold her sex in higher regard and waited for her to issue a cutting defense. He could easily imagine Miss Templeton agreeing with the baron to such an excessive degree that his opinion would begin to seem absurd.

But the Marchioness of Huntly was no Tuppence Templeton. Rather than extend the interlude, she offered up a reason as to why she had to leave. "It's been an age since I've seen my sister, and I imagine she's wondering where I've wandered off to. I trust you'll excuse me," she explained, then she turned to the earl and said it had been a pleasure to meet him.

He didn't doubt her sincerity. If Miss Templeton's version of events was accurate, then surely the lady inventor knew exactly what he was up to.

Verily, the baron was inclined to linger over conversation, for the desecrated rug was the least of the indignities he'd suffered in pursuit of an efficient drainage system, but Gage had no further use for the gentleman and abruptly walked away. Assessing her ladyship's knowledge of rubber and turpentine had been only half of that evening's mission, and he still had another victim to seek out.

To his surprise, he found Lord Tweedale alone on the terrace quietly enjoying a cheroot. It was unexpected because the man was widely known to be as much of a chatterbox as Lady Jersey. Indeed, he had once famously treated the patroness of Almack's to a forty-five-minute dissertation on Napoleon's affair with Countess Walewska, as illicit romances, particularly imperial ones, were a consuming passion. "Silence" had never been so silent for so long.

In addition to pontificating on matters of salacious interest, his lordship enjoyed boxing with Gentleman Jackson, raising roses and losing at faro. Despite his penchant for gossip, he was generally respected by his peers and considered to be a reasonably entertaining fellow as long as he wasn't in his cups. Too much madeira and his rumor-mongering tipped into garrulous pedantry. His encounter with Lady Jersey, though bandied about for a month, was hardly his worst exploit. Mr. Walter Hayes reported being subjected to a recitation of every rumor ever bandied about regarding Lord Byron's relationship with his half-sister that topped two hours.

For this reason, as well as several others, including a general lack of interest in his person, Gage had had little contact with Lord Tweedale. But both men belonged to the same club and had played a hand or two of faro together, so it was not the oddest thing in the world for the earl to greet him amiably and ask if he perhaps had another cheroot.

Certainly, Tweedale did not observe anything strange in the interaction and immediately produced a second cigar.

Knowing his lordship was the target of Miss Templeton's scheme and not a participant, Gage saw no reason to tip-toe around the matter. His association with the Patent Bill Office was well known, and his interest would be interpreted as merely academic.

"I must congratulate you on your invention, Tweedale," he said after lighting the cheroot. "I read your application. It's very impressive stuff."

Tweedale was a substantial man—well over six feet, with broad shoulders, a wide neck and a thick head of hair despite being well into his sixth decade. Nevertheless, he simpered at the compliment. "Thank you, my lord. I'm very pleased with it. In fact, I'd never aspired to be an inventor, as most of the devices I've come across in my life satisfied my needs, but as soon as something fell short, I resolved to improve it immediately. I am a man of action."

"Indeed," he said. "It was very clever of you to use Amazon rubber."

Tweedale agreed. "It has the greatest elasticity of all the rubbers. There are so many different types to choose from, but I knew instinctively that the rubber from the Amazon River would be most suited to my project."

Gage nodded. "And settling on copper arsenate to increase its malleability. That was quite clever too. More instinct?"

"Experience," Tweedale explained firmly, "which is an important as instinct when it comes to inventing new devices. As a man of science, I have to rely on prior knowledge as well. The ingredient makes many things malleable."

In fact, it did not. Copper arsenate was a blue-green powder used in paint. "How did you figure out a liter was the right amount to add?"

"I wonder how you can even ask," Tweedale said. "As I've explained, my instincts are finely honed, and as a scientist, I have a keen sense of what is required at any given moment. I know things innately. It's a part of who I am. It's why I'm such an outstanding inventor."

Gage could not think of anything more grating on his nerves than the man's pompous complacency. Despite his rising annoyance, he kept his expression smooth and asked with surprise, "It was not a matter of trial and error?"

Tweedale lifted his chin. "My dear sir, I do not make errors."

Gage rather thought he'd just did, a big one, in fact, but he kept that information to himself, preferring to take two more puffs on the cheroot in silence, then extinguishing it below his heel and bidding the other man good night. Without question, the self-important fool didn't know the first thing about inventing an elasticized rubber hose. There was no such thing as Amazon rubber, and one didn't use liters to measure a dry ingredient like powder. He was such a sanctimonious buffoon, he hadn't even bothered to read the application before handing it in. The earl found the man's sloppiness almost as appalling as his overweening self-confidence. Surely, the first thing you do when submitting a false claim to a governmental office is memorize the details of it. He'd made a sworn declaration before a judge only a few weeks ago. Had he truly forgotten everything so quickly?

As he reentered the drawing room, the earl felt his anger turn to fury as he realized he had taken this imbecile's side against Miss Templeton. He could not admire such an undisciplined female such as she, but she'd earned his respect with her lively mind and her refusal to back down. She had spine. That was why she'd readily admitted to the ruse rather than cravenly deny it. Any other woman would have batted her eyelashes and trilled in feigned delight at the accusation in hopes of charming him out of his temper. But not she. Tuppence Templeton owned the truth, absorbed his abuse and pleaded her case.

And now he owed her an apology.

That did not sit well with him.

No, indeed, it sat very poorly.

It would be one thing if he'd simply doubted the truth of her story. It was entirely natural for him to credit the creation of the modern watering hose to a man, as Miss Templeton herself had made this very point. As a general rule, women didn't invent things. Instead, as Sir Charles had so recently observed, they selected the color of the drapes and rearranged the furniture in the drawing room. If he'd left their exchange there, then an apology would be a minor business between the parties. He'd offer a bow, perhaps unbend his shoulders a little and offer a sincere expression of regret. But he hadn't stopped there. Oh, no. He had continued to lash out at her, piling vicious insult on top of vicious insult in an attempt to soothe his damaged pride.

And it was, he acknowledged now, damaged pride that had made him act with such brutality. He'd thought the source of the wound was her seeming contempt for his intelligence with her outlandish story. But in truth it went deeper than that. He'd experienced a new sensation during the carriage ride, a sense of camaraderie with a female, and it was the betrayal of that feeling that had made him act so cruelly.

Damn and blast, he thought, looking for Letty in the crush of the drawing room to announce his departure. Apologizing wouldn't be enough. An apology was what you offered when you stepped on a woman's hem or splashed your friend with port. It smoothed over minor misdeeds. But this transgression exceeded the humble apology's authority. It required something far more substantial. It required amends.

Prickly Perceval *hated* making amends.

CHAPTER NINE

It was a real cold.

Yes, it gave Tuppence, who still felt the sting of the Earl of Gage's insults, the excuse she needed to avoid attending events, but it was also a genuine physical ailment. Her nose was runny, her eyes were puffy, and her throat felt as if it had been scraped by a fire iron.

Even her mother, who usually scoffed at any assertion of illness, had pronounced her too unwell to accompany Hannah to the dressmaker and insisted that she return to her room at once. Since that moment four days ago, Mama had been sending up broth, lozenges, herbal tea infusions and toast at regular intervals. The treatment was consistent but not very filling, and Tuppence, suffering from hunger as well as congestion, wondered if her mother was trying to trim her figure in addition to curing her cold.

She was saved from starvation by Caroline, who was so grateful for the suspension of her French lessons that she eagerly smuggled in food.

Reading in one's room and surreptitiously eating meat pies was not the worst way to spend a few days.

If only she could overcome her scruples, for recuperating in the confines of her bedchamber felt far too much like hiding—and not just from Prickly Perceval. There were other people she dreaded seeing, such as the Harlow twins, who did not yet know the truth. As far as they were aware, their plan was still proceeding apace. Any day now, the Marchioness of Huntly would be awarded the patent she deserved.

Thank you, Miss Templeton!

All Tuppence had to do was send a note to one of their houses. She didn't have to convey the information in person, and since their plot had been exposed, it no longer mattered if a line could be drawn from her to them. There was absolutely no reason why she couldn't write a brief missive explaining how she'd failed to hold up her end of the arrangement—except her head felt so fuzzy and filled with cotton she couldn't quite get the words right. She'd made several attempts in the past few days, and each one had been worse than the last.

As soon as her head cleared, she would write the letter. Probably tomorrow, for she was still too tired today.

Even as she had the thought, Tuppence knew it was all a hum. Her cold was almost entirely gone. Her cough lingered and her lips still felt dry, but she could breathe with ease. Her thoughts remained muddled, though. That was due, however, to her situation, not her condition. She *was* hiding, and the fact that she had a legitimate excuse to do so made her feel only more cowardly—because she was desperately grateful to have a legitimate excuse.

That this complicated mixture of emotions could be laid at the Earl of Gage's door made it all the more demoralizing. Tuppence Templeton wasn't afraid to take her lumps. She made bold choices and understood there would be unexpected consequences from time to time. She accepted that. But did those consequences have to be dispensed by the same man over and over again? Couldn't circumstance contrive to supply a variety of lump-givers to create a more-interesting assortment? Society hostess Lady

Courtland seemed like a daunting and formidable woman. And Mr. Westerbrook's gout made him thoroughly disagreeable. Couldn't they cut her to the quick once in a while? Must it always be the earl who reduced her to an incoherent mass of jelly?

Deciding she had sought refuge long enough, Tuppence resolved to compose a letter to the Harlow sisters immediately. She put her book to the side, climbed out of bed and retrieved a blank sheet of stationery from her escritoire. There, now all she had to do was write.

But no, she couldn't write like this, in her dressing gown with her hair around her shoulders and her teeth unwashed. If she was going to do something useful, she needed to feel neat and proficient—like a young woman of authority, not the resident of a sickroom.

She rang for her maid and requested Lila help her get dressed.

A half hour later, Tuppence, wearing her best morning dress—a deep cerulean color that actually flattered her skin tone—sat down at her desk to try again. She took a deep breath, dipped her pen in the ink and wrote, "Dear Lady Huntly."

Or should she address it to both sisters? Perhaps she was obligated to write two separate notes? Did they have to say different things or could she write the same letter twice?

She leaned back in her chair to contemplate the matter and noticed how untidy her escritoire was. Nibs were everywhere, and different sizes of paper were stacked together in a jumbly mess. Obviously, that would never do, for everyone knew stationery should be sorted by size. And writing utensils belonged in the little box next to the inkwell.

At once, she put down her pen and began to straighten up the mess, creating three different piles to accommodate the various sizes, then adding two more to sort further by color.

When it was all arranged neatly, she examined her handiwork with satisfaction and decided there was nothing to stand in the way of a productive note-writing session.

I will begin now, she thought, holding her pen above the sheet.

A minute later, she was still holding her pen above the sheet, as if the device were fated to stay there, suspended a mere inch from the paper for the rest of time, when a knock sounded at her door.

"Oh, thank God," she muttered with relief as she dropped the pen onto the desk. Finally, a legitimate excuse not to write. Had the interruption not occurred, she might have been forced to rearrange her wardrobe by width of hemlines.

With undue eagerness, she strode to the door and opened it. Her sister Caroline, thirteen years old and already as tall at her sister, darted into the room and hastily closed the door behind her.

"I'm on a secret mission," she announced.

Given that her sister had spent the past seventy-two hours sneaking food into her bedroom, Tuppence wasn't surprised by this declaration. What did take her aback was Caroline's empty hands. Meat pies were usually delivered on a plate or wrapped in a linen square.

Surely, she wasn't hiding lunch under her skirts.

"The Earl of Gage is downstairs waiting to see you," Caroline said, grinning widely. "Papa tried to kick him out because he finds the man detestable, but I told Smudge to show him to the front parlor. Papa never uses the front parlor, particularly in the middle of the day when he's going over the accounts with his secretary, and Hannah is out shopping with Mama, so nobody is likely to discover him there. I asked Smudge to bring him a fresh pot of tea, which rather made his shoulders stiffen because, while it's one thing to show an unwelcome guest to the front parlor, it's another thing altogether to supply him with refreshments. Truly, I don't know what his quibble is, as all I requested was a pot of hot water with some leaves. It wasn't as if I'd asked Mrs. Weathers to bake a fresh batch of scones with currants. I'd thought about it, of course, as I do so love fresh scones with currants, and I'm particularly hungry right now because I haven't eaten a thing since breakfast. Oh, my, breakfast! You must be hungry too. I completely forgot to bring you something to eat. Mrs. Weathers made… "

On and on Caroline rattled, jumping from one topic to another like an exuberant puppy playing with a ball, while Tuppence's mind stayed rooted to the spot. The Earl of Gage *here*? *The Earl of Gage* here?

She didn't doubt for a moment that such an ornery and tenacious man would seize another opportunity to hurl invectives at her head, but making morning calls in order to do so seemed needlessly inefficient. Certainly, that pleasure could wait until he saw her again at a social event. There were several excellent opportunities in the coming week alone: Lady Brackton's musicale, Mrs. Williams's ball, Almack's again. Why take time out of his day to insult her? He was a busy man with fellow members of Parliament to abuse and an ungainly patent process to overhaul.

"…not really sure the source of the antipathy, as Papa was too agitated to explain, but he mentioned an elephant, which, with his aversion to nuts, might explain it somewhat. But what would an elephant be doing in the House of Lords. And, more to the point, would an elephant fit inside the House of Lords? I suppose Mama might know…"

Ultimately, it didn't matter why he felt compelled to interrupt his schedule to insult her. He was here, and now she had to deal with it.

Suddenly her head was clear. The wooliness of just a few minutes ago, which had kept her from writing a coherent letter to the Harlow twins, was gone, driven way, she realized, by the injustice of the visit. Prickly Perceval was free to wallow in his resentment, for it was not her place to decide how long a gentleman's fit of pique may last. But coming into her own home to berate her was beyond the bounds of accepted incivility.

Infuriated by his audacity, she marched out of her room.

Caroline, who was trying to figure out which animals from the African veld would fit easily through the entrance of Parliament ("...it would depend, I suppose, on how far down a giraffe could bend its neck..."), abruptly stopped talking and trailed her sister down the stairs. She would have followed her into the front parlor as well, but before she could enter the room, Tuppence shut the door a mere inch from her nose. Insulted to be excluded from a meeting she'd thoughtfully arranged, Caroline huffed loudly and called to Smudge to cancel her order of tea.

Tuppence walked up to the earl, who was standing by the window in the late-morning light, and said, "Let us align our schedules. I'll be at Lady Brackton's musicale tomorrow night. Will you?"

The question surprised his lordship, for his black eyebrows drew together almost as if suspicious of her intention, and Tuppence wondered if he was taken aback by the unconventionality of her greeting or annoyed that he wasn't in control of their conversation. Regardless of the cause, he answered immediately, "No, I will not."

She nodded and moved on to the next available opportunity. "The following evening I'm to attend Mrs. Williams's ball. Are you attending as well?"

"Letty has requested my escort," he said.

Although the reply was noncommittal, Tuppence took it as a firm yes. "Very good," she said, satisfied that the matter could be arranged so quickly. No need to linger over a pot of tea that wasn't coming. "Let's plan on that, then. Say, after the first waltz but before we're called into dinner. I trust you don't need the extra days to hone your attack, but do take the time to ensure your remarks are as cutting as possible. Listing my inadequacies as a daughter is particularly fertile ground for causing me pain, so perhaps you should focus your attention there. If that is all, my lord, thank you for calling and have a lovely day."

Tuppence relished a good exit—the sweeping of one's

skirts as one brushed carelessly through the door without a backward glance—but her movements were halted by the look on the earl's face. She was used to seeing anger there. Anger, annoyance, boredom, confusion, impatience, surprise, even humor—these were all familiar expressions deployed regularly by the earl, who felt no obligation to hide his emotions behind a pose of civility. But this was something altogether new, and although she could scarcely credit it, the new thing looked a lot like devastation.

It was gone in a flash. A split second later and his lips were pulled into a familiar line, firm and disapproving. His forehead was smooth and his black eyes were courteously blank. The expression disappeared so quickly, Tuppence wondered if she'd imagined it. But why would she do that? What purpose would she have in ascribing unexpected depth of feeling to a man she detested? Was some part of her mind determined to make him appear more likable?

The question was so absurd, she refused to even consider it. If she had seen devastation on Prickly Perceval's face, it was because Prickly Perceval's face had displayed it. It had been as fleeting as a flicker of lightning but just as real, and her proof, she realized, was staring her in the face, for when had the famously argumentative peer ever been courteously anything? The answer was never, and the fact that he felt the need to affect polite indifference now clearly indicated an attempt to disguise a deeper emotion.

Even as she tried to decipher the meaning of his devastation, she decided it didn't matter. As unpleasant as he was, he was still a human being, with the right to the same range of emotions as she. Her objection was only to his giving vent to them in her front parlor. As agreed, he could resume his disparagement of her two days' hence in Mrs. Williams's ballroom.

With that in mind, she dipped into a gracious curtsy, determined to make a more considerate, if less satisfying, departure from the room. "I trust you can show yourself out, my lord."

This time when she turned to leave, her movements were sedate and even, almost placid, and although the calm exit was significantly less rewarding than a furious spin on her heels toward the door, it presented a picture of high-minded aloofness she found pleasing. He may deport himself in any unruly and disruptive way he wanted, but she would be the epitome of well-mannered womanhood.

Then he said, "I owe you an apology," and Tuppence's astonishment was so acute she tripped. She didn't fall, only wobbled a little and immediately righted herself with a bracing hand on the settee, but her balance remained uncertain. Indeed, it felt as if someone could tip her over entirely with the slightest tap.

Disconcerted, she turned around slowly to give herself time to gather her wits. Without question, she knew herself to be owed an apology, but the possibility that the Earl of Gage was there to issue it seemed extremely improbable. He was, as far as she could discern from their previous interactions, constitutionally incapable of admitting to a mistake. If he didn't believe he'd truly done something wrong, then his intention toward her must be false. His so-called apology was either a hoax or an insincere maneuver to get her to reveal a weakness.

As plausible as the prospect of a trick appeared—and it struck her as several times more likely than an apology—Tuppence knew the earl would never resort to deception. He held himself in too high esteem to sink to spouting falsehoods, especially to an aging spinster whom he already considered beneath his touch.

No, despite all sense and reason, the Earl of Gage had presented himself at Curzon Street to apologize to Miss Tuppence Templeton.

She had no intention of making it easy.

"That is kind of you to say, my lord, but I'm sure you do not," she insisted, as she strode across the room to stand next to the window. "Your assessment of the Fitz-Walter affair was reasonable and accurate. What right did I have to save a defenseless young girl from a conscienceless fortune hunter? The fact that I managed to route him entirely on my own, that every part of my scheme fell effortlessly into place at precisely the right moment, only proves how poorly suited I was for the task. Of course, it *seemed* as though the success of my plan was due to careful thought and meticulous plotting, but you knew it was only sheer luck that nothing went awry. And what if something had gone awry? My poor, feeble, female brain would have crumpled from the pressure of trying to come up with solutions so quickly."

Tuppence kept her head tilted down as she spoke, her eyes focused somewhere between the bottom of Gage's coat and the windowsill. Although the pose indicated a docility she didn't feel, she was genuinely reluctant to look him full in the face. She knew how little the earl enjoyed being teased about anything and the matter of Mr. Fitz-Walter remained a particularly sensitive topic. She imagined his anger was so intense by now that steam might be pouring out of his ears in an effort to escape his body.

Nevertheless, she persisted. "As you pointed out over and over again, it's only thanks to Providence that your sister isn't trapped in a loveless marriage to a heartless villain. So, please, my lord, don't ask me to stand here and permit you to apologize to me now. If I were a better woman, perhaps less of a spinster and a quiz, I would be gracious and let you have your say. But I have far too much respect for you to let you condescend to my feelings."

Tuppence finished her taunting speech, at once gratified by her own audacity and fearful she might have gone too far. She told herself she had nothing to worry about, for she had already seen the earl at his most irate and the only thing he could do was belittle her further. No, she thought, not further because he had already dragged her to the bottom of a very deep pit. There was no more harm he could do her.

Comforted by the thought, she decided there was no

reason to prolong the inevitable. She had poked the bear, spurred on by bone-deep perversity and the recuperative benefits of four days of books and meat pies, and now she would accept the consequences. Her shoulders stiff and sure, her heart beating only a little harder than normal, she raised her eyes.

The earl was smiling.

Tuppence closed her eyes for the count of three, confident his agreeable expression was either a trick of light or the product of her woolly brain. But when she opened them again, he was still smiling.

No, he was grinning.

His amiable response undercut her equanimity entirely. She knew how to handle Prickly Perceval and Angry Perceval and Incensed at Being Manipulated Perceval, but this convivial gentleman with the black eyes sparkling with amusement was a terrifying new puzzle. He even looked like a stranger, his countenance younger, lighter, gentler, the harsh angularity of his features softened by humor. All at once, she was noticing how well shaped his lips were, pillowy and red, and the appealing line of his jaw.

He was, she thought with astonishment, a wildly attractive man.

Clearly, all those meat pies and novels had corrupted her mind.

Quick, she ordered herself, think of something mocking to say.

For once, Tuppence's brain wasn't fast enough, and the earl spoke before she could make a dampening observation.

"Try as you might, Miss Templeton, I won't let you sway me from my purpose," he said good-naturedly. "I came here to apologize for my behavior the last time we met. I was angry about several things and spoke more harshly than I intended or the situation called for. By your own admission, several of my remarks cut you deeply, and for that I'm particularly sorry. Letty will tell you I have an innate ability to find a person's weak spot and that's where I tend to strike.

I'm not proud of the ability and hope you can forgive me."

Tuppence didn't know what to say. Having realized his intent to apologize was real, she'd expected something cold, stiff and formal, not honesty expressed with earnestness and warmth.

After an extended period of silence, perhaps the longest she'd ever observed in a conversation, she managed to thank him with a modicum of composure. She didn't stammer or stutter, which seemed to her in that moment to be a great achievement.

His lordship looked at the settee. "May we sit down?"

Now she stumbled as she tried to make sense of the question. "You want to…yes…no…I mean, I'm sorry, of course. You must sit down," she said with conviction, wondering why the idea of sitting in the front parlor with the Earl of Gage was so unsettling. It was a perfectly normal occurrence for two adults to sit down on a settee while having a genial conversation.

And yet it felt disturbingly similar to a romantic tête-à-tête.

Five and twenty years old and half a decade on the shelf, Miss Tuppence Templeton was mortified to discover she somehow still harbored girlish illusions.

To hide her embarrassment, she walked over to the tapestry ribbon by the door and rang the bell. When a footman appeared a few moments later, she requested a pot of tea, for there was nothing less amorous than a steaming cup of common bohea.

"I would offer you scones as well, but I understand from my sister there's a crisis in the kitchen regarding currants," she explained as she sat down on the settee. The mundanity of the task had calmed her nerves.

"Tea is sufficient, thank you," he said, also taking a seat.

Tuppence nodded and wondered if it was her turn to make a comment. Had he asked to sit down so that they may have an insipid conversation about the weather or her mother's health?

"I would also like to apologize for treating your explanation for the events at the patent office with such contempt," he announced. "I have investigated the matter thoroughly on my own and discovered that everything you told me was accurate. The Marchioness of Huntly is the true inventor of the modern elasticized garden hose, and Lord Tweedale is an imbecilic pretender who can't tell the difference between a cord and a card. I'm very sorry for doubting you."

"An apology isn't necessary," she said with sincerity, her tone and intent aligning with her words for once. She was, to her utter amazement, charmed by his lack of self-consciousness. Having decided to express his regret, he was doing it straightforwardly and without equivocation. He wasn't making excuses or justifying his behavior, and Temperance, perverse to the end, found herself determined to do it for him. "The situation was quite implausible, and I would have been surprised if you had taken me at my word. As soon as I said the phrase *rivalrous horticulture organization,* the preposterousness of the situation struck me. Truly, I don't blame you for your response."

The earl shook his head. "You are being too gracious."

But Tuppence disagreed. The Harlow twins had hatched such an elaborate plot because they knew the truth was too outlandish to be believed, and she couldn't fault the earl for falling within the bounds of expected behavior. Any man would have reacted in the same way. "No, my lord, you are."

Gage laughed, and suddenly the room was filled with the bright, rich sound. "Now that's one charge that's never been leveled against me before."

Well aware how true his statement was, Tuppence smiled. "As I said, the situation is preposterous."

His lordship grinned in appreciation, and she marveled again at the difference between this earl and his notorious alter ego who went around sniping and frowning all the time. She could hardly believe they were the same person.

A knock sounded at the door, and Smudge entered with a pot of tea. Despite Tuppence's advancing years, he grimaced to see her sitting in such companionable repose with an unmarried gentleman. Determined to rectify the circumstance, he placed the tray on the Hepplewhite table in the corner by the small window overlooking the side street.

Then he looked at her, his eyes narrowed in mild disapproval, and said, "Is everything satisfactory, miss?"

As the tea was several yards away across the room, everything was obviously not satisfactory. Tuppence, however, was too familiar with the butler's machinations to rise to the provocation. If she acknowledged the great distance, he would explain that the draft by the settee wasn't suitable for the serving of a hot beverage or the rickety legs of the table would cause unnecessary spills.

Smudge always had an explanation that befit his opinion.

"Everything is perfect, Smudge, thank you," she said cheerfully.

The butler nodded, clearly disappointed by his failure to get a rise out of his mistress, and examined the room for another option. Tuppence smothered a smile as she noted the calculating glint in his eye. It was futile, of course. Short of putting the tea out the window, there was no farther spot in the room than the one he'd chosen.

"That will be all, Smudge, thank you," she said, sending him back to the kitchens, where he would no doubt launch into a lurid description of the scene he'd witnessed. Tuppence knew she should be horrified at the thought of being gossip fodder for the servants, but she was too amused by the novelty to work up the outrage.

As soon as Smudge left, Tuppence stood up to bring the tray closer. "I must apologize for what must seem very odd behavior on the part of my butler. Seeing me in conference with a man has so befuddled his brain, he accidentally put the tea in the wrong spot. I don't think he even noticed, and to point it out would have been churlish."

The earl accepted this fiction, as ridiculous as it was, without comment and waited silently as she poured the tea.

"How did you discover the truth?" she asked as she handed him a cup. "You said you investigated the matter yourself. By what method?"

"I quizzed each applicant on his invention," Gage said before launching into a full account of both conversations. Although his intent was to tell the story in a single thread, from beginning to end, he frequently had to stop and go back in the narrative to address Tuppence's many questions. At first, she thought she was annoying him with all her interruptions, but she soon realized he relished her attention to detail, for it seemed to match his own. And he genuinely appreciated the way she always brought him back to the place in the conversation where he'd left off, regardless of the length of the digression.

"And your expression didn't change when he announced himself to be a man of science incapable of making mistakes?" she asked, as amused as she was appalled by Tweedale's boundless self-assurance. How did a man who knew nothing about the elasticized hose answer questions about its invention with the confidence of an expert? Why did he not feel like a fool or a phony? Tuppence herself had pulled off many bold schemes in her life, adopting the gestures of others to create a more believable character, but even she would balk at claiming knowledge she didn't possess. "I'm sure I would have broken into a fit of giggles."

"I was too disgusted to laugh," the earl said, laughing now at the memory. "But his pomposity, the way he sort of fluffed up his feathers when I asked if he'd employed trial and error to find the correct measurement for copper arsenate, was the stuff of pure farce. Imagine Kean playing Polonius and you might get a sense of how entertaining his performance was."

"I wish I had witnessed it," Tuppence said with true regret.

"I wish you had too, as I was a very unappreciative

audience of one," he said, finishing his last sip of tea. The pot was empty and would remain that way, for she wasn't reckless enough to ring for more. "I was too angered by the fraud he'd perpetrated to enjoy the comedic value of his act. The patent system is not perfect. It's riddled with complexities and redundancies, and it takes far too long and costs far too much than is reasonable. But its foundational principle is sound: that an inventor should reserve the rights to his invention. That is only fair, and I believe, on the whole, that the world is fair. That is why Tweedale's deception is so unacceptable and must not stand. It disrupts the balance for everyone."

The afternoon had been lovely, Tuppence thought as she listened to his pretty speech in defense of fairness. In this convivial mood, the Earl of Gage was everything a young woman could want in a conversational partner: clever, insightful, courteous, respectful, earnest, interesting, droll. He was patient with her questions, considerate of her opinions, and genuinely funny in his answers. Sitting there on the settee next to him for the past hour, she felt as if she had finally accomplished her goal of securing his friendship. It had taken much longer than she'd expected and involved a considerably more circuitous route than she could have imagined, but she felt certain that when they met at Mrs. Williams's ball on Tuesday, he would look upon her with kindness.

But like the patent system, she had a few foundational principles of her own, and one of them was to draw attention to hypocrisy when it sat in her front parlor sipping tea.

She didn't want to, of course, for to do so would bring an end not only to a lovely interlude but to their détente as well. She wished she could smother the compulsion, to drown it in tea and laughter, but she had been this way her entire life. It was why she'd never attached one of those second sons, for she refused to compromise her own beliefs to promote the comfort of another. Principles made cold bedfellows, she knew, and yet without them she wouldn't even have the bed. They were called *foundational* for a reason.

Her heart picking up speed, she moved a few inches farther from the earl under the guise of smoothing her dress, for she knew in a moment he would draw away and it seemed important than she do so first. "I'm sorry, my lord, but your perception that the world is generally fair is grossly inaccurate. You see, it's been my experience that you can extricate a young girl from an unfortunate situation with competence, skill and discretion and still be chastised for being a rash and inept female. This happens because many people believe women are inferior to men, and I don't see how you can have fairness in the world without equality. Of course you've formed a different opinion based on your own experience, and the best we can do is agree to disagree."

Tuppence spoke steadily and kept her eyes trained on his. She saw the moment her words penetrated, the glint of anger that sparked in his eyes, and she braced for the tirade that was sure to come. As much as she wanted to run from the room, she forced herself to stay exactly where she was and not give another inch.

But the outburst did not come. Perhaps mindful of the insults he'd dealt her the last time they'd disagreed, perhaps deferential to the afternoon's agreeable tone, he simply nodded his head and said, "Yes, we must agree to disagree."

Inexplicably, his polite response, which was the best she could have hoped for, disappointed her in its mildness. She'd been prepared for an argument, for an opportunity to make her point and perhaps score a few, and now she felt like a balloon that had lost all its air. At a loss, she sat there silently, feeling wilted and limp, marveling at how swiftly the mood had gone from convivial to stilted. It was the last thing she'd expected.

Unable to bear the awkwardness, she jumped to her feet and said with the aggressive good humor usually reserved for teaching her apathetic sister mathematical equations, "Well, my lord, I believe that concludes our business. I shall inform Lady Huntly that the matter has been taken care of and that the patent will be issued as quickly as the system will allow. Thank you again, my lord, for being so gracious and understanding. It is due to you that we're ending the matter on such a satisfactory note."

The smile on her face was too big, too bright, but she felt incapable of subduing it. She looked around the room, her gaze settling on the tapestry ribbon along the opposite wall. "I'll ring for Smudge to show you out."

"It's not at an end," the earl said.

Tuppence halted midstride. "Excuse me?"

"Our business," he explained, "it's not concluded. The matter has not been resolved satisfactorily."

She stared at him, baffled. "But you said you believed Lady Huntly to be the true inventor."

"I do," he readily agreed.

"So her application can go through," she said. "The office will alert Lord Tweedale to the mistake, and Lady Huntly will be awarded the patent."

"That was the original plan, yes," he said as he took several steps in her direction. "But now there's an asterisk."

"An asterisk?" she repeated.

"Yes, an asterisk," he said firmly. "It's an internal designation that indicates there's something of further interest to the clerks."

"But why would they apply an asterisk to the matter?" she asked.

"That's my fault, I'm afraid," he said, his eyes tilted down. "When I realized there was a scheme afoot, I told Jeffries to hold off on informing Lord Tweedale of the invalidity of his application. Inevitably, he wanted to know why, and I explained that the situation was more complicated than we'd originally thought, and, well, complicated situations are automatically marked with an asterisk. Because they are complicated, you see."

But Tuppence didn't see. She was too disheartened by

this sudden new obstacle that had risen up in her path to properly understand how it had gotten there. They'd been so close to attaining their goal, and now it seemed as far away as ever. She would have to write another letter to the Harlow sisters, informing them of this discouraging new development. Given that she lacked the wherewithal to compose the first missive, it seemed unlikely she would manage to produce the second.

Perhaps a private conversation would be better.

At once she pictured the look of disappointment on her ladyship's eager face and knew herself lacking courage as well as wherewithal.

With a sigh, she sat down on the settee.

"I hate to see you so discouraged, Miss Templeton," the earl announced, taking the cushion next to her. "It's really not necessary, for I have a plan to remedy the situation. All we need is a caveat."

At his cheerful tone, Tuppence found herself perking up immediately. Prickly Perceval was hardly the sort of gentleman to concern himself with the feelings of someone else. If he said the situation could be remedied, then the situation would be remedied. "A caveat," she said, recalling vaguely a conversation on that topic with the clerks in the Patent Bill Office. If she remembered correctly, a caveat was a means by which an inventor put in a claim for a device before he finished inventing it. "Didn't Jeffries say that he'd searched for a caveat before approving Tweedale's application? He didn't find a caveat at that time, and I'm not sure how he will find one now. Two files lost behind two different cabinets strain credulity."

"I agree, Miss Templeton, but fortunately we don't have to rely only on faulty filing to achieve our goal. It would be an easy thing for a clerk to overlook a caveat if the name of the invention differed slightly on the application. Even Jeffries's eagle eye would have overlooked the form if Lady Huntly's elasticized gardening hose was described as an elasticated watering line," he explained with unprecedented enthusiasm. Not even when he was relaying his absurd conversation with Lord Tweedale had his voice brimmed with so much excitement.

Tuppence stared at him, not sure which unsettled her more: the endearing glint of mischief she saw in his eye or the surly lord's willingness to cast aside the laws he was charged to protect.

Both were so uncharacteristic.

Too uncharacteristic, she realized with suspicion. "And I suppose after I've broken into the Patent Bill Office following your precise instructions, I *won't* be discovered skulking in the dark by a magistrate who will cart me off to prison."

At once, the hint of playfulness was gone, replaced by a stern look of offense. His voice stiff with outrage, he said, "My dear Miss Templeton, I wonder at the company you keep that you would imagine that any gentleman would seek to entrap a lady at all, let alone through such nefarious devising. No one of my acquaintance would stoop to such contemptible behavior, and I'm astonished to learn that this is the low opinion you have of me."

"Really, my lord?" she asked with a bright smile, delighted by his effort to shame her. Certainly, she was far too sensible to fall prey to such a facile maneuver, but it pleased her to realize he wasn't too stuffed with his own conceit not to make the attempt. "But surely your intention has been for me to have as low an opinion of you as possible. Your treatment of me from the first moment we met would indicate that has been your plan all along. And do let me be the first to congratulate you on succeeding admirably."

The earl laughed and shook his head. "You're giving me far too much credit, as any offense I've given has been entirely inadvertent. Indeed, one might begin to suspect that you're perhaps a little too sensitive to slights. However, we digress from the point, which is something that happens with alarming regularity when I talk to you, Miss Templeton. You have the most distressing ability to distract me. Nevertheless, to return to the topic at hand, I would never consent to exposing you to danger. Naturally, I'll break in to the Patent Bill Office on my own and covertly place the document in the cabinet."

Tuppence stiffened her shoulders and raised her chin to an obstinate angle, for there were few things in the English language more calculatingly designed to rile her up than the word *consent*. For years and years her life had been ruled by the authority of others, leaving her with little recourse but to seek consent and earn approval and await permission. Leave was rarely granted, of course, as her parents believed her only chance of success on the marriage mart was to remain silent and smile prettily. She did her best to comply with both commands, feeling with increasing humiliation more and more like a prize pig on an auction block. It was only now that they'd given up on her that she had any freedom at all. Relegating her to Hannah's companion had been the kindest thing they had ever done for her, for it also put her beneath their notice. Now she sought no one's consent.

"You are gracious to offer, my lord, but I cannot shirk my responsibility to the Harlow sisters," she said firmly. "I made a commitment to them and am bound by honor and obligation to see it through. Naturally, *I'll* break in to the office on my own, as I'm sure you find this whole matter unseemly and not worthy of your attention."

This line of reasoning, as logical as it was, failed to sway the earl, who refused to see himself as blameless. "'Twas I who instigated the asterisk in the first place. This problem is more my doing than yours."

"True, my lord, but a man has the right to be upset when he discovers he's been manipulated and so easily too," she observed.

Although she expected the prickly earl to bristle at her description and had used the word *easily* for just that purpose, he paid it no heed. "There is also the little matter of the caveat itself," he pointed out. "I know exactly what the document should say and how to create it."

He didn't forthrightly state that he would provide the form only if he was the one to plant it, but the implication was clear. Either she would have to accept his condition or ask the Harlow Hoyden and her sister for help in procuring the document. "Very well," she said on a lengthy sigh, "I shall allow you to accompany me."

Thank you," he said, dipping his head in gratitude.

His tone was sober, the nod respectful, yet she thought she could detect a hint of laughter in his eyes. It was slightly unsettling, she realized, not to know if one was the source of amusement or the object of it. Strongly suspecting it was the latter, she said, "You're welcome, my lord. I trust you can have the document prepared quickly?"

"It won't take more than a day," he said.

"And you're certain a caveat is all that's needed to ensure Lady Huntly gets proper credit for her invention?" she asked.

Now the earl smiled. "Oh, yes, without question, this will resolve the matter. An asterisk requires a clerk to recertify a petition for the attorney-general. In practice that means Jeffries will go through all the steps of certification once again. This time, he will discover the caveat that Lady Huntly filed—let's say six months ago—and feel confident that the patent is rightfully hers. As he will start that process as early as tomorrow, there's no time to lose. You're attending Lady Brackton's musicale tomorrow night. Can you extricate yourself from the commitment?"

Although her health had improved greatly in the past twenty-four hours, there was no reason why she couldn't suffer a setback. Some sneezing, some coughing, a little grumbling about the ache in her head, and her mother would confine her to her bedchamber for another full week. "Of course. What time shall we meet at Lincoln's Inn?"

"Jeffries usually closes up the office around five o'clock, but the building remains busy for several hours after, and then there's the janitorial staff to consider. I think we should aim for eleven at the earliest," he said thoughtfully. "But meeting there is far too risky. We will travel together in my coach."

Shocked by the impropriety, she gasped, then immediately turned bright pink at the utter ridiculousness of her response. The Earl of Gage wasn't proposing an elaborate scheme to get her alone in a dark coach so he could press his attentions. He was merely suggesting the most efficient way for them to fulfill their mission. That she could believe otherwise for even a fleeting moment horrified her. She was no schoolroom miss to entertain such romantical notions. Indeed, even when she *was* a schoolroom miss, such romantical notions had somehow found her person to be an inadequate host. She'd always been too practical to waste time pining for impossible things.

To hide her embarrassment, she agreed to his plan with an enthusiastic yes, then launched into a detailed timetable of their caper—and, yes, she was so disconcerted she actually called it a caper—mapping out their movements minute by minute. Accounting for traveling, skulking, planting, and returning, she calculated that she would place her left foot on the bottom branch of the oak tree outside her window at 1:27 a.m.

She was rambling, of course, talking nonsense at a frightfully quick pace for no other reason than she was incapable of stopping herself. It was another new and mortifying experience brought to an end by Smudge's sudden appearance. He claimed he was there only to see if she wanted more tea for her guest, but his disapproval was engraved in every line of his stance. With their business concluded, the earl saw no need to linger and graciously accepted the butler's offer to see him out.

He left with a formal bow, and Tuppence stayed where she was, on the settee in the front parlor, her thoughts in shambles as she tried to understand these sudden, new emotions caused, inexplicably, by a man she detested. He'd humiliated her time and time again.

And yet all she could think about was the glint of

mischief in his eyes, the hint of laughter in his voice, the pillowy redness of his lips. It was the thought of these features that kept her tumbling and turning in her bed all night, so that she wasn't able to fall asleep until only a few minutes before dawn. Even then, her rest was fitful and uncomfortable, and when a few hours later she stumbled, pale and wan, into the dining room to have breakfast, she was sent immediately back to bed by her mother, who feared a relapse or a frightening new infection.

Too exhausted to argue, Tuppence complied, with a pointed look at Caroline, who, still offended by yesterday's ill treatment, pretended not to notice her sister's interest in the plate of bacon. Smudge was likewise nursing a grudge and refused her request for tea on the grounds that the brewed beverage would be too stimulating for her frail condition.

"You need to rest," he said with faultless sincerity.

Tuppence glowered in response and waited until he was called to answer the door to sneak downstairs to the kitchens. She compiled a collation of cold meats, bread and cheese, which she ate as soon as she returned to her room. Feeling satiated, she fell asleep while rereading Coleridge's "The Rime of the Ancient Mariner."

When she woke hours later, it was dark and quiet, and she could see the crescent moon shining over the roof of the town house next door. Without looking at the clock, she knew it was time to get serious about that evening's activity, and with a sigh, she climbed out of bed to examine the prime skulking options in her wardrobe.

An hour later, she was ready.

CHAPTER TEN

As Nicholas Perceval, Earl of Gage, contemplated the silent figure of Miss Tuppence Templeton in the darkness of his carriage, he entertained the very real possibility that he was losing his mind.

It wasn't the fact that they were on their way to Lincoln's Inn to break into the Patent Bill Office that had him worried—although that development was certainly worrisome. In one and thirty years, he'd never crossed a threshold without being explicitly invited.

Nor was it the fact that he'd come up with this ludicrous scheme at a moment's notice. An asterisk! Who had ever heard of anything so preposterous as a star indicating that a petition needed to be recertified? It was complete drivel. Truly, he couldn't have been more surprised by the words coming out of his mouth if they'd been sung to the tune of *The Beggar's Opera.* Despite its lunacy, it had somehow been the perfect thing to say to extend their association, as Miss Templeton had fallen in with the plan immediately.

That he didn't want their association to end had come as an unsettling surprise in the middle of their conversation, for up until the moment when she'd announced their business to be over, he'd believed that was the conclusion he sought as well. Indeed, arriving at her house to offer his apology had been excruciating. He couldn't remember the last time he had to say he was sorry for something, and to have to make that statement to the impertinent Miss Templeton seemed particularly unjust. The moment he'd stepped into the sunlit front parlor, he'd wanted to step out again. Then she breezed into the room, determined to arrange a more convenient time for him to resume abusing her and full of advice about how best to go about it, and he was appalled to discover how deeply he'd injured her.

More than ever, he'd wanted to be gone.

Yet when she told him he could leave, something inside him rebelled and began inventing asterisks and creating procedures and concocting plots. It was madness.

And she believed it, all of it, even the part about altering the name slightly in the caveat in order to convince Jeffries he'd missed the invention during the first search. It had sounded feeble to his own ears, and yet Miss Templeton, who had impressed him as one of the cleverest people he'd ever met, male or female, had accepted it without blinking.

Clearly, she was so desperate to prove herself to the Harlow twins that her judgment was impaired.

Although these two things—inventing a harebrained scheme and following through on it—were indications of reduced mental capacity, they weren't the reason he feared he was losing his mind. No, the source of that apprehension was far more unsettling: He desired Miss Tuppence Templeton.

He didn't know how it had happened. Indeed, he couldn't believe it *had* happened. She was everything he detested in a woman: willful, independent, insolent, satirical, confident, disrespectful, proud, irreverent.

And the package itself was as nondescript as a parcel from a minor governmental office: listless brown hair, dull-colored eyes, unremarkable features, slight build. There was nothing about her that would capture a man's attention or set his heart racing.

But as he stared at her in the seat across from him in the passing glow of the streetlamps, his attention was wholly captured. As much as he wanted to look away from her, to examine the buttons on his gloves or the stitching on the cushion, he could not remove his gaze from her person. She wore a particularly ugly gown of chalk gray that was a little tight in the shoulders and wholly unflattering to her complexion. If anything, she looked like a disapproving governess on her way to a funeral, and yet her vibrancy shone through. Even sitting quietly in the carriage, she radiated liveliness and humor. It was her eyes, he thought, ordinary brown and yet fathoms deep, always sparkling with intelligence and irreverence and hints of gold as she formulated her next plan. Inconceivably, he was fascinated by the way her mind worked, the way it schemed and devised and never backed down until she had the upper hand.

Never in a million years could he have imagined the intense longing to be touched by the hand that held the advantage.

It was irrational, he knew, to crave her taunts, to crave her laughter, to crave her ire, to crave *her*. All his life he had been a sensible man—a responsible son, a devoted brother, a committed parliamentarian—and he could not understand this sudden streak of perversity that seemed to have washed over him like a tidal wave. Naturally, a man desired to be challenged at his club or in the House of Lords or while drinking a glass of port after dinner, but no man sought a debate in the bedroom.

The undeniable truth, however, was that he did. During their short acquaintance, he'd come to look forward to their disagreements, a development that both baffled and thrilled him. He had no advantage over her, no privilege of intellect or reason, and somehow that had become wildly exciting. Inexplicably, he found a chalky gray dress and silence to be utterly arousing.

Oh, he was very depraved indeed.

The insanity had started yesterday afternoon in her front parlor. He could even pinpoint the exact moment—when she'd blushed so prettily and thoroughly at the prospect of being alone with him in his carriage. She'd tried to cover up her discomfort with a barrage of words, but it was the lack of discipline in her speech, the way she chattered almost seemingly without point, that confirmed the direction her thoughts had taken.

And that was the spur: All he'd needed to become aware of her as a woman was her awareness of him as a man.

But no, he thought, it had started before then. In the coach on the way to the Patent Bill Office, he'd felt a connection to her, a sense of mutual enjoyment, which was why he'd responded so viciously when he'd discovered the truth. Her trickery, her manipulation of his good intentions, nullified the unexpected pleasure he'd found in her company and he was furious with her for taking that away.

Absurdly, he'd felt betrayed.

He'd barely known her then and yet his reactions had been so intense. That should have been a clue that something was amiss.

"I'm not going to stumble over a chair," she announced suddenly.

Although he'd been studying her quite intently, he'd been deep in his own thoughts and wondered at this seeming non sequitur if he'd missed an earlier comment. "All right."

"Or upset a tea tray that will clatter loudly on the floor," she said.

"Of course not," he said evenly.

"I say that to put your mind at ease," she explained, "as you're staring at me as if trying to figure out how to clean up the untidy mess I'm sure to create during our escapade. I promise you, I will not be the source of any contretemps. If anything, you should be concerned about yourself, my lord."

His lips twitched. "Myself?"

"Yourself," she repeated firmly, her tone sober but

her face alight with merriment. "You are far too upstanding a citizen to participate in skulduggery and nefarious deeds, and thus have no experience with the stealth and furtiveness required to carry out a successful breaking and entering. I'm quite worried you'll make a misstep—for example, knock over that tea tray you're so worried I'll topple—and get us hauled before the magistrate. If that does happen, my lord, I expect you to exert your influence to extricate us from the situation. Usually, I don't approve of politicians using their position for personal gain, but in this case I'm willing to make an exception because you are a neophyte."

"I assure you, Miss Templeton, I have not been thinking of tea trays," he said, smiling wryly at how very far from the truth her assumption was. She would be shocked to discover what was really on his mind. Indeed, there was no shade of red that would properly display her embarrassment. Thinking of her response did little to curb his desire, and he sought to distract himself by focusing on her words. "A neophyte, you say? Are you so experienced, then?"

"A lady doesn't discuss her conquests," she said with exaggerated primness, "but you would be wise to follow my lead. I will keep you out of trouble, my lord."

The Earl of Gage very much doubted that. "Can a lady discuss her conquests if she uses vague descriptions that in no way reveal the names and circumstances of the individuals involved?"

She shook her head. "Even that little would be a violation of the code. However, I can get you a general accounting of my accomplishments. I've snuck into one gentleman's study, two carriages, one stable, the backroom of a gaming hell, and the highly crowded kitchens of a London town house. The last one, by the by, was my own, which might seem like a less impressive achievement, but it's actually harder because you can't fade into the woodwork when you're among servants who knew you in leading strings. That's the secret to successful skulduggery—

being able to fade into the woodwork. Here, obviously, the dowdy spinster has the advantage over the diamond of the first water."

Gage recognized the insult as one he'd lobbed at her during their scene at Almack's, but he couldn't quite decipher the tone with which she repeated it. Clearly, the snub had stung, otherwise she would not have recalled so easily that he'd issued it, but she seemed to savor the description as well, as if being a dowdy spinster imbued one with special powers.

Regardless of how she felt about the insult, he was disgusted now, as he had been yesterday, by his cruelty to her. He sat there silently, wondering how to make amends. To tell her the truth—that she shimmered with so much wit, devilry and joy, she was by far the prettiest woman of his acquaintance—would be to risk exposure. Apologizing again seemed like the safer course, and yet he feared descending into sincerity in the confines of the small carriage posed its own dangers. One act of intimacy might lead to another and another.

Rather than say anything at all on the topic, he asked her to describe the woodwork of the gaming hell she'd invaded, and when she refused to give any information other than that it was dark and wooden, he questioned the veracity of the claim. "I don't believe anyone could pull off such a lark."

Offended by the assertion, she launched into such a detailed account of the interior that he immediately recognized it as 26 Bennett Street.

Gage smothered his smile, for he didn't want her to know how smoothly she'd been maneuvered. Although their association had been short, he already felt as if he knew her better than many of his lifelong friends. Yesterday, in the front parlor, all he had to do to get her to come with him on this furtive mission was tell her she could not. Indeed, he had only to utter the word *consent* for the light of battle to enter her eye.

Perhaps that was the moment he first desired her, for, he realized now, he relished the light of battle in her eye. And he'd thoroughly enjoyed letting her browbeat him into submission until they were agreed: They would both go.

It seemed as if he was even more perverse than he'd imagined.

Talk of gaming hells occupied the rest of the ride, with the earl specifying the layout of various gambling houses and Miss Templeton explaining how she would infiltrate the back room of each one. With every new location, her exploits grew more lavish and daring until she was swinging on a silk rope through the garden window of the Red Corner House. The earl said such an approach would more likely end with a sharp thud as the lustrous knot slipped and dropped her on the hard brick of the terrace, but she insisted that she'd been practicing how to make a reliable fastener with her sheets for years.

Before he could ask her why—or even ascertain if the claim was true—the carriage stopped and they climbed out of the hack. In the light of the moon, she could see the building that housed the Patent Bill Office several hundred feet away. As a precaution, they would traverse the last distance soundlessly by foot. To ensure they had a coach waiting when they were done, the earl dropped several coins in the driver's hand.

"We won't be above thirty minutes," he said, wondering if that was indeed true. As Miss Templeton had rightly pointed out, he was an inexperienced skulduggerer and had no real sense of how long their task would take.

When his skilled companion didn't correct him, he assumed his estimate was somewhere in the vicinity of accurate.

Silently, they walked toward the building, for which, through his work overhauling the patent office, he had been able to obtain the key. It hung on a hook in the attorney-general's office and it had been an easy thing to slip it off and deposit it in his pocket. Tomorrow, he would have his secretary drop it under the nearest clerk's desk so that it would appear to have accidentally dropped should anyone notice it missing.

Gaining access to the Patent Bill Office would be just as easy, for he himself had been issued a key when he'd taken on the responsibility of reforming the system. It had hardly seemed necessary at the time, but he was glad now that he hadn't bothered to refuse it.

"There are two night watchmen on duty and a cleaning crew," he said softly in her ear even though they had already gone over this information in the coach.

"There's one," she whispered, pointing to the guardhouse, where a lone head could be seen by lamplight. "The second might be patrolling."

Without discussing it, they both began to walk faster, and Gage, matching his gait to hers, discovered the unexpectedly sweet pleasure of having an accomplice. He'd hatched this plan in reckless impulse, giving into the foolishness of a moment, but he knew now that even if he'd had months to weigh its merits, he would have still proposed it. He liked having this thing—this caper, as she'd called it during her self-conscious ramble—in common with her.

Swiftly, they arrived at the building, and Gage unlocked the door, which let out a startlingly loud creak when he pushed it open. Alarmed, Miss Templeton punched him lightly on the arm and raised a finger to quiet him. It hardly seemed fair to blame him for a poorly oiled hinge, but he held his tongue, for even he recognized that defending oneself while sneaking into a building and dodging cleaning crews was the behavior of a neophyte.

Once inside, he closed the door with deliberate slowness. The hinge groaned but refrained from making any piercing squeaks. With a sigh of relief, he started down the corridor, with Miss Templeton beside him. They turned right at the first intersection, then left into a stairwell. As they arrived on the second floor, they heard the chatter of voices echoing through the hallway. They were too far away to understand the specifics of the conversation, but Miss Templeton and the earl stayed in the stairwell for several minutes, their shoulders pressed against the wall, waiting for the sound to fade away.

Eventually it did, and fearing the men's return, they ran as quickly as possible to the patent office. Gage opened the door with extreme caution, grateful that it moved noiselessly on its hinges, and then shut it with equal care. Then he used the tinderbox he'd brought to light the candelabra by the door.

In the safety of the office, Tuppence commended the earl on his performance. "You almost gave the game away with that door, but for the most part you are acquitting yourself adequately."

Even now, in the middle of an unlawful entry, she was still a provocative little minx. He looked at her, her face gleaming in the candlelight, and wondered how he could have ever thought her plain.

"Caveats go in this set of drawers," he said, leading her past Jeffries's desk to a cabinet along the far wall. He placed the candelabra on the nearby desk and pulled a document out of a pocket in his overcoat. He handed it to her to do the honors. After all, she'd come all this way to fulfill her promise to the Marchioness of Huntly. "They're arranged chronologically."

She needed both hands to search the drawer, so he offered to hold the candle for her and she solemnly accepted. As she looked through the files at the other caveats, he was grateful he had taken the time to ensure the false document looked as real as the genuine ones. Although his steward was a skilled artist, the young man had never before done a drawing requiring technical accuracy. It had taken several attempts before his elasticated watering line looked identical to Lady Huntly's elasticized gardening hose. Ultimately, it didn't matter because this whole scheme was mere pantomime. Jeffries would never search the files for a caveat because nobody would ask him to. In

the morning, he would tell Jeffries to approve the marchioness's application and the petition would continue to
the next stage of the laborious process.

"There," Miss Templeton said, a hint of satisfaction
in her tone as she gently closed the drawer.

"You are performing quite adequately yourself," he
said approvingly, then turned to seize the candelabra from
the desk. He misjudged the distance and knocked over a
silver platter. It landed on the floor with a sharp clatter,
and Miss Templeton stared in horror as pieces of a broken
porcelain cup rolled under the chair.

By all that was holy, it was a tea tray!

Miss Templeton started to laugh. Like a summer gale,
it seemed to come out of nowhere. One moment the room
was silent, the next it was filled with uncontained mirth. It
echoed off the walls, it seemed to him, as loud as thunder,
reverberating with unadulterated joy. He could not imagine
a happier sound. He could not imagine a purer one. It
seemed almost to lift him up and suspend him midair on a
pillow of elated glee.

It had to stop.

Yes, this visit was a ruse, a hoax perpetrated by him
to further their association, but the consequences if they
were discovered would be all too real. He would look like
the veriest of fools, breaking into the Patent Bill Office in
the dead of night when he was free to enter in the bright
light of day, and she would be ruined. Being found alone
with him in a deserted building would compromise her
completely. She would be forced to wed him at once or
face social ostracism.

Neither option was acceptable.

Desperate to end the interlude as quickly as possible,
he did the only thing that seemed reasonable: He cut the
sound off at its source. Barely thinking of anything but
coveted silence, he pulled her into his arms and pressed his
lips against hers. As much as he desired her, the only thing
he was thinking about in that moment was saving her from

a future she could not control. His intentions were virtuous; his morals were good.

But the second his lips touched hers, lust like he'd never experienced, lust like he hadn't thought possible, lust like a conquering army seizing an enemy hill, overcame him. He pressed his mouth to hers with a devouring hunger, his tongue demanding—and receiving—entry. He wrapped his arms around her, pulling her body closer to his, then closer and closest, his hands running along her back and around her font, feeling the tightness in the fabric. He groaned with arousal, then moaned her name, as he tried to absorb her body into his.

He felt her stiffen, then slowly relax her limbs as she melted into the feeling, her response at once sweetly innocent and ferociously sure.

She didn't understand what was happening, that much was clear from the way she held on to his shoulders, as if grasping a lifeline.

How could she understand, he thought with what was left of his mind. He was the author of two dozen love affairs and he could barely comprehend what was happening. It was frightening to discover one's control was as frail as a dry twig, capable of snapping under the slightest pressure.

If he was frightened, then she must be terrified.

Good God!

He pulled away.

In the faint light of the candles, he could see the flush of her face and her struggle to regain her breath. She looked down at the floor, at the shattered pieces of porcelain, as she tried to hide her confusion and embarrassment.

Gage was horrified by what he'd wrought. Many times he'd wanted to pierce the intractable wall of her confidence, but not like this. Never like this. To use her own body against her was the act of a cad.

And it had been days since he'd felt anything but admiration for her poise and her courage. He admired her more than any woman he'd ever met.

Unsure how to proceed, a feeling he'd never experienced before, he sought to explain. "You were laughing."

He recognized the prickliness of his tone at once, for one cannot make one's reputation on peevishness and not know its sound, and the words came out more as accusation than explanation.

"Yes," she agreed quietly.

She kept her head tilted down, and the earl felt a pang in his chest at the thought of this brave woman being humbled by shame.

The earl tried again, striving to speak gently and place the blame where it belonged—on his shoulders. "The thing was, you were laughing and I wanted to halt your laughter as quickly as possible because I was afraid members of the cleaning staff would hear it and discover us. My methods were inappropriate, even reprehensible, but it was never my intention to frighten you. I assure you, Miss Templeton, the last thing I want to do is frighten you. I wanted to protect you from the unintended consequences of your actions. No, I mean *my* actions. I'm the one who knocked over the tea tray, just as you said I would. But you were laughing, you see, quite uncontrollably, and I wanted to stop it as swiftly as possible. Before the cleaning staff heard it. I acted rashly, and I apologize. I didn't mean to frighten you. I just…you were laughing and I feared discovery."

He could have gone on, saying the same words over and over again until he was convinced she believed him, but he made himself stop. The situation was bad enough without him descending into gabsterish fiddle-faddle.

It had seemed as if he'd talked just the right amount because as soon as he finished with his rambling speech, she looked up at him. The color in her cheeks had faded and her breathing had returned to normal, but her eyes didn't glow with quite the same intensity. For that, he was deeply sorry.

Nevertheless, she gamely replied, "I'm a practical woman, my lord, and will always appreciate a sensible solution. As it has been made remarkably clear, you're a neo-phyte, but even with your lack of experience, you have ac-quitted yourself adequately. Now do pick up the tray and the broken pieces. We don't want to leave a suspicious trail."

Gage hadn't thought it could get any worse. Hearing her describe the single most exhilarating experience in his life, the single most intoxicating and passionate, as *adequate* was devastating. With one remark, she'd repaid him for all the insults he'd dealt her at Almack's. The score was even.

And then to be ordered to clean up the floor like a lackey!

In that moment, the score tipped entirely in her favor, for nothing he'd ever done or said to her required her to drop to her knees.

Now was not the time to indulge his bruised pride, of course, for they were still on the second floor of Lincoln's Inn and, as Miss Templeton had so helpfully pointed out, there were shattered pieces of a teacup to be disposed of. Submitting to the humiliating task, he resolved to save his brooding for when he was alone in his study with a glass of port.

But having made the resolution, he discovered it was impossible to keep it. It would take a man of far greater discipline than he to put the matter entirely from his mind—and the Earl of Gage sincerely believed there was no man of greater discipline than he.

One by one, he tossed the shards into the trash bin, muttering under his breath about having to suffer the un-warranted abuse of strong-willed spinsters.

"What are you doing?" Miss Templeton asked as she laid the silver tray on Jeffries's desk next to the inkwell.

As her intelligence was quite keen, he knew the ques-tion wasn't as simple as it appeared, but he had no re-course save to tell her the truth. "I'm throwing away the broken teacup."

She looked at him in horror. "You can't do it here. The clerks will find the pieces there in the morning and wonder what havey-cavey business went on in their absence."

"Perhaps I should put them in my pocket and use the bin in my study," he said, his tone satirical, as he considered such a measure to be excessively cautious. Surely, the natural assumption would be that a member of the janitorial staff had broken the cup while going about his duties. Or if she was really worried about Jeffries or one of his colleagues seeing the pieces, they could just throw a few sheets of paper on top to hide the evidence.

"An excellent suggestion, my lord," she said with an approving smile. "Now you're thinking like a beginner who has advanced to the next stage."

Although he knew her answer wasn't meant to tease, he found her combination of approbation and condescension—along with her complete lack of respect for his dignity—maddeningly arousing. Truly, he thought, retrieving shards of porcelain from the trash bin, he could take her right there on the floor of the Patent Bill Office.

How had he come to this?

When every piece of the broken teacup was in his pocket, he stood up, wiped the dust from his trousers and blew out the candles. The room returned to darkness save for a sliver of moonlight shining wanly through the narrow window.

Leaving the building was as easy as entering—easier, in fact, because he knew to take special care with the creaking front door—and they returned to the hack without incident. Taking his seat inside the carriage, Gage was more than ever aware of the intimacy of the confined space. He felt as though he could feel every breath of air Miss Templeton took.

If his companion found anything about the situation uncomfortable or awkward, she did not reveal it by word or deed. She was quieter than usual as the carriage pulled through the city streets, but she responded to all his questions with coherent thoughts and met his gaze every time. He talked of trivial things during the ride to her home, mentioning the upcoming ball at Mrs. Williams's and Letty's plans for the next day. He extended an invitation to go for a drive in Hyde Park on his sister's behalf and complimented the plumed hat he'd observed her wearing on a previous occasion.

Every word he uttered was proper and courteous, and although he knew it was futile, he was determined to counter the indecency of the patent office with the circumspection of the drawing room.

When the hack stopped on the side street next to her house, Miss Templeton shifted forward in her seat and held out her hand. "I'm sincerely grateful, my lord, for what you did for me tonight," she said with grave intention. "Thank you."

Although Gage had never shaken hands with a woman, he recognized the act for what it was—a gesture between equals—and graciously accepted it. As he had crossing the field to Lincoln's Inn, he felt a gratifying sense of closeness to her. They shared a secret no one else would ever know. They were coconspirators now.

It was clear that Miss Templeton did not conceive their experience in the same sentimental light, for her goodbye seemed determinedly final, as if *now* their business had been satisfyingly resolved. She was, by all indications, relieved their association was finally at an end.

As he helped her down from the carriage, as he watched her cross the lawn beside the house and climb onto a low branch of an oak tree—of course she'd climbed down a tree!—he considered how very far from satisfied he was. He understood why she would want to be done with him. He'd insulted her and called her names and belittled her thoughts. Nevertheless, he could not let the matter rest. 'Twas not just pride that made him determined to earn her good opinion. It was something deeper, something unsettling, something that went beyond sheer perversity or contrariness. Even if he couldn't identify it by name, it was real and it spurred him on, and he knew that before he and Miss Tuppence Templeton were done, she'd say that he'd acquitted himself superbly, magnificently, better than any man she'd ever met.

He would not accept anything less.

CHAPTER ELEVEN

The first thing Tuppence did upon waking the next morning was write a letter to the Marchioness of Huntly, assuring her that her application—and hers alone—would now proceed smoothly through the system. She kept the missive brief, eliding many of the details, and thanked her for entrusting her with the responsibility. Helping to secure the patent was not a task she would have sought and it definitely had its fraught moments, but now that a happy resolution had been attained, she was pleased to have had a hand in achieving it.

Justice had been served, and the posturing Lord Tweedale could go water a row of turnips with a bucket.

After she sent the note, she summoned her maid to help her get dressed, then dropped by the schoolroom, where her sister was sewing a sampler while her nurse looked on in quiet satisfaction. The scene was lovely and bucolic in its own way, but Tuppence found the calm silence intolerable and insisted they begin their French lesson right away. After two hours of drilling Caroline on partitive articles, she turned their attention to mathematics and made her do her sums for thirty minutes. By the time she left, Caroline was calling her names and threatening to make sure she never got a currant scone ever again.

"Smudge likes me better," Caroline taunted. "I know it and you know it."

Next she visited Hannah, who was reading a magazine in the front parlor, and suggested that now might be a good time to make a thorough evaluation of her wardrobe to assess the condition of all her dresses.

Without looking up from the pistache silk gown she was admiring, Hannah said, "How silly you are, darling. That's not something people do. If Mary notices anything amiss, she fixes it and returns it to the closet without bothering me."

"It's something I do every season," Tuppence said, although in fact she had never taken more than a brief survey of her items. "Now that you've had your come-out, you need to do it too. Come, you lazy cawker, I'll help. It won't take above an hour."

Remarkably, her sister was unmoved by this appealing offer and insisted she was resting for Mrs. Williams's ball, which was still ten hours away.

Lazy cawker indeed.

Undaunted, Tuppence went to her sister's room and made a careful study of her wardrobe on her own. Although she was dismayed to see the lavish abundance with which her parents had outfitted their second-oldest child, for there were enough pelisse and bonnets and pairs of silk gloves to clothe a small village, she was grateful for their excessiveness because sorting through it took twice as long as she'd anticipated.

As soon as she was done, she presented herself to the library to make sure all the books were alphabetized by the last name of the author. The accuracy was almost one hundred percent, but she managed to find a few stragglers in the wrong place and happily took them to task as if they had personally set themselves down on the wrong shelf.

After the library, she organized her mother's escritoire in her sitting room.

She readily acknowledged that some of these chores weren't fully necessary, as her mother's writing desk was sufficiently organized without her dividing the nibs by size, but her intent wasn't to perform an actual service. No, her sole purpose was to keep herself busy. Busy, busy, busy. So busy she couldn't think of the Earl of Gage.

The effort, of course, was patently futile. It didn't matter how many verbs she forced her sister to conjugate or how many stains she tallied or how many nib boxes she subdivided with improvised partitions made of folded stationery. Not thinking of the Earl of Gage was impossible.

He was there with her constantly, trailing after her like a shadow or a puppy that wouldn't be brought to heel.

Well, no, she thought, that comparison made absolutely no sense, for there was nothing puppyish about the earl. He was a man—a strong, attractive, exciting man.

Just recalling his strength, the way his arms seemed to crush her, made her heart skip a beat.

Stop it, she ordered herself and stalked into her room to rotate the linens on her bed. Mrs. Flagston usually did it or one of the housemaids, so it was a domestic task with which she had only passing familiarity, but it seemed like a rather straightforward thing to remove a sheet, turn it around and put it back on.

Ten minutes later, she sighed with frustration and dropped wearily to the mattress. She didn't know what she was doing. With the sheet, yes, of course she did—she simply didn't have the skill to make the linen lie flat and smooth—but the method by which she was handling the problem with Gage was out of character for her. She wasn't the sort of person who hid from a problem or pretended it didn't exist. She confronted matters head-on: eyes steady, shoulders straight, mind focused. She was no insipid mouse to run from a challenge: That cold that had kept her bedridden for almost a week had been the genuine article. One night her nose had been so stuffed, she'd slept sitting up.

Yet now she was working herself to the bone in hopes of making herself too exhausted to think of Gage.

It was cowardice, pure and simple, and it disgusted her.

Perhaps if it had worked, she wouldn't be so angry with herself. But here she was, an entire day's worth of menial labor under her belt, and still he was all she could think of.

How could she *not* think of him? Nobody had ever treated her like that before. She hadn't known that an embrace could be so searing, that a man's lips could burn themselves onto your soul. The only kiss she'd experienced, bestowed by a cavalryman in the Light Dragoons during her first season, had been mildly pleasant, like a soft breeze on a warm spring day. But the earl's kiss—that was a summer storm, wild and fierce, unexpected and unrelenting. It had made her body ache for something she couldn't name, and the aching hadn't ended with the contact. She felt it now, again, always.

Damn him, she thought, falling back on the mattress.

It would be one thing if she thought he'd felt the same fever she had, the same driving need, but it had been immediately apparent that he was unmoved by the experience. As soon as he knew the danger had passed, he'd pulled away with abrupt determination and explained his behavior. He was so worried that she, a dowdy spinster with no prospects, might misread the situation that he repeated himself several times in a rush to make the situation clear.

Yes, yes, Tuppence understood: She was laughing. He feared discovery.

Enough, please.

What truly mortified her was his obvious assumption that she was so desperate for male attention that she would misinterpret his intentions. Did he really think she would stride from the steps of Lincoln's Inn to the entrance to her father's study and announce their engagement?

The fact that he clearly did was the gravest insult

she'd ever been dealt in her life. It was funny, for just two days before, she'd decided he could do her no further harm. And now this.

Would Prickly Perceval always prove her wrong?

It was realizing the thoroughly staggeringly low depth of his opinion that had helped her pull herself together in the aftermath of the kiss. Overcome with emotion, she'd wanted to wallow in sensation, both desire and anger, but to respond with anything other than benign good humor would have been to reveal weakness. It took every speck of control she had to calmly state that she not only understood his actions but also applauded his quick thinking.

The carriage ride back to her house had been excruciating, with the earl doing everything possible to make it clear there was nothing between them but the polite discourse of social acquaintances. If she hadn't been so miserable, she would have found it excessively amusing to watch the notoriously peevish lord striving so hard to be a pattern card of civility. That was how much the thought of being romantically entangled with her terrified him—he'd betrayed a lifetime of rudeness.

But knowing the truth did not extricate her from the service he'd done her, for he had not been obligated to provide the caveat or make sure it was put in the correct cabinet. For whatever reason, he'd been kind to her and so she, mustering all the dignity she had left, thanked him for his help with a sincerity she was far from feeling. She'd offered her hand like a gentleman to ensure there would be no awkward contact. She couldn't imagine anything more unbearable than his placing a tepid kiss on her hand.

And now, as she'd observed before, their business was satisfactorily resolved and they need not have any more interaction. It seemed unlikely they would meet up again, for she was naught but a glorified companion who spent her time in the corner with women of similar stature. They were a largely invisible cohort, only seeming to appear when there was a need to be met. Tuppence knew such thoughts would make her seem bitter to anyone who overheard them, but she truly didn't mind her lot. Being on the fringe of the ballroom as well as the beau monde meant that everyone left her alone. She was free to pursue her own interests, rather than her parents' or even her husband's. No doubt matrimony offered its own compensations, but having failed so spectacularly at being a covetable item on the marriage mart, she could imagine them to be only meager at best.

Tuppence thought again about the awfulness of her first season. How endless it had been, with her mother's constant exhortations to be less dull, to pose thoughtful questions, to make clever observations, to glow with the effervescent sparkle of youth. Nothing could be calculated to make a shy girl less interesting than the command to be more interesting. It didn't help that her father kept pressing the opposite advice, for the only thing a plain woman had to offer, he insisted, was docility. "Agree with everything," he said. "Smile often, say yes and respond to every comment with a compliment."

For years, she'd struggled to comply with their demands, and as soon as it became clear she'd never attain the level of success they desired of her, they'd dropped her like any other unproductive social connection. She'd been cast out of their hearts so effortlessly, she realized she'd never actually been in them. To them, she'd always been a bit of goods for the trading.

Discovering that her parents had only a transactional interest in her released her from the obligation of trying to please them. A bolt of fabric that failed to satisfy its buyer was not required to worry about the feelings of its purchasers. With relief, Tuppence surrendered the stage to her sister for a comfortable life in the wings, where she was free to disagree with gentlemen as much as she wanted and thwart fortune hunters when the opportunity arose. All in all, she was satisfied with her life, and she wouldn't let the unsettling ache she felt for the earl undermine it.

Without any doubt, she knew it would subside in time, for everything went away eventually, and pretending it didn't exist would do nothing to speed up the process. For now, she had to live with the fact that she had strong feelings for the Earl of Gage. It was a daunting prospect to consider, but she knew it was merely the unexpected side effect of the devastating kiss. As a woman of little experience, it was inevitable that she'd find the force of the interaction overwhelming. Surely, every woman felt swayed to some extent by her first taste of passion. Tuppence's thoughts weren't so corrupted that she'd developed a tendre for the earl. She still knew him to be rude, impatient, short-tempered, insulting and mean. If he had some positive qualities, such as a lively mind, an interesting perspective, and a willingness to consider other opinions, it was only because no human being was entirely one thing. Everyone had dimensions.

Settling the matter cheered her up considerably, and feeling calm enough of mind, she decided to read for a little while. Selecting the volume, however, proved more challenging than she'd anticipated, as she decided to stay away from anything that might remind her further of the earl. That meant Coleridge was out of consideration, as well as all Gothics and anything from Minerva Press. *The Improvement of Human Reason, Exhibited in the Life of Hay Ebon Yokdhan,* a philosophical tale translated from the original Arabic by Simon Ockley that had been sitting on her shelf for years, seemed like a safe choice, but the title character's insistence on reason was too reminiscent of Gage.

Disgusted, she threw the novel to the floor and fetched a history of the sailing vessel from the library. She'd spotted it earlier while straightening the books, and it had struck her as deadly dull reading.

Now it seemed perfect.

Although she had no affinity for the subject, the writing was engrossing and when builders developed the large merchant ship called the carrack, which could withstand the ravages of the ocean, she silently cheered the invention, then immediately wondered who held the patent on that innovation. Inevitably, the earl flashed through her mind again, but with little effort she was able to return to the narrative. It was a relief to discover that her odd fascination with the earl wasn't so intractable that it couldn't be overcome by a good story.

Clearly, she wasn't as sunk as she'd thought.

Buoyed by the realization—and amused at her thematically appropriate use of a nautical term—she dressed for Mrs. Williams's ball in her best gown, a pink crepe with Vandyke points edging the neckline. Like the other gowns in her closet, it was no longer the height of fashion but its edges were smooth, not frayed, and the fabric still had a pleasing sheen. It was the opposite in every way of the gray rag she'd worn the night before to break into Lincoln's Inn, which was almost as old as the decade. It had been made for her grandmother's funeral.

Recalling that mean old biddy, with her petty resentments and cheek-pinching claws, she smiled. How horrified she would be if she knew the fervor with which the Earl of Gage's hands had clutched the well-worn fabric. Every feeling would be outraged! The image of her withered face contorted in shocked disapproval amused her so much, she decided the turmoil over the kiss was almost a fair price to pay for the moment of levity.

Her mood stayed buoyant during the carriage ride, despite Hannah's claim that her recent ailment had somehow damaged her appearance. "You were confined to your room for only a week and yet you look as though you've been living on the trauma ward of a hospital for a month," she said, staring at her in confusion in the dim light, which should have flattered her sister's haggard features. "I don't know how you do it. Anyone else would look refreshed after a sennight in bed."

Tuppence knew her sister was only trying to understand a baffling phenomenon, so she didn't take offense at the unkind observation. "I suppose we all have our special talents," she said with a bland smile.

"I suppose," Hannah agreed, although she didn't sound convinced that her sister's ability to rapidly degrade her looks counted as a skill.

They arrived soon after at the Williamses' town house, and the moment they entered the ballroom, Lord Hughland greeted the sisters with gratifying enthusiasm. He timed his reception so precisely to their entry, Tuppence could only assume he'd been lying in wait for their appearance. Although clearly eager to sign her sister's dance card, he lingered for several minutes in polite conversation with Tuppence.

It was, she thought in amusement as she watched them walk toward the dance floor, a singular act of chivalry.

She knew her opinion was entirely immaterial, but she decided Hughland was by far Hannah's most appealing suitor. He did not possess the fortune that accompanied Mr. Quilltop's vast estate, but he was kinder and more genuine in his manners. She recognized, of course, how easy her approval had been to court, for all it had taken was a few kind words to win her to his corner, but that just made her like him more. Mr. Quilltop was impervious to the feelings of an older sister, though appeasing them would require little more than a how-do-you-do.

Tuppence wondered which suitor her parents would prefer. A title versus vast wealth pitted two of their favorite things against each other. Amused, she watched the dancing, enjoying the light touch of the orchestra, as she tried to decipher which side would win.

"I'd hoped you'd be here," said Martha. "If you weren't, I would have sent around a note in the morning."

"Martha!" Tuppence gasped in surprise at her friend, whose journey home to care for her sick mother had been subsidized by the sale of her grandmother's garnet-and-opal ring. "I thought you were still in Liverpool. Your mother…"

"Is much better, thank you," Martha said, correctly reading the expression of concern. "The doctor didn't think it was possible, but all she needed was love and tireless nursing, both of which I could provide in spades. I now know everything there is to know about restorative jellies, so if you're torn between Dr. Gilbertson's Curative Pork Jelly and a homemade formulation, do apply to me."

Tuppence laughed and said she hoped she'd never have to make that application.

"Me too," Martha said.

Keeping one eye on her sister, who was now waltzing with Mr. Quilltop while Hughland looked on in envy, Tuppence asked about her friend's current situation. She was delighted to discover it had improved dramatically since her return. Apparently, in the months she'd been gone, her employer had had the pleasure of learning that far from being an avaricious gadabout who burned through the tapers, Martha was actually a diligent and dependable companion for her daughter. For one thing, she didn't steal from the other servants. For another, the laxity of her morals wasn't the subject of constant debate.

"Also to my advantage," she added, "is the fact I don't say 'lawks alive,' which Susan now does with startling regularity. Mrs. Carsdale is convinced she has merely picked up the bad habit, but I can tell from the look in Susan's eyes that she does it with the sole purpose of teasing her mama."

"It's incumbent on parents to hide the source of their minor annoyances from their children, lest they become daily trials," Tuppence said with a grin as the waltz came to an end. Hannah had no sooner curtsied graciously at one partner before the next one appeared to claim her. Susan returned to Martha's side and pronounced herself parched. The pair excused themselves and went off in search of refreshments.

As the next set formed—a cotillion—Tuppence was amused to see her father in conversation with Lord Hughland across the room. Clearly, the young man was determined to ingratiate himself with every member of Hannah's family. He would have little trouble earning Lord Templeton's favor, for he liked and respected anyone who had the good sense to remain quiet and listen to him, something a suitor in the early stages of courtship would be inclined to do regardless.

"I trust I'm not late," the Earl of Gage said genially, suddenly appearing at her side.

He was dressed simply—blue coat buttoned at the waist, buff-colored pantaloons, pure white cravat, shiny black Hessians—and although Tuppence was able to appreciate the dignity of his form, she was annoyed at having to perceive it. Less than four and twenty hours ago, they'd agreed their association was over, and now here he was, talking to her with an air of expectation, as if they still had business to discuss.

She glared at him balefully out of the corner of her eye, then returned her attention to the dance floor. "I have no idea, as your schedule is no concern of mine."

"I must beg to disagree," he said with mild amusement. "Given that we have an appointment, it is *some* concern of yours."

Tuppence knew he was teasing her, for if they'd arranged such an assignation, it would have figured prominently in her thoughts, but she couldn't decide what he hoped to gain by playing such a game. The night before, he'd treated her with the cool indifference of a passing acquaintance, as if determined to prove he owed her no more consideration than a random stranger who might be seated next to him at Covent Garden. And yet now he spoke to her with the good-natured familiarity of an intimate. She couldn't fathom why. Was he offended by her easy acceptance of his apathy? Was he insulted by her lack of hysterics? Had she pricked his vanity by not clinging to his arm and demanding an offer at once?

The possibility of such perversity confounded her.

Surely, no gentleman could be so contrary as to go from grateful to disgruntled in less than a day.

Determined to bring their conversation to an end, she said with curt directness, "I'm sorry, my lord, but our meeting is of such little significance, I'm afraid I've forgotten it entirely. I suggest you do the same."

"Forget an opportunity to talk to you?" he said with exaggerated surprise. "You ask the impossible, Miss Templeton. I do understand, however, how it might have slipped your mind amid the events of last evening. Nevertheless, I assure you my memory is sound. We'd agreed to meet sometime after the first waltz and before dinner. The first waltz ended not twenty minutes ago."

Now she remembered. Of course she did, for it had been only two days ago when she'd insisted he issue his insults at Mrs. Williams's ball rather than in the front parlor of her own home during morning calls. That he would dare to keep the assignation shocked her, for it signaled a level of mean-spiritedness of which she hadn't thought him capable. Yes, he was famously testy and impatient and carried himself with an air of superiority, as if nobody could accomplish anything with the same efficiency or ingenuity as he, but he wasn't known for his spite. He was called Prickly Perceval, not Petty Perceval.

The disappointment Tuppence felt at discovering his true nature was out of proportion to the revelation. Most people were worse than you expected. Her parents, certainly, but also Mr. FitzWalter, with his determination to see a young girl ruined rather than settling his debts honorably, or Martha's employer, assuming the whole world was determined to take advantage of her kindness, which was, in reality, a miserly thing.

It shouldn't have mattered to her at all, and yet she felt as if some unarticulated ideal had been sullied.

"You're correct, my lord," she said calmly, determined to accept his criticism with equanimity. She would not allow herself to be provoked into an argument or a futile defense of herself. He was welcome to his own opinion, and once he shared it, their association would truly be done. "It had indeed slipped my memory, but I recall it now. Please proceed."

Without hesitating, the earl said, "That cap you're wearing is a hideous accessory, as it hides the lovely silkiness of your hair, and that dress is a dreadful shade, for it fails to bring out the appealing gold in your eyes."

His comments astonished her.

No, she thought, not astonished. Stupefied.

She was stupefied by the Earl of Gage's compliments, and that was why she was staring dumbly at him.

Were they compliments?

Perhaps they were insults sporting the pretty patina of praise.

Or was it praise sporting the pretty patina of an insult?

Did he truly think her eyes were appealing?

Don't be a peagoose, she scolded herself. He was mocking her and making no attempt to hide it, for describing the drab brown of her eyes as gold was such unambiguous flimflammery that even a small child would recognize it as ridicule. Her own mother had once observed while lamenting her misfortune in having a daughter who couldn't sparkle that their dull shade made ditchwater seem vibrant in comparison.

If he'd really wanted to bamboozle her, he wouldn't have chosen an attribute she contemplated daily in her own mirror.

He knew what he was doing, and he wanted her to know it as well. Evidently, he was still smarting over the FitzWalter affair or her treatment of him during their first visit to the Patent Bill Office. Perhaps his resentment was of more a general nature, and he simply bore her a grudge for all the time he had been forced to spend in her presence. She didn't know the cause and realized she didn't care. She was too disheartened to discover the depth of his pettiness.

'Twas as if she didn't know him at all.

The overweening conceit of such a notion—imagine: believing for even a moment that she *did* know him— shook her from her stupor, and she resolved to say something. She couldn't stand there as mute as a joint of mutton indefinitely. At some point, the orchestra would cease playing and the company would be called to supper. Surely, their scene would conclude well before then.

She considered her options. For one, she could return his praise with over-the-top compliments that carried the same sincerity as his. Or she could turn his stratagem on its head by offering an insult in the comforting language of assurance—for example, claiming that despite what everyone else said, she thought his nose was the perfect size for his face. Or she could dispense with embellishments and insult him with straightforward honesty. There was nothing, she thought, like making a clean breast of it. Another possibility was to thwart him altogether by simply walking away. Or she could change the subject to one that was sure to rile him up, such as asking if he'd heard from Mr. Fitz-Walter recently.

All of these alternatives had their merits, and while she was still weighing one against the other, the earl said, "The orchestra is striking up a waltz, Miss Templeton. Would you please do me the honor?"

Tuppence stiffened, unable to conceive what he hoped to accomplish with this new tactic but confident it would lead to her downfall. It had been many years since the plain-faced Miss Templeton had stepped onto the dance floor with any gentleman, let alone a handsome lord, and her doing so now on the arm of the Earl of Gage would cause a stir. People would talk and what dreadful things they would say. They would ridicule her for having expectations. They would scorn her for nourishing girlish dreams. They would deride her naiveté and jeer at her optimism and sneer at her desperation.

That was what he sought to expose her to out of a desire for petty revenge.

Patently, she would not comply. Although she knew herself to be a quiz, she could not knowingly turn herself into a figure of fun. She didn't doubt she was already the target of mockery, with her three failed seasons and dashed hopes, but she would not don a clown costume. If people wanted to laugh at her, they would have to find their own fodder. She would not provide it.

She opened her mouth to refuse his offer with quiet dignity, for it would do no good to take to task a man who was inured to shame. But when she looked into his face, she didn't see contempt or disdain. She saw hope and sincerity and perhaps even worry about the answer. His eyes beseeched her to say yes, and she, like a ninny with no will of her own, took his hand. He grasped hers tightly for a moment, then loosened his grip and led her onto the dance floor, where they took their place among dozens of other couples.

They danced silently, the earl's hold on her at once light and commanding, unnerving and comforting. She felt the pressure of his hand on her back, keenly aware of its heat transferring itself to her body, and she wondered if anything had ever affected her so. She tried to recall the last time she had waltzed with a man. It had been during her third season, she decided, when one of the many second sons—the issue, this time, of a marquess—had made a half-hearted attempt to woo her. Her portion had been described to him as being "sufficient," and he thought they would rub together tolerably well as long as they kept their expectations in check. He'd thoughtfully explained this while they whirled around the room so as to minimize the amount of time they would have to spend in courtship, something else he kindly made clear during their dance. Again, to help her keep her expectations aligned with reality.

Although Tuppence generally appreciated anyone who paid her the compliment of assuming her to be practical-minded, she resented more the implication that she deserved less than other girls simply because she didn't sparkle.

That was, she realized now, the moment she gave up.

Pretending that she would one day nab a husband was a waste of everyone's time. The longer she stayed on the market, the more gratitude the market expected her to feel, and she would never feel grateful for scraps from someone else's feast. She would have her own feast or nothing at all.

Several months would pass before her parents too recognized the hopelessness of the endeavor and switched their affection to Hannah, who was fifteen at the time and still young enough to mold into the perfect product.

Tuppence would have expected these melancholy recollections to have a dispiriting effect on her mood, but they did not. She felt oddly buoyant and happy. At first, she was relieved the earl didn't speak and ruin the pleasure of the experience for her, for it was such a lovely experience. Slowly, however, it dawned on her that he was the source of her pleasure. He moved with such fluidity and grace, and although he tried to pretend he was focused solely on the space to the left of her shoulder, she caught him looking at her several times with an expression of bemused delight.

It was impossible to understand what was happening, and as long as the orchestra played, it was unnecessary. She would enjoy every moment while it lasted.

The music ended far too soon, and Tuppence felt her spirits dip as she realized it meant the resumption of hostilities. To complete his plan of reprisal, the earl would now walk away and leave her alone, the target of malicious gossip and idle speculation. She braced for it, knowing the response was entirely justified, for she'd behaved like the veriest school miss, practically blushing from pleasure.

But Gage did not leave her side, lingering instead to ask about her fondness for Coleridge and "The Rime of the Ancient Mariner" and to ascertain if her interest in polar exploration was sincere or something concocted in the moment to tease him. He listened to her answers patiently and responded thoughtfully and revealed an abiding affection for the poet, which she had not begun to suspect.

Before she knew it, supper was announced, and suddenly reminded of her responsibility as chaperone, she craned her neck to find Hannah.

"She's with Mr. Quilltop and his mother, I believe," he said, as if reading her mind. "She's only several feet away from Letty, who is with my Aunt Millicent and an eager young suitor named George Halesowen, whose fondness for Gothics seems to rival your own."

Tuppence didn't know what to say except thank you. Then she accepted his arm and allowed him to lead her in to supper.

Gage remained attentive for the rest of the evening, expressing seemingly sincere regret when it was time to say good night. He promised to pay a morning call the next day, which he did, at the earliest hour it was deemed polite, and stayed well past the customary thirty minutes. She met with him in the front parlor while Smudge tinkered with the grandfather clock in the northwest corner of the room. As soon as she and the earl had sat down, the butler had strode in with a butter knife and spoon and announced his intention to get "the old girl" working again.

"Don't mind me," he said as he opened the front to reveal the gears of the device.

The clock hadn't worked in over a year, and after the servant's careful administrations, it seemed unlikely it ever would.

"All right, Smudge. Thank you," she called back, then met the earl's gaze over the tray of refreshments. His eyes were twinkling with amusement, and she stared at him for almost a full minute before she remembered to pour the tea.

The following day he took her for a drive in Hyde Park with Letty and discussed several pieces of legislation he was working on in the House of Lords. Not only did he seek her opinion on the proposals, but he also listened to her answers and resisted any attempt his sister made to turn the conversation in the general direction of her new beau. Being the second son of a minor baronet in the south, Mr.

George Halesowen fell well short of Gage's expectations, and Letty, aware of her suitor's shortcomings, sought Tuppence's support by listing all of his interests.

"He's read every book by Mrs. Radcliffe and has all the correct ideas," Letty explained with almost breathless excitement. "The heroine of *The Sicilian Romance,* for example, is generally lauded for her bravery, but just as I do, he finds her to be an insipid hedgehog, burrowing and fleeing with such dreary repetition. And he adores the plays of Marlowe, just like me, and of all the strange coincidences in the world, muscadine is his favorite ice."

Given her own fondness for muscadine ice, Tuppence did not quite think Halesowen's preference for it was quite the rarity that Letty did. But she understood the girl's enthusiasm, for it was unusual to find a young man with whom one's interests aligned so nicely.

Gage, however, did not seem as impressed, and the next evening, when Letty was again listing the very fine attributes of her suitor, this time to Hannah, who had accompanied them to the theater, he kindly requested she leave off for the duration of the play.

"Merely as a courtesy to the actors, you understand," he rushed to explain. "Personally, I could listen to a catalog of Mr. George Halesowen's wonderful qualities for days on end, as, indeed, I have."

Although his tone was sharp with impatience, his demeanor remained amiable and Tuppence found him to be the perfect host, going so far as to politely seek her sister's opinion on the play. His expression revealed no disgust when Hannah observed that Oberon and Titania were merely a pair of foreign villagers, most likely French. He caught Tuppence's eye, of course, and his lips twitched, but he said nothing cutting or corrective.

By the end of the sennight, Tuppence had no choice but to come to the same conclusion as the rest of the *ton*: The Earl of Gage was courting her.

What nobody could agree on was why.

Her mother assumed he was using her to spur the interest of another woman. "Most men make the mistake of lavishing attention on a beautiful woman in the hopes of making their target jealous, but that's a strategic mistake," she explained over breakfast while Dover refilled her coffee cup. "Seeing one's beloved toadying up to an Incomparable makes one feel so inadequate one abandons the field. He becomes unattainable. But seeing him with someone like Tuppence? Now, that emboldens a woman, for she thinks, Am I truly going to concede an earldom to a plain-faced nobody like that? Of course the answer is no, and she redoubles her efforts to win the gentleman."

"Don't be a fool," her father said.

Although his tone revealed disgust for his wife's theory, Tuppence knew better than to think he was outraged on her behalf.

"Obviously, this is about me," he announced, rustling the morning paper, which he'd read during the meal after a brisk nod of acknowledgment to his family. "Gage is seeking my support for an upcoming bill on tariffs, and he believes he can soften me up by courting my offspring, as everyone knows I'm a fond father. I would tell him such an effort will come to naught, but I enjoy watching him put himself out. There seems no reason not to, as the only person he's harming is himself."

These statements were a vicious way to talk about anyone, let alone one's own daughter, but nobody in the room took exception. Hannah asked Dover for a cup of chocolate, Caroline requested another plate of eggs, and Tuppence silently reviewed that morning's lesson plan on geography. Although she might wish her parents had a better opinion of her than random members of society, she could hardly blame them for saying to her what everyone else was saying to one another. Nobody could fathom the earl's interest in her being sincere. Surely, he had a secret agenda, and as confident as they all were that something devious was afoot, nobody could figure out what it was. At Brooks's, wagers had been placed as to whether he was trying to win a bet or lose one. Truly, it was impossible to tell.

As the only member of society who didn't doubt the earl's sincerity, Tuppence thought the endless chatter and speculation were vastly amusing. She understood their suspicions, for she herself had shared them. In the beginning, she'd looked for an explanation that that would give his sudden change in behavior meaning. It was like a puzzle, trying to decipher his secret agenda, and the friendlier he got, the warier she grew. She kept herself removed from him, examining his every act with a jaundiced eye, determined to figure out what he wanted from her before she fell prey to his charm.

Because he was, she discovered with dismay, remarkably charming.

For two weeks, she held herself aloof, mistrustful of everything he said and did. Then he escorted her to Hatchards not, as she'd assumed, for him to buy her his favorite book on polar exploration but for him to buy her favorite for himself. In that moment, standing between the stacks of history tomes and maps of the Continent, she decided the simplest explanation was the correct explanation: He liked her. To ascribe any other motive to his enduringly kind and endearing courtship would be to turn him into a monster, and she could not do that. Despite his reputation for prickliness, he was neither ogre nor beast. He was merely a man of strong opinions who expected everyone else to feel just as deeply. When they did not or could not defend their position, he grew impatient.

Understanding the earl's intentions solved one problem and immediately created another, for Tuppence didn't know how she felt about the information. At times, it made her ecstatically happy, as she'd never expected to meet someone whom she could hold in such high regard or who would share her esteem. She didn't doubt for a moment that the respect she felt for him was earnestly and generously returned.

But Tuppence's feelings were not confined to mere respect and regard. There was that ache too, the one that hadn't left her since the kiss in the Patent Bill Office. It was mortifying, but sometimes Gage would be speaking to her about something trivial or laughing over an offhand comment and he would look a certain way—jaw cocked, eyes crinkled—and in a moment she would be back in that room at night, his eyes gleaming in the candlelight as he pressed his lips to hers and the ache would swallow her whole.

What a thing it was, to suddenly grow hot and flushed whilst standing in the middle of Hatchards discussing the career of Vitus Bering.

If the earl felt the same way, he gave no indication, and Tuppence worried that respect and regard were the extent of his affection. He was one-and-thirty, the age when many men began to think of setting up their nursery, and why shouldn't he contemplate doing so with the first woman he found bearable.

Tuppence couldn't resent him for taking such a practical approach to matrimony. Indeed, it was to his credit that he'd waited for someone with whom he could hold a sensible discussion, for few gentlemen counted engaging conversation at the breakfast table to be among their requirements for happiness. But she knew it would not be enough for her. She hadn't settled into aging spinsterhood on a whim. During her three seasons, she'd met and considered many second sons with whom she thought she might indeed rub tolerably well. They were friendly enough and kind.

But if that was really all there was to marriage—a lack of friction, the ability not to annoy each other—then she would much rather have her freedom and her independence.

Could she sacrifice both now simply because the gentleman made her body flush with desire? The arrangement he offered was the same as all the others, and if it wasn't good enough three years ago, how could it be good enough now?

This was the question that echoed endlessly in her head—while she was eating breakfast, while she was teaching the girls, while she was brushing her hair, while she was dancing with Gage, while she was lying in bed at night. At all times, she wondered what part of herself she would give away to be with the earl.

The question consumed her and the answer terrified her, two states that she found exhausting, so it was almost with relief that she spotted a man who looked vaguely similar to Mr. FitzWalter deep in conversation with Letty's suitor behind an overly large fig plant in Lady Gardiner's drawing room.

CHAPTER TWELVE

The only person in the household who objected to Tuppence launching a comprehensive investigation of Mr. Halesowen was Smudge, who found her in her father's study while she was rooting through his desk in search of a spyglass. Ostensibly, he'd entered the room to dust the shelves, for he had a rag in his left hand and expressed surprise at her presence, but she knew his discovery of her was a calculated event. As industrious a servant as the Templeton butler was, even he did not wander the house looking for surfaces to dust at two-thirty in the morning.

No, Smudge was doing now what he'd been doing from the moment he realized the Earl of Gage's interest in her was pointed: watching her movements with the piercing gaze of a hawk. Like the whole of London, he could not conceive of his lordship's attentions as being anything but nefarious.

"I'm looking for my father's spyglass," she told him smoothly, sliding the top drawer closed and opening the one below it. It contained two snuff boxes, a broken pair of spectacles, a miniature of her grandfather on a horse, a packet of letters wrapped in a dark blue ribbon and a breakfast roll as hard as a paperweight. "The one Lord

Dunmow gave him upon his return from Africa. Have you seen it?"

The butler stiffened his shoulders. "I will not aid and abet the pilfering of cherished heirlooms of my employer. I suggest you leave this room at once and retire to your bedchamber for several months to think about what you've done."

"It's brass with a wood veneer," she said, wondering what her ethical obligation was in regards to stale foods in private quarters. Was she supposed to discard it so it wouldn't attract mice and other vermin to the house, or should she respect the sanctity of the room and leave everything the way she found it—except, of course, her intended object. "He used to keep it on his desk, as a sort of memento of Dunmow's inability to pass the Covington tariff. If my father cherishes anything at all, it's the failure of others."

She shut the middle drawer and opened the one on the bottom: more letters, some notebooks, quills, another petrified baked good (this time a muffin). "I say, Smudge, you might want to talk with the parlor maids about inspecting the drawers for debris when removing meal trays from the room."

This suggestion, which was as well intentioned as it was practical, seemed to pain the butler further. "It's not my place to decide which pastries my lord may or may not store in the privacy of his own study, which is precisely why you shouldn't be here. This is my lord's *private* study."

"And I will leave as soon as I find his spyglass," she said agreeably. "I'm not poking around out of idle curiosity. I need that spyglass for an important investigation into a potentially iniquitous man."

Smudge smiled. "You mean Lord Gage?"

"No, not the earl," she said impatiently. "He's everything honorable and good. No, I mean the man who is courting his sister, Mr. George Halesowen. Information has come to light that indicates his intentions toward Lady Letitia are odious and corrupt. But I don't want to draw any hasty conclusions, which is why I must investigate the matter thoroughly, and to do that I need my father's spyglass."

"That doesn't sound like a very good idea, miss," Smudge said, quietly shutting the door to the study and walking toward her, the rag clutched in both hands now. "That sounds dangerous."

Tuppence closed the bottom drawer with a sigh. "It's not."

"What if you get caught? If he's the villain you think he is, he will not take kindly to being spied on," he pointed out.

It was a reasonable observation, but it failed to take into account her skill and expertise. "I won't."

"I find it appalling that his lordship would embroil you in such an ordeal," the butler said, his color high as he vented his outrage. "A good and honorable man would resolve this problem on his own, not rely on a mere girl who doesn't know better."

"He isn't," she said matter-of-factly. Although her tone indicated no emotional distress, his words cut her to the quick, for it was the first time she heard aloud what she'd been thinking to herself all night. The earl would not welcome her interference. On this subject, he'd made himself remarkably clear time and again, and she was willfully ignoring his wishes. It made her desperately sad to think about the end of their relationship, to imagine the expression on his face as he realized she'd done it again, sallied into the fray with no consideration of her inferiority, but she could not do anything else. Though he did not know it yet, they were at an impasse: He would never forgive her for meddling in Letty's future a second time, and she would never forgive herself if she went running to him for a solution. She'd routed FitzWalter once, and she would rout him again. It was not hubris to have faith in one's own competence.

Tuppence knew the earl would disagree. As much as he liked and admired her, he would never credit her with having as much sense and intelligence as a man. Understanding that, grasping its meaning on a visceral level, broke her heart in two, for it made her realize that their problem had always been bigger than mere respect and regard. Even if the earl loved her passionately, even if he longed for her with the same unquenchable desire she felt, he'd never consider her his equal—no woman was—and she was far better off alone than diminishing herself to fit inside his pocket.

And that was the end of that. Weeks of deliberating and debating and wringing her hands had come down to one essential truth, and that truth was the only thing that mattered. It was the exclamation point at the end of a long, dreary sentence.

Resigned to the relentlessness of reality, she stated candidly, "The earl will disapprove of my actions when he learns of them and immediately end our connection."

Smudge brightened at once. "Lord Dunmow's spyglass is in the cabinet to the right of the settee on the second shelf behind the Islington clock and beside a desiccated orange," he said, then yawned widely and smiled. "I believe it's time I retired. Do let me know if there's any other way I can be of assistance. I'm here to serve."

Tuppence retrieved the spyglass from the cabinet and employed it the next morning from the back of a hack in Dean Street to keep a steady eye on a black door flanked by austere white columns. This address, though less fashionable than where his guardian lived in St. James's Square, had hosted FitzWalter during this previous visit to London, and if he was indeed back in town, as she suspected, this was the likely place where he would be staying. It belonged to his cousin, who was reputed to cheat at cards, though no one had ever been able to prove it. They were, she thought in disgust, two peas in a pod.

As she had responsibilities at home, she could not spend the entire day pretending to run a single errand and when noon approached, she reluctantly gave up her surveillance and went home. In case circumstances required

her to get closer to her subjects, she was wearing an elaborate disguise that made her resemble an old fishwife, but
nobody in her family examined her closely enough to notice and Hannah called out a greeting without looking up
when she walked by the drawing room.

Only Smudge observed her costume, and he merely
winked in encouragement.

The next day was likewise disappointing and the day
after that as well. But on the fourth morning, her suspicions were confirmed when the tall, rounded-shoulder
form of Mr. FitzWalter emerged from the town house and
skipped quickly down the steps. As at Lady Gardiner's
rout, he'd taken pains to hide his appearance, for his hair
was longer and lighter and he sported a thick beard, which
was far from fashionable. At first glance, he looked like an
entirely different person, but one cannot alter the shape of
one's nose or the shifty look in one's eyes.

Tuppence had been convinced she would recognize
the weasel anywhere, for true villainy was impossible to disguise, and she was happy to have this conviction validated.

FitzWalter reached the sidewalk, paused for a moment and turned right. At the corner, he hailed a hack. She
instructed her driver to follow the carriage at a discreet
distance, which he did without question, for he had participated in these sorts of intrigues with Miss Templeton before. He furthermore wasn't surprised when she ordered
him to stop before entering the lane. She knew this was
where Mr. George Halesowen lived, two doors in from the
corner, and didn't want to run the risk of his seeing her.
Like Mr. FitzWalter, she'd donned a costume to alter her
appearance, but even without the gigantic wart on her nose
and the soot-stained mobcap, her plain face made it unlikely that either man would take notice of her. Most wom-
en lamented their lack of beauty, particularly in the hal-
lowed halls of Almack's, but she knew her plain appearance was much more practical. An ordinary-looking person
could go anywhere.

After a few minutes, Halesowen stepped out of the house, strode down the walk and warmly greeted FitzWalter. The two men chatted briefly next to the hack, then climbed inside. The coach pulled away from the curb and drove to a public house a few blocks from the Thames. It was on an alleyway so narrow, sunlight didn't reach the pavement.

The two men dismissed their carriage and went inside. Tuppence stayed put for a few minutes, then asked her driver to wait for her return and followed the pair inside. Per her usual procedure for stealth operations, she had her pistol in her reticule should she need to defend herself in a forceful manner, but she didn't expect trouble. In her experience, nobody bothered with wart-ridden hags with a limp—either in taprooms or ballrooms. Her assumption was validated the moment she crossed the threshold, for the few patrons who looked in her direction immediately looked away.

As she shuffled slowly to a table, she surveyed the room. Like other establishments near the docks, the Black Horse Inn was dark and long, with low ceilings and a wide-planked floor stained with several decades of spills and brawls. The suspected conspirators were seated to the right, at a small square table near the fire. Halesowen's tall frame perched awkwardly on the low wooden stool as he clutched a tankard of ale. They spoke quietly, their heads tilted together as they discussed something of great amusement to them both, and Tuppence realized they must be old friends. She was sure if she investigated their histories, she'd discover a long-standing connection that went back to their childhoods. Maybe they were neighbors in Sussex or schoolmates at Harrow.

Confident in her disguise, she walked to the long wooden table next to her quarry and sat down. She grunted, as if exhausted by the effort, and proceeded to breathe loudly like a tired nag or a wild boar. Halesowen and FitzWalter looked at her in disgust, then resumed their conversation. The only person to pay her any extended attention was the barmaid, who came to take her order.

"By far the easiest fruit I've ever plucked," Halesowen said with a satisfied grin. "She's thoroughly besotted and will do anything I say. If I told her to jump into the river, she'd ask which bridge to propel herself from."

"That's due in no small part to my providing you with all the information you needed to woo her," FitzWalter pointed out, clearly unable to allow his associate to have too high an opinion of himself. "She's a gullible twit, yes, but don't overestimate your charms, my friend. Knowing her favorite books and favorite plays and favorite food in advance so you could profess the same preferences paved the way for an easy conquest."

"Of course, of course," Halesowen rushed to agree. "Knowing what to say gave me a huge advantage. Some men might argue that knowing *how* to say something is just as important, if not, perhaps, more, but not me. I'm well aware of the favor you did me by providing this opportunity. It's just the thing I've always wanted—to marry a dimwitted heiress who worships the ground I walk on. I will never be grateful enough."

"Pay me my share," FitzWalter said, "and I don't care how grateful you are."

"That goes without saying," Halesowen insisted. "When have I ever squelched on a debt?"

FitzWalter laughed and rattled off a list of names.

His friend smiled. "Those were debts of chance, not debts of honor, for who among us is morally accountable to a turn of a playing card or a roll of the dice? Trust me, my friend, you have nothing to worry about. I have known you far too long and been through far too many scrapes to leave you dangling in the wind now. I would be insulted by your comment if I wasn't aware of how deeply your pockets are to let."

"Your situation is not much better," FitzWalter said.

"True," Halesowen admitted, "very true. But my brother might well die yet."

FitzWalter raised his glass. "Here's hoping."

They grinned at each other and drank, then turned their attention to the details of their plan. Although the two men believed themselves to be diabolically clever in devising their scheme, in fact it varied little from every other plot ever conceived to cheat an underage heiress out of her fortune: woo under false pretenses, propose hasty marriage, elope to Gretna, treat abominably while draining accounts.

The world of villainy had very little range.

Although, Tuppence conceded, employing the insights FitzWalter gained from his courtship to smooth the way for Halesowen's was an astute use of information. Any woman would feel an immediate connection with a suitor with whom she had so much in common.

"Ollie, my good man, there you are," FitzWalter said, rising to welcome the newcomer, who wore a black greatcoat, scuffed boots, and a patch over his right eye. He was a big man, intimidating in both height and breadth, with a neck as thick as a tree stump and tangled hair that fell to his shoulders.

If depicted in a novel by Mrs. Radcliffe, the description under his image would read, "Ruffian."

Ollie smiled, revealing a missing incisor on the top row, which Tuppence thought was taking matters a bit too far. Even in the most gruesome of Gothics, the scoundrels all had full sets of teeth. His voice was a low rumble as he returned FitzWalter's greeting and sat down at the table, which seemed to shrink with the addition of his large frame.

As FitzWalter made the introductions, Tuppence was reminded of the griminess of her surroundings, for she was suddenly accosted by the stench of rum and manure. Scrunching her nose in distaste, she darted an annoyed look at the obvious culprit: a sailor in a tricornered hat who clearly had a healthy disgust for bathing.

If the others were bothered by the smell, they gave no indication. Rather, Halesowen examined his new associate warily, as if unsure what to make of him. He seemed particularly unsettled by the missing eye, for his own intact set was continually drawn back to the black patch, no matter how many times he forced himself to look away.

Nevertheless, he professed pleasure at the meeting.

Ollie nodded abruptly and called for a tankard of ale, which was delivered to him immediately at the table. His ability to demand and receive instant service impressed Halesowen even more.

Delighted by his friend's response, FitzWalter grinned and took another drink from his own tankard. "Ollie is only a precaution," he said, "and most likely an unnecessary one at that. A young lady is a capricious thing. One never knows when she's going to take a fright or start to worry about her family's opinion or simply desire to return to the comforts of home. If that happens, a fond fiancé will naturally concede to her wishes and stop the coach. And that's when our precautionary measure will appear to make sure she understands the world outside your carriage is more dangerous than the world inside it. Ollie, look menacing."

Not a single muscle on the ruffian's face moved, except one or two in his lips, which arched into a slight smile.

"There," FitzWalter observed with satisfaction, "isn't he terrifying? Lady Letitia will cling to you in terror and you will insist that you continue onto Gretna to ensure that you will always have the right to protect her from danger. Her mind addled with fright, she will naturally agree."

As depraved and immoral as the plot was, Tuppence had to respect its elegance. The challenging part of any plan was getting your target to go along with it, and fear was an excellent way to gain compliance, for, as FitzWalter pointed out, it dulled one's mind. The more scared a person was, the less considered her decisions would be.

Although Halesowen clearly appreciated the scheme, he felt it could do with one or two slight improvements. "Is offering the girl a refuge from the dangerous world enough? Shouldn't I demonstrate how ably I can protect her from it as well?" he asked thoughtfully. "To truly overcome her scruples, mustn't I jump into the fray and save her from the evil scoundrel seeking to destroy her? It behooves us, I believe, to get into a bit of a brawl. Nothing very serious, of course, just a few jabs here and there, perhaps a well-placed facer or two, and then Mr. Ollie falls to the ground vanquished and I emerge as hero."

Informed of his easy defeat at the hands of the other man, Ollie constricted a few more muscles in his face, sharpening his smile and menace in equal degrees.

Halesowen cringed in response and said, "Please understand, I'm only sharing ideas as they come to me. They're neither deeply considered nor well thought out. As FitzWalter has more experience manipulating young women through fear, I'm happy to defer to him."

"A brawl, certainly, will keep the fair maiden on the edge of her seat," FitzWalter agreed, "but for it to be truly effective, Ollie will have to land a few blows. Letty won't be able to nurse your wounded brow if you have no wounds."

His friend blanched at the word *wound* but gamely allowed the value of his getting a little marked up in the pursuit of a fortune. "Perhaps we can try out the steps beforehand to ensure there are no mistakes in the moment."

"Of course," Ollie said with surprising agreeableness. "My time is your time as long as you're willing to pay for it."

FitzWalter found this statement to be entirely reasonable. "It goes without saying that the more work you do for us, the more you shall be compensated. Do tell us your fee so we may proceed to the next order of business, which is selecting a date for the elopement."

Ollie named an amount that struck Halesowen as exorbitant, for the gentleman's features pinched and he stammered in surprise. Perceiving his distress, FitzWalter explained that the charge was based on time and effort, and if Halesowen was willing to forgo some services, such as rehearsing the steps of the brawl, the price would come down.

Halesowen was willing.

He was also open to amending the details of the fisti-cuffs, as each strike had a monetary value attached to it, so that knocking Ollie to the ground cost twice as many pounds as landing a blow on his left cheek. A glancing blow was cheaper still, although considerably less impressive to the frightened young lady watching from the window of her lover's coach, and Halesowen struggled to arrive at an appropriately awe-inspiring display that also suited his budget.

As Tuppence listened to the protracted negotiation, she tried to decide if she admired Halesowen's frugality, for it demonstrated a considerable amount of respect for Letty's fortune, or horrified by his penny pinching, which seemed needlessly miserly for a man who expected to come into a large fortune in a matter of days.

"So we are agreed," FitzWalter said. "Three punches, two jabs and one poke in the vicinity of Ollie's eye patch."

Halesowen nodded uncertainly, for the brawl now sounded more like a scuffle. His disappointment at not quite getting the value he'd sought for his money was forgotten, however, when he learned he must pay half the fee in advance of the event. The reason, he was told, was an elopement was a tricky deal to lock down and you could never be sure one would turn out the way you planned. Ollie's explanation was meant to comfort Halesowen, for it indicated not a lack of faith in him as a schemer determined to mislead and impoverish an innocent young woman but rather a lack of faith in the process itself. Being warned of the possibility of failure by someone with years of experience in misleading and impoverishing innocent young women, however, did little to comfort him. Nevertheless, he promised to deliver the sum by noon the next day.

FitzWalter smiled with satisfaction and suggested the evening of Lord Bawtry's ball, which was nine days hence, for the elopement, for nothing fogged up a clear head like waltzing and a few glasses of ratafia.

"You will begin laying the groundwork tonight?" he asked his friend.

Halesowen nodded. "I will make myself disagreeable to Gage at once. It won't be hard, as he's rebuffed my efforts of ingratiation for weeks. Just last night, I made several insightful observations about some dreary law crippling factories with onerous regulations and he raged at me about soot-ridden orphans. He's a standoffish bastard," he muttered with annoyance, "who has made it clear I don't meet his qualifications for his beloved sister. Lady Letitia is aware of his disapproval, so it will be an easy thing to win her over to my plan. Her love for me is sincere and binding."

Well aware of Letty's fondness for the young villain, for the girl could scarcely talk of anything else, Tuppence worried that his understanding of the situation was indeed correct. Halesowen's betrayal would hurt her terribly, possibly causing deep and lasting pain, and extricating her from his clutches would require skill and consideration. It was not like last time, at Mrs. Shipton's weekend party, when Letty considered thwarting FitzWalter to be a great lark.

No, this time Tuppence would have to tread very cautiously lest she alienate the girl and risk pushing her deeper into his corner. If she was truly besotted with the charlatan, she might resist the truth and rise passionately to his defense. She might even decide that Tuppence was scheming against her on her brother's behalf and fall in with Halesowen's plan to elope.

As unlikely as the prospect was, Tuppence couldn't dismiss it entirely, for she knew love often had a deleterious effect on a person's good sense. From her place along the wall at balls and soirees and garden parties, she'd witnessed the desperate behavior of lovers and scoffed at their antics. She'd assumed herself above such dramatics, but considering the facts of her current situation— bewarted in a tavern near the Thames eavesdropping on a trio of villains—she had to allow for the possibility that she was just as susceptible as everyone else.

It wasn't the wart itself that made her question her invulnerability, nor the tavern nor the villains nor the particularly bitter ale she was consuming one meager sip at a time. None of that was remarkable, for she had made a career of observing unpleasant people in unlikely places. No, what presented a problem for her was the knot in her stomach indicating anxiety and concern that dispensing with FitzWalter on her own wasn't the right decision. Tuppence wasn't used to uncertainty, and experiencing it now underscored how compromised she already was by her feelings for the earl. That she would even consider for a moment the other option—running to him for help—revealed a weakness of character she'd never suspected.

It was one thing to contemplate marriage to a man whose regard for her didn't rise above respect and admiration, for surely there was a sort of freedom to be found in the frank appraisal of each other's worth. What she lost in independence she might gain in honesty. In truth, she believed much of the unhappiness in the world was caused by unrealistic expectations.

But it was another thing entirely to consider an arrangement that required her to be less than herself, to always temper her natural response with anxiety about how Gage would respond. If she was to confide in him now to stay in his good graces, it would ineffably harm her sense of self. It would turn her into a smaller person, a somehow more venial one, and it would affirm forever what he already believed: that she wasn't his equal, that no woman was.

That sort of relationship was intolerable to her. It would never end—the concessions she'd have to make to keep his esteem—and her disgust of herself would grow and grow and seep into every corner of their union. It would always be between them, for she would never be able to forget the sacrifice she'd made to be with him, and in the end it would be resentment, not desire, that swallowed her whole.

She knew this, knew it in her bones as surely as she knew her own name, and yet she was still tempted. Somehow being unhappy with Gage was as appealing as being happy without him.

Such madness could be attributed to only one thing: She loved him.

Under her wart, Tuppence turned white at the thought.

She'd known, of course, that she'd developed feelings for him, as she was an intelligent woman with a keen understanding of the situation. If she'd been unsure of how things stood, the quick stab of relief she'd felt at FitzWalter's sudden reappearance had made it remarkably clear that she was in much deeper than she'd suspected. Desire and fondness had meshed into a thick web of emotion, creating uncertainty and turmoil about the future, and she had been grateful that something had emerged to take the decision out of her hands.

Any sensible woman would choose a clean break over the slow dissolution of affection.

But even with the quick stab of relief, even with the grateful abdication of having to make the decision, she hadn't put all the pieces together. It was only now, as she sat in a dingy dockside tavern feeling an inexorable pull to do that wrong thing, that she grasped the truth: The thick mesh was love. The ineffable lightness was love. The spirited debating was love. The giddy impatience was love. The quiet respect was love. The ache was love.

It was all love.

Tuppence felt hollowed out by the revelation, as if everything inside her had spilled onto the pockmarked floor. A sensible girl with too much character and too little beauty, she'd never sought out love, and it struck her as patently unfair—wrong, cruel, sinister—that *it* had pursued *her* to the farthest reaches of the ballroom to torment her with the last gentleman on the face of the planet she would ever consider suitable. No doubt fate was having a merry laugh at her expense.

At that moment, FitzWalter broke out into a menacing cackle as if responding to a stage cue, and the unpleasant sound shook Tuppence from her stupor. She'd never been one to rail against the unjustness of the universe, despite extensive provocation, and she refused to do so now.

Halesowen remained a threat as did her own weakness. The only solution was to settle the first matter as quickly as possible, thereby resolving the second. As soon as Gage discovered what she'd done, the episode would be over and she would be free to move on to the next project: mending a broken heart. She had little hope of a speedy recovery, for just the thought of removing the earl from her life caused her significant pain.

If she wasn't careful, she would start weeping into her ale and the glue that held the lump on her nose in place would dissolve. The last thing the situation needed was a wandering wart.

With their business arranged for one week hence, Ollie announced he had another appointment and took a brusque leave of his fellow conspirators. Halesowen watched his departing back with an expression of awe mixed with anxiety. "He does understand that the fight is just for show, right?" he asked. "I mean, I'm paying him to intimidate Letty into submission, not to cause me lasting harm."

FitzWalter shrugged off his concern. "Ollie knows what's what. No need to worry about him. Worry rather about gaining the girl's consent. I don't think you want to pay Ollie for an abduction. The greater the penalty for the crime, the steeper the charge."

Halesowen seemed to blanch at the thought of an out-and-out kidnapping of Letty, or perhaps it was the suggestion of handing over more blunt. "I assure you, that won't be necessary. I will play my part. As I said, she will be easy enough to sway given her infatuation with me. I do say again, Fitz, this was a brilliant plan. I've always desired physical comfort but lacked the necessary willingness to discomfort myself to attain it."

"I understand exactly, my friend. Exactly," he said, then sighed loudly, as if contented with the world and his place in it. "I don't know which I'm looking forward to more: getting my hands on all her lovely money or getting one over on her nasty brother. He bought up all my vowels, you know."

"I do know," Halesowen said. "You've mentioned it before."

"Like they were baubles from a jewelry store! As if that would deter me from taking further action. Quite the opposite. It spurred me to be more creative in my methods. I can't wait to settle my debt with him using his own ready. It will be one of the greatest pleasures of my life."

The boast was so demonstrably false, for FitzWalter was far too miserly to ever settle a debt, even out of spite, it drew a smile of genuine humor from Tuppence, who had, moments ago, believed she would never smile again.

Halesowen, also recognizing the comment as empty, nodded with exaggerated approval and said, "Yes, I'm sure it will."

FitzWalter reviewed the plan once more for his friend's benefit, determined, it seemed to Tuppence, to ward off failure with minutiae. He advised his friend on the right flowers to send, the best waistcoat to wear, and the right way to offend Gage to ensure his staunch disapproval.

As if there were a *wrong* way to offend the earl, Tuppence thought with amusement.

While the two men worked through the final details of their plan, Tuppence began to formulate her own. Obviously, issuing threats would serve no purpose, for Gage's efforts had only roused FitzWalter further and her promise to expose his sins to his guardian worried him not at all. Perhaps he believed he could explain away all the charges in the damaging letter she would send, and not knowing Lord Wallasey personally, she allowed for the possibility that his assumption was accurate.

If that was the case, she needed to gather more convincing evidence. How exactly she would do that, she didn't know yet, but one thing was clear: FitzWalter would not stop. If he failed in this scheme to secure Letty's portion, he would devise a new one. The target might be another young woman, perhaps one with fewer champions to protect her, but his determination to secure a fortune through devious means would remain unchanged.

It wasn't enough to rescue Letty. She must come up with a plan to rescue his next victim and his next.

The thought of saving all of womanhood from his evil clutches lifted her spirits considerably, for there were few things she enjoyed more than having a mission. It gave her life purpose, as represented by the fact that she now had several clearly defined objectives: foil FitzWalter, rescue Letty, astonish Gage, return to genteel spinsterhood.

Tuppence wasn't naïve enough to believe achieving her goals would be as easy as listing them. Indeed, she wasn't naïve at all. She knew the challenges ahead were manifold, the most daunting of which was settling back into her existence as indifferent ape leader. She'd been content in that life before, with its industriousness and good deeds and intelligent exchanges with women of a similar bent. It had been minor, yes, and narrow—in many ways as self-contained as a fiefdom—but its autonomy suited her. For years, it had been all she'd known and it had been enough.

Now she knew more, and going back felt like going backward.

All she had to do to stop the regression was simply stop. Cease her scheming and tell Gage everything, and let the world resume its forward motion.

How easy it would be to just submit.

The more she wanted to give in, the more disgusted she became with herself and with the earl for revealing the breathtaking depth of her weakness. She truly wasn't the person she thought she was, and realizing that over and over again demoralized her.

Fortunately, that dejection had the felicitous effect of stiffening her resolve. As FitzWalter and Halesowen left the tavern and she was assaulted by another wave of rum-manure stench as the open door drew the smell forward, she returned her attention to formulating a plan. She would keep it simple, with as few moving parts as possible, for the more gears a device had, the more likely it was to fail. Her scheme would be straightforward and use Halesowen's worst trait against him—namely his greed.

It was, she decided as she climbed into the waiting hack, only the merest outline of a plot, but one had to start somewhere. Every complex conspiracy and complicated contraption began with an idea. She had all day to work out the details, and she did, in the quiet privacy of her room, where no one bothered her, except Smudge, who requested the return of her father's spyglass, while offering to use it in the service of her mission.

"I'm quite skilled in surveillance," he announced before she could politely decline. "The trick is to remain still and not call attention to oneself. Being a butler, I am, of course, naturally inclined to invisibility. Nobody notices me or my ilk unless the doorbell rings."

Tuppence smothered a smile and thought Smudge was rather more likely to use the glass to spy on her. "Thank you for your gracious office. I will keep it in mind."

Although this wasn't the enthusiastic response he'd been hoping for, he accepted it with an abrupt nod and remained firmly planted on the threshold until she handed over the small telescope. After he left, she closed the door, her despondent mood at the thought of ending her relationship with Gage somewhat lightened by the butler's antics.

CHAPTER THIRTEEN

Although he'd earned the epithet Prickly Perceval through years of impatient sneering and irritable sniping, the Earl of Gage actually considered himself a fair-minded, even-tempered individual. He'd embraced the nickname out of utility, for having a reputation for prickliness kept fools at bay and caused even the boldest among his peers to tread lightly. It was a matter of practicality, not personality.

And yet as he raged at his valet for not securing his cravat properly on the first attempt, he was forced to allow that perhaps the general assessment of his character was in many ways accurate.

He was certainly prickly now, for Thomas's inability to create a simple knot—the Mail Coach, for God's sake, not the Mathematical or an elaborate piece of nonsense like the Waterfall—caused him to snarl peevishly and shrug off the man's efforts.

"I'll do it," he growled.

Stricken, the valet mumbled an apology and stood helplessly to the side as his employer ruthlessly twisted the starched linen square with angry fingers. He winced as the cloth wrinkled under the rough treatment, and Gage, noting his expression, sighed deeply and dropped his hands.

"I apologize, Thomas," he said. "You are much better suited to this task than I am. Please resume your administrations and I will endeavor to remain calm no matter how many tries it requires."

As his valet skillfully arranged the cravat into the desired form, Gage conceded that his fuse had been frightfully short lately. Just that morning, he'd snapped at Mathers for asking if he would like butter with his toasted bread. True, it was a bloody stupid question, for he wasn't an ascetic who preferred his toast as dry as a bone. But calling the footman an asinine weevil for showing him the expected deference was entirely out of place. He'd done the same thing with Letty just the night before, when she'd dared to ask him which conveyance he'd like to take to Lady Swivenell's rout. (The carriage, obviously! He couldn't very well escort her on horseback!) And that was nothing compared with the stream of insults he'd directed at Mr. Halesowen when the man tried to engage him in conversation about the Health and Morals of Apprentices Act. Everyone knew the earl was a staunch supporter of regulations requiring proper ventilation and cleanliness of factories, so advocating for the law's repeal would have driven his temper in the best of circumstances.

Ignorant puppy!

Even if the earl were open to considering a suitor for Letty who wasn't on the approved list, he would never agree to a second son with a minor portion and middling prospects. Broad-mindedness was one thing; criminal negligence was another.

Nevertheless, the brutality of his response to Halesowen was uncalled for, and he knew an apology was in order. It also wouldn't hurt, he thought now as Thomas helped him into his coat, to take the opportunity to warn him off. He was clearly enamored of Letty, and although his sister seemed to return his affection, the relationship could never amount to more than a flirtation.

Gage would make sure of it.

Such a conversation wasn't suited to one's club or the

corner of a ballroom, and he determined to visit the other man's residence that morning. It was better to resolve the matter immediately rather than let it drag out.

But deciding to do the right thing made him feel more churlish than ever, and he had to bite back a cross remark when Thomas handed him an ornate watch with enamel and pearls. He took a deep breath, shook his head and calmly observed that the gold watch with the repoussé case would be more appropriate to the situation. Thomas, whose preference for embellishment was well known, returned the elaborate timepiece to the drawer without comment, but Gage felt his disapproval buzz in the air like a fly.

It required every ounce of his self-control to walk sedately out of the room without muttering annoyed curses under his breath—and even then he made it only as far as the staircase before he began to stomp.

Despite being famous for his prickliness, the Earl of Gage wasn't used to feeling constantly displeased with the world and found his increased exasperation with minor irritants to be extremely exasperating. He didn't know to what to attribute it, and as he waited for Whiting to bring around his horse, he considered possible sources.

Letty was the obvious explanation, for she continued to assert her independence despite his insistence that she heed his wisdom. This visit to Halesowen, for example, would be entirely unnecessary if she'd limited her interest to the assortment of suitors he'd deemed worthy of her attention.

Gorleston was another likely cause, for he continued to push hard for the repeal of the factory reforms the earl so strongly supported. As the owner of a textile mill, the viscount from Cheshire found it logistically onerous and financially burdensome to have to ensure the safety of his workers. His lordship deeply resented the government's interference and seemed to consider it his own private business if he wanted to maim or mutilate one of the hundreds of laborers who worked for him, a stance that infuriated Gage whenever he considered it.

But he'd been clashing with Gorleston and others of his ilk for a long time. Prior to introducing the move to repeal, the viscount had proposed establishing a tax on every baby born in the country, and before that he'd advocated for a law that would allow pickpockets as young as fourteen to be hanged for their crime. It was the same with Letty, who, though obviously not a repugnant human being like the miserly lord, had long made her strong opinions known.

No, it was something new that was responsible for his unusually harsh disposition, and if Gage were to be completely honest with himself, he already knew the cause: Miss Templeton…Tuppence.

Of course it was she.

He'd spent two weeks exerting all his energy in the struggle to at once earn her good opinion and keep his desire in check. Every moment in her presence was a balancing act between enjoying the present and imagining the future, which typically entailed them in various states of undress inappropriate to their setting. While waltzing with her at Mrs. Williams's ball—the first time he'd held her since the devastating kiss in the patent office—he pictured them writhing together on the very floor on which they were dancing. It had even happened in Hatchards. Hatchards! The den of high intellectual fervor and genteel enlightenment! He never imagined he had so little control over his own thoughts, and yet there they were, looking for one of Tuppence's favorite books, and suddenly he saw their entangled bodies pressed against the bookshelf like mindless animals. It made no sense, for she was wearing the most dowdy dress he'd ever seen, ill fitting and years out of fashion, and her hair was again hidden by one of those dreadful mobcaps. But her face was flushed and her eyes seemed to sparkle with surprised delight and passion swept through him. Indeed, the drabness of her clothes only heightened the contrast and made his desire for her more intense.

Sometimes in her presence he felt like a callow youth

unable to catch his breath, and that alone would be enough to blacken his mood.

And yet that wasn't the cause. He knew it wasn't, because in truth he actually relished the sensation, for it was novel and created an almost unbearably delicious anticipation. Even when he *was* a callow youth, he'd never experienced such heedless excitement or eagerness. His affairs of the heart had always been enjoyable and satisfying, even rewarding, and as he'd watched Tuppence browse the shelf at Hatchards, it had struck him with knee-wrenching force that the paltry words he chose to describe the encounters, so pleasant in their benignity, amounted to little more than adequate.

He would not settle for adequate.

In that moment, his entire purpose shifted—indeed, his entire world shuddered—and his pursuit ceased to be a sop to his ego and started to be a sincere campaign to win her heart. He wanted Tuppence, and the true revelation was that he wanted everything about her: the book she was searching for among the polar explorers almost as much as her body.

It was a disconcerting discovery, to be sure, but it still didn't account for his frayed temper, for he'd left Hatchards slightly bemused and wholly delighted at having found a woman who aroused both his passion and his intellect.

The very next day, he began to court her in earnest, and although he'd expected her to respond to his increased interest with wariness, she didn't appear to notice anything different in his behavior. She'd remained the same maddening, fascinating, engaging, insightful, clever young woman she had always been.

Except, he thought now as Whiting helped him onto his horse, the night of Lady Gardiner's ball. On that occasion, she'd been unusually quiet during supper, responding to his comments with solemn nods of her head or one-word answers. Indeed, she'd been almost sullen, which was highly out of character. He hadn't thought too much of it because the next day her spirits had been restored.

Restored, yes, but something about her remained altered, something so minor he hadn't bothered trying to identify it. Indeed, he'd halfway convinced himself he was imagining it. Yet part of him had known something was deeply wrong, for it had been reflected in his temper.

He gave the matter his full consideration now as he rode to Halesowen's residence on Stanhope Street.

The change wasn't in her manner, for she smiled at him as much as ever and answered his challenges with the same straightforward determination. Tuppence Templeton had never backed down from a fight and he doubted she ever would. The difference was more subtle than her responses. It was her eyes, he thought. In the past few days, they hadn't sparkled, not even when she teased him.

And then he realized, she hadn't teased him, not in days, not even when he'd remarked that Mr. Redhill, with his black eyes and thick brows, had the ridiculously ferocious look of a Minerva Press villain. She'd laughed, as he'd intended, and complimented him on his astute observation, but she hadn't taken exception to his description. She hadn't cocked her head in that aggressively thoughtful way and defended the archetype as an element of all genres regardless of publisher or pricked his ego by calling attention to his own dark brows, which weren't entirely unferocious.

Rather, she'd responded with common courtesy, he thought now as a knot of dread formed in his stomach. He might as well have been a dowager duchess she'd met but a few minutes before for all the familiarity her manner exhibited.

Clearly, he'd done something to unsettle her.

He didn't have to ask himself what that thing was because he already knew it: He'd started to treat her as a prospective bride, not as an obstacle to be overcome. As his feelings had warmed, so had his demeanor.

Gage cursed under his breath and felt a wave of hot anger at himself for handling the matter with such ineptitude and clumsiness. He wasn't a clunch. He'd been wooing women for years and knew how to show measured interest without causing his quarry to scurry in the opposite direction.

The problem, of course, was the kiss in the Patent Bill Office, for those moments had been anything but measured. If Tuppence, perceiving the change in his attitude, feared a proposal of marriage, it was no doubt because of the unbridled passion she'd been forced to endure. Like any other innocent girl, she recoiled at the idea of being subjected to it again and was gently but firmly making her own intentions known by severing the relationship with cool politeness.

As angry as Gage was at himself for not treading more carefully, he was furious at Tuppence for the display of cowardice. The fearless woman he loved—yes, he said *loved*—would tell him straight to his face that she had no interest in him as a husband. Then she would volunteer to help him find a suitable replacement.

That she would try to slink away under the cover of amiable good humor was the first and only time she'd disappointed him.

It wouldn't stand, he decided with petulant obstinacy. Tuppence was free to spend her life without him. She was welcome to make any number of earls, tenacious or intelligent or otherwise, the object of her derision if that was her wish. But first she was going to deal plainly with him.

No stealthiness.

No furtiveness.

No pretending it wasn't happening.

The resolution cheered him considerably.

Having never been in love before, Gage had little concern that it would reveal itself to be a stubborn emotion. He assumed anything you fell into with little design could be overcome with logic and determination. Indeed, the way people described love made it sound more like an accident that happened to unmindful victims than an enduring condition. Surely, all he had to do to overcome the feeling was list the many ways in which he was better off without her interfering presence in his life.

Thoughtfully, he began to tick them off: Not loving Tuppence Templeton meant he'd be free from her ridicule. He'd be liberated from her constant harassment and expectation that he consider other points of view. He'd be able to make decisions on his own again, without a nagging sensation that her input would help him make a better choice. He'd be unmocked, unpestered and self-sufficient.

And alone.

The stray thought, as unwelcome as it was unexpected, struck him as inexplicable, for the notion of being alone was not one he'd ever contemplated before. It simply did not exist for him in any sense—neither as a condition to be feared nor as a concept to be embraced. He merely lived his life with the independence afforded a man of his stature and accepted the freedom from having to consider the opinions of others as his due.

Suddenly, that freedom felt like loneliness.

Annoyed at the maudlin turn his thoughts had taken, Gage urged his horse to move faster. What he really needed now was a head-to-head battle over a clear-cut issue, and confronting Halesowen would surely provide that.

Just let the man *try* to argue that he was a fit husband for Letty.

Gage would annihilate him.

The earl turned on to the appointed street, and spotted the gentleman in question already in close conference with an associate. He was still too far away to positively identify the other individual, but there was something oddly familiar about him.

The curve of his shoulders…

Could it be…?

No, of course not.

He hung back, stopping his horse a few houses away to observe from a secure distance. He couldn't see clearly because Halesowen was blocking the other man as they walked down the front path. Perhaps if he climbed off his horse, he could get a closer look.

Gage didn't have time to employ the tactic, for he no sooner had the thought than the two men climbed into a carriage. It pulled away from the curb, leaving the earl with little choice but to follow in order to confirm once and for all that the other man wasn't Horace FitzWalter.

He knew it was ridiculous and yet...

The earl urged his horse forward, then brought him to a stop as the hack directly in front of him pulled into the street. Like Halesowen's conveyance, it turned right at the end of the block. Appreciating the tactical advantage of putting a little distance between him and his target, Gage followed from behind the second coach. Naturally, he assumed the path of the hack would diverge from his own sooner or later, but it held its course, somehow turning left and right whenever Halesowen did.

This development made the situation even more curious, for as convinced as Gage was that his sister's suitor wasn't in the company of the confirmed villain he'd routed so thoroughly only a few months before, he couldn't shake the sense that something outrageously bizarre was going on. There was no other way to explain the fact that the coach he was following was also following the coach he was following.

Halesowen's carriage stopped in front of a rundown tavern on a narrow street, causing the hack to come to an abrupt halt. Gage pulled up his horse and watched from a distance as the door to the first coach opened. The two men stepped out of the carriage, giving the earl his first clear view of the second face.

No, Halesowen's mysterious companion was not FitzWalter, for this gentleman's hair was far lighter and his chin did not have the same pointy aspect. Even with whiskers obscuring the lines of this feature, Gage could tell that its shape was rounded.

Relieved, he watched the two men disappear into the tavern, then turned his attention to the hack to see what would happen next. Although he was confident Letty's suitor wasn't conspiring with the fortune hunter who sought to ruin her, he knew something not quite on the level was going on. The coaches of entirely innocent men weren't trailed by suspicious-looking hacks.

Something was definitely afoot.

Gage held his position and waited. After a few minutes, the door of the conveyance opened and a woman in a gray-colored dress climbed out.

He stiffened at once, for he knew that dress. That drab gray dress, which he'd fantasized removing so many times he felt sure he was going insane.

It wasn't Tuppence.

How could it be Tuppence?

Was this how it would be going forward—his mind would create visions of her everywhere he went?

But even as his heart wrenched at the lunacy, she turned her head slightly and he recognized her features.

For a moment, for just the briefest span of time, he felt such delight in seeing her that he almost called out as if hailing her on a path in Hyde Park.

The surge of joy passed as quickly as it came, supplanted forcefully with horror at her presence. What in God's name was she doing there?

Why was she following Halesowen?

It was madness, no doubt, but as soon as she entered the tavern, he secured his horse and crept like a thief to a window to look inside. The Black Horse Inn wasn't particularly crowded, but the glass through which he peered was dirty and it took him a moment to locate Tuppence among the smudges. To his dismay, he found her sitting at a table no more than two feet from Halesowen. If the gentleman reached back with his arm, he'd brush her on the nose.

Fortunately, Letty's suitor did not seem interested in stretching his arms. Engrossed in conversation, he showed no awareness of anyone but his mysterious companion.

Frustrated by the filthy glass and his inability to hear

anything but muffled chatter, Gage considered his options. Having arrived by horseback, he didn't have a groom to accost, so he settled for the first man he saw, a sailor with several days' worth of stubble, a tricornered hat and a torn navy coat that smelled like rum, lavender and manure. Although he cringed at the odor, he knew now was not the time to be too fine in his notions and gamely proposed a swap: his coat for the sailor's. But as soon as he made the proposition, he realized how absurd it was, for the man could have little use for Weston's finest. Indeed, the earl's beautifully cut garment would only attracted ruffians and thieves. So he switched tactics, naming a more than generous sum, and struggled to hold on to his temper while the sailor weighed the pros and cons of the offer.

For a full minute, he mumbled a series of calculations under his breath, then countered with an amount that was twice as much. "And ye coat too," he said.

Too anxious to be annoyed at the other man's savvy horse-trading, Gage handed over the money and the garment and gratefully tugged on the navy coat. He was immediately assaulted by the stench of manure, and while swallowing a nauseated gurgle, he decided it was a good thing, as the unpleasantness would stop people from giving him too careful a perusal. But just in case someone did, he snagged the sailor's hat. He opened his mouth to protest the abuse but settled for a glum nod when he met the earl's impatient glare. He'd gotten the sharp end of the deal and knew it.

Gage wasted no time, reaching for the door of the tavern at the same moment a wide-shouldered man grabbed it. Since the other patron was as big as a tree and would provide just as much coverage as an oak, the earl eagerly deferred to him and entered the room in his shade. He kept his eyes studiously trained on the scuffed floor until he was sitting down. Although he knew the safest position in the room was behind Tuppence, he couldn't resist the urge to see her face, so he took a table to her right and immediately had to stifle a laugh when he spotted the wart on her nose.

He knew by any objective measure she looked awful. Her hair was greasy, her skin was sallow, and her dress bulged in the strangest places, as if she'd added layers of padding to her body in the dark. Taken together, the elements of her disguise made her appear old and sickly, like a dowager with the rheumatic complaint, and yet when he looked at her all he could see was her beauty. It was like a light that radiated from her core, and noting its implausibility, the earl had to wonder if perhaps this thing he felt for her—this emotion called love—might be a bit more intractable than he'd previously assumed.

The thought made him angry, and when the barkeep appeared at his table to take his order, he glowered at him.

"What'll ye have?" he asked undaunted.

Gage wanted a glass of brandy, a comfortable chair and a quiet room to clear his head but knew that was impossible. He settled for a tankard of beer.

While he sipped the warm brew, he watched Tuppence watching Halesowen and tried to make sense of the scene. Nothing in her behavior had revealed a suspicion of Letty's suitor. If anything, she'd displayed a genuine fondness for the young man, praising his goodness and kindness as if those traits compensated for a lack of wealth or standing.

Truly, he was absolutely baffled as to why she would don a wart and follow him to the docks. Perhaps she had done so on his sister's behalf?

If Tuppence put herself in danger at Letty's request, he would banish the silly chit to the attics for a month with nothing but bread and water.

His anger at his sister abated as soon as the mysterious stranger stood to greet the oak tree whom the earl had followed into the tavern. All he had to do was speak and Gage knew the truth.

"Ollie, my good man," he said, his voice ringing loud and clear throughout the room, "there you are."

Without knowing anything else, Gage knew everything.

FitzWalter and Halesowen had hatched some scheme to rob Letty of her portion, and somehow Tuppence had uncovered it. He didn't wonder how. She was clever and observant and well skilled at inserting herself in places where she didn't belong. Perhaps she'd seen through FitzWalter's disguise. Perhaps, like him, she'd needed to hear him speak to know the truth. Regardless, she'd figured it out and devoted herself to scotching it.

Of course she had.

She was Tuppence Templeton and believed she could do anything. If he announced tomorrow that he would no longer occupy his seat in the House of Lords, she would don breeches and present herself to Parliament in his stead.

Make no mistake: Gage respected her confidence, and although it made him anxious for her safety, it was infinitely preferable to the simpering misses one usually had to endure. That said, he would naturally assume responsibility for the matter going forward. Now that he was aware of the problem, it was incumbent on him to solve it—not only because it was his sister whom FitzWalter's sinister plot targeted but also because he was more suited to the task. As capable as Tuppence considered herself, she was still subject to the weaknesses of her sex. Letty's future was far too important to leave in her hands.

Gage listened as the three men revealed the details of their plan and conceded that it might have worked. While he liked to believe Letty was far too dutiful to agree to an elopement, her love of elaborate plots and high drama made her unpredictable. It would be just like her to assume herself persecuted by a cruel brother who didn't understand the tenderer emotions and run off to Gretna Green at the first opportunity.

He shuddered at the thought, unable to imagine anything more infuriating or uncomfortable than a midnight race to the border. 'Twas a very good thing he'd uncovered the truth. Now he had a week to decide how to rout Fitz-

Walter permanently and punish Halesowen appropriately. Both would be his pleasure.

" You mustn't wear a fawn-colored waistcoat, as fawn is the enemy of infatuation," FitzWalter observed, switching from flowers to clothes after concluding a five-minute treatise on the romantic viability of posies. Ollie had left a while ago, but there were still important matters to discuss. "Despite Brummell's insistence on neutrals, I can assure you with one hundred percent certainty that nothing will kill a young girl's fancy faster than a muted shade."

FitzWalter also dismissed puce with a protracted explanation involving fleas, dogs and blood, even though Halesowen stated clearly that he didn't own any garment in that particular color.

The nonsensical chatter went on and on, and Gage, listening from his perch one table away, decided that if the man's lack of conscience hadn't already made him a confirmed blackguard, his deeply rooted conviction that he was an expert on every conceivable subject did. He was, by any measure, intolerable.

"Gage's range of interest is so narrow, you have no choice but to stick with airing political views that are antithetical to his," FitzWalter said, having dispensed all his insights on color and courtship. "He tends to champion factory workers and chimney sweeps and filthy street urchins who try to steal your coins in Leicester Square. No wonder he's so prickly all the time—he picks the losing side of every argument. To keep him in a constant state of irritation, complain about how unsightly and annoying the poor are. Tell him that if you were in Parliament, you would propose a law requiring impoverished orphans and widows to hide behind a bush or an unoccupied carriage whenever a member of the gentry walked by. He will have an apoplectic fit and ban Letty from ever mentioning your name again."

Rather, Gage thought with amused disgust, he would simply walk away from Halesowen without saying a word, for some ideas were too stupid and ignorant to dignify with an answer.

While FitzWalter prattled on about legislation designed to offend his sensibilities, the earl kept his eyes trained on Tuppence and wondered what she made of this representation of him. Surely, a champion of orphans and widows was the sort of person with whom a high-minded, self-sufficient young lady would want to align herself. He was kind to puppies, treated his staff with respect and never whipped his horse, no matter how staunchly it refused to take a fence. He was principled and honest, and he discharged the civic responsibilities that came with his rank and position virtuously and without complaint.

He was, by anyone's calculation, a worthy suitor.

If Tuppence didn't appreciate his value, the problem was hers, not his. He wasn't the one sacrificing his only chance at a comfortable future with a compatible mate. A man with his fortune and title would have many more opportunities to secure a wife. Indeed, if he would but allow it, a bevy of hopeful mamas would line up before him every season to present their daughters for his consideration. Even with his reputation as a stickler, he had his choice of Incomparables.

A spinster of a quarter century with no manners or desire to ingratiate herself with others would surely spend the rest of her life alone, whilst he made a brilliant match with a diamond of the first water.

Everyone would stare in envy.

But even as he celebrated this future triumph, Gage winced at the horrifying picture it created, for he couldn't conceive of anything worse than being admired for his wife's beauty. What a hollow victory that would be for both parties. He hadn't even met the young lady yet, and already he was annoyed at her insipidness, the way she agreed with everything he said, the implicit trust she placed in all his opinions.

Disturbed by the turn his thoughts had taken, the earl

shook his head silently and stared into his tankard of beer. What was he thinking—to find fault with everything he'd been raised to expect? Only a cracked-pot would quibble over the prospect of a deferential wife.

What other comfort was there to be had in marriage, other than aligning with a woman who left you to the solitude of your own counsel?

And children, he reminded himself, for that was the true point of such an arrangement: to beget heirs and secure the succession. Could you imagine, he asked himself in disgust, how that transaction would turn out with Tuppence at the helm? If Letty was unmanageable, Tuppence's daughters would be defiant.

No rational man wanted to raise defiant daughters. The idea was as appalling as it was preposterous.

Moreover, no creature still capable of rational thought craved a woman who had so little respect for him that she would run roughshod over his preferences. She knew exactly how he felt about her interfering in Letty's business. He'd made himself entirely clear the first time FitzWalter threatened her future, and yet there she was, handling the matter on her own once again. It was a deliberate rebuke, and the message was clear: I don't need you.

Well, he didn't need her either, and as soon as FitzWalter and Halesowen left the tavern, he stood up, fully intending to poke her on the shoulder and put an end to their association once and for all. He reached out his hand...

And froze.

He was staring at his fingers a mere inch from her ugly gray dress, but he kept seeing Tuppence's daughter—a pert little girl with her mother's bold gaze and bright golden eyes. She was no bigger than a bear cub and yet had all the confidence of a lion.

No rational man wouldn't want that.

Profoundly unsettled, Gage stood there, his hand hovering in the air, his breath trapped in his throat.

Touch her now and it would all be over, he told himself. Just touch her now and be done with it.

And that was the moment—the moment when he couldn't get his arm to move even a fraction of an inch, no matter how stridently he ordered it—when he knew he couldn't outreason love or overcome it with logic or free himself from its grasp with a list of disadvantages. He could walk away from it, for despite the strange malfunction of his hand, he still had free will, but he would leave something of himself behind. A part of his soul belonged to Tuppence now.

Inexplicably, the revelation made him feel whole.

But it wasn't his emotions that mattered—it was Tuppence's, for she was the one who'd decided a few nights before to quietly expel him from her life. Less than two hours ago he'd accepted that decision with equanimity. Now he found it intolerable. It required every ounce of his self-control not to grab her by her shoulders and demand that she love him.

Then a terrifying thought struck him: What if she couldn't love him?

She'd said as much once, hadn't she? In the front parlor, when he'd gone to apologize for his appalling behavior at Almack's. They'd gotten into a discussion about the state of the world—whether it was generally a fair place—and perceiving no common ground between them, she'd announced that the best they could do was agree to disagree.

He'd felt such unfathomable sadness at hearing those words, as if he were standing on the opposite side of a vast gulf. Even then, even when she was just a brazen curiosity he couldn't stop thinking about, he'd known he wanted to be on her side. It was the reason he'd proposed the ridiculous escapade to the Patent Bill Office. The desire to extend their association by any means possible had been visceral, instinctive, primal.

Now, as he stood only an inch from her, Gage felt

the gulf widening, for *he* had been her example. It was *his* conduct she'd submitted as evidence that the world was unjust to women: "It's been my experience that you can extricate a young girl from an unfortunate situation with competence, skill and discretion and still be chastised for being a rash and inept female."

How could it be that he, the Earl of Gage, champion of orphans, widows and stray dogs, was unequivocal proof of the world's great injustice?

It didn't make sense.

Indeed, it was nonsensical and grossly unfair. As Letty's brother, he had been doing only what both nature and the law required: shepherding his sister into a suitable arrangement that would ensure her happiness and security. Tuppence's reckless interference jeopardized that, and if she chose to take exception to his responding as a responsible guardian, then it was her problem.

But, no, he thought, it's my problem.

He could continue to argue the point, staking out an ever larger swath of land on his side of the gulf— Tuppence, for her part, expected nothing less—or he could concede ground.

The thought presented itself like it was one of several options, but in fact it was the only option. If he wanted a future with Tuppence, he would have to admit that her ideas were sensible, her schemes were practical, and her ability to successfully carry out a maneuver was as refined as his own. He would have to acknowledge that she was as intelligent and capable as he.

In short, he would have to accept her as an equal.

It was an outlandish notion, to be sure, for he considered few men of the world to possess the necessary traits to attain such categorization, and if you'd asked him before that moment if a woman could ever aspire to such heights, he would have shrugged off the query as both diverting and ridiculous. And yet as soon as he proposed the idea to himself, he accepted it as fact. Indeed, nothing in the whole of his life had been as easy to accept as Tuppence as his equal. What would have been hard, he thought with surprise, was loving and respecting her as much as he did while withholding his trust.

Dumbfounded, he slid back onto the stool, draped his arms around the tankard of beer and tilted his head down to disguise himself further. Trusting Tuppence meant allowing her to proceed with her plan to foil Fitz-Walter without his interference.

The decision did not sit lightly with him, for he had too much faith in his own judgment to believe anyone could do anything as well as he. But Tuppence had deftly extricated Letty from a dangerous situation once before, and he had little doubt she could do it again.

Only a very little doubt, he thought, unable to completely smother the concern that he was leaving his sister's happiness in the hands of a mere slip of a girl.

A mere slip of a girl who looked entirely at home among the rough patrons of a seedy dockside tavern, he observed with silent amusement. Even in that drab gray gown, she should have stood out like a rose among weeds, and yet she blended in so well with her surroundings he would have assumed she frequented the establishment daily. And that wart! Rather than make her appear absurd, the berry-sized blob on the tip of her nose gave her an air of misfortune and sincerity.

Gage smiled into his beer, at once comforted and entertained by the depth of his depravity, for only a man besotted beyond reason could admire a malformed lump in the middle of his beloved's face.

The irrationality of his appreciation made him happy in a way he'd never expected to be, and as he watched Tuppence bide her time before leaving, he felt buoyantly optimistic that, yes, she could love him.

Pieces of it were already there: He made her laugh. He challenged her. She clearly delighted in any opportunity to challenge him, for never did her eyes sparkle more than when she was about to issue a teasing remark. There was affection between them and a fondness he felt every time he led her onto the dance floor to waltz. She always settled easily into his arms, her movements assured and unself-conscious. Desire, of course, was a much harder emotion to pin down, but the passion that had exploded between them in the patent office was too fervent to be only on one side.

Tuppence Templeton felt something for him, and if it wasn't love yet, he would woo her patiently, ardently, thoughtfully until it was. Trusting her to thwart Halesowen, protect Letty and rout FitzWalter was a very good start, for it proved unassailably that the gulf between them had narrowed. Ten years of listening to his fellow members of Parliament bluster had taught Gage one thing above all else: Deeds carried more weight than words. Oratory could soar, but actions changed the world.

Suddenly, Gage, who often felt impatient for minutes to pass but not days, couldn't wait for next Friday. He wanted all of this nonsense with FitzWalter behind them so he could start courting Tuppence properly. He would announce his intentions to her father and ask his permission.

No, he thought, shaking his head, that was a terrible idea, for if Tuppence's insistence on independence meant anything, it meant the right to decide for herself whom she married.

Instead, he would take the case to her, declaring his feelings and describing point by point their remarkable evolution. He would detail the many things he admired about her, outline the numerous ways they were suited to each other, and catalog the abundant benefits of their union. Inevitably, such a conversation entailed discussion of settlements, but the thought of broaching the topic with the lady in question, even one as unconventional as Tuppence, ran a little too against the grain. He would request permission to take the matter directly to her father.

Gage felt confident that such a display of thoughtful forbearance would earn her approval and affection.

It was a good plan, he decided, surprised yet pleased to discover that a public taproom and a tankard of beer could be as conducive to thought as a private study and a glass of brandy.

While he was settling his future, Tuppence was assessing the present and determined that enough time had passed since FitzWalter and his accomplice had left. Calling no more attention to herself than a mouse in a church, she stood up and walked—good God, was that a limp?—out of the tavern.

Not nearly as cautious, Gage waited only a minute before following her out of the establishment. He emerged into the weak sunlight of the alley to see her hack pulling away. Grateful, he tugged off the filthy navy coat and hat and dropped the items on a bench in front of the tavern where either its original owner could retrieve it or another lucky fellow could claim it.

Though *lucky* was a relative term, he thought with a grim smile, given their offensive odor.

Although such circumspection wasn't necessary, he followed the hack to make sure it deposited Tuppence safely on her doorstep. 'Twas obvious she wasn't in danger from the driver, who had waited patiently for more than an hour for her meeting to conclude, and if some misfortune should happen to befall her, he was confident she would contrive an escape. No, his decision to trail her coach home had nothing to do with necessity. He simply wanted to be near her a little bit longer and to enjoy the unexpected pleasure he derived from inconveniencing himself further on her behalf.

He was a man in love for the first time in his life and delighted in feeling foolish.

CHAPTER FOURTEEN

If Tuppence had learned one thing in her many years of scheming, it was never hinge a plan on an heiress. Young ladies who lived in expectation of inheriting a large fortune were reluctant to enter into elaborate schemes, a disinclination that made sense when one considered how many problems access to vast wealth solved. Furthermore, heiresses, as fortune hunters everywhere had discovered to their detriment, were difficult to come by. Their number was simply far too sparse to satisfy everyone's needs.

Tuppence's list, therefore, of heiresses who might be available to draw Halesowen's attention away from Letty was distressingly short. It had just three names on it, and the last two were included only to make her feel as though the pickings were not quite as slim as they were. But obviously, neither woman would do, for Miss Garstang's mumps were unlikely to miraculously disappear in time for her to attend Lady Sophia's ball four days hence, and Lady Agatha was too sincerely devoted to her fiancé to convince anyone she'd thrown him over for Mr. Halesowen.

No, the only viable contender was Miss Kennington, an Incomparable in her fifth season who had eluded all attempts to attach her. At twenty-four, she'd been out for almost as long as Tuppence, but her beauty and her wealth ensured that she remained popular. With bright-red curls, green eyes and ninety thousand pounds, she was sought after by suitors of every age, rank and distinction. Despite the constant assault, which Tuppence imagined would make her as prickly as Gage, she remained good-natured and affable. In addition, Miss Kennington was kind, clever and thoughtful.

She was also a close friend of the Harlow Hoyden.

That fact—more than her lack of mumps or fiancé—made her the ideal candidate, and Tuppence promptly sent a note to the duchess requesting an interview at her earliest convenience. She kept the tone even, giving no hint of her visit's confidential nature, and yet when the response arrived, it contained instructions for how to enter the residence via the side entrance if such discretion was necessary.

Although Tuppence didn't believe the precaution was called for, she certainly wasn't going to turn down the opportunity to enter a duke's house through the parlor window. As promised, there was a little footstool positioned against the building to make one's entrance graceful and elegant. Even with the added height of the low bench, she caught her skirt on a branch and—mortified by her own lack of agility—gave the mustard-yellow dress a hard tug. The material pulled free with a faint rip.

The duchess gave no indication she heard the tearing sound as she helped her over the frame of the window, and Tuppence ruthlessly pushed aside concern for her gown. Another day, she thought, another repair.

While Emma greeted her warmly, Tuppence examined the room, which seemed too bright and cheerful to be a solemn command center requiring a side entrance and a footstool.

"Thank you for agreeing to see me on such short notice," Tuppence said with a grateful smile. Despite the fact that she had done the Harlow sisters a good turn, she was still keenly aware of the elevated status of the woman before her. It wasn't every day that she had a tête-à-tête with a duchess.

"I was delighted to get your note," Emma insisted, leading her to the settee and gesturing for her to sit. "Do make yourself comfortable and tell me how we may be of assistance. Vinnie will be here any moment with refreshments."

The duchess had no sooner said the words than the door opened and her sister entered carrying a tray of tea and scones. She laid it on the table next to a daffodil-colored armchair and sat down.

"We weren't sure from your note what the appropriate level of furtiveness was for the visit," the duchess said, "so we settled on maximum stealthy."

The Marchioness of Huntly laughed. "*You* settled on maximum stealthy," she pointed out. "*I* settled on the front door and was told to go fetch the tea from the kitchens."

"To protect Miss Templeton's identity, of course," Emma explained reasonably to Vinnie, then turned to their guest. "Given your history of quietly sorting out other people's problems, it seemed likely that you wouldn't want anyone to know about your visit. The fact that you arrived via the side entrance would seem to confirm that."

"That window is wretched," her sister said sternly. "I hope you didn't get a cut or a splinter. Emma has destroyed more gloves climbing over that sill than I have in an entire career of gardening. Regardless, we're happy you're here and are eager to help. What can we do?"

Grateful for their generosity and enthusiasm, for neither woman seemed hesitant to lend her assistance, Tuppence accepted a cup of tea and launched into an explanation

"As Emma suggested, I'm indeed trying to sort out the problem of a friend. You recall Mr. FitzWalter, whose scheme to compromise Lady Letitia Perceval I scotched a few months ago?" she asked, tipping her eyes down as she realized what a ridiculous question it was to ask. Of course they recalled the incident, as it was the whole reason they'd sought her out. If she hadn't interfered in the Earl of Gage's personal business, they would never have met. "Despite my machinations, he's reappeared to try once again to charm Letty out of her portion. He has recruited a confederate who is equally without conscience and that is where I need your help. I have a plan to thwart him and I'm afraid it requires an heiress."

Given their well-known scarcity, Tuppence fully expected one of the Harlow sisters to ask her why she didn't enlist the earl in her efforts instead of such an elusive creature. Would it not be much easier to seek help from the man who had been living in her pocket for weeks?

She knew they had noticed because the whole world had noticed. Gage's incomprehensible courtship of her hadn't escaped the jaundiced eye of any member of the *ton*. After years of obscurity, she was the *on-dit* of the season, with most of the beau monde wondering with vague annoyance why such a mousy little nothing had suddenly risen to their attention. Surely, her relationship with Prickly Perceval was of particular interest to these two women, who knew precisely why her association with him had been renewed.

Bracing for the question, Tuppence couldn't figure out what answer she would give in response. Patently, it wouldn't be the truth, for despite the informality of their relationship, she couldn't very well launch into an agitated dissertation on the soul-destroying concession of accepting respect and admiration in place of love.

They would think her suited for Bedlam.

Alternatively, she could make up a convoluted story about why asking the earl for help simply wasn't possible. He was working on a very important act for Parliament that would affect the fate of the nation, for example, and couldn't be distracted with minor business. Or he was suffering from an egregiously pernicious illness and the troubling truth of his sister's situation might permanently derail his recovery.

Immediately dismissing both excuses as blatantly false and embarrassingly feeble, Tuppence felt even more demoralized by her inability to invent a plausible, last-minute fiction. Coming up with believable lies was one of her most reliable talents, and failing to do so now made her feel like less than herself.

Fortunately, neither sister broached the subject of the earl. Despite her concern, they were more interested in the details of her plan than the necessity for it.

"All the best schemes require heiresses," Emma observed.

Although she wasn't convinced that was true, Tuppence appreciated the encouragement and promptly explained FitzWalter's plot and Halesowen's place within it. "Letty seems to be genuinely in love with the gentleman, who is obviously a confirmed scoundrel, and I fear any attempt to enlighten her about his true nature might have the opposite effect. Women in love are not known for their rationality. Therefore, it's necessary that he demonstrate clearly and without any ambiguity who he really is."

"Enter the heiress," Vinnie said, holding out the teapot to offer her guest a refill.

Tuppence agreed to another cup and smiled at her host's ready grasp of the facts. "Yes, enter the heiress, who will welcome his attentions with such enthusiasm, he'll chuck Letty over the fence like muck from a stable."

"Because he won't have to give FitzWalter a share of the fortune, as he had secured it all on his own," Emma observed.

"Exactly," Tuppence said with satisfaction.

"If Letty is really in love with him, she will be devastated," Vinnie said sadly.

Tuppence couldn't deny the truth of the statement, but surely there were worse things than a broken heart, such as tethering yourself for all of eternity to a man who didn't love you. If one must endure pain regardless of what decision one made, then a short period of intense suffering was infinitely preferable to an interval that extended over years. It was the decision she had made for herself, and she knew Letty would be better for it over the long term.

"Devastated, yes, but smarter and stronger for it," the duchess said with calm practicality. "But let's not assume the worst. She's a young lady making her debut, and as a whole the species is prone to falling in love many times before the first season is over. With any luck, Mr. George Halesowen will merely be the second or third in a series."

"In the normal course of events that might very well have turned out to be true," Vinnie said, "but once his iniquity is revealed, he might take on a mythical quality and this incident could become the great blight of her life."

"Come now, Vinnie, you're doing it a bit brown," her sister said impatiently. "Every woman suffers a disappointment or two in her youth. No need to pitch a tent and set up a circus. Now, let's return to the matter at hand: A well-placed heiress will take care of one villain. What's your plan for the other?"

Grateful for Emma's pragmatism, as talk of great blights had had a disheartening effect on her spirits, Tuppence quickly outlined the second phase of her scheme. "During our first encounter, I threatened Mr. FitzWalter with exposure to his guardian, an upstanding gentleman who I'm sure would be appalled by his wicked behavior. That threat, however, was insufficiently daunting, so I'm left with no choice but to follow through and expose him fully. Anything less would leave other young ladies open to equally depraved treatment. The only way to do that unequivocally is to have his guardian as well as an infamous chatterbox discover him in the act of conspiring. I believe such a scene can be arranged by sending him a letter from Halesowen announcing the end of their agreement and his pending engagement to the heiress."

"FitzWalter will rush to confront him," Emma said with a nod of approval, "and you will ensure his guardian is there to witness the encounter."

"Hiding out of sight in the voluminous folds of the Petersons' drapery," Tuppence said, recalling her impromptu meeting with the Harlow Hoyden behind a curtain at Lord Clerkenwell's ball. "Lady Sophia's parents are throwing her a lavish ball on her birthday, and I noticed when I visited her after the run-in with Featherweight that the front parlor of their town house has several windows. I merely need to ensure that his guardian is amenable to such an arrangement."

"Who's the guardian?" Emma asked.

"Viscount Wallasey."

"Ah," Vinnie said, grasping at once the contrivance she hoped to use.

Experiencing no such flash of comprehension, Emma looked from her sister to her guest and then back again.

"Viscount Wallasey is a member of the Society for the Advancement of Horticultural Knowledge," Vinnie explained. "Tuppence wants to use the watering hose as a pretext to get Wallasey behind the curtain. What will you tell him? That you will trick me into confessing that I stole the invention from Tweedale?"

Emma shook her head. "No. You will do nothing that puts Vinnie's authorship at risk."

Although Tuppence had expected to encounter many obstacles to the fulfillment of her plan, this objection wasn't on her list of things to worry about, for it didn't matter what fiddle-faddle she promised Wallasey—or Tweedale, whose compliance was also necessary for her scheme to succeed. It would all be mere pretense. Nevertheless, she was mortified by the duchess's assumption and rushed to clarify her intention. "Naturally, I would never—"

"Of course you wouldn't," Vinnie said smoothly. "And neither would I. Your telling Wallasey a whisker to gain his compliance in no way puts my authorship at risk. I have no intention of confessing anything, and I'm sure Tweedale, who will have to witness the event for it to have any success, will forget all about my dreary watering hose as soon as FitzWalter opens his mouth, for he will have the *on-dit* of the century. I'm firmly convinced his lordship loves nothing more than a sensational story he can vouch for personally."

"As am I," Tuppence said, earnestly leaning forward as she sought the duchess's gaze. "I know it sounds self-serving, but I truly believe that witnessing such a scene will permanently distract Tweedale from the patent issue. All he really wants is to be at the center of a great drama, and what greater drama can there be than one seemingly respectable young man railing against another seemingly respectable young man for spoiling his plan to compromise an innocent young lady out of her fortune and being caught in the act by his stickler guardian? I'd be surprised if his lordship ever talked about anything else ever again."

"When you put it like that," Vinnie said, "I'm not sure I'd talk about anything else ever again either."

Emma sighed and conceded the soundness of Tuppence's reasoning. Nevertheless, she turned to her sister and sternly ordered her not to say a word in Tweedale's presence.

"You mustn't worry," Tuppence said. "Vinnie won't even be there."

The marchioness tilted her eyebrow in surprise. "I won't?"

"All I seek from you is permission to use your name," Tuppence explained. "Your presence isn't required for the success of the plan."

This announcement didn't sit well with the Duchess of Trent either. "Come now, my dear," she said, her tone stiff with rebuke, "surely you're not going to be so miserly with your spectacle as to deny us a front-row curtain. If we were plotting a display of equal magnificence, you'd be the first person we'd invite to observe."

Even though the actual number of curtains in Lady Peterson's front parlor eluded her at the moment—she could picture two large windows in the front, but were there two windows along the side wall or three—Tuppence immediately apologized and assured both women they were welcome to view the proceedings. "My intention wasn't to exclude you from the denouement but to minimize your involvement, as you must have more important things to do. But I'd be very grateful if you did stay, for additional, unimpeachable sources would be very useful. Tweedale's penchant for embellishment makes some of his stories difficult to swallow. If you recall, in the first telling of Mr. Askern's accident, the horse was of fairly average height; in the second account it had grown to twenty hands; and by the time he was telling the tale to Prinny, the horse that threw Askern in the Serpentine was as tall as a giraffe."

"Something more important than exposing a villain?" Emma asked. "You credit us with lives far more interesting than the ones we lead. Now that the general plan has been explained, let's return to the important details and the real purpose of your visit: You wish me to arrange an interview with Miss Kennington and vouch for the merit of your scheme."

Although Tuppence was startled by the Harlow Hoyden's ready deduction, she wasn't entirely surprised, as the scarcity of heiresses was a problem known to everyone. "Correct. I have considered all the likely prospects and decided that Miss Kennington fits my requirements the best."

Emma's dimples glinted as she smiled. "You mean, because she's not stricken by illness or engaged to be married?"

Tuppence shrugged, as if helpless. "Yes."

"She'll listen," Vinnie offered. "I'm not sure if she'll consent, but she would certainly keep an open mind as you explained the predicament. Don't you agree, Emma?"

Her sister agreed at once and walked to the large mahogany desk near the side entrance to write her friend a missive. "I'll ask the footman to stay to receive her reply. Vinnie, run down and get a fresh pot of tea while we wait."

The idea of the Marchioness of Huntly fetching anything for her, let alone tea from the kitchens, embarrassed Tuppence and she said with firm conviction, "My tea is still quite warm."

To her guest's horror, Vinnie scoffed at the notion of serving tepid tea and promptly stood up to remedy the situation. Tuppence, her cheeks bright red, suggested that they send for a servant instead, as her visit did not require secrecy. Vinnie rang the bell over the protests of her sister, who argued in favor of extreme caution in this circumstance and urged Tuppence to quickly hide under the desk before Caruthers entered.

Although the thought of scurrying under a large piece of furniture, especially in a dress that was already torn, held little appeal, Tuppence rose to her feet, as it seemed like the only polite thing to do. After all, the Harlow Hoyden wasn't merely a duchess, she was also her host. She sat down again, however, at Vinnie's insistence.

"Emma thinks every circumstance requires extreme caution," she observed.

"Not every," her grace countered with obvious offense. "Most."

Vinnie laughed and claimed there was very little difference between the two, an opinion that further offended her sister. Emma, who was capable of writing a letter to her friend and defending her point of view at the same time, broke off when a knock sounded at the door.

"Excellent," her grace said, sealing the missive in an envelope as Caruthers entered carrying a tray with freshly brewed tea and another batch of warm scones. She handed off the note to the footman, sat down next to her sister on the settee and promised Tuppence they would hear back from Miss Kennington within the hour. "Kate is always very prompt."

Her estimate struck Tuppence as overly optimistic, but rather than quibble about timing, she accepted another cup of tea and raised the next issue to be settled: forging in

Halesowen's own hand the letter to FitzWalter that announced his pending engagement to the heiress.

"I assume you have someone on retainer, as your forgery of the patent application was impeccable," she explained.

"Indeed we do," Emma said and agreed to contact her forger should the plan go forward with Miss Kennington's approval.

Grateful, Tuppence nodded, selected a scone with currants and settled into conversation with the two women. Although she had responsibilities at home—among them resuming Caroline's lessons, which had come to a halt five days before when she'd begun her surveillance of FitzWalter—she gave them no further thought as Vinnie entertained them with stories of the most recent meeting of the British Horticultural Society and Emma discussed their latest scheme to help a friend gain entrance to the Royal Academy of Arts.

It was, Tuppence decided, a lovely way to spend an hour, with warm buttery scones and lively conversation. And yet even as she enjoyed the experience, she was made keenly uncomfortable by how thoroughly they kept the topic away from her and the Earl of Gage. The effort had to be monumental, as several times the exchange seemed to veer suddenly down that path only to be nimbly thrust in another direction by one of the sisters. It was a feat both impressive and oppressive, for she could feel their curiosity weighing on her like a heavy blanket. Surely, they were dying to know how the ape leader and the prickly lord had managed to forge a romantic relationship, especially when she'd been so resolute in her determination never to speak to him again.

And now she appeared to be on the verge of marrying him.

Just wait a few days, she thought cynically, and everything will change again. Gage will drop her like a rotten turnip, and she will return to spinsterish obscurity. The natural order of the *ton* will be restored.

She was at once terrified of the moment and impatient for it to come, for inhabiting the middle space of inevitably was intolerable.

"And then Mr. Capell replied, 'I named the roses Margaret and Melanie, not my daughters,'" Vinnie said in a low voice meant to imitate her horticultural colleague's baritone, "which deeply offended Lord Morton, who *had* named his twins Margaret and Melanie."

"An insult of the highest order," Emma said with admiration. "Did Capell plant him a facer? I wager he did. Capell is a pugnacious fellow. He once threatened to clean Phillip's clock for spilling some brandy at White's."

"They had tea," Vinnie said. "Mr. Berry brought in the serving tray, and we all partook of refreshment."

"If I didn't already find your horticultural society to be a bafflingly dull institution, I'd give it that designation now. Souchong instead of boxing," she said, shaking her head, clearly as confused as ever.

"I think it's delightful," Tuppence said, imagining a roomful of sullen gardeners sitting down for tea.

Before Vinnie could agree to this observation, Caruthers knocked on the door and announced the arrival of Miss Kennington. Although her visit was unscheduled, Emma calmly received her as if she'd been expecting her at any moment. "I knew you wouldn't be able to resist the lure of an escapade."

"If by 'lure,' you mean the insuppressible obligation to talk you out of it, then, yes, I wasn't able to resist," Miss Kennington said with amusement. "But I'm surprised to see Vinnie here. She can usually be relied upon to temper your more outlandish ideas."

"It was my idea," Tuppence said immediately, a slight blush rising in her cheeks as she stood to address the new arrival. Although they'd never had occasion to meet, she was quite familiar with the sought-after beauty, for she had a quality that made her stand out in any surrounding, even the sunny interior of the duchess's study. With her shiny red curls and vivid green eyes, she sparkled with precisely the sort of vibrancy Tuppence lacked, a fact that had been pointed out to her with deadening repetition by her father. It hardly mattered to her sire that, five seasons in, Miss Kennington's success on the marriage mart was no more impressive than hers, for her physical perfection assured that she was judged by a different standard. Not a single eyebrow was raised when she summarily cut Lord Hastings, whom everyone expected her to marry. The assumption, which was widely bandied about with ruthless indifference for her victim, was that she could do better than a mere viscount. Someone with her appearance and fortune could look as high as a royal duke.

As much as Tuppence resented the existence of a second set of rules for people of beauty, she bore no ill will toward Miss Kennington. It wasn't her fault the world was grievously unfair, and despite the many advantages of her situation, she remained unaffected and kind.

Nevertheless, Tuppence felt her courage falter as she raised her eyes to meet the gaze of the other woman. To formulate an elaborate scheme based entirely on a complete stranger's willingness to court a scoundrel suddenly seemed like foolish presumption, especially when the stranger in question clearly disapproved of escapades.

And yet even as she wondered if she truly had the impertinence to make such a request, she launched into an apology that doubled as an explanation. "I'm the one who came up with the outlandish scheme, and I'm truly sorry you felt compelled to come straight here to dissuade the duchess from implementing it. I understand your concerns and applaud the good sense that questions its soundness. Nonetheless, I cannot conceive of another way to save an innocent young woman from misery and lifelong disappointment, so I hope you will hear me out and consider what I propose. I am Tuppence Templeton," she said, vaguely aware that she should have introduced herself sooner, perhaps before mentioning misery and lifelong disappointments, which were rather heavy subjects for strangers. "We've never met, but I've admired your sense of independence for quite a while."

Although Tuppence knew the value of a well-placed compliment and wasn't above employing one when it suited her purpose, she was entirely sincere in her statement. Despite the many offers Miss Kennington had received—and Tuppence had to assume they numbered in the dozens by now—she'd decided to remain unwed until an aspirant met all her qualifications. Even Lord Hastings, a top-of-the-trees Corinthian with an excellent seat and an affable demeanor, fell short of her requirements and was abruptly shown the door. Like Tuppence, she expected more from marriage than the approval of her parents and society. Unlike Tuppence, she'd managed to hold on to both despite her failure.

Miss Kennington, her manners corrupted by more than a decade of friendship with the ill-bred Harlow Hoyden, forthrightly held out her hand in greeting. "Thank you, Miss Templeton. It's a pleasure to meet you. I do tend to keep my own counsel, it's true, and have been blessed with parents who trust me to know what is best for myself. More important, however, I'm in possession of a sizable trust, and in my experience the person with the largest fortune in the room is always correct. This gives the appearance of independence but is in fact just plain old sycophancy."

Expecting neither the handshake nor the ruthless candor, Tuppence stared at the heiress for a few moments before belatedly gripping her hand. "Now I admire your honesty."

"And I admire yours," Miss Kennington said, sitting down in one of the armchairs. "Let us waste no time, then, in discussing the particulars of your plan. My immediate impulse is to politely decline, as I can see no value in poking at Mr. FitzWalter, who, though immature for the age of twenty-three, is far from spoiled. He simply needs a bit of seasoning, which a few years in London will give him."

"On the contrary, Miss Kennington," Tuppence said sharply, "he's rotten to the core."

Struck by the severity of her tone, the other woman tilted her head and asked thoughtfully, "Is he?"

Tuppence nodded, sat back down and gave her new acquaintance a comprehensive account of her history with the unseasoned young man. She provided the place, date and time of each encounter and named all the players, including Lady Letitia, for she trusted the heiress and knew that sparing the details would undermine her case. She even produced FitzWalter's letter to Mrs. Shipton, the society matron who, whilst hosting a weekend party for her niece's friends, had agreed to get Letty drunk in order to lead her to the wrong room.

"You have only my word that the missive is authentic," she conceded while Miss Kennington read the note, "but I hope you'll believe that I'm not trying to harm an innocent young man for malicious and private reasons. FitzWalter has ensnared a dear friend of mine in an evil scheme, and all I hope to do is free her from it in the most effective way possible and ensure that no other young lady is subjected to his mistreatment. I think this plan would accomplish both objectives."

"I agree," the duchess said, endorsing the scheme. "It's a little more convoluted than I'd like, as arranging people behind curtains is an inexact science, but it will get the job done."

Her friend smiled. "Yes, you do prefer a more forthright approach, like blackmail or pistols at dawn."

Emma scoffed. "Don't be absurd. I've never engaged in a duel."

"Not for want of trying," Vinnie observed with a trace of humor as she reached for the teapot to refill her guests' cups. "By my count, you've issued the challenge three times, including once to my husband."

"He shouldn't have called you a nickninny," Emma said.

"*You* called me a nickninny. Felix only agreed," she said, skillfully pouring the tea with one hand while removing the lid from the sugar basin with the other.

"Exactly," Emma said, as if Vinnie had just proved her point. "I'm your sister and have earned the right to call you a nickninny or a ninnyhammer or a peagoose—all of which you were for not filing a patent application straightaway. Huntly has not. He may consult with me again in twenty years and petition for the privilege. Until then, he will continue to receive challenges."

"And there's Mr. Jarrow," Miss Kennington said, "of whom you demanded satisfaction during the floral exhibition at Kew."

Vinnie looked with surprise as she handed Tuppence a fresh cup of tea. "My Mr. Jarrow? From the horticultural society?"

"He called Trent's roses blowsy," Emma said, her tone implying that this statement explained everything.

"'Twas a compliment," her sister said, shaking her head. "It meant they'd bloomed fully."

While the duchesses protested the use of ambiguous terminology in describing flowers, Tuppence smiled blandly and ordered herself to remain patient. As frustrating as it was to listen to the conversation digress toward trivial topics, she couldn't fault the women for teasing each other. Miss Kennington had been their friend for a long time, and it was clear that the bond was deep and firmly established.

Eventually, after a painfully long catalog of adjectives Emma considered acceptable, Miss Kennington returned the conversation to the matter at hand and consented to encourage Halesowen's suit.

"Not because Emma gave it her seal of approval," she was quick to point out, "but because Vinnie did. I agree it's a sound plan and has a very good chance of succeeding. When do we begin?"

"Immediately," Tuppence said, at once relieved to have her help and anxious at how many ways the plan could go awry. "Lady Sophia's ball is in six days, so we have no time to lose. I will drop hints in Halesowen's ear this afternoon when he accompanies Letty and me on a drive in Hyde Park. Perhaps you might be interested in taking the air during the fashionable hour as well?"

Miss Kennington announced that a drive around six o'clock sounded delightful, and arrangements were made.

CHAPTER FIFTEEN

Given how assiduously Letty hung on Mr. Halesowen's sleeve, Tuppence was forced to employ an extreme tactic to extricate the young suitor from her custody.

"It's terribly unfair of you to assert, Lord Gage, that all Minerva Press novels have a corrupting influence on the thinking ability of their readers," she said when the earl paused for breath in his defense of the Health and Morals of Apprentices Act, which Halesowen had criticized yet again. Having provoked Letty's guardian into a satisfying lather once by arguing in favor of factory owners, he'd returned to the topic over and over in hopes of replicating the outcome. Although Gage dutifully complied every time, raising his voice in scorn at the outrageously ignorant opinion expressed, his language became increasingly simplistic, and he spoke slower and slower until it was clear that he thought he was talking to an imbecile.

Tuppence was vastly encouraged by the display, for surely a man of such limited intelligence and creativity would easily swallow the nonsensical story she was about to feed him.

"Letty, for instance, remains as sharp as ever," she added, observing the confused expression on the earl's face, "and it's deeply insulting of you to suggest otherwise."

Although profoundly distracted from most mundane matters by her infatuation with Mr. Halesowen—or George, as she had lately taken to calling him—Letty raised her head sharply at this information. "Excuse me?"

Tuppence kindly explained further. "Regardless of what your brother thinks, I don't consider the fact that you left your reticule in the carriage last night a sign of reduced mental capacity. I believe you're as clever as ever."

The color in her cheeks rising with her outrage, Letty stepped away from Halesowen to confront her brother, whose baffled look had switched to shock. "How dare you impugn my intelligence!"

Gage opened his mouth, clearly prepared to deny the charge, which, to his credit, he'd never actually made, but first he darted a quick glance at Tuppence. Finding something in her expression, he changed his mind and said, "Well, it *is* the first time you've left anything behind, and I did see you reading two different Minerva Press novels this week."

Tuppence had no idea why he would do something so illogical as to decide to draw Letty's ire, but she was grateful and sent him a smile.

Only it wasn't a smile but rather a bright, beaming grin of surprise and delight that she and the earl had somehow arranged their thoughts in synchronicity so that he seemed to know what she required without her asking.

The smile was so bright, Gage stared, transfixed, while Letty rang a peel over his head for his small-minded notions.

With effort, Tuppence pulled her eyes away from the earl and glanced briefly to her left to confirm that Miss Kennington was in the appointed spot.

Very good.

"Mr. Halesowen," she said, threading her arm through his, "you must allow me to tell you how very ardently I admire you."

If he found the unprecedented familiarity disconcerting, he was too pleased by the compliment to display it. "Of course, Miss Templeton. It would be surly of me to try to dissuade a lady from speaking her mind."

"You have such charming manners," she said approvingly. "It's no wonder that Letty is so smitten."

"You think so?" he asked, his tone a mix of uncertainty and satisfaction.

"Does that please you?" she asked. "I think it does. And naturally that makes me only admire you more, for any other gentleman would have had his head turned by an heiress such as Miss Kennington. But you are steady, Mr. Halesowen. Steady, reliable and honorable."

"Certainly, Miss Tuppence, I'm smitten with Letty...I mean, Lady Letitia...too and I would never—" He broke off as the conviction with which he spoke gave way to confusion and curiosity. "I'm sorry, did you say Miss Kennington?"

Although a light, teasing chuckle perfectly suited the moment, Tuppence laughed with sincere appreciation at the hopefulness of his tone. "You don't have to pretend with me. I know you've noticed Miss Kennington's interest. It's all right. I won't tell Letty. Her happiness is very important to me, and I would certainly never cause her needless worry about such a trifle. We both know you're too honorable to throw her over for a fortune, no matter how many lures the heiress casts in your direction."

Halesowen wasn't clever enough to disguise his blatant interest. "Of course. Of course. Far too honorable indeed. But, tell me, Miss Kennington has been casting lures in my direction? Are you sure?"

Tuppence giggled again to underscore her incredulity. "As if you don't see the young lady in question right there"—she tilted her head to the left to indicate the heiress's position—"looking at us."

Not bothering to replicate the discretion of her nod, he tilted his entire head to the left and looked straight at Miss Kennington, who returned his gaze unflinchingly. Then she curled her lips into a hesitant smile and lifted her hand a little to greet him shyly. Tuppence watched in fascination as his expression went from disbelieving to doubtful to unsure to certain. It took only a dozen seconds and little more than a bashful wave.

"And that is exactly why I admire you so much, Mr. Halesowen, because you aren't tempted by her vast wealth, not even a little," Tuppence added, smothering a grin as she watched his eyes narrow in consideration of all that lovely money at his disposal. His interest had clearly been whetted, and she leaned in a little to deliver the coup de grâce. "It must be so appealing to imagine a fortune like hers without an older brother to interfere in your business and disapprove of your opinions, which are so well articulated, by the way. No doubt it's daunting to think of someone like Prickly Perceval always looking over your shoulder, always trying to control your life. Indeed, Miss Kennington doesn't have any siblings and is wholly in possession of her fortune so you wouldn't have to share it with anyone at all. It would all be yours—yours and your wife's without anyone else involved. What a lovely prospect that would be for some men. But not you, Mr. Halesowen. Your head isn't turned by thoughts of an easier life. You're a man of true mettle, and for that I will be eternally grateful."

Afraid she might be doing it a bit too brown, Tuppence ceased talking and gave him an opportunity to ruminate on her words. She could tell by his abstracted air that he was giving serious contemplation to the alternate future she described—one without the Earl of Gage always at his elbow disapproving, one without FitzWalter taking half of a fortune he wasn't entitled to.

He was hooked, Tuppence thought, and she remained silent as they strolled down the path. It was easy enough to do, as he had no interest in conversation. Rather, he turned his head around at regular intervals to stare at Miss Kennington, who maintained a pose of abashed interest with brilliant precision. She never quite looked up. She never quite looked down. She never quite averted her gaze.

Tuppence was genuinely impressed and couldn't wait to congratulate the young woman on playing her part so beautifully.

While Halesowen reassessed his options for a comfortable future, Letty continued to berate her brother over his uncharitable and narrow view of Minerva Press novels, demonstrating fully that her ability to quarrel had in no way been affected adversely by Gothic stories. If anything, the repeated exposure to the overwrought and erudite tales of Mrs. Radcliffe and her ilk had expanded her vocabulary and honed the tenor of her argument. She even made a detailed list of the countries she'd learned about, thanks to the books' foreign settings.

The earl submitted meekly to this treatment, listening to Letty's tirade without saying a word and intermittently glancing at Tuppence with an exaggerated expression of defeat.

His decision to silently accept a punishment he'd done nothing to earn endeared him to Tuppence in a way she had never imagined possible, and she felt a wave of affection sweep through her. Suddenly, all she wanted to do was wrap her arms around him, lay her head on his shoulder and hold on to him with all her might. The sensation was so strong, she almost couldn't breathe, and recognizing it as love, she ruthlessly pushed it away.

When Letty decided her brother had been sufficiently admonished—or, Tuppence thought with amusement, when she'd simply run out of insults—she reclaimed Halesowen's attention. He gave it to her at once, complimenting her on having the proper amount of feeling while suggesting her arguments might be more persuasive if she could keep her passions in check. To Tuppence's annoyance, she accepted the criticism with a placid smile and calmly asked him which Gothic he'd found most educational in terms of its location.

Having overheard the details of his plot with FitzWalter, Tuppence knew his interest in such books had been feigned to manufacture a bond between him and Letty, and she wasn't surprised when he floundered for an informed response. First he stalled for time by listing all the countries he'd always wanted to visit (France, Switzerland, Italy, Greece—the grand tour essentially), then explained why travel to those places had always been beyond his means (sickly mother, bad investments, monsoon off the coast of India), and ended with an observation about foreign governments' bearing respect for their factory owners and not burdening them with unfair regulations that minimized their profits.

Naturally, Prickly Perceval could not let such an assertion stand and immediately leaped to the defense of the Health and Morals of Apprentices Act. As the conversation devolved into yet another lecture on the necessity of laborer protections—this time pitched to a half-wit and limited to words of one syllable—Tuppence wondered why Gage allowed himself to be so easily provoked. Surely, he had more important things to do with his time and temper than to try to reason with a simpleton who showed no capacity for learning.

Although he was perhaps not entirely a simpleton, Tuppence thought with amusement, as the conversation never did return to the topic of Gothic novels. The earl held court for ten minutes on his pet subject before they were hailed by a friend of Letty's who proposed an excursion to Vauxhall Gardens to watch the fireworks in a few days.

"That would be delightful," Letty said, looking eagerly from her brother to her suitor for agreement. "I should enjoy that above all things."

Halesowen, his neck craning as he examined the surrounding crowd for the sight of bright-red curls, absently fell in line with the plan.

Tuppence could not have been more satisfied with how well the first phase of her scheme had gone and was gratified even more when, the next day, Miss Kennington reported that she had successfully bumped into Halesowen in front of the Elgin marbles at the British Museum. As he was unencumbered by Letty at the time, he was able to converse freely with the young heiress, who gaped with astonishment at his impressive knowledge of antiquities.

"I don't think he knows where the marbles came from," Miss Kennington said to Tuppence several hours later at Mrs. Settle's rout. "The first time he said Pantheon, I assumed it was an oversight, as the two names are easy to confuse. But then he spoke of it being in Turin, though I suspect he meant Rome, and I realized he doesn't have a clue. Nevertheless, I plied him with compliments in my giddiest tone, which actually wasn't that difficult, as everything he said was genuinely remarkable to me. To be honest, I'm shocked we have to make any effort to thwart him, as he seems a little too stupid to cause anyone harm. Can't we simply turn him in another direction and advise him to walk off a cliff?"

Tuppence laughed at the image of Halesowen blithely toppling over the edge of a precipice because he was too dim-witted to realize there was a drop. "That's exactly what we're doing."

Miss Kennington smiled. "I'm the cliff?"

"You're the cliff," Tuppence said.

The heiress paused a moment to consider the description and decided she rather liked it. "I wonder if I can have visiting cards drawn up that say precisely that."

Her fortune was so vast, Tuppence thought, she could have visiting cards drawn up that said she was the Prince Regent. "He will be here tonight, as Mr. Settle is friendly with his father, who cannot attend as he is home in the country nursing a broken foot."

"Yes, he said something similar when I asked him this afternoon. As he's already arranged to fetch me a glass of lemonade, I assume Lady Letitia will not be in attendance?" she asked.

"No, Letty is attending the theater with her aunt and

Gage went to his club this evening," Tuppence said, then immediately felt her face flush as she realized there was no reason for her to mention the earl. Miss Kennington did not ask for his movements, nor did she care about them. Fortunately, her inordinately red cheeks could be attributed to the overly warm drawing room, which had more guests than space. Even though the two women had secured a private corner to conduct their conversation, they found themselves constantly jostled by the company.

If Miss Kennington thought the reference to the Earl of Gage was bizarre or revealing, she gave no indication. "Very good. I shall flirt shamelessly with him, though, of course, with discretion, as I do not want to alert his friend to the possibility of a match. That must come as a surprise at the right moment."

"Agreed. And although Halesowen is a dolt, I think he's clever enough to understand on a visceral level that his friend shouldn't discover the truth until he's resolved his future," she said, then swallowed a yelp of pain when a passing elbow prodded her forcefully in the back. "Now, I should probably locate my sister in this crush before it becomes entirely impossible to move."

"Yes, you should," Miss Kennington said firmly. "And I shall find myself a comfortable spot where I can keep a cautious eye on the front door, so I can see when he arrives. And while I'm arranging things, I shall also make sure I'm talking to a rich, handsome lord who is a few years his senior so that he doesn't think the matter is entirely resolved. He might grow suspicious if he doesn't have to pursue me at all."

Tuppence appreciated the soundness of her logic as well as the natural confidence that assumed a rich, handsome lord of approximately thirty years of age could be conjured at the precise moment one was needed.

Her appreciation continued to grow in the days that followed, as it became increasingly apparent that Halesowen was fully convinced of the heiress's affection. Another man, perhaps one with less self-assurance and more introspection, might wonder why the glittering prize of the beau monde, who had withstood the charms of dandies, bucks, rakes and Corinthians, had quietly slipped into his pocket.

Halesowen, however, considered it his due and blithely began canceling plans with Letty. First he was an hour late for their appointment at the circulating library, owing to an unavoidable family emergency involving an illness, a bad investment and a monsoon off the coast of India. That it was the same excuse he'd given for why he'd never taken a grand tour escaped Letty's notice, most likely because she was too concerned about the health of his mother (or father or sister or uncle—it was impossible to know which, as he hadn't said). But Gage observed the similarity and raised his eyebrow at Tuppence.

Next, Halesowen withdrew from their outing to Vauxhall on the vague pretext that he had to review accounts with his steward. It was a confusing excuse, as one's ledgers were usually perused during the day and it seemed churlish to make one's steward work through the night when there was a perfectly good morning in the offing. Letty accepted it with equanimity and even volunteered to hold off on the excursion until they were both free to attend, an act of particular maturity and generosity, as she was very much looking forward to the fireworks.

Her suitor insisted he didn't deserve such consideration, which Tuppence heartfully agreed was true, and said that she must go without him. "So you can give me a detailed description of the display."

Despondent, Letty nonetheless rallied to the cause and went to Vauxhall fierce in her determination to remember every single thing that occurred. She even wrote notes after she got home, so that she could give Halesowen an accurate report when he called the next day.

But he didn't call the next day, despite his intention, nor did he send a note explaining his absence.

More than disappointed, Letty was simply confused

by his failure to appear, convinced that some great misunderstanding had happened or that his letter had been inadvertently misplaced. It was, she insisted, lying forlornly in a tray by the door buried under a stack of calling cards and invitations.

If only Hobson the butler knew to look for it.

A note finally did arrive two days later, on the day before the Peterson ball, when Tuppence was paying a call. Ostensibly she was there to return a book of Gage's that she had borrowed, but in reality she simply wanted to spend as much time with him as possible. The final phase of her plan had arrived at last, and now only thirty hours remained before the earl knew the truth. Only thirty hours until he discovered that she'd openly defied him, that she had once again solved the problem of his sister's future without turning to him for help. Only thirty hours until he ended their association.

There was no way his affection would overcome his indignation.

Disheartened, she gave no indication of her true feelings as she sat in the front parlor and entertained him with Dr. Singleham's opinion of *An Illustrated History of Trepanation of the Skull*. It went without saying that the fictitious doctor, whom she'd invented during their first carriage ride to the patent office, had many outlandish ideas, only some of which were based on actual science.

"The disparity in understanding can be explained very simply, I think," she said, employing the same tone she used when lecturing Caroline on history or science, "by the fact that Mr. Bell is considering only the male brain and Dr. Singleham considers both the male and female brains in his study. He works from the assumption, which is radical in some circles, I know, that women are human beings too, with differing processes that are equally legitimate. This is why his map of the brain contains an area called the 'hyper-hypocritus,' which is devoted exclusively to defending ourselves against male hypocrisy."

Although Gage smiled at the clarification, he observed with equal solemnity that there must be a corresponding region in the male brain focused solely on creating hypocrisies.

Tuppence was about to alert him to the presence of the hypo-hypocritus when Letty entered the room, a letter held aloft in her hand.

"Here it is," she said, pulling the note from its envelope, impatient to discover what it said. "No doubt Hobson *finally* sorted through the invitations and found it gathering dust under Lady Carmichael's garden—"

The letter fell to the floor as Letty let out an anguished shriek, covered her mouth with her hand and ran from the room. With a baffled glance at Tuppence, the earl picked up the letter and quickly perused its contents. It was brief, reducing a six-week courtship to half as many lines stating that he no longer believed they had enough in common to make a match of it. He was sorry for the pain this information might cause, hopeful she would recover swiftly from the blow and eager to meet again as friends.

Even though she knew a few days of heartache were infinitely better than a lifetime of regret, Tuppence still felt like a monster for causing Letty's distress. How quickly her countenance had changed, how swiftly the color had drained from her cheeks—from happy to hopeless in a fraction of a second.

The way he did it, with a letter, was an act of needless cruelty.

With all that she knew of Halesowen, it had never occurred to her that he'd end the relationship any way other than honorably and in person. To break a young girl's heart via the post was craven, callous and caddish.

Everything you needed to know about the gentleman was contained in that single deed.

She hoped Letty would realize that when the misery subsided.

If she didn't, Tuppence would be happy to explain it.

The more pressing matter at the moment, however, was how the earl would respond. Autocratic, of course, and high-handed, he was still a fond brother, and she couldn't imagine his taking this treatment lightly. No doubt some part of him would be relieved to be spared an endless string of family suppers with that dullard, to never have to painstakingly explain the merits of the Health and Morals of Apprentices Act again, but that nugget of gratitude would be overwhelmed by disgust and fury.

Would he call Halesowen out?

Could this situation, which she'd had so tightly under her control, veer wildly into chaos like that, with Gage's life suddenly and horribly at risk?

No, she thought, her heart pounding. No. She wouldn't accept that as a consequence, and if he was determined to storm out of the room and order Halesowen to name his second, then she wouldn't let him leave the room. She would imprison him in the front parlor using...using...her eyes swept the room...the cord from the curtains! She would tie him to a chair using the cord from the curtains until the anger passed.

Obviously, the plan presented some logistical challenges, namely, how to get Gage in the chair while at the same time removing the cord from the drapes without arousing suspicion. It seemed daunting, to be sure, but there were two things largely in her favor: a pair of bergères located within convenient proximity of the curtains and the fact that wrath dulled one's awareness. If she stoked his ire further, he would be too distracted to notice her fingers making quick work of the cord knot. To get him into the chair, all she had to do was sit down herself, for he was far too much of a gentleman to loom menacingly over a lady.

But how to strengthen his anger without driving him directly from the room? It would require subtlety. She couldn't simply announce that Halesowen deserved to be run through with a sword. Rather, she could remark on how unexpected this turn was and that he'd always *seemed* like a perfect gentleman and perhaps then list ways in which he obviously was *not* a gentleman. The plan hinged on the tone she used, for she did not want to sound as if she was chastising Gage for his obliviousness while at the same time chastising Gage for his obliviousness. It would require—

Tuppence did not get any further in her scheming, for she was suddenly and abruptly encased in the earl's arms with his lips pressed ardently against hers.

How did it happen? She didn't know. A moment ago, he'd been consumed with fury and now he was acting in lust.

It made no sense. Did he not care that his sister's heart had just been ruthlessly crushed under the heel of a callous fortune hunter? Was he indifferent to her suffering?

These questions went unanswered as the part of her brain devoted to making sense of the world was overtaken by the ache. With breathtaking swiftness, her body was awash in desire, in sensation, in awareness, and she felt a longing so intense, she was positive she could merge her body with his if she could simply press against him hard enough. Every moment that she remained separate was equal parts painful and delightful, and when he tugged the bodice of her dress down to reveal her breasts, when he took those eager peaks into his mouth, it felt as though something unbearably elusive had suddenly drawn closer.

It wasn't fulfillment, no, but it was a satisfaction of sorts, and she dropped her head back and whimpered. She wanted so much more. How could she get it? What did she need to do?

She would do anything.

"Marry me," the earl said, his voice barely a husky whisper as he issued the request. "Marry me this instant." He pressed his lips against her cheek and her chin and her ear as he spoke, making her shiver with the intimacy of his tone. "Marry me. You must. I have never…you are…"

Unable to finish the thought, he tightened his arms and kissed her again, his tongue ravaging her mouth, his hands exploring her body, the rough fabric of his shirt pressing against her breasts and driving her mad.

"Marry me," he said with fervent urgency. "Marry me."

Tuppence might have said yes. In her mind, she screamed it vehemently over and over and over: yes, yes, yes, yes, yes. In the embrace with Gage, she might have murmured it incoherently.

But despite the yearning and the desperation and the passion that seemed to turn her entire body into a quivering mass of molten lava, she was still Tuppence Templeton, ape leader and pedant. No matter how compromised her faculties were by desire, she couldn't let herself make a rash decision. Sure, she could say yes now and savor the giddy thrill of belonging to Gage for a little while. She could revel in the joy and the novelty and the unprecedented freedom to follow an impulse to its natural conclusion, but it would all come to an abrupt end when the earl discovered the truth. In just thirty hours, every aspect of her plan would be revealed, and Gage, seeing her clearly perhaps for the first time, would understand just how inured she was to his expectations. He would know that he'd engaged himself to a headstrong harridan who wouldn't comply with his demands, no matter how staunchly he issued them. He would realize he'd bound his future to a woman who would blatantly disregard his own conscience every time it was in conflict with hers.

At that moment, he would have two options: rescind his offer or keep it in place. Of course, for a man like him, there actually weren't any options. His sense of decency would never let him break his bond, and he would go to the altar with her regardless of how much he loathed her in his heart. He was just honorable enough to make them both miserable.

It would fall to her, then, to end their association, and what a commotion that would cause—the long-in-the-tooth Miss Templeton having the gall to throw over any suitor, let alone one as rich and high on the flagpole as the Earl of Gage. The scandal wouldn't last long, for she wasn't important enough to engender lasting interest from the *ton*, but in general she thought it was better to avoid being a nine days' wonder if one could.

Knowing she had to break them apart, Tuppence pressed herself closer to Gage, her tongue ravaging his mouth now as she sought to imprint every moment on her soul. She never wanted to forget what it felt like, to be desired beyond reason by the man she loved.

She kissed him again and again, arms wrapped so tightly around him it was as though she would never let go.

And then she stepped back.

Calmly, as if her heart weren't pounding wildly, as if the fingers straightening her gown weren't trembling madly, as if tears weren't threatening to dissolve her hard-won resolution, she said, "No, thank you, my lord."

It was a splash of icy water, her rejection, and he stiffened at once, his eyes shedding the veil of desire so quickly and forcefully she could almost believe she'd imagined it.

When he didn't speak, when he didn't say a single word in response, she realized he was too surprised to formulate an immediate reply.

Of course he was, for he had every reason to expect an exhilarated yes. He was the Earl of Gage, by God, and met every woman's requirements for a suitable husband: wealthy, titled, handsome, respected. So what if he had an ornery disposition? He was not immune to reason and could be brought to agreement if the disputant was able to make a sound argument.

He was, in common parlance, a catch, and no woman in her right mind would turn him down.

Was she in her right mind?

Tuppence didn't know the answer to that.

As she watched Gage struggle to absorb the shock of

her rejection, as she saw the disappointment mingle with confusion, she found herself wanting to offer him comfort. Despite what this looks like, she longed to say, I'm doing you a favor. Give it thirty hours, my lord. Just one more day and you'll be grateful for the bullet you dodged.

She couldn't say that, of course, for to reveal her plan now might mean undermining it, so she could do nothing to mitigate his bafflement and dismay. Instead, she thanked him for the monumental honor he'd done her in making an offer and assured him she would be forever grateful.

"But, no, I cannot marry you," she said and walked out of the room with quiet dignity, her head straight, her shoulders back. She didn't run or scurry, although she wanted to both run and scurry so that the tears and the pounding and the trembling could finally be free to overtake her. Rather, she kept her pace steady as she passed through the hall, crossed the front path and turned onto the sidewalk. Her stride remained smooth long after she was out of view of the earl's town house and even after she'd climbed the steps to her own home. She kept her emotions in check as Smudge greeted her and Hannah asked where the books she'd promised to pick up were and Caroline chided her for missing tea. She held herself together until she was alone in her room and the door was shut behind her and she could bury her face in a pillow. And when it was and she could, she wept and wept and wept for the unfairness of the world with all the misery in her heart.

CHAPTER SIXTEEN

Although his behavior following Tuppence's rejection of his suit closely resembled pouting, Gage would have boxed the ears of anyone who dared suggest such a thing, as his valet very nearly had while helping him dress for the Peterson ball. Correctly interpreting the expression on his employer's face, Thomas quickly changed the word *sullen* to *sullied*.

"Yes, yes, my goodness, indeed," he stammered nonsensically. "Far too sullied indeed to be worn out tonight. Do allow me to remove the offending shirt from your presence and find a pristine one that will do you credit. It will take only a moment, my lord."

The earl knew it was ridiculous to pretend the immaculate shirt bore a disqualifying stain, but he didn't have the heart to argue and allowed Thomas his pantomime. A moment later, the valet returned with the exact same shirt, which he lauded for its cleanliness while wondering aloud how the old shirt (though, in fact, *that* shirt) had gotten so dirty.

"If I had to guess"—of course he didn't—"I would say Perkins left the back door open and one of those dogs got inside again. Those blemishes looked a lot like paw prints."

Although Gage knew he should take exception to his valet blaming a fictional problem on a real-life nemesis, he couldn't be bothered to care. The prospect of addressing the petty squabbles of his servants was as unappealing as attending the Peterson ball.

He had no choice in the latter, as Letty was adamant about appearing at the affair with a bright smile on her face to demonstrate to Halesowen how little he meant to her, but he had full control over the former.

Hobson could sort out matters between the two men.

As Thomas secured the cuffs of his shirt, he once again cursed Letty's fortitude and resilience. Why couldn't she take to her bed and sink into a decline like a normal girl? Why did she have to make a brave showing to prove she was unaffected?

Gage did not want to make a brave showing. He wanted to sit in his study, drink brandy and draw up a list of all the ways Tuppence Templeton was an abrasive fishwife who didn't know her place.

But of course he would go to support Letty. He would have to be a very cruel brother indeed to make her face the *ton* alone, especially when he knew how very deep the wound went. She was devastated by Halesowen's treatment and confused by his change of heart. A few times she'd turned to her brother to ask if he'd observed anything she'd done that would make a suitor beg off.

Was I too demanding? she'd asked. Was I too boring? Did I not pay enough attention to him? Should I have offered him more praise?

No, Gage assured her. No, no, no.

And it was true: It wasn't anything that Letty had done. Halesowen's betrayal was entirely due to Tuppence's manipulations—and for that he would be grateful for the rest of his life. He still couldn't believe how smoothly she had engineered his defection, somehow convincing the elusive Miss Kennington to pry him away with coy smiles and shy giggles.

Truly, he'd never seen anything so masterful as the way Tuppence engineered the knave's downfall, and to have had her there at the moment of its culmination, to be standing beside her when the letter ending the relationship arrived, was more provocation than he could withstand. Full of love, brimming with admiration, humbled by respect, he'd indulged every impulse he'd ever had and captured her in an embrace that still brought an agonizing heat to his body all these many hours later.

He hadn't intended to propose like that, without grace or a finely honed speech or even a declaration of his feelings, but when a man held in his arms everything he'd ever wanted, he tended to act on impulse. And as much as he respected the persuasive power of soaring oratory, he knew her refusal wasn't about the way he'd proposed. He'd seen it in her eyes—the rejection of him, not his words.

Something about him was unacceptable to her and there was nothing he could do to change it.

Unlike Letty, he did not feel defiant or determined to show Tuppence how little he cared about her refusal. He felt sad and tired and wanted some time to organize his thoughts and get a firmer grasp on his emotions.

He had no idea how he was going to get through an entire evening of lively chatter and dancing.

In the carriage later, it seemed as though Letty was wondering the same thing, for she was quiet and downcast, but as soon as they arrived at their destination, she assumed a mask a blithe amusement. The difference was startling, and watching her greet Lady Sophia and her parents with sparkling eyes, he found himself trusting her judgment for the first time in his life. Clearly, she had complete control over her emotions and knew exactly what she was about.

His opinion of her rose again when she calmly addressed herself to Halesowen while he was at the refreshments table fetching a glass of lemonade for Miss Kennington, whose side he'd been reluctant to leave all evening.

"I wanted to thank you, Mr. Halesowen, for removing me from a very awkward situation," she said with relief that sounded so sincere even her brother believed for a moment that it was genuine. "I'd been trying to figure out how to gently extricate myself from a relationship that was not quite to my liking, and you kindly spared me the effort. It relieves my mind greatly that you have found an admirer who is more suited to your intelligence and temperament. I wish you nothing but the best."

The parade of expressions that marched across the young man's face—from wary to relieved to outraged to angry to disbelieving—was so entertaining to observe, Gage felt like laughing for the first time in more than a day. Halesowen didn't know how to respond, whether or not to waste precious moments away from his heiress to refute Letty's statement, and he looked back and forth between the two women, his face alternately glowering and smiling.

It was, the earl conceded, quite the funniest thing he'd ever seen.

After what seemed like an eternity of head twisting, Halesowen decided it was more important to consolidate his gains with his new target than to argue with his old one, and he returned to Miss Kennington's side after huffing with frustration.

The heiress accepted the glass of lemonade with a shy smile and tilted her eyes down as if she was too embarrassed to look her suitor in the eye.

At once, the earl was alerted to something strange, for what cause did Miss Kennington have to simper at Halesowen? She'd been recruited by Tuppence to lure Halesowen from Letty and that goal had been achieved with reassuring efficiency. The game was over, and all the pieces should be removed from the board.

And yet Miss Kennington remained firmly on her square.

That meant only one thing: Tuppence was still playing. Why?

The question stirred his interest like nothing else had done since Tuppence had rejected his proposal, and his eyes swept the ballroom searching for a graceful figure in an unfashionable dress. From the moment they'd arrived, he'd forced himself to keep his gaze steady and not look for her along the perimeter of the room, where she usually hid. He had too much pride to pine for her like a lovesick puppy and too little vanity to feign indifference like Letty.

It would be a while before he could address himself calmly to her.

At least, that was what he'd thought when they'd entered the ballroom, but now that he knew a scheme was afoot, he was too curious to care about his pride or his vanity. He wanted to know what she was up to.

Gage located her on the edge of the dance floor, her head bowed in close consultation with—and this was even more intriguing—Lord Tweedale of all people. He watched in fascination as she nodded earnestly a few times and then drew another gentleman into the conversation. It was, the earl noted with some surprise, the imposing form of Viscount Wallasey.

He was confounded by the development for a moment, unable to imagine what business Tuppence could possibly have with the famously prim lord, then he remembered whose guardian he was.

FitzWalter.

This evening's manipulations were about thwarting Horace FitzWalter.

Without uncovering any more details, the earl knew Tuppence intended to finish the project she'd begun months ago with Letty: dispensing with FitzWalter once and for all. This time she was determined to make the banishment stick by enlisting his guardian in her plan.

It would work, Gage thought, familiar now with the care and precision she took with all her plotting. Wallasey was far too straight an arrow to put up with any of his ward's nefarious antics.

He felt a spike of pride at her resourcefulness, which was immediately followed by a dart of sadness at the thought of all he'd lost when she'd turned him down. Although he knew it was better not to think about it at all, her bizarre next step—leading the two gentlemen out of the ballroom to the front parlor at the top of the staircase—made him acutely aware of how much more interesting his life was with her in it.

After the trio disappeared into the room, Gage approached the door silently and pressed his ear against it, too curious to worry how it would appear if a servant were to stumble across him arranged in such a strange position. Having lived his life forthrightly until now, he had little experience in the art of spying and wasn't sure how to proceed. He could understand only a few muffled words, most of them Wallasey's, as he seemed the most affronted by Tuppence's proposal, which, if he was hearing correctly—and there was no reason to assume he was—required him to hide behind a curtain.

The silence that followed seemed to indicate compliance, and the earl scuttled down the hallway looking for a crevice to hide in before Tuppence came out. He settled for a dark corner next to a bust of the fourth Lord Peterson, a round-faced fellow whose second chin offered more coverage than the crouching earl had a right to expect, and while he waited there, his body huddled in an uncomfortable squat, his head tucked into his chest, he decided he would propose to Tuppence again. Previously, he'd thought it was beneath his dignity to make a second offer to a woman who had rebuffed him. But this—crouching on his haunches, listening at doors—was truly beneath his dignity and he hadn't hesitated to do it.

Surely a chance at lifelong happiness deserved as much consideration.

Or, rather, as little.

He heard the door open and watched as Tuppence emerged from the room alone. She closed the door, rested her back against its surface and closed her eyes for several seconds as she sighed deeply. It was, he realized, a revealing moment, for he could see for the first time that it wasn't effortless for her. All these machinations, though carried out with passion and conviction, required determination, energy, fortitude and focus.

In the next instance, she was off, striding down the stairs to get the next set of players in place. He realized then he had a decision to make: Either he could continue to follow her around the house, observing her every move while assiduously evading her notice, or he could establish himself in secret in the parlor. The latter came with the greater risk of Wallasey and Tweedale discovering his presence, but it also offered the greater reward, for if he could hide himself behind a curtain as well, then he would have a first-row seat to whatever scene Tuppence was orchestrating.

Obviously, there was no choice at all, for he was desperate to know what the impertinent miss was scheming. He stood up, crept down the hallway and opened the door with wary uncertainty, fully prepared to meet the startled gaze of Wallasey or Tweedale and yet hopeful he would not. If he did, of course, it would be no matter to grumble in credible annoyance at their presence in the only quiet room in the house. Having cultivated a reputation for prickliness, nobody took exception when he displayed it.

Fortunately, the room appeared to be empty, which meant the gentlemen had obligingly remained behind their assigned drapery. Knowing he had to do the same, he considered the three sets of curtains and tried to reason out which ones already had occupants. He considered Wallasey's penchant for decorum and history of gout and decided Tuppence would have stowed him behind the curtain closest to the door.

Gage, therefore, settled on the farthest pair, which overlooked the street. He crossed the room swiftly and silently, slipping behind the heavy velvet fabric with what he considered to be admirable stealth. He was not as used to moving in the shadows as Tuppence was, as the incident with the tea tray had clearly demonstrated in the Bill Patent Office, but his skills weren't entirely lacking.

Satisfied, he adjusted his position to make himself more comfortable in the confined space and cried out in surprise when he realized he had company.

He was immediately shushed.

In the murky light from the dozens of lanterns illuminating the front walk, he could make out the outline of the Harlow Hoyden.

"What...?"

She shushed him again.

Or maybe she hadn't. Her sister, the Marchioness of Huntly, was also sojourning behind the curtain and glaring at him with staunch disapproval. As his eyes adjusted to the gloom, he could make out the expressions of both women clearly, and neither one was pleased to see him.

"We are hiding," the Harlow Hoyden whispered.

"Yes, I can see that," he said, his voice equally soft.

"No, I meant *we*"—she indicated all three of them with her hand—"are hiding. If you continue to make a ruckus, *we* will not be hiding anymore. We will be disclosing our location."

"I beg your pardon, your grace," he said stiffly, surprised to find himself offended by the criticism. It was one thing for Tuppence to take issue with his inability to sneak around and quite another for this brazen young lady whom he'd met only a handful of times. "I didn't expect to discover anyone here."

"Pray, do not blame us for your insufficient preparation, Lord Gage," the duchess said crisply. "Everyone else booked their curtain in advance. You are hiding *and* interloping."

The earl very much wanted to protest the sentiment and the scorn with which it was expressed, but he could not bring himself to mount a defense, heated and whispered, while concealed in the folds of Lady Peterson's primrose drapes.

That was also beneath his dignity.

But even if there was a graceful way to squabble sotto

voce with a duchess behind a velvet curtain, he was too disconcerted by the discovery that the Harlow Hoyden and her sister had arranged their presence with Tuppence to focus his attention.

No, not disconcerted.

Hurt.

He was actually pained by the fact that Tuppence hadn't invited him to participate. Surely, if anyone deserved to reserve a curtain to witness the downfall of Mr. FitzWalter, it was he. It was his sister, after all, who was the injured party.

That she would withhold the pleasure from him confirmed in what little esteem she held him, and he resolved not to propose a second time. There was no reason to compound the many indignities he'd already suffered that evening with yet one more.

And why would he—when he was clearly better off without her? Although that conclusion might appear to be merely his opinion, he knew it was in fact objectively true because before he'd met Tuppence Templeton, he'd never broken into an office that he was legally allowed to enter at any hour of the day or exposed himself to a woman's unholy glee or cowered behind the voluminous chin of a marble statue or been accused of insufficient preparation.

Clearly, not reiterating his offer was the best decision he'd ever made, he thought in sullen triumph.

"But there *is* plenty of room," the marchioness said softly, leaning forward to speak with him, "and you are more than welcome to share our curtain. I'm actually grateful for the opportunity to thank you for your assistance in the matter of the patent. I know deceit does not come naturally to you and I appreciate your bending the rules to help us."

In the darkness, Gage smiled, for the formality of her tone hardly seemed appropriate for their setting. "I do not consider it bending the rules to make sure the appropriate person gets credit for her invention."

Her ladyship raised her hand to her mouth to smother a laugh. "So Lord Tweedale did not stand up well to your interrogation? Did he in fact use nonexistent rubber from the Amazonian forest to create his hose?"

"As well as a chemical used in paint," he said.

Now she giggled, unable to stop herself, and the Harlow Hoyden was forced to shush her as well. "What part of *hiding* is too difficult for the two of you to understand?" she asked in an exasperated whisper.

Before her sister could answer, FitzWalter entered the room, his voice shrill and furious as he spit out insult after insult: "You sniveling coward, you rotten cur, you malignant toad, you imbecilic, puerile sack of grotesque flesh passing for a human being!"

CHAPTER SEVENTEEN

Wallasey was the problem.

He didn't think it was ethically appropriate to observe a young lady without her permission, even one so lost to morals and good sense as to be a member of the British Horticultural Society.

"But you're not observing her," Tuppence patiently explained to FitzWalter's guardian. "Only listening. You won't see a thing, I promise."

That, of course, only made the situation worse as far as the older gentleman was concerned, as a woman's true meaning could be discerned only by watching the expression on her face. To listen just to her voice would be to open one's self up to all sorts of improper assumptions.

He simply could not do it.

Tweedale, whose impatience to get on with the project convinced Tuppence that he truly believed he was the hose's actual inventor, suggested they ask another member of the Society for the Advancement of Horticultural Knowledge to witness the confession. "Cowle is here, and I just saw Neston by the refreshments table. Either one would do. We need not pester Wally to sacrifice his scruples."

Tuppence tried to recall what she knew about the

gentlemen in question. In preparing for her scheme, she'd investigated only the primary players. It hadn't seemed necessary to investigate the entire membership of the organization.

Neston was Alfred Neston, eighth Marquess of Frodsham.

She tried to recall what she knew about him—Neston...Neston—but drew a complete blank. The gray-haired peer had never crossed her path or kicked up enough dust to be covered in the dailies.

Very well, then, she thought. "Of course, Lord Neston. He will do just as well. I'm sure his poor hearing won't present a problem at all."

"Poor hearing?" Tweedale asked.

"He and I just had a lovely chat by the refreshments table," she said brightly before adding a note of uncertainty. "Or at least I think we did. He left his ear trumpet at home, so I'm not sure how much of our conversation he heard. But he was delightful nonetheless, and I'm sure he would agree without hesitation to lend you his assistance."

Tuppence's smile was tense as she waited for one of the men to contradict her, for both seemed confused by this news that their friend relied on a listening device. But neither one was quite sure enough of that fact to speak up.

"Neston's a reliable fellow, but I wouldn't want to bother him if he's out of sorts," Tweedale said quickly. "Much better to ask Cowle for his help. He owes me a favor anyway."

"Perfect," Tuppence said, hoping the rumors she'd heard about Mr. Cowle's gambling problem were accurate. "He's noted for his concentration with cards, and no doubt he will devote the same attentiveness to this situation. I saw him go into the cardroom a little while ago. Shall we go drag him away? I'm sure he won't mind our interrupting his play."

If her ability to be everywhere and see everything struck either gentleman as strange, Wallasey refrained from saying so. He merely made a moue of disgust at the mention of his associate's intractable habit, and Tweedale frowned as he realized that he actually did need to pester Wallasey into sacrificing his scruples.

It took just seven minutes of Tweedale's incessant pleading to gain Wallasey's consent, which he granted because it was the only way to get his fellow society member to stop talking. His patience was severely frayed by the time Tuppence directed him to the curtain to hide, and he protested loudly at the indecency of the arrangement.

Everyone knew the only way to spy on a private conversation was from an armchair pointed in the opposite direction.

Tweedale also began to complain about the awkwardness of the accommodations, forcing Tuppence to make a grandiose speech about the glory of discovery, the sublimity of invention and the prodigious acclaim that came from fabricating a brand-new device that would be used by gardeners for generations.

Both men decided it was worth bearing up under the mild discomfort.

Relieved to finally have them in position, Tuppence closed the door to the front parlor, rested her shoulders against it, closed her eyes and sighed heavily. Now she needed them to *stay* in position, something she had little faith in their being able to do for long. If Tweedale opened his mouth to talk about anything, anything at all, even the mildness of the weather, she could easily imagine Wallasey stomping out of the room.

Tuppence allowed herself ten seconds of silence, then straightened her shoulders and rushed down the stairs to oversee the final stage of her plan. She knew it would be only a matter of minutes before FitzWalter marched into the party demanding justice. Her scout—a seemingly capable man named Mr. Squibbs, whom Emma had recommended to her—had reported the delivery of the letter and its satisfying reception. According to the account, FitzWalter's face turned such a bright shade of red, he resembled an apple.

At the bottom of the staircase, Tuppence turned right and reentered the ballroom in time to see FitzWalter's feral grin as he spotted his friend. Although the scoundrel hadn't expected to go to a ball that evening, his dress was appropriate enough to fit in, and nobody raised an eyebrow as he stalked past. Only Halesowen had a reaction, and his jaw all but dropped to the floor when he saw the savageness in his coconspirator's expression.

As they'd planned, Miss Kennington swiftly jumped between them to avoid a scene and suggested they take their disagreement to a deserted room, such as the front parlor upstairs.

Halesowen, desperate to stay in her good graces, immediately agreed and strode to the staircase without another word. FitzWalter had no choice but to follow.

Tuppence was astonished to discover her heart was racing a dozen beats per second as the two men climbed the stairs.

"You were brilliant," Miss Kennington said.

"Me?" Tuppence said with confusion. She was far too anxious about how the next few minutes would play out to make sense of the compliment. "You're the one who convinced them to fall in line with our plan."

"Only because you told me what to say and how to say it," she insisted. "I followed your script down to the last word. Come, I think I just heard the door slam. Let's go up and watch the rest of the scene unfold."

Tuppence nodded, for she had no intention of missing the final act of the drama. For this one moment, she'd renounced an entire lifetime with Gage.

No, she wouldn't miss that.

And yet she couldn't bring herself to go up those stairs without one last glance at him. Her entire body itched with the desire to say goodbye, as if her refusal to marry him had not been the ultimate farewell. There was nothing left to say, and when her eyes could not find him in the crowd, she allowed Kate to lead her up the staircase.

They heard FitzWalter's expletives clearly through the door before they managed to open it a crack to watch. He was so incensed, he would not have noticed he had observers if the entire audience for that evening's performance of *A Midsummer Night's Dream* at the Drury Lane had relocated to the room.

Halesowen remained calm and kept his expression even as his friend snarled insults at him.

"You putrid mass of craven humanity, how dare you?" FitzWalter said, standing mere inches from Halesowen's face, his hand raised as if to strike him. "How dare *you,* an insignificant nobody who was courting a country lass with only a barn to her name, dare betray me? I *made* you. I gave you everything. And this is how you repay me? This is the gratitude you show? If I hadn't handed her to you on a silver platter, you would be a muck farmer."

Despite the imminent threat of physical abuse, Halesowen held his ground and maintained his poise. "I appreciate your concern, but I don't see why my romantic life should be of any interest to you, sir."

FitzWalter growled like a wild beast and picked Halesowen up by the cravat. "We had a deal!"

Halesowen didn't struggle as FitzWalter's grip became tighter and tighter. "I'm sure I don't have any idea what you're talking about. You and I are both far too honorable to strike any kind of deal that would affect the future of a young lady."

This repudiation enraged FitzWalter further, and he released his former associate from his grasp to stalk around the room like a furious bull. Watching, Tuppence wondered what Wallasey was waiting for. Hadn't he heard enough to condemn his ward? Even if the details were vague, FitzWalter's intent was clear.

"You won't get away with it, you won't," FitzWalter said, reason returning as he realized the other man was playing a deeper game. Remaining calm gave Halesowen the edge and now he sought to emulate his composure. "I won't let you get away with it. I'll tell the heiress everything, every minor detail of your sordid little scheme to woo Lady Letitia under false pretenses, and Ollie will testify that the plan was yours all along, not mine. I will paint you as the blackest blackguard that ever roamed London, and when I'm done, she won't be able to look at you, so filled with contempt and disgust she will be."

"You must do what you think is right, however misguided and evil your motives," Halesowen said, as if prepared for this line of attack, and Tuppence realized with sudden insight that he was. He'd known from the moment he'd broken off his relationship with Letty that a scene with FitzWalter was inevitable and he had already decided how he would approach it. Having long considered him an extension of FitzWalter, more an instrument than an actual person, she was impressed by the foresight and planning.

"Miss Kennington is aware of your jealousy of me," he continued, "and your dedication to doing anything necessary to make me unhappy. I am confident she will see through your lies and remain committed to me. You wouldn't understand, sir, but our affection for each other is real and sincere. Obviously, you have had some distress in your life if you are driven to undermine the happiness of an innocent woman, but I forgive you for succumbing to base desires you cannot control."

The hypocrisy of Halesowen's outrage and gracious pardon was too much for even FitzWalter, who, despite being a dyed-in-the-wool villain on a vitriolic rampage, paused in his bluster to laugh with genuine humor. It was fleeting, of course, his amusement, and Tuppence tensed as she saw the light of violence enter his eyes. This time, he would not be satisfied with only threatening to strike his associate. No, this time the skin of his palm would meet the flesh of Halesowen's cheek, and the victim, aware of what was coming, raised his hand as if to ward off the blow.

Rigid with expectation, Tuppence watched in horror at the unfolding brutality.

And then it stopped as a cry of distress rend the room and two men fell out of the curtains onto the floor, one on top of the other as they struggled to free themselves from the voluminous folds of fabric.

FitzWalter's and Halesowen's heads swung violently to the side in response to the noise and they both stared, dumbfounded.

"You will unhand me at once, you scoundrel," Lord Wallasey said as he tried to throw off Tweedale, whose knee was pressed into his fellow society member's back.

"I told you, it's rude to interrupt a private moment," Tweedale said with ferocious impatience, seemingly unaware of the pairs of eyes goggling at him in astonishment. "We will stay here until it is finished."

Wallasey, unable to stand, despite several attempts, settled for a humiliating roll, which succeeded only in causing their positions to switch. He was on top now, but he still couldn't break free of his opponent or the drapery.

"I will not spy on my own ward," he said, breathing heavily from his struggle. "It's indecent."

"It's your ward that's indecent," gasped Tweedale, who was also fatigued by the battle.

Neither man was the picture of good health.

Halesowen realized first what had happened and began to laugh with such wild abandon, he could scarcely draw air. FitzWalter was too stunned by the site of his guardian flopping on the floor like a suffocating fish to object. Wallasey seemed to have finally managed to place a foot firmly on the floor, but as soon as he tried to lift his considerable weight, Tweedale's elbow knocked him in the belly and he curled over with pain.

"Don't you get it, old man?" Halesowen said to his fellow conspirator. "You've been had. Someone set up this elaborate scene for the benefit of your guardian." Even as he described with perfect accuracy the events of the past few minutes, it didn't occur to him to wonder if he'd been dealt the same hand. He truly believed his friend's wickedness had been punished and his own rewarded with one of the largest fortunes in London.

Villains, Tuppence thought, could be so obtuse.

Once the truth had been pointed out to him, FitzWalter began to put it together, and his face paled as he realized what discovery by Wallasey meant for him and his future.

As if awaking from a dream, he suddenly seemed to notice everything. He looked toward the door and saw Tuppence watching from the threshold. He glanced across the room and spotted the Harlow sisters and Gage in front of the front window, seeming to have materialized out of the air like ghosts.

And the last piece of the puzzle fell into place.

Roaring with fury, FitzWalter charged at Gage, hurling the entire weight of his body at him and toppling him to the ground. He raised his fist and pounded it into the earl's jaw.

Tuppence's understanding was no more keen than FitzWalter's, for there was something very specter-like about Gage's sudden appearance, and her reaction was almost identical. With a cry, she raced across the room to fling herself onto FitzWalter's back, determined to remove the threat.

Gage mustn't get hurt, she thought.

He couldn't get hurt.

It was all her fault.

She was halfway across the room when Gage whipped his legs up, then slammed them down, propelling his chest forward and dislodging FitzWalter. A second later, he had his hand on the other man's throat.

Tuppence skidded to a halt.

"I don't believe attacking me is in your best interest," Gage said smoothly, as he straightened his shoulders and tugged FitzWalter to his feet. "Your guardian, Lord Wallasey, abhors violence and this demonstration can only harm your cause further. You do still have to explain to him how you planned to fleece my sister of her fortune."

Hearing his name, Wallasey, who had extricated himself from Tweedale's grip and now had only the drapery to contend with, stood up with as much grace as he could muster in an unbuttoned waistcoat and mussed hair. He stomped and kicked the offending fabric as he announced with excessive dignity that his feelings and opinions on the subject were a matter of privacy between him and his ward.

The earl's lips twitched and he tilted his head in the direction of Tweedale, whose eyes were glittering with almost fevered excitement. "On the contrary, it's a matter of public spectacle."

FitzWalter sputtered with impotent rage and sneered at Gage, "You did this and I'll never forget it. Never."

Now the earl smiled beatifically. "No. Not at all. I didn't have a single thing to do with it. Tonight's revelations were brilliantly conceived and superbly executed with precision and perfection by Miss Templeton. She's the one you should have tackled," he explained, before adding, "although if you try to harm one hair on her perfect, impertinent head, I will be forced to kill you. And that is no idle threat, so do think carefully about your next move."

Tuppence, whose bewilderment at Gage's presence had been intensified by the brutish simplicity with which he'd overcome FitzWalter, for who would ever have supposed that lithe body could contain so much power, understood in a fraction of a second what the earl's words meant.

No, not even his words.

She'd grasped it from the sublimity of his smile alone.

All those weeks of worry, all those days of indecision, all those hours of overwrought anguish, all those endlessly ticking minutes reminding herself that spinsterhood was preferable to soul-destroying compromise—all of it needless, pointless, a waste of weeks, days, hours, minutes.

Held her in esteem and regard?

Oh, no, this man loved her.

This man loved *her,* every perverse, imprudent, impertinent corner of her being.

Light-headed with relief and giddy with excitement and impatient with the time they had wasted—all that self-pitying self-abnegation when they could have been making love—she went to him. Her eyes steady, her pace deliberate, her smile as beatific as his, she strode across the floor and launched herself into his arms, giving him barely enough time to do anything other than toss FitzWalter to the floor before catching her.

With a dizzying mix of hunger and affection, she pressed her mouth against his and kissed him, her hands running over his shoulders and across his back as she imagined his body, supple and strong, exposed to her.

How long would she have to wait?

She couldn't wait.

Embracing the ache, oh, that wonderful, delightful ache, she tightened her arms and pulled him closer. He responded in kind, pressing her so tightly against his torso she could hardly decide where he ended and she began.

At no time did she forget her audience. Even as she succumbed to the ache, she was mindful of FitzWalter and Halesowen, Wallasey and Tweedale, Emma and Vinnie, and somewhere nearby, perhaps still by the entrance, Miss Kennington. She simply did not care if a handful of spectators witnessed her accepting the earl's marriage proposal. It was a social transgression, no doubt, to embrace one's affianced husband with wild abandon in the front parlor during a young lady's birthday ball, but the outpouring of emotion was sincere and somehow the most decorous thing to occur in the room all evening.

Despite feeling justified in her behavior, Tuppence knew modesty demanded she put an end to their exhibition before one of them actually did forget their audience. Gage, however, did not agree, and when she tried to raise her head, he pressed forward to maintain the contact. Again and again and again, he kissed her.

When he finally did pull away, it was only to rest his forehead against hers and smile.

"Mr. Tweedale," she called sweetly, turning her head slightly to watch him step forward, his movements so light and eager he might have been waltzing. Far from being disappointed that he hadn't been vindicated as the inventor of the modern elasticized watering hose, he appeared delighted with his good fortune, as if providence, not Tuppence, had arranged for him to witness so many scandalous events.

"Yes?" he said as he stepped over FitzWalter, who lay on the floor where Gage had dropped him.

"You may announce that Miss Templeton and the Earl of Gage will be married tomorrow by special license," she said.

Although the gentleman was slightly disappointed that their salacious conduct would soon be condoned by God and man, he was still delighted to have the information first and the opportunity to spread it.

He assured her it would be his pleasure as the earl, straightening his posture, explained that he might not be able to secure the license quite that quickly.

Tuppence's eyes sparkled with humor. "Breaking your promises to me already, are you?" she asked.

Such unfair abuse warranted retribution and he kissed her again—deeply, thoroughly, briefly—while Tweedale weighed the value of leaving the room now, before anyone else did, so that he might truly be the first to relay the details of these stunning *on-dits,* or staying to gather more of them. It was the single toughest decision he'd ever had to make in his life.

Having settled one pressing matter, Tuppence turned her attention to the other, which, though sprawled on the floor like a little boy, stared at her with the savagery of a full-grown man.

She crouched down so that her eyes were level with his and said, "As you rusticate in the country or in France or wherever your admirable guardian decides is the most appropriate place for a reprobate such as yourself, Mr. FitzWalter, I want you to think about how unnecessary this dreary little scene was. I had made one simple request of you: Leave Lady Letitia alone. That was all. I didn't demand that you forgo harassing other young ladies for their fortunes or insist that you give up the pleasures of polite society. I merely asked you not to interfere with the future of my friend. Instead of complying, you chose to intensify your efforts with a new scheme more contemptible than the last. That left me no option but to respond. I did warn you what would happen. The first time I threatened to tell your guardian of your behavior, but as that threat failed to intimidate you, I was forced to provide your guardian with a demonstration. Everything that happened here today is entirely on your head."

Then she stood up and turned her back to the villain to address Lord Wallasey, whose expression of outraged virtue was undercut by his frantic attempts to flatten unruly tufts of hair. "I must apologize, my lord, for the discomfort you have suffered. I had assumed you would be safe behind the curtain, and I'm truly sorry if the experience in any way caused you harm."

Growling was ordinarily beneath his dignity, but Wallasey, realizing the game was already up, left off patting his hair and indulged in a loud harrumph. "You are the most disagreeable young lady I have ever had the misfortune to meet, and be assured that I *will* report your deplorable behavior and questionable morality to your parents. And that is the *only* acceptable response to a situation like this, missy, you should have done the same when you discovered a moral failing in my ward. Private matters should be handled privately and at the discretion of one's guardian. What you've chosen to do here"—the look he darted at Tweedale that was equal parts enraged and embarrassed—"is a type of lawless justice that's almost as depraved and unconscionable as what my ward has done. You had no right to decide his punishment, no right at all."

Although Tuppence found his criticism to be both unfair and poorly reasoned, she made no effort to respond out of respect for the difficulties he had endured. She rather thought he had a right to be cross with her, for nowhere in her calculations had she allowed for the possibility that Tweedale would physically restrain Wallasey to prevent him from interrupting a revealing conversation. Knowing how voraciously the former consumed gossip, she probably should have.

The Duchess of Trent, however, had no such scruples, and immediately rose to her friend's defense, arguing that it wasn't Tuppence's responsibility to make sure FitzWalter was an upstanding citizen who made only positive contributions to society. Vinnie, as well, believed that molding the moral character of one's ward fell to his guardian and chastised Wallasey for failing to do his duty. The two women spoke in tandem, sometimes saying the exact same words at the exact same time ("appalling abdication," "obvious inadequacies," "harrowing escape"), and Halesowen, seeing the direction the wind blew, added his voice to the cacophony. Lacking the twins' penchant for aligned speech, he repeated their words only a second or two after, like an echo, creating the sense of a united front, which was precisely the effect he was striving for.

"Yes, a very ineffective worm," he said and promptly closed his mouth when he realized they had reached the end of their collective tirade.

The treatment distressed Wallasey so much, he stormed out of the room in high dudgeon, vowing to speak to all of their parents, even the earl's, whose forebears had passed from the world more than a decade ago. His dignified exit was marred, however, by his return a moment later to retrieve his recalcitrant ward, an oversight that seemed to confirm the Harlows' argument that he was a less than attentive guardian.

As Wallasey left with his charge, Miss Kennington entered and was immediately greeted by Halesowen, who assumed she had come looking for him.

"I was gone too long," he said, pressing his hand to his heart in a show of remorse. "I'm sorry, my love."

At once, her features hardened into a frown and she looked at him like a bug she hoped to squash. Tuppence smothered the urge to clap her hands at the convincing performance.

"Excuse me?" Miss Kennington said, her tone as frosty as a wind off the North Sea in January.

Although her response was not everything a lover could want, he pushed aside any concern and barreled through. "You're cross with me, of course, and I won't say that I don't deserve it, getting into a quarrel in the middle of a party. It's definitely not the thing. But I was the victim, you see, and it's all been resolved now. His guardian has him firmly in hand, and we may return to the ball. Come, my love," he said, holding out his hand. "I believe the next waltz is mine."

Miss Kennington took two very deliberate steps backward, and Halesowen, perceiving the distance to be not just physical, lost the color in his cheeks.

"I comprehend my mistake now and apologize, sir," she said coldly. "If I had realized you would turn a dance or two into a full-blown courtship, I would have been more cautious."

"But...but...my eyes," he stammered, looking from Miss Kennington to their audience and back at her again. "You said my eyes are more beautiful than the sky over the heath on a cloudless day."

"Are they blue?" she asked, her tone awash in boredom. "I hadn't noticed."

Halesowen whimpered, Tuppence swallowed a smile, and Tweedale salivated as he realized his extraordinary luck had somehow improved with a titillating third scandal. He'd never imagined the world could be filled with so much wondrous information waiting to be disseminated. He didn't even know with which story he should start. Logically, it should be with the spinster's engagement, as soon it would be announced in the paper and he'd have to compete with *The Times*. But FitzWalter's depravity was the much better tale.

The earl laughed at Halesowen's crestfallen expression, wrapped his arm around the other man's shoulders and said, "You're certainly not the first man to misunderstand a woman's kindness. Come, let us seek solace in politics. Are you familiar with the Health and Morals of Apprentices Act? Yes? Maybe? No doubt. But it's a complicated matter that you might not grasp the first, second or eighth time"—here, he winked at Tuppence—"so I will explain it to you in minute detail."

Thoroughly defeated, Halesowen submitted without a peep.

Tweedale watched them leave the room, then turned to the ladies with expectation in his eyes as if to say, What else do you have for me?

All four women regarded him in silence.

Then Tuppence said, "I should return to the ball as well. My sister has no idea I'm engaged."

With almost comical swiftness, Tweedale hastily bowed to the ladies, whirling like a dervish to do justice to each one, and darted out of the room as if a rabid dog were at his heels.

Tuppence, grateful for the consistent venality of his nature, for he was the only player who had performed his role according to expectation, asked if they could not throw a small invention his way, perhaps a nozzle or a knob for Vinnie's watering hose, to thank him for his service.

EPILOGUE

If Tuppence had realized that becoming engaged to the earl would make conversation between the two of them impossible, she would have acted very differently in Lady Peterson's front parlor. Rather than instructing Tweedale to announce her pending nuptials, she would have lamented her ruin, embraced social ostracism and enjoyed a lovely evening chatting with Gage in a quiet corner.

Instead, she found herself in the middle of a melee, waylaid permanently by a cadre of well-wishers, who, though intent on offering their best on her marriage, seemed incapable of understanding why they had to. Tweedale's announcement revealed itself, to the surprise of all present, to be an accurate assessment of the situation, but it was maddeningly sparse of details and provided no answer to the burning question on everyone's lips: Why in God's name would an imperious lord like the Earl of Gage, who demanded perfection in everything, settle for a mousy little nobody over all the glittering beauties of the *ton*?

It was a mystery of vast proportions, and few of the guests who accosted her scrupled to seek her assistance in solving it.

"You say you're Lord Templeton's *eldest* daughter?" Mrs.

Garstang asked, her nose crinkling as she struggled to make sense of the information. "Lord *Templeton's* eldest daughter?"

Tuppence smiled blandly and said yes.

"And Lady Templeton is *your* mother?" Mrs. Garstang pressed, approaching the problem from another angle.

Tuppence's answer remained the same. "Yes."

As if unable to believe it, the widow with two daughters of marriageable age shook her head. "I thought for sure Hannah was her eldest daughter."

Having heard this exact same observation seven or eight times in the past hour, Tuppence merely nodded and said yes.

Her parents were no better.

"The *Earl* of Gage?" her father asked hours later when she and Hannah had returned home from the ball. Lord Templeton had passed the evening at his club, where a report of the engagement had reached him. Being a reasonable creature with a long association with the girl in question, he'd immediately assured the fellow his information was inaccurate.

"Yes," Tuppence said, too familiar with her sire's opinion of her to take offense at his tone.

"The Earl of *Gage?*" he said again, as though the problem were with the way he'd asked the question as opposed to the question itself.

"Yes," she said.

"The Earl of Gage who is known by the sobriquet Prickly Perceval?" he asked. "The Earl of Gage who bedevils me on an almost daily basis in the House of Lords? *That* Earl of Gage?"

Tuppence sighed and said yes.

Lord Templeton was still trying to make sense of the news when his wife arrived home from a card party and announced that she'd heard the most remarkable story. While they were discussing the implausibility of her engagement, Tuppence left the study and returned to her bedchamber.

Exhausted, she dropped onto on her bed, lay back and closed her eyes. A dozen minutes later, she felt the press of a warm kiss against her neck. She bent her back luxuriously and said, "You found the oak tree."

"It's big and oak-like," the earl said softly, moving his lips along her jaw. "I'd have to be a fool to miss it."

"Yes, well, I haven't ruled that out yet," she said teasingly.

He laughed with delight and captured her lips in a kiss that started soft and sweet and quickly turned hot and insistent. She groaned as the burning ache began to spread, and she pulled him down onto her bed, determined to deny herself nothing. Returning her enthusiasm with searing passion, he seemed as lost to reason as she, but when her hand slipped under his shirt to feel the warmth of his skin, he pulled back.

"I'm an honorable man," he said sternly, "and you will not succeed in corrupting me. I only agreed to climb through your bedroom window because I haven't had a private word with you all day. Indeed, it feels like years since we last spoke." He looked at her smile, so happy and carefree, and shook her gently as he recalled their exchange in his drawing room. "How dare you turn down my proposal? I have been miserable for days and days and days."

"I thought I was doing you a kindness," she explained as she marveled at his restraint. Although she too felt as if they'd been separated for years, the last thing she wanted to do was talk. "Given how cross you were the first time I intervened with FitzWalter, I naturally assumed my interfering a second time would be the end of our association. My intent was only to spare you the indignity of having to marry a sadly misguided woman of questionable intelligence and an overdeveloped sense of her own competence."

Recognizing an echo of his own words, the earl grimaced. "Did I sound as asinine as Wallasey?"

"Worse," she delighted in telling him, "for Wallasey's objection was brief. Yours went on for several minutes.

The exact number I cannot recall now, but it was long enough for me to resolve a dozen times to have no further contact with you."

Although the resolution had long been broken, Gage still felt as if he'd narrowly avoided a horrible future and had to affirm the present with contact—so much contact that he was soon breathing heavily and his limbs were shaking from the effort of restraining himself.

'Twas ridiculous to have believed he could conduct an intelligent conversation with her when there was a bed in the room and she was warm and willing in his arms.

No matter what it entailed, he would get that special license tomorrow.

With a sigh, he drew away and announced that he owed her an apology.

Although her eyes were still hazy with desire, the shake of her head was clear and firm. "No, you made your amends. This evening, in the parlor, your comments to FitzWalter settled everything. I was so sure you would resent my interference and end our connection. Indeed, that was my primary reason for conceiving of the scheme—to save myself from the helplessness of my own emotions. You'd become too important to me, and I had started to crave your approval. So I did something that I knew would earn your ire," she explained, then smiling with wonder, added, "And yet somehow I did not. I still don't know how you wound up tucked behind a curtain with the Harlow sisters, but I will forever be grateful that you did. Your words moved me, unbearably so, but it was the pride in your tone that undid me entirely. I have never felt so swamped with love in my entire life."

Her confession, so simply stated, had a similar effect on her listener, and in a matter of seconds, her shoulders were once again pressed against the bed pillows and her mouth beneath his. Inconceivably, impossibly, his desire seemed hungrier, greedier, more voracious, and she met it with delight and a thirst of her own, determined not to let anything undermine her satisfaction. If Smudge walked into the room at that very moment, she would calmly wave him away without breaking contact.

Gage, of course, had a different opinion on the matter and raised his head to gaze down at her. "I thought you'd never say it."

"What?" she asked, genuinely baffled.

"Love."

Because she could feel the emotion radiating off him, she didn't need the words and was astonished to discover that he did. Nevertheless, she had no desire to deny him anything. "I love you, my lord."

He sighed with pleasure and kissed her again. "Nicholas. My name is Nicholas, and I would dearly love to hear it on your lips."

She readily complied. "I love you, Nicholas."

"I love you, Tuppence," he responded immediately.

She grinned. "I know."

"I realized how much in that tavern," he said, amazed that he could affect nonchalance so convincingly given the situation. "You know, the one near the docks where Fitz-Walter and Halesowen met with their friend Ollie?"

Shocked, Tuppence shot straight up in the bed and stared at him.

Her reaction could not have pleased him more, for his ability to surprise her boded well for their marriage. It would not do for her to *always* have the upper hand. "The wart was a marvel, by the way," he said with sincere admiration. "If I hadn't already been besotted beyond reason, the confidence with which you wore that disfiguring mark would have sunk me entirely."

Although she usually appreciated compliments on her ability to wear a convincing disguise, for such remarks were rare, she was too distracted by a review of the tavern's interior to respond. She pictured Halesowen at the table in front of hers and FitzWalter beside him and Ollie across—

And then she knew. "The sailor who smelled like rum and manure! That was you!"

He conceded the truth with a brief dip of his head. "Not my best moment, to be sure. But lacking your fore-thought and preparation, I had to make do with what was available to me in the moment, which was limited to the inhabitants of the alley. Had I known when I left my house that morning that I would end up surveilling the Black Horse Inn, I would have dressed more appropriately."

Although the world had changed the moment she'd noticed the earl standing there, in the Peterson parlor next to the Harlow twins, she hadn't understood how radically it had been altered until this very moment. Everything she'd thought impossible had been true for days. While she had been silently mourning the end of their relationship, the earl had been quietly trusting her with the safety of his sister.

The problem, she realized now, had never been his lack of faith in her but *her* lack of faith in *him*.

What a humbling revelation to have at three in the morning, she thought, her anxiety at the disparity under-mined by her joy. The situation certainly demanded restitu-tion of some kind, but she was too curious about his movements just then to think about it.

"I'm amazed you were able to restrain yourself," Tuppence said.

She was referring to FitzWalter and his vile plan, but the earl took it another way. "I almost didn't. As soon as I realized you'd taken it upon yourself to rescue Letty again despite my disapproval, I resolved to give you a sharp set-down."

Very familiar with his stinging reprimands, she smiled with sly humor and said, "You impertinent miss, you inso-lent hussy, you deluded chit, you overconfident fishwife, how dare you."

He nodded with good-natured amusement. "That and more. I took it exactly as you'd supposed and determined to end our association right then and there. I stood up to issue a rebuke, but I couldn't do it. My body simply wouldn't let me. Because the truth was, I didn't want to end our association. I never have. From almost the very beginning. So I sat back down at the table, reviewed my options and realized the only way to have a future with you was not to interfere. As the presence of the wart indicated, you clearly had the matter well in hand and I had to trust you to see it through. It was, to my surprise, one of the easiest things I've ever done."

This endorsement, so simply given, overcame her curiosity and she pressed her lips against his in an enthusiastic show of gratitude and appreciation. Eventually she pulled away to ask how he'd come to arrive at the tavern and he damped his desire enough to explain how entirely unnecessary their midnight foray to the Patent Bill Office was. They both giggled like children at the absurdity of the tea tray—so loudly, in fact, Tuppence thought for sure Smudge would appear at her door to eject Gage.

But nobody came and an hour passed and another as they entertained each other with all the misunderstandings and hurt feelings they had suffered for weeks. At five in the morning, unable to deny how quickly time was passing, Gage announced his intention to leave. If he was going to pester the Archbishop of Canterbury for a special license in the morning, he should at least look as though he hadn't stumbled in from a card game. And there was Letty to consider. She claimed to be unaffected by the exposure of Halesowen and FitzWalter's plan, but he refused to believe she wasn't disturbed to discover how deep the deception ran. He needed to take a moment to reassure himself of her welfare before heading out to Doctors Commons. And while he was seeing to matters, it wouldn't hurt to make sure Perkins didn't suffer any ill consequences for sullying a shirt that remained pristine. And of course there was the matter of settlements to be discussed with her father.

Yes, the earl had several important things to do in the

morning and staying with Tuppence would only hinder his ability to accomplish them. As it was, they were lucky to have had these quiet hours together, and the longer he stayed, the more likely they were to be discovered. That would be unacceptable, for he would allow no hint of scandal to mar their union. There was no away around it: Leaving now was for the best. He pressed his lips gently against hers one last time, then pulled away.

"I must go," he said.

Tuppence yielded at once, agreeing readily with his statement and saying with all due sincerity that she understood. She too needed some sleep to deal calmly with her parents' bewildered felicitations, and of course *she* would discuss settlements with her father. And there were her sisters to consider, for they would no doubt have hundreds of excited questions. It mattered little anyway, for they would see each other later, after he'd secured the special license.

How reasonable she sounded.

And yet her hand tightened on his and her eyes sparkled with mischief and she tilted her head alluringly to one side and her smile—

Oh, yes, her smile.

It was impertinent.

ABOUT THE AUTHOR

Lynn Messina is the author of more than a dozen novels, including the best-selling *Fashionistas,* which has been translated into 16 languages. Her essays have appeared in *Self, American Baby* and the Modern Love column in the *New York Times,* and she's a regular contributor to the *Times* Motherlode blog. She lives in New York City with her sons.

CPSIA information can be obtained
at www.ICGtesting.com
Printed in the USA
LVHW091300250619
622298LV00001B/41/P